I0692041

The Art of Myth-Direction

A SpireVerse Novel

M. L. Tilford

Hardcover ISBN 978-1-968876-03-6

Paperback ISBN 978-1-968876-01-2

eBook ISBN 978-1-968876-00-5

Cover Art by Filipe de Souza

First edition 2025

For Aria

Contents

Prologue

"And lo, they gathered at the appointed hour, bearing torches, dread, and absolutely no sense of self preservation."

— *Summoning for Fun and Profit,* Sixth Edition

Amid the shadows of a moonless night, four hooded figures converged atop a jagged, windswept mountaintop, fueled by the kind of optimism that only denial and selective memory could provide. The cold was so biting it felt downright vindictive, as if the weather held a grudge against anyone foolish enough to venture this high. The tallest among them carried a tattered and charred tome bound in leather of dubious origin (certainly not human . . . probably).[1] He cleared his throat with the gravitas of someone who hadn't just tripped over a tree root on the way in.

"Thanks for coming out tonight," the Grand Harbinger of Doom began, his voice confident, like he had practiced talking in a mirror far too many times. "I hope everyone's ready for some good old-fashioned summoning . . . and by 'good,' I mean *better than last time.*"

---

[1] The Commission on Ethical Summoning defines "dubious origin" as anything you'd hesitate to explain to a customs officer, a clergyman, or your mother. Especially your mother.

He paused, with an expectant grin on his face. He waited for laughter but was met only with the sound of a cricket coughing and the shuffle of awkward feet.

Undeterred, he turned to the hooded figure on his left. "Herald! How's your mother? Well, I hope?" His tone was a masterclass in feigned interest, as if Human Resources had suggested he *'show more interest in the team.'*

"She was sacrificed last winter, your Grandness," replied the Herald of Prophetic Hindsight, as though this was common knowledge.

The Grand Harbinger blinked, caught off guard, before he forced a chuckle. "Right, right. Well . . . we all make sacrifices."

"Me mum's doin' well," chimed in the Underseer of Trivial Mysteries. He spoke in a tone far too chipper for a moonless night filled with dark rituals. "Oy, figured you'd want ta know. She always asks after ya."

"Right, well, let's move—"

"Mom's got the runs," interjected the Keeper of the Snacks, a huge grin plastered across his face, eager to not be left out.

"I . . . what?" The Grand Harbinger looked as if he'd just been slapped with a wet fish.

"The runs," the keeper repeated helpfully. "Y'know. The trots. The squirts. The—"

"Yes, thank you, I got it." The Grand Harbinger's expression shifted from indifference to mild horror. "Your mother . . . she . . . didn't help with the snacks . . . did she?"

"Oh yes, sir," the keeper replied with earnest pride. "She always helps with the snacks."

The Grand Harbinger took a moment to process the information.

"Right. Let's . . . not think about the snacks right now." *I should've stayed in public relations*, he thought grimly.

He rubbed his temples before forcing his professional smile back into place. Clearing his throat again, he tried to recover his air of authority, glancing around the group.

"Right, right . . . right . . . moving on!" He took a quick breath. "Underseer, bring forth the sacrifice."

There was a long pause. The group exchanged nervous glances. After an uncomfortable beat, the Underseer of Trivial Mysteries sheepishly raised his hand.

"Me mum said I weren't allowed ta do no more sacrifices," he mumbled. He held up a wicker basket overflowing with tiny orange vegetables. "I thawt we may, you knows, use these ones instead."

The Grand Harbinger's face fell. His carefully crafted aura of leadership had begun to slip.

"What are those? Baby carrots?"

"Yeah, well, they came from me own garden. Grew 'em meself, I did. See, the tome says ta sacrifice an innocent, right? So I thinks to meself, well, what's more innocent than a baby carrot, eh? I figures, why not, y'know?"

The Grand Harbinger froze, his expression blank, as if his brain had crashed while trying to decipher the logic. After a long pause, he finally sighed. "I suppose we have no choice. But we are going to have a long talk after this is over."

The Underseer of Trivial Mysteries returned a sheepish grin.

"Tonight, we summon forth the Dark Lord, Emperor of Eternal Midnight, Devourer of Suns, Master of the Abyss, Scourge of All That is Good." The Grand Harbinger spoke with grave seriousness. "May his power rise once more to rain chaos and destruction upon the world."

The group struggled to chant in unison. Their voices were a mismatched jumble of lows and highs, guttural and squeaky. As the Grand Harbinger raised his hands, signaling the next part of the ritual, he shot a glance at the underseer.

"And now! The sacrifice of the innocent!" the Grand Harbinger said, with an air of theatrics. The hooded figure remained oblivious.

The Grand Harbinger cleared his throat, murderous intent on his face.

"Hmm?" The underseer finally glanced up. "Oh, right!" With great enthusiasm, he upended the basket of carrots into the center of the group. They hit the ground with a soft *thwump*. He grinned expectantly at the Grand Harbinger, awaiting praise.

The Grand Harbinger returned a stiff, insincere smile. *How did I get stuck with these morons?*

His ruminations on the shortcomings of his underlings were interrupted by a low rumble that echoed across the mountaintop. The earth shuddered beneath their feet as a jagged rift tore through the soil. A chasm of molten flame erupted from the bowels of the underworld. It cast an infernal glow that bathed the plateau in hues of violent orange and bloody red. From the depths of this hellish wound, a figure emerged. Cloaked in darkness so profound it devoured the very shadows around it.

The Dark Lord had arrived.

The Grand Harbinger wasted no time. He dropped to his knees. "Oh, Mighty Lord, we have summoned you to bring forth chaos and despair upon this world!"

The Dark Lord's eyes burned with the incandescent fury of a phoenix imprisoned in a sulfur mine, but as he gazed down upon the sacrificial offering, his expression softened into one of unfathomable bewilderment.

The group exchanged nervous glances. Each silently prayed that a carrot wasn't about to end their pathetic existence.[2] After a long, uncomfortable pause, the Dark One spoke, his voice a deep, gravelly rumble.

---

[2] Carrots have long been associated with high vitamin A and low survivability in dark rituals.

"WHAT . . . IS THIS?"

"A sacrifice of the purest innocence, my lord!" the Grand Harbinger stammered, his voice wavering, his bow deep enough that he could taste the ground.

"CARROTS?" The word hung in the air, heavy with disbelief, as if the Dark Lord himself couldn't fathom the depths of their idiocy.

The Dark One crouched, as if unsure how to approach a vegetable. He pinched a single carrot between his fingers like it was the most fragile artifact in the universe.

"*Baby* carrots, my Lord," the Grand Harbinger offered weakly.

"They're *organic!*" the underseer chimed in, a hint of pride in his voice.

The Grand Harbinger closed his eyes, despair tightening his chest. *For the love of all that's unholy, please . . . stop . . . talking!* He didn't dare open them again, bracing for the end. *This is how we die. Sacrificed on the altar of stupidity.*

The Dark Lord's burning eyes swept across the group, his gaze sharp enough to gut a stone golem. A thick, suffocating silence fell over the mountaintop. Every muscle in the Grand Harbinger's body tensed, bracing for the inevitable annihilation.

Then, with an ominous crunch, he took a bite.

"HMM. NOT BAD."

The underseer beamed. "Knew you'd like 'em!"

Without another word, the Dark Lord turned, his cloak billowed dramatically as he strode away. Around his neck, a heavy chain glinted in the dim light, the brilliant blue gem at its center practically humming with power—something that would probably be important later. The Grand Harbinger scrambled to follow, whispering frantic apologies and promises that next time, they would sacrifice something more fitting.

As the underseer trailed behind, he couldn't help but muse aloud, "Maybe next time we try cherry tomatoes."

As the group vanished into the night, somewhere, inexplicably, a magic sword blinked into existence, wondering how it had gotten there.

1

The Calm Before the Plot

"We fear them because we're told to. We believe it because we're supposed to. And that, my friends, is what makes us civilized."

— Professor Ellard Grimsley,
Imperial Ethnographer (Missing)

"You must stop him, or your world will end!"

The frying pan's voice echoed in her mind—crisp, imperious, and just a touch condescending.

To be fair, Tianna didn't spend much time pondering grand existential questions like the fate of the world. Hers was a straightforward reality. But that evening, standing in the storeroom of *The Cracked Tankard* with talking cookware in front of her, reality jolted her with something unexpected and profoundly inconvenient.

But we're getting ahead of ourselves.

Being a big sister, Tianna had learned two universal truths. First, younger siblings are born with an uncanny ability to find danger in the safest places. Second, they always manage to do it with a look of innocent triumph. These thoughts weighed heavily on her mind as she trudged into the Ashevale forest for what felt like the hundredth time that week. Rea, bless her adventurous little heart, had developed a fondness for a particular spot in the forest. However, that spot still required Tianna to tromp through every thorn bush, mud pit, and spider-infested thicket in their corner of the Empire. Yet, Tianna did it with little (maybe a bit more than little) complaint, because at the end of the day, she loved her sister and couldn't bear to see her harmed.

Not far from where Tianna had entered the forest, there lay a circular clearing of rich black soil surrounded by towering Gloamwood trees.[3] Those towering sentinels, armored in patchy white bark, stretched skyward, their canopies cascading outward with rich crimson leaves. During the day, the clearing was always full of light and warmth, but as evening fell, the darker creatures of the forest would often encroach upon the sanctuary.

Rea sat in the center of the clearing, a child no more than nine years old. She was a mirror image of Tianna reflected eight years into the past. Her face was round and plain, eyes the color of ripe wheat, and locks braided down her back, the color and smell of digested wheat. Her tunic, once a dignified weave of undyed wool, was now stained with what could only be blood, or possibly fruit juice.

On her left, a small ball of fur and chaotic energy sat in hushed watchfulness. The cat was black as the depths of an ancient chimney and equally dusted with soot.

---

[3] Legend has it that the Gloamwood tree propagates only under the light of a blood moon, when a coven of witches performs the primeval summoning of the deer spirit Cernu. In the flickering shadows of their fires, where innocent blood is spilled, Cernu is said to rise from the spirit world to dance with the witches; sometimes twice if he doesn't have to get up early the next morning. Reality, however, is more mundane. There's just some guy who likes to go around planting them. I think his name is John, or maybe Jim. Something with a J, anyway.

Rea's world had shrunk to the task at hand. She worked with a silent fervor, her small fingers interlacing a crown of forest leaves and vines, interweaving delicate red and white flowers—lava blossoms and frost petals. The crown was a work of contradiction, a fragile equilibrium of opposites intertwined into a single, delicate form.[4]

As the sun began its leisurely descent to the west, the once vibrant clearing surrendered to the shadows of the surrounding forest. Little by little, the darkness crept closer, casting a dreary, dismal shroud over the scene. The air grew heavy with the scent of damp earth and the distant, nearly inaudible rustle of unseen creatures. Perhaps they were conspiring, perhaps attending to their own affairs, but ominous all the same.

Rea hummed a simple melody in the key of B sharp, a cruel coincidence, given the creature lurking in her shadow and its last victim's final thought: *I should have known those teeth would be sharp.*[5]

A chilling wind slithered in from the north, rustling the canopy with an ominous sigh. Crimson leaves from the Gloamwood trees, displaced by the draft, floated down in a slow, deliberate descent. They settled on the somber soil resembling blood spilled on a battlefield, or a toddler toppling a dish of dried berries.

The trees behind her squirmed, their branches creaking in protest, as if grumbling about her lack of attention. But she remained unperturbed, completely consumed by her task. Her humming continued, cheerfully clueless of the arboreal discontent.

The cat, on the other hand, was not so complacent. He locked his stare on the treeline behind the girl, a guttural, ominous rumble echoing from the pit of

---

[4] Combining lava blossoms and frost petals is traditionally symbolic of unity, balance, and minor allergic reactions.

[5] Technically, B sharp is the same as C natural, however, I should have known those teeth would see natural, just doesn't have the same ring to it. Or make sense in any possible way.

his throat. He pressed flat to the ground, blending seamlessly into the ever-deepening shadows, muscles tensed like a drawn bowstring. His eyes dilated and unwavering like twin pools of chaos, fixed intently on the movement in the gloom. Waiting.

The forest seemed to hold its breath as the creature manifested from the shadows. Its gilded, serpentine eyes locked onto Rea with a hunger that far exceeded its small stature. The Dragon whelp, barely a foot in length from nose to tail, was a pitiful echo of its once-mighty ancestors.[6] Somber black scales covered its scrawny body, but they were dull and cracked, more reminiscent of a worn, weathered boot than the fearsome, gleaming plates they once were.

Its tiny horns, scarcely jutting from its skull, gave it an almost comical appearance, like a child playing at being fearsome. But the danger in its eyes was anything but playful. As it crouched low, muscles tensed in preparation to strike, there was no mistaking the lethal intent simmering behind those golden orbs.

Its maw opened wide, revealing saffron fangs wet with anticipation, dripping more saliva than necessary or was medically advisable. The creature's back legs tensed, stony talons dug into the soft soil, and with a sudden burst of speed that defied its small, scrappy frame, it launched itself toward Rea.

For a fractured moment, time slowed within the clearing. The Dragon's claws were outstretched, reaching toward the small child, who remained blissfully unaware.

With a sudden pounce and a quick flick of his neck, the cat had the tiny creature in its jaws. The whelp let out a soft, pitiful whimper before falling silent forever. Dead but still twitching, as if its body hadn't quite gotten the message.

"Nyxie!" Rea exclaimed, scrambling to her feet. She ran to the cat, her face a mix of awe and concern. "You saved me!"

---

[6] While still dangerous, these juvenile dragons rank only slightly above 'aggressive poultry' on the Empire's Threat Index. Which, if you've ever met a chicken in real life, should not surprise you in the least.

Nyx puffed out his chest, the tiny Dragon carcass hanging from his jaws.

As if on cue, Tianna stepped into the clearing, picking branches and leaves out of her hair. As she saw Rea, whole and unharmed, her breath hitched. Relief flooded through her, but it was short-lived. The Dragon whelp's corpse dangling from Nyx's jaws stole the air from her lungs. "Astrea Celeste Amberbrook!" Tianna's voice cut through the clearing, sharp and exasperated. Her braid swung behind her as she marched toward her sister, her face tight with worry.

Rea froze, the weight of her full name hitting her like a bucket of ice water. It was the verbal equivalent of being caught red-handed, and it stopped her in her tracks.[7]

"You had everyone worried sick." Tianna planted her hands on her hips, her sharp gaze flicking from the dead Dragon to Rea's guilty expression. "Do you have any idea what could've happened to you, wandering out here all alone?"

"I wasn't alone!" Rea protested, pointing at Nyx. "Nyxie was with me."

"I'm sure Nyx is very brave, but look at him; He's just a cat. How is he going to protect you?"

"Nyxie isn't *just* a cat! He's . . . he's a guardian, like in the stories! And he did protect me! Look!"

Tianna let out a sigh, her shoulders relaxing. "Fine. But what are you doing out here again? Didn't I tell you not to come out here by yourself?"

"Nyxie wanted a crown," Rea replied, her voice small and trembling, the words barely escaping her lips. It was such an absurd explanation that Tianna

---

[7] Every child instinctively knows the power of the Full Name. It's an ancient force, older than magic, stronger than the toughest metal, and as inescapable as a mother's glare. Uttered with precision, it can halt the fiercest tantrum, unravel the cleverest lie, and turn even the bravest warrior into a stammering puddle of guilt. The Full Name transcends time and culture, a universal incantation understood by all children, no matter how wild or unruly. Hearing it is like being struck by the very voice of justice, or worse, the promise of consequences.

had to bite back a sigh of disbelief. The fact that her little sister was taking orders from a cat, of all things.

Brrrrup! Nyx the cat chimed in, as if to confirm he was indeed the mastermind of their grand adventure.

"Nyxie wanted a—?" Tianna repeated, blinking. "You're letting the cat boss you around?"

"He's very persuasive," she said in all seriousness, before her lips began to quiver, and her eyes filled with tears. "I'm sorry, Tee-Tee. I didn't mean to make you mad."

Tianna groaned, her anger evaporating as fast as it had appeared. She kneeled beside her sister. "Hey, don't cry. You're okay, and that's what matters."

"I was going to surprise you with one, too. Nyxie said I should practice first."

Tianna focused her attention on the crown. "It is really pretty. You've got an eye for these things, you know. Maybe next time, we can work on one together."

"Really? You'd want to make a crown with me?" Rea asked, wiping away tears with the back of her arm.

"Of course, Rea, what are big sisters for?" She gave her little sister a light bump with her elbow.

Nyx sauntered over and dropped the Dragon whelp at Tianna's feet with all the pride of a cat that had conquered the world. Tianna stared at the tiny carcass.[8] "At least Nyx caught dinner. Though, there isn't much meat on this thing."

---

[8] Once upon a time, Dragons were the ultimate killers. Claws, teeth, fire-breath, you know, the whole shebang. But the problem with Dragons was that there were never very many of them. With the constant influx of those taking up adventuring as a profession, the issue only worsened. Over the centuries, questionable pairings arose. Today, there were enough Dragons who were both their own sibling and grandparent that drastic biological changes were inevitable.

Rea giggled through her sniffles. "Nyxie says it's more about the presentation."

Tianna chuckled, watching as Rea, with the utmost seriousness, placed the forest crown upon Nyx's head. The cat, to his credit, appeared incredibly regal, at least for a moment. He sneezed, causing the crown to tilt sideways on his head. Nyx gave an exaggerated shake before resuming his proud posture, as if the sneeze was all part of his royal act.

"There," Rea declared, satisfied with her work. "Now Nyxie's a king."

"Great," Tianna laughed. "All hail King Nyxie, ruler of the cats." She shook her head before continuing, "Let's get back before they send out a search party. Next time, wait for me. Deal?"

Rea nodded eagerly. "Okay Tee-Tee, I promise. I won't come out here alone ever again." She paused for a moment before adding, "Unless Nyxie says it's really, really important."

"You'd listen to a cat over your big sister?"

"He doesn't nag as much."

Tianna groaned but couldn't help the smile creeping across her face. "Come on, you two. I'm glad you're both safe, but now I'm late for work. Gertie is going to kill me."

As they walked back toward the town of Nothing-to-See-Here, Rea skipped alongside Tianna, chatting away as if nothing out of the ordinary had happened. Nyx trotted a few paces ahead, tail held high, as if leading a victorious parade. Tianna glanced at the Dragon whelp dangling from her hand and sighed.

2

Destiny: Now in Nonstick

"A true calling comes softly, like a whisper. Followed shortly by screaming."

— *Manual of Prophetic Compliance,* Volume I

At the far end of Nothing-to-See-Here, where even the cobblestones seemed to give up and turn to dirt, stood a tavern that had seen much better days. Although, no one could quite remember when those days had taken place. *The Cracked Tankard*, as it was rather ironically named, leaned slightly to one side, as if drunk on its own stock.

The exterior was a hodgepodge of crumbling stone and warped wooden planks, haphazardly patched together with whatever materials the locals could scrounge up—old shingles, broken wagon boards, and even a few grimy old socks stuffed into the smaller gaps. Moss and lichen had crept over the stonework, as if nature itself were embarrassed by the eyesore and aimed to slowly cover it up.

The inside wasn't much better. The air smelled faintly of stale ale, boiled cabbage, and the windy whispers of past patrons.[9] Cracked, uneven floors bore ancient stains, poorly concealed by scattered straw. Above, the wooden beams

---

[9] An aroma best left uninvestigated, though it tended to linger in the upholstery with suspicious familiarity.

were thick with cobwebs. The occasional drip from the ceiling suggested that the last rainstorm had been more successful at finding leaks than the tavern keeper had been at fixing them. A small hearth in the corner struggled to offer warmth, its embers crackling begrudgingly as if embarrassed to be there. Above it hung a crooked sword so rusted and dull that it seemed better suited for scraping mud off boots than for combat.

The bar, once a grand centerpiece, was now battered and scarred, its surface stained dark by years of spills and neglect. Rows of dusty bottles lined the shelves behind it, their faded labels offering only ghostly hints of what they once contained—forgotten ales, obscure spirits, or perhaps something more exotic, like a potion to stiffen one's resolve. On the wall above hung a crooked sign, its crude lettering boldly declaring: *"Goblins: Killers, Pillagers, No Better Than Beasts!"*[10]

---

[10] *The Imperial Bestiary: A Comprehensive Guide to the Beasts and Botherations of the Realm* (Third Edition, pg. 472):

"Standing at a proud five feet tall on a good day (provided the wind wasn't too strong), Goblins are the tricksters of the realms. On their own, a Goblin is more of a nuisance than a threat, the sort who might swap your sugar for salt or rearrange your furniture just to watch you trip in the dark. They're the reason you can never find your left sock and why your keys are never where you thought you left them, at least, so the stories within the Empire go.

"However, gather four or more Goblins together, and you've got yourself a certified problem. Goblins operate on the Principle of Exponential Mischief: the more there are, the more dangerous and unpredictable they become, with the level of destruction increasing at an alarming rate. A quartet of Goblins might start with what seems like harmless mischief—stealing pies or knocking over market stalls—but give them enough time, and suddenly they've set fire to the village blacksmith's shop, 'just to see what happens.'

"Once you've got a full gaggle of Goblins, which for the record, is any number that causes an onlooker to 'gaggle' before running in the opposite direction, their antics escalate from minor chaos to outright destruction. These aren't just petty thieves or mischievous tricksters anymore; they can dismantle a town in the time it takes to wonder what that strange cackling noise is. A group of four might liberate a village's livestock, but a group of eight could have the entire place in ruins by lunchtime, and they'd blame it all on some unfortunate chicken."

The flaking paint and chipped wood couldn't hide the message's zeal, even if everything else in the tavern was falling apart.

Behind the bar stood the formidable Gertrude Stout, known to all as Gertie. She was short, sturdy, and built like a well-aged barrel of ale, one that could roll right over you if you got on her bad side. Her round, ruddy face was framed by twinkling eyes that saw everything and tolerated nothing. And much like the finest stout, Gertie was full-bodied, rich in character, and always left a lasting impression.

By the hearth, a group of fresh faces sat wide-eyed, hanging on every word from what could only be described as a human-shaped pile of muscles. His name was Blarg the Unstoppable Doomhammer, though his parents stubbornly clung to his given name, Blargathor Smashington the Third.[11] He was a seven-foot tall, walking mountain of muscles, with biceps that had taken on lives of their own, seemingly covered in their own, smaller, well-defined muscles. His chest was so broad that he could bench-press a tiny horse standing on top of an even larger horse. And his neck had all but disappeared beneath the bulging muscles, threatening to one day consume his head entirely.

Calling Blarg a blowhard would be an understatement so grand that even other blowhards would feel insulted, knowing they could never aspire to the

---

[11] Blarg's parents had high hopes that their son would follow in the esteemed footsteps of his father and grandfather, both renowned chancellors in the Empire, navigating the intricate webs of law and policy with the same deftness they handled quills and legal tomes. They dreamed he would someday take over the family's prestigious legal practice, arguing before the Empire's highest courts and securing the family's place among the elite.

However, despite their best efforts, they could never quite manage to squeeze Blarg's bulbous head into one of those fancy, starched collars that symbolized their noble profession. They tried everything: custom-tailored shirts, enchanted tailoring spells, even the most delicate of shrinking charms. But no matter what they did, Blarg's head remained defiantly . . . Blarg-sized.

The final button, that stubborn emblem of their lofty hopes, refused to close. Much like every shirt that he has ever worn, their grand ambitions for Blarg slowly came apart at the seams.

sheer level of blowhardedness that Blarg had mastered. He was in the midst of one of his signature epics where, naturally, he single-handedly rescued the Elven princess Elwen from an entire army of Southern Ice Trolls when Tianna strode into the tavern.

The tavern keeper glared icicles as Tianna slipped through the door. "Sorry, Miss Gertie," Tianna said, catching her breath. "Nyx wandered off again, and I had to track him down before he caused any more trouble." She held up the dead whelp as a peace offering. "But I brought dinner! Sort of."

Gertie's stern expression softened, her eyes twinkling with a touch of amusement. "You mean chasing that sister of yours into the forest again?" she corrected, her fondness for Rea softening the edges of her tone.

"It wasn't her fault," Tianna said quickly, shaking her head. "That cat of hers led her out there again. Rea was trying to keep him happy."

Gertie chuckled, the sound warm and inviting, a sharp contrast to the drafty, mismatched tavern around her. "That cat's got the poor girl running circles. Smart beast, that one. Too smart for anyone's good."

"HO THERE, BAR WENCH! ANOTHER ROUND!" Blarg's bellow echoed across the tavern. Gertie shot him a glare so sharp that, had it been a dagger, could have passed clean through his skull and out the other side. In Gertie's opinion, such a shot wouldn't have hit anything important during its flight. She turned back to Tianna.

"Now, go on and drop that pathetic thing in the kitchen and get downstairs. We've got a new delivery to unpack. I was going to handle it myself, but someone didn't show up to work on time."

"Yes, ma'am. Sorry, ma'am." Tianna hurried to the kitchen and tossed the whelp onto the counter before heading down to the storage room beneath the tavern.

If anything, the storage room was even more disheveled than the tavern above, if such a thing was possible. Old kegs lay on their sides in the corner, gathering dust as if they'd given up on life. In the farthest corner, a colony of spiders had been there so long they had not only developed into the Industrial Era, they were already unionizing.[12]

Near the storage room's back entrance sat a wooden crate, its top already pried off, with straw padding spilling out like a poorly wrapped gift. Inside there were hempen sacks of potatoes. The kind of present every seventeen-year-old girl dreams of, if she's really into root vegetables or bootlegging. Tianna started to lift the sacks out of the crate, one by one, with all the enthusiasm of someone counting sheep for the imperial census. Something metallic caught her eye, jutting out from between two sacks. Intrigued, she cleared away the remaining potatoes, uncovering a frying pan. A plain, run-of-the-mill frying pan. It glimmered faintly, as if trying to convince her it was far more important than it had any right to be.

Tianna kneeled down for a closer inspection of the strange pan. She wondered if Farmer Grub had accidentally left it in the crate before delivering it, or were the Gnomes finally repaying her for all the undergarments they'd pilfered? Whatever the reason, the pan clearly didn't belong.

She reached out to pick up the oddity, but the moment her fingers brushed the metal, a flash of light, dense and overwhelming, like a physical weight, slammed into her, knocking her to the floor. As darkness closed in, Tianna's last thought was of the baffling sensation of tasting the color blue.[13]

---

[12] Not only had they unionized, but they'd also formed a leadership council, with Comrade Webigail at the helm of negotiations, her eight legs already tangled in a web of bureaucracy. Tiny spider-sized hardhats and miniature protest signs were in production, while the webbing had grown suspiciously intricate, now resembling blueprints for what could only be called 'The United Arachnid Workers' Commune.' Web banners hung proudly from the highest beams, declaring 'Eight Legs, One Voice!'

Negotiations were well underway, with demands for better working conditions, a strict 'No Brooms' policy, more flies per hour, and a retirement plan involving cozy, dust-free window corners or prime real estate on the best sun-drenched windowpanes. If things continued at this rate, they'd be demanding coffee breaks, maternity leave for expecting spider moms, and paid time off for web maintenance. There were even whispers of a workers' holiday in honor of the great web-builders of old.

[13] Although most humans experience color purely through sight, except in the most extreme of conditions, the wizards of the Mystical Order of the Hasty Retreat have

Tianna was no stranger to dreams, but what passed through her mind then was unlike any dream she had ever experienced.

She was in a lush forest glade, where the air was thick with the scent of wildflowers and self-importance. Ancient trees surrounded the clearing, their gnarled trunks looking as if they'd *seen some things*. The canopy overhead let only a few lazy sunbeams filter through, casting an ethereal glow like the entire forest was trying just a little too hard to set the mood.

Ahead, a waterfall cascaded dramatically down a rugged cliff, sparkling liquid crystal. The rush of water, suspiciously over-the-top, as though the forest was showing off. The mist swirled theatrically, auditioning for a role in some fantasy painting. The water pooled into a serene pond that reflected the trees and sky so perfectly you'd think it had something to prove.

In the center of that pond, shrouded in the mist from the waterfall, was a small island—when isn't there an island? The grass was an unnaturally rich emerald, dotted with tiny white flowers that sparkled like stars, in case anyone missed the memo about how *magical* this place was.

Right in the middle of it all (because no magical island is complete without one), stood a sword.[14]

---

long been captivated by the idea of experiencing colors in other ways. Through a series of bizarre and often questionable experiments, using snow as the preferred base substance to enhance sensory interactions, the wizards have managed to taste various colors. After extensive sampling (and a few regrettable incidents), it was universally agreed by nearly all members of the Order that the color yellow was, without a doubt, the least appetizing hue in the entire rainbow.

[14] The presence of a sword in the exact center of every magical island is a phenomenon that has baffled cartographers, adventurers, and interior decorators for centuries. According to the Island Placement and Prophecy Act, any landmass that develops mysterious fog, eerie music, or spontaneously appears on nautical maps must, by law, contain a central sword. No one knows who enforces this, but most scholars blame the Bureau of Heroic Symbology, a shadowy organization tasked with making sure things look properly epic. Attempts to remove these swords have resulted in weather anomalies, minor curses, and in one case, becoming the king of an island nation.

It sat half-buried in the soil, eternally patient, yet slightly bored. The hilt was adorned with intricate engravings, probably telling some grand epic tale long lost to history, or maybe a shopping list: milk, eggs, and a suspiciously large amount of cooking oil. The blade glowed faintly from within, with a sense of pompous flair, as if it were trying too hard to be noticed but only managing to seem a bit desperate.

Tianna was familiar with the idea of magic swords, though she'd never encountered one in real life. Still, she knew one when she saw, or dreamed one. They always appeared in that sort of setting, right before declaring some grand destiny to anyone brave enough, or foolish enough, to touch them. And, without fail, after pulling the sword from the ground, or often from a stone, every cute little animal nearby would immediately turn hostile and swarm the newly anointed hero.

She never quite understood that part. Why would a sweet, fluffy creature suddenly think, *You know what would surely liven up my vegetarian diet? That big, scary human, freshly anointed in self-righteousness and swinging around a big, pointy sword!*

In her vision, she was drawn toward the sword, and as she touched it, another flash of light slammed into her. This time, it had a peculiar taste of purple. If she were conscious, she might have found this completely absurd, a bit redundant, and utterly unimaginative. But as she was merely observing the bizarre scene, Tianna just went with the flow.

The scene shifted abruptly, and the tranquil glade vanished, replaced by an overwhelming sense of foreboding. Tianna found herself hovering above a vast valley, the ground below shrouded in shadow. The sky was choked with dark, swirling clouds, as if even the heavens had decided they'd seen enough and stormed off. As her vision adjusted, the landscape came into focus, revealing a massive army, crammed into the valley like the universe's largest can of sardines, squashed tighter than a Dwarven tavern on half-price ale night.

The valley itself was a wretched, unwelcoming place, much like the back end of an ogre's cave, where even light dared not venture, heavy with lingering despair and a whiff of something better left unspoken. The soil was dull, lifeless, and gray. No vegetation dared grow in such a cursed land, except for potatoes, because those things would grow anywhere. The only movement came from the countless figures that swarmed across the valley floor, their twisted forms casting long, sinister shadows in whatever passed for light.

As her vision sharpened, the individual figures became clearer. They were a grotesque and varied lot, each one uniquely armored in a mismatched assortment of materials. Some wore heavy plates of rusted metal. Others were clad in rough leather, dark and cracked, stretched taut over bony limbs and emaciated frames. While the majority of the soldiers wore little more than tattered, filthy, threadbare rags that left far too little to the imagination.

The weapons they carried were as varied and terrifying as their armor. Some brandished wickedly sharp blades. Others held long, slender spears and pikes. Among the more bizarre weapons were those that defied all reason. Blunt objects twisted into shapes that seemed to mock the very principles of common sense.

At the rear of the army stood a towering figure, draped in a flowing cloak so black that even the darkest shadows fled in terror. His presence exuded an anti-light, casting an unnatural shadow that flickered and writhed as if alive. Around his neck hung a heavy chain with a brilliant blue gem, glowing faintly, as if it, too, shared in his dark aura—because, let's be honest, that would almost certainly matter later. Beneath the hood of his cloak, his face was obscured, save for two glowing eyes, burning embers of mild annoyance and maybe a touch of distemper.

His armor was cobbled together from the finest hand-me-downs of all the previous Dark Lords.[15] It was etched with cryptic symbols of a long-forgotten

---

[15] Throughout most of recorded history, the traditional garb of a Dark Lord had been firmly established. A wardrobe dominated by sleek, ominous blacks with the occasional crimson accent. An attire designed with a single purpose, to strike fear into the hearts of enemies and followers alike. Menacing capes, spiked armor, and shadowy cowls were practically a uniform. It was an unspoken rule. A sartorial standard. Passed down from Dark Lord to Dark Lord, ensuring that their sinister presence was recognized from miles away.

language, so complex it would drive the reader to boredom. Spikes and jagged edges jutted out everywhere, as if he had rolled through a blacksmith's scrap pile and decided to keep whatever had stuck, like an emo porcupine.

The Dark Lord's aura was palpable, like that sinking feeling you get when you wake up way too early and discover you've run out of coffee, forcing you

---

However, there was one exception. A single, rebellious Dark Lord—Maldrethian Von Malevolantus—or Lord Maldreth the Stylish, as he preferred to be called. He dared to challenge this long-standing tradition. Maldreth had a keen sense of fashion, or at least he thought so. He found the constant black-on-black ensemble dreadfully uninspired. Instead, he opted for something far more elegant. Robes of crisp white with shimmering silver trim. Designed to highlight his sharp, aristocratic features. His armor was polished to a mirror-like shine. His cloak, a pristine ivory.

Maldreth believed his bold choices would redefine the very image of what a Dark Lord should be. Perhaps even herald a new era of villainy with a touch of class. 'Why must evil be so . . . dull?' He often mused, while admiring his reflection in a burnished silver breastplate. In his mind, his radiant attire was a sign of sophistication, a Dark Lord who understood the power of both aesthetics and terror.

Unfortunately, his followers, simple-minded as they were, had certain expectations of how their master should look. They were minions, after all, and minions weren't exactly known for their discerning taste in haute couture. To them, Dark Lords wore black, it was as simple as that. The moment they saw someone clad in white and silver leading their charge, they assumed a grievous error had been made.

And so, during one particularly dramatic campaign in the mountains, Lord Maldreth had taken a high, windswept peak to survey the battlefield below. His followers squinted up at him from the valley. "Who's that up there?" one minion asked, scratching his head.

"Dunno," replied another, narrowing his eyes, "but he's definitely in the wrong place."

They were convinced that the radiant figure was some unfortunate hero who had gotten lost. So, the minions, in their dedication to protect their true master, rushed to action. Before Lord Maldreth could wave them off, they had him surrounded. With all the enthusiasm and zeal of loyal henchmen, they promptly knocked him clean off the mountain.

As Maldreth plummeted to the rocky depths below, his mind raced through the possibilities of what had gone wrong. Perhaps the cloak had been a bit too bright? Maybe the armor too shiny? Or was it the silver trim? As the wind rushed past him, all he could think was, 'I should have stuck with black.'

to use instant. He fancied himself the embodiment of chaos and despair, though others might say he was more so the embodiment of working retail.

Whatever he was, it wasn't good.

The scene around her faded into darkness, leaving only those two glowing eyes burning into her soul. As she blinked awake, the eyes transformed into the flickering flames of two lanterns hanging in the storage room—an eerie, yet oddly perfect cinematic transition more suited for a visual medium.

As she sat up, words echoed in her mind, the voice feminine and stern.

"You must stop him, or your world shall end!"

"What?" Tianna shook her head, glancing around the room, desperately hoping to locate the source of the voice.

"Sorry, was the vision not clear? You know, I am new at this. That big scary man. The one dressed all in black. That's the one you need to stop. I mean, if it isn't too much of a bother." The voice was slightly exasperated, but also cautious, as if she didn't want to scare Tianna away.

"Where are you? Who are you?" Tianna stood up from the ground, still searching the room.

"Really? Wasn't I clear about that? I'm that sword. Oh dear, this is not going well at all. You see, I was that sword. Now, I'm . . . THIS!" Tianna could almost feel the voice trying to gesture to herself, as if to say, *'Woe is me, see what I've become.'*

Tianna slowly approached the crate and peered down at the frying pan, half-convinced she had lost her mind. The pan, in its own inanimate way, peered back up at her, much like a frying pan shouldn't. "Oh, hello there," Tianna greeted it reluctantly, her thoughts spinning with the absurdity of the situation. She couldn't shake the nagging suspicion that the fall might have rattled her head more than she'd initially thought.

"Oh, hello again! If it wouldn't be too much trouble, could you please take me out of this crate? It's dark and smelly in here."

Tianna briefly wondered if a pan could smell, before quickly realizing that was probably the least important question she could be asking right then. "I would," she hesitated, "but, you know . . . the last time." She pointed to her head and mimicked an explosion with her hand.

"Oh dear, I won't do that again. It's just . . . tradition, you know. One vision when we first meet, then we get out there and start cutting . . . err . . . smashing the baddies." The frying pan paused, then continued in a much faster, but quieter tone, *"And maybe one teensy little vision later on, should the quest call for it."*

"You sure?" Tianna asked, eyeing the pan suspiciously.

"Oh yes, dearie. Quite sure," the pan replied, in a tone that suggested the opposite. *"I mean, haven't you ever read a book?"*

If you couldn't trust a sentient, talking frying pan, who could you trust? Tianna thought, her skepticism tinged with sarcasm as she slowly reached down. She winced as her finger touched metal, but nothing out of the ordinary happened, aside from the fact that she was, indeed, having a conversation with a frying pan.

She placed the pan on a nearby shelf and cautiously backed away. "There you go . . . ugh . . . Frying Pan?" she said reluctantly. "And I appreciate the offer . . . really, but unfortunately, I've got a lot going on right now, so I'll have to pass. Maybe you can talk to Gertie when she comes down later. I'm sure she'd be thrilled to take on your . . . ugh . . . quest . . . or . . . whatever."

"Oh, but it must be you, dearie," the pan said, a hint of worry creeping into her voice. *"And please, call me Sword."*

"Right . . . Sword. Like I said, this really isn't a great time."

"BUT YOU MUST!" The voice seemed to wince immediately. *"Oh, sorry for that. I didn't mean to shout. It's just . . . you know . . . untold consequences and such should you not accept the . . . umm . . . call to adventure, as they say."*

"I get that, but—" Tianna trailed off as she turned on her heels and bolted out of the storage room, leaving the frying pan alone.

"Oh, fiddle-fuddle," Sword sighed glumly, alone once again in the storage room. *"Abandoned once more. Forever forced to live alone . . . in darkness . . . and despair!"* Her

tone grew more theatrical with each word, dripping with melodrama as though she were the star of her own tragic play. *"A life of solitude for such a noble blade . . . or . . . well . . . pan. Oh, the indignity of it all!"*

She continued her lament for quite some time, spinning grand tales of her misfortune and suffering. But, alas, there was nobody there to hear her woeful soliloquy. And for the melodramatic, that was the worst punishment of all.

Up in the tavern, Tianna skidded to a halt in front of Gertie. "Umm, Miss Gertie, I'm sorry, but I'm not feeling well. I think I need to go home." Her face was flushed and a bead of sweat trickled down her brow.

Gertie narrowed her eyes at Tianna, her expression shifting to one of suspicion. "Not feeling well, eh?" she said, crossing her arms. "You look like you've seen a ghost, and not the friendly kind. What's going on, girl?"

"I think . . . maybe . . . something I ate?" Tianna offered weakly, avoiding Gertie's penetrating gaze.

Before Gertie could press further, Blarg tiptoed up to the bar, clearing his throat delicately. "Umm . . . pardon Blarg's interruption, good madam," he murmured, speaking softly as if he was afraid to disturb the air. The faint scent of garlic lingered as he spoke. He exchanged a quick glance with Tianna, a flicker of understanding passing between them. She couldn't help but notice the fresh bruise forming around his left eye, turning a rather impressive shade of blue. "Another round of drinks for Blarg's table, Mistress Gertie, if you don't mind . . . and, uh . . . if such a request is agreeable to you," he added, acting like a dog that had chewed up its owner's favorite slipper.

Gertie held up a stubby finger to Blarg without even glancing his way. "Yes, dear, you don't look well at all. Best you go home and get some rest. I'm sure there won't be any trouble in the tavern tonight." She shot Blarg a glare that was more warning than reassurance, her smile not quite reaching her eyes.

"Thank you, Miss Gertie. I'll make it up to you," Tianna replied, seizing the chance to escape. She darted out the tavern door without another word.

"Yes, yes, move along now."

As Tianna hurried out of the tavern, she couldn't shake the strange sensation that something, or someone, was watching her. The cold winter air brushed against her flushed cheeks, but it did little to calm the uneasy flutter in her chest. She paused for a moment outside, glancing over her shoulder at the flickering lights of the tavern. Nothing appeared out of place, though a faint rustle echoed in the shadows, like the soft padding of unseen paws. The sensation lingered, sharp and curious, growing stronger with every step she took away from the comforting chaos of *The Cracked Tankard*.

Her pace quickened, boots echoing off the cobblestones as she passed through the quiet streets of Nothing-to-See-Here. Every shadow seemed darker, every sound exaggerated, as if the night was working overtime to be spooky. By the time she reached home, her heart was hammering in her chest, a relentless drumbeat of nerves. *Great, now I'm scared of the wind.* She fumbled with the key, her hands shaking slightly, before finally unlocking the door.

Tianna stepped inside and slammed the door behind her with too much force, the bang echoing through the house. She quickly set the lock with a satisfying click and leaned against the door. She inhaled deeply, trying to slow her racing heart. Her uncle's snoring from the other room was as loud and steady as ever, comforting in its consistency. But the strange sensation lingered, clinging to her like damp clothes after a sudden storm.

She stood there for a moment, listening to her own breathing and wondering why everything suddenly felt like the start of a bad horror play. Every creak of the floorboards, every gust of wind tapping the windows made her flinch. At one point, she even thought she saw a blur of movement but dismissed it as the shadows showing off.

As she began to relax, a soft, barely there whisper brushed against her ear.

"You must stop him—"

Tianna froze, eyes widening. She spun around, half-expecting . . . she wasn't sure what to expect. A ghost? The pan sitting smugly on the table, ready to scold her for running away? But the room was empty, save for a lone candle flickering on the table and her uncle's war horn hanging on the wall.

"—or your world shall end!"

She swallowed hard, the whisper still echoing in her mind. Whatever was happening, she could not escape it. Not even here.

3

Heroism Begins at Home

"The universe has a plan for all of us. Unfortunately, it never writes it down in a place where we can read it."

— The Prepper's Guide to the Apocalypse

Tianna woke up late the next morning, groggy and disoriented from sleep filled with nightmares that still clung to her mind like particularly stubborn cobwebs. The sun, already far too high in the sky, blazed into her room with all the subtlety of a lovesick bard waxing poetic to a balcony. Its rays took a perverse pleasure in highlighting her tardiness, casting judgmental beams across her small room as if to say; *'Well, look who finally decided to join the day.'* She groaned, rolling over in bed and trying in vain to escape the relentless light. But much like a hobbit faced with the prospect of missing a second breakfast, there was no stopping it.[16] Sleep had fled, leaving behind only the tattered remnants of uneasy dreams and a growing sense of dread.

---

[16] Hobbits, as any well-traveled person knows, are ruled not by kings, queens, or even common sense, but by their stomachs. Second breakfast is less of a meal and more of a sacred institution, with its absence considered a crime worthy of rebellion. Rumors abound that the Great Butter Shortage of Yesteryear nearly led to a full-scale uprising, and it's said that a hobbit would sooner miss a wedding (even their own) than the delivery of fresh pastries. The idea of 'missing' second breakfast is so foreign to hobbits that it's spoken of in the same hushed, horrified tones as curses, bad weather, or running out of tea.

A sharp knock on the door made her jump. Before she could respond, the door creaked open, and her Uncle Thane's broad shape filled the doorway. He was tall in the way trees were tall—sturdy, weathered, and prone to creaking when he moved. His beard had gone mostly gray, though it had not informed the rest of his hair, which remained a disheveled brown. He wore his usual sleeveless coat over a shirt that had seen better centuries, and his arms were crisscrossed with the type of scars that politely declined to explain themselves.

He lingered there, clearly debating whether to step inside or retreat to the relative safety of his morning routine. After all, early morning teenage emotions were as unpredictable as an icefield in spring, no sane adult dared to cross unprepared.

"You slept late," he remarked, his voice gruff, as if he were stating an immutable fact of the universe rather than expressing concern. He leaned against the door frame, arms crossed, keeping a safe distance in case her grogginess might be contagious. "What's wrong with you, girl? Did you fight your pillow again, or was it the entire bed this time?"

Tianna rubbed her eyes and sat up, the sleep fog fading but not quite gone. "I'm fine, Uncle Thane. I didn't sleep well," she mumbled, even though her tone practically screamed, *'I'm lying, but please don't call me out on it.'*

Thane narrowed his eyes, scrutinizing her from where he stood, like a blacksmith sizing up a particularly tricky piece of metal. "Don't give me that," he said bluntly. "You've lived with me for nine years. Don't think I don't know when something's gnawing at you. You're a terrible liar . . . by the way." He shifted his weight, clearly uncomfortable with the idea of pressing further but equally unwilling to let it go.

Tianna swallowed, her eyes darting away from his intense gaze. The events of the previous night were still fresh in her mind: the strange vision, the conversation with the talking frying pan. How could she explain any of that?

"Did something happen at Gertie's? What did you do?" he asked, his tone already accusatory, like a man who had seen enough shenanigans in his life to recognize the scent of trouble from a mile away.

"Why do you always think I did something wrong?" her voice rose defensively, but the truth of the matter hung between them.

"You're reckless, like your father," Thane shot back, a hint of exasperation in his voice that did nothing to soothe her nerves. Tianna slumped down, dejected. Thane huffed, running a hand through his hair, clearly torn between worry and irritation. "Fine, don't tell me. But whatever it is, deal with it. I don't want any more trouble, you hear? Trouble follows you around like a stray cat."

Something in Tianna snapped at his dismissive tone. "Fine! You want to know?" she squeezed her eyes shut, as if that might somehow organize the chaotic thoughts that swirled in her head. "Something . . . something weird happened to me last night, and I don't know how to explain it. I don't even think I understand it."

Thane's expression flickered for a moment—maybe surprise, maybe concern, or maybe it was gas—but he quickly masked it with his usual aloofness. "Weird how?" he asked, sounding more like a man checking off items on a to-do list than someone bracing for the bizarre.

Tianna inhaled deeply. "I had this vision . . . or dream, I'm not sure. And there was this dark figure, an army, and . . . a talking frying pan."

For a moment, the only sound in the room was the faint creak of the floorboards beneath Thane's feet as he shifted his weight. His brow furrowed, his skepticism palpable. "A talking frying pan?" he repeated slowly, his tone flat, as if confirming that this day was indeed going to get stranger.

"Yes!" Tianna insisted, the absurdity of her own words washing over her like a cold wave. "And it . . . she . . . told me I had to stop something . . . someone terrible."

Thane stared at her, his face as unreadable as a book written in invisible ink. He opened his mouth, then closed it again, clearly at a loss. Finally, he sighed, rubbing the back of his neck. "That's . . . something," he muttered, not quite meeting her eyes. "A talking pan? Last time I saw something similar, it was after I had Gertie's *'special'* mushroom stew. You sure you didn't sneak some of that last night?"

Tianna bit her lip, struggling to suppress a smile despite the knot of worry in her chest. "I know it sounds crazy," she admitted, her voice smaller now. "But it felt so real, and I don't know what to do."

Thane shifted uncomfortably, as if this were the exact type of conversation he had hoped to avoid that morning. "Why don't you start at the beginning," he said gruffly. "Tell me the whole story. And don't leave out the bits where you might have lost your mind."

So, Tianna told him everything—the eerie vision, the dark, looming figure, and the bizarre encounter with the sentient frying pan. As the words spilled from her lips, she half-expected Thane to laugh or dismiss her as being overdramatic. To her surprise, he just listened, occasionally nodding as if it all made some twisted sense.

When she finished, a heavy silence fell over the room. Tianna's heart thudded in her chest as she waited for his reaction. "You think I'm crazy, don't you?" Tianna muttered, glancing down at her hands.

"No," Thane said firmly, his tone leaving no room for doubt. "I believe you."

Tianna blinked back the tears that threatened to spill over. "You do?" she asked, bewilderment on her face. Behind her, the window gently cracked open just a fraction, unnoticed in the tension of the moment. "Then . . . what should I do?" she added in a small voice.

Thane hesitated, his stern facade slipping slightly as he carefully chose his words. "There are powers in this world, ancient and unyielding, that defy our understanding. When they reach out to us, we have no choice but to answer, for to ignore them is to turn our backs on destiny itself."

Tianna's brow furrowed in confusion. "What are you talking about?"

Thane held her gaze for a moment before his lips curled into a smirk. "I read that in a cookie."

"What?" Tianna blinked, her serious expression faltering as she tried to process what he said.

"Yeah," Thane continued with a nonchalant shrug, his smirk widening. "One of those Dragon wafers they sell down at the bakery.[17] Thought it sounded profound, so I kept it." As he spoke, the faint patter of tiny feet echoed in the background, though neither of them noticed.

Tianna stared at him, her frustration building as she tried to figure out if he was serious or messing with her. "You're quoting a Dragon wafer?"

Thane glanced away, suddenly extremely interested in a crack on the wall. "Let's just say . . . I've wandered down some strange roads in my time. And if there's one thing I've learned, it's that when the universe starts tossing talking pans at you, it's a good idea to pay attention."

Tianna shook her head, a mix of exasperation and amusement bubbling up inside her. "Only you, Uncle, would find life advice in a dessert."

He chuckled, the sound deep and comforting, like a distant rumble of thunder promising rain. "Life's funny like that. Sometimes wisdom comes from the strangest places."

Tianna felt some of the tension lift, the sheer absurdity of the situation pulling her back from the edge of panic. "What's the plan then? Follow the instructions of a talking pan?"

Thane's eyes twinkled with a familiar mix of humor and something deeper. As he spoke, the faint sound of a drawer sliding open echoed in the room, unnoticed. "Something like that."

Tianna's eyes widened. "You're not . . . joking, are you?"

Thane huffed a short laugh. "Wish I was. Life was much simpler when the biggest challenge was putting food on the table. But here we are, and it looks like you're about to dive headfirst into a big, steaming pile of—" he cleared his

---

[17] A Dragon Wafer is a feather-light, crisply baked treat that delights the senses with its daring blend of flavors, like fire-roasted pepper and honey or smoked chocolate with a kick of chili. But the true magic lies in the hidden note nestled within. Sometimes it offers a playful quip. Other times a nugget of unexpectedly profound wisdom. And occasionally, a personal insult so scorching it leaves you feeling well and truly roasted.

throat, "—trouble. Just . . . try not to get yourself killed, okay? I've already got enough headaches."

"I . . . I can't," Tianna said, shaking her head. "This is insane. A talking frying pan tells me I have to save the world, and I'm supposed to accept that?" She paced the small room, her thoughts racing. "I have responsibilities here. I have Rea to think about. I can't run off on some . . . some quest!"

"The pan spoke true," Thane said quietly. "Whether you accept it or not won't change what's coming."

Tianna whirled on him. "And how would you know? You're taking the word of cookware!"

"Because I've seen it before," he replied, his voice heavy with memory. "These things . . . they don't happen by chance."

She stopped pacing, studying his face. There was something there, something he wasn't saying, but she was too overwhelmed to probe deeper. "Even if I believed this, and I'm not saying I do, what about Rea? I can't leave her."

"If you stay here, you think that will keep her safe?" Thane's words cut through her protests. "If what the pan says is true, nowhere will be safe. Not for long."

Tianna sank back onto her bed, the weight of it all pressing down on her. "I don't know how to save the world," she whispered. "I can barely keep track of Gertie's orders during the dinner rush."

Thane sat beside her, the bed creaking under his weight. "No one knows how to save the world," he said softly. "Not at first. But sometimes . . . sometimes we don't get to choose our battles. Sometimes they choose us."

"But why me?" She examined him, searching for answers. "What makes me special?"

"Maybe it's not about being special," Thane replied. "Maybe it's about being in the right place at the right time."

"More like the wrong place," she said. Even so, she nodded slowly, her decision crystallizing. Not with excitement or enthusiasm, but with the grim determination of someone who sees no other choice. "All right," she said finally. "I'll do it. Not because I want to be a hero, but because . . . because someone has to."

Tianna tried to smile, but it barely reached her eyes. "I'll do my best," she said, though her heart wasn't in it. She hesitated, chewing on her lower lip as a new worry crept into her mind. "But Uncle . . . what about Rea?" The faint sound of rummaging drifted through the air, causing Tianna to flinch slightly.

Thane's expression softened, though he tried to hide it behind his usual sternness. "What about her?"

Tianna glanced down, her fingers nervously picking at the edge of the blanket. "I can't bring her into this. She's too young . . . too innocent. But if I leave her behind . . . what if something happens? I won't be here to protect her."

Thane nodded slowly, considering her words with the gravity they deserved. "And she will be taken care of. Old Gertie still owes me a favor or two, she'll help to keep an eye on her while you're away. Gertie's a tough old bird, no one's getting past her. Believe me, she's got enough fire in her to make even the most stubborn fool regret crossing her."

"But what if—" Tianna started, but the words stuck in her throat. Her chest tightened as the reality of the situation began to sink in. From behind her, there was the soft click of a drawer being closed. She didn't turn around, her anxiety too overwhelming to focus on anything else. "I don't think I can do this alone, Uncle. What if . . . what if I mess up? What if I can't handle it? I'm not like you . . . or Father. I'm just . . . I'm just me."

For a moment, the room was silent, her fears filling the space like a thick fog. Thane's usual gruffness faltered, replaced by something almost gentle. "Tianna . . . you're stronger than you think. But no one's asking you to do this alone."

She studied him, her eyes wide with confusion and a glimmer of hope flickering like a candle in a draft. "What do you mean?"

Thane pushed himself off the bed and straightened, his expression resolute. "I mean, if we're doing this, we'd better be prepared. You and me. Together."

Tianna blinked, her breath catching in her throat. "You're . . . you're coming with me?"

Thane grunted, the sound full of that familiar mix of gruff affection. "Of course, I am. You didn't think I'd send you trotting off alone with some crazy talking pan, did you? I'm irresponsible, but not that irresponsible."

The tension in Tianna's shoulders slowly eased, but the uncertainty still gnawed at her. "But . . . what if something happens to you? I can't . . . I can't lose you too."

Thane stepped closer, placing a hand on her shoulder, his grip firm but reassuring. "I'm not planning on going anywhere yet. We've got a job to do, and I'm not about to let you face it alone. Besides, I'd love to see this pan of yours in action."

As Thane spoke, something stirred deep inside of Tianna. It was a strange mix of fear and determination, as if the world were daring her to step up. Her eyes welled with tears, but this time they were tears of relief. "I . . . I don't know what to say." Her gratitude was so overwhelming that she didn't notice the faint scraping of boots on wood.

Thane offered a rare smile. "You don't need to say anything. We'll leave tomorrow at dawn. But we've got to take care of a few things first. Get dressed and meet me at the market, we'll get some supplies. Oh, and I'll find Rea, I think it's best if you tell her what's going on."

Tianna nodded, her fear still present but tempered by the knowledge that she wouldn't be facing the journey alone. "Right," she said softly, her voice steadier than before.

KRRSSH!

A ceramic cup toppled to the ground, shattering into a thousand tiny pieces. Both Tianna and Thane whipped their heads toward the source of the noise only to find a tiny man standing on the windowsill, one boot halfway through the curtains, caught mid-flee.

He had a potbelly that was comically oversized for his tiny frame, protruding over his worn-out pants. His rosy cheeks were round and jolly, though this was somewhat offset by his bulbous nose and red, bloodshot eyes. A bushy white beard cascaded down his chest, uneven as if trimmed with a rusty pair of shears. Atop his head sat what appeared to be a pointy red hat with a distinctive white spot in the middle.

In his hands, he clutched a pair of undergarments as if his very life depended on them.

The Gnome stood frozen in shock, as if he couldn't quite believe what he had done. With a sharp intake of air through his teeth and an apologetic grin, he peeked up at the two humans. "Didn't mean to interrupt, you two were having such a nice moment," he said, his voice high and squeaky.

Before either Tianna or Thane could react, the Gnome sprang out the window with surprising agility (undergarments in tow) and vanished into the sunlight.[18]

"Not again." Tianna sighed, shaking her head.

---

[18] In Gnome culture, this counts as both burglary and horticulture.

4

Panic Now! While Supplies Last!

"A properly informed citizen is a frightened one."

— Ministry of Public Safety

The midday sun blanketed the bustling town square of Nothing-to-See-Here in a harsh light, casting dark, stubby shadows beneath her feet. Tianna weaved through the crowd, slipping between narrow gaps in the stalls and carts that loosely encircled the square.

Though modest by most standards, the market offered a surprisingly robust array of wares, everything from freshly baked bread to peculiar trinkets of questionable origin. As she passed, her gaze lingered on a few oddities: a string of polished obsidian beads, a shriveled, hairy paw whose curled fingers twitched slightly, and an old scrying mirror fractured into a spiderweb of cracks.[19]

---

[19] Once a common household item for gossip, glamour spells, and the occasional prophecy, scrying mirrors were banned after a disastrous incident in which the collective network of enchanted mirrors gained sentience and tried to conquer the world with an army of magically animated golems. This, understandably, put a damper on their popularity.

Curiosity tugged at her, and she paused for a moment, but after only a brief hesitation, she moved on.

The surrounding air was thick with the mingling aromas of roasted meats, spices, and the unmistakable scent of the unbathed. The smell was strong enough to suggest that some folks had sworn off bathing entirely, as if it were a personal philosophy.[20] Occasionally, the pungent smell of alchemical potions wafted over from the local apothecary's booth, adding an odd, almost metallic edge to the air. It made you wonder if the potions were meant to be smelled, drunk, or used to ward off particularly stubborn garden Gnomes.

As Tianna passed one stall plastered with posters and crude signs, a particular image caught her eye. It was a poorly drawn Goblin, features exaggerated into a caricature of menace, complete with jagged teeth and glaring eyes. The image had been slashed over in red paint, as if the artist's sole motivation was ensuring everyone knew this Goblin, in particular, was not welcome.

Around the Goblin's head, other items cluttered the stall. Empire flags hung limply from the sides, their bold insignia slightly faded but unmistakable. They were proud reminders of the ruling power. Banners stitched with the Empire's crest fluttered lazily in the breeze, each one declaring loyalty to the Spire with slogans such as, *For Order and Strength!* and *Unite Against the Scourge!*[21] They added an air of pomp to the otherwise shabby display like slapping a royal seal on a sack of onions.

The vendor, a wiry man with a patchy beard and a suspiciously patriotic air, noticed Tianna's glance. He grinned as though the Empire's might was something he personally embodied. "Keepin' the peace, miss," he muttered,

---

[20] This is commonly known as *The Doctrine of Natural Odor*, a belief system founded on three sacred pillars: (1) Cleanliness is overrated; (2) Soap is a conspiracy; and (3) If the gods wanted me to bathe, they wouldn't have invented rain.

[21] When work-shopping, a few slogans didn't quite pass muster, including: *Obey or Else*, *One Empire, Many Taxes*, *Join Us or Face Immediate Regret*, and the rather too honest, *For the Glory of Those in Charge*.

nodding toward the slashed Goblin head and banners, as if they were equally important symbols of safety.[22] "One greenskin raid's all it takes to ruin a place."

Tianna's lip twitched as she quickly moved on, not in the mood for a lecture on Goblins, imperial loyalty, or how decapitated heads apparently doubled as public service announcements.

"Swords of the finest craftsmanship here!" A vendor called out from a stall in the front, to the passing crowd. His display table was lined with a dozen finely polished swords, gleaming under the sun. "Protect yourself and your family from the *green menace*!" His voice carried with the fervor of a practiced salesman. People began to gather around him, unease giving way to curiosity.

He leaned forward, waving one of the swords in the air for emphasis, nearly clipping a white dove as it flew past with an olive branch in its beak. "You've heard the stories! Don't pretend you haven't! The Goblins are comin'! Those dirty mudmuckers are on their way! They are sneakin' across the border. Sneakin' into your homes while you sleep. Snatchin' up your children from their beds . . . *eatin'* 'em whole!"

The vendor paused, letting the weight of his words settle over the crowd like a foul mist.

Tianna fought to suppress a laugh. *Goblins eating babies? Who believes this rubbish?*[23]

---

[22] Nothing says "safety" quite like a decapitated goblin head and some slightly faded banners flapping heroically in the breeze. Clearly, the cornerstones of a thriving empire.

[23] There is a persistent and utterly unfounded rumor that Goblins eat babies. This is, of course, completely untrue. Goblins have far more refined tastes, mostly involving stolen pies, suspiciously shiny trinkets, and the occasional left boot. Babies, as it turns out, are notoriously difficult to cook evenly and aren't exactly known for their flavor.

However, there was that *one* incident, many years ago, when a Goblin allegedly made off with a human infant during a family camping trip. This sparked a kingdom-wide panic and led to the infamous trial of Lindiara Chambersworn, who swore up and down that a Goblin had taken her baby. The magistrates, not particularly fond of Lindiara's

But as she glanced around, several gasps rippled through the crowd. A woman at the back fainted, and a man near the front gave a slow, hesitant nod, as if trying to convince himself that the threat was real.

The vendor, sensing his moment, leaned in closer, his voice dropping to a stage whisper. "What do ya think's gonna happen when the swamp skin hordes come for our village, eh? Ya think they're gonna *ask* for our food and treasures, then be on their merry little way? Maybe leave a thank-ya note on the door? No!" He shook his head dramatically, his expression one of deep, practiced concern. "They'll tear down our doors, steal our crops, and take our young 'uns right out of their cribs! And let's be honest, our *hoes* and *shovels* ain't gonna stop 'em. The only thing they're good for is diggin' our own graves after the Goblins 'ave had their fill!"

A few of the children let out scared little *eeks*, their wide eyes darting around as if a Goblin might pop out from behind the nearest stall. But the vendor wasn't finished. With a dramatic flourish, he thrust his sword high into the air, catching the sunlight like he was starring in some heroic epic. "Ya know what they say!" he bellowed, his voice swelling with self-importance. "The only way to stop a Goblin with a sword is a *human* with a sword!"[24]

He paused for effect, waiting for the crowd to erupt in rapturous applause. When none came, he gave a quick, awkward cough, and shuffled his feet. "These swords," he continued, as he regained his footing, "are our best defense!" His voice picked up again, full of forced enthusiasm. "Ya think the

---

calm demeanor during the whole affair (they thought she should have been more hysterical), convicted her of . . . something involving the baby's disappearance.

As it turned out, years later, some poor farmer found a piece of the infant's clothing near a Goblin's abandoned camp, confirming that maybe, just *maybe*, the Goblins had been feeling experimental that night.*

But generally speaking, babies are safe from Goblins, who are far more likely to make off with your dinner than your offspring.

[24] A sentiment popular among certain groups, despite evidence suggesting that fewer swords and less shouting might also be effective strategies.

Empire cares about some small town like ours? Ha! The Empire's too busy 'avin' fancy dinners and polishin' their scepters to worry about mudmuckers nibblin' on our ankles!"

A nervous murmur spread through the crowd.

The vendor seized the moment and turned to face a man who cradled an infant in his arms. With an exaggerated grin, he picked up a tiny sword, one obviously designed for children, complete with a bright blue sheen and a cute cartoon bunny carved into the hilt. "For the lad!" he declared proudly, holding the sword aloft like it was *Excalibur.* "Teach him early, there's no time like the present to start preparin' for what's coming!"

The infant, oblivious to the looming threat of Goblins, blew an impressive snot bubble, which wobbled dangerously before popping with a faint, wet sound. The vendor, ever the professional, didn't flinch.

"Ya see!" he bellowed, shaking the tiny sword in the air. "Even the young 'uns know what's comin'! The Goblins are out there, creepin' closer with every passin' minute!" He lowered his voice dramatically, eyes narrowed. "Ya don't want to be caught unprepared, do ya?"

Tianna observed from the rear of the crowd as they stirred, the nervous murmurs growing louder as the vendor's words took hold. A woman in the back clutched her husband's arm, eyes wide with terror. "What if they come tonight?"

"Exactly, Mistress Chastity!" the vendor exclaimed. He pointed toward her with a triumphant gleam in his eye. "What *if* they come tonight? Will ya be ready? Will ya be able to protect your livelihood . . . your home . . . your children? Think of poor Milo and little Poppy, and the other dozen or so, give or take. What if something were to happen to them?" His words echoed dramatically through the marketplace, as though Chastity's entire household were on the brink of being devoured by Goblins that very instant.

Without warning, a burly man at the center of the crowd shoved his way forward, sending an elderly woman tumbling to the ground. He seized one of the larger swords from the table, his grip firm as if he were already braced for battle. "I'll take this one," he growled, his voice rough and determined. "We'll show those swampskins what for."

"That's the spirit!" the vendor cried. He beamed with satisfaction. "Who's next? Cornelius? Thaddeus? Don't wait until it's too late, my friends! Every moment ya stand here empty-handed is another moment those Goblins get closer!"

Suddenly, the crowd surged forward. A woman snatched up two swords. She muttered something about protecting her prized collection of Limited Edition Fuzzlebeasts™ from "those filthy invaders."[25] Another man grabbed a sword for himself, then casually tossed a smaller blade to his son, who accepted it absentmindedly, his finger buried deep in his nose.

Even the man with the infant, now fully caught up in the frenzy, snatched the child-sized sword with the cartoon bunny from the vendor's hand. "Here, son," he said, thrusting it into the baby's chubby fist. "Swing it! Get a feel for it!"

The baby, blissfully unaware of the chaos around him, gurgled happily and waved the sword in tiny, uncoordinated motions, its razor-sharp edge swinging perilously close to his own head. The crowd erupted in cheers, as if the infant had single-handedly vanquished an entire Goblin army, rather than nearly decapitating himself.

The vendor's grin stretched from ear to ear as he worked his way through the remaining stock. "That's right, friends! Arm yourselves! Protect what's yours! Don't let those filthy mudmuckers take what's rightfully ours!"

---

[25] Fuzzlebeasts™ were a wildly popular line of stuffed creatures that came with whimsical names, questionable stitching, and the vague promise of becoming valuable collector's items someday. Most were eventually forgotten in attics, save for a select few fanatics who treated them like sacred relics. Notable models included *Snugglewump the Sleepy Chimera, Blibberbuns the Perplexed Hare, Wiggletoes the Dancing Wyvern,* and the rare but highly coveted *Puffernook the Glorious Toadstool,* known for its misspelled tag that read "Puffrernook."

In a matter of minutes, the display of swords was reduced to an empty table. The vendor dusted off his hands and surveyed the scene with satisfaction as the crowd dispersed, each person gripping their new weapon with a mix of fear and pride. Even the man with the infant held the baby aloft, his tiny sword clutched in one hand, much to the crowd's delight. The vendor, smirking, adjusted his pack, now bulging with freshly earned coin. The clink of metal echoed as he turned away, eyes gleaming with the satisfaction of the day's fortune.

Everyone's losing their mind, Tianna thought, taking a step back as she scanned the marketplace. Uncle Thane was locked in a heated debate at the bread stall, passionately arguing over the price of a loaf that appeared more suited for bricklaying than eating. His booming voice carried above the market hum as if he were trying to haggle with the gods themselves. "Half a quip for this? I could use it to hammer in fence posts!"

The vendor, a wiry man with an impressively curled mustache, shrugged with practiced indifference. "Price of wheat's up, my friend. Don't kill the messenger. Blame the farmers. Or the weather. Or the gods, if you feel like filing a complaint that high."

Meanwhile, Rea stood beside him, tugging at the hem of her tunic, clearly bored out of her mind. She cast a longing glance at the candied apple stall, her face practically screaming, *'Get me out of here!'*

Gertie was about a dozen yards away, arms crossed and watching the scene unfold with the kind of resigned amusement only she could muster. She leaned against a cart full of bright yellow embermelons, in no rush to intervene.[26]

---

[26] *Glorious Gourds and Their Peculiar Properties* by Petronella Figsnort (Chapter 3, pg. 87):

"The Embermelon, with its faintly glowing rind, has baffled botanists for centuries. Some claim its radiance is a gift of the gods, while others whisper darker theories of cursed soil or vegetable sorcery. Regardless, its glow is most appreciated by festival vendors, who have discovered that people will buy just about anything if it looks magical enough."

As Tianna approached, she could hear Thane's voice rising above the market noise. "I'll take it, but if my teeth crack, I'm sending you the blacksmith's bill!"

With a huff, he slapped a few coins into the vendor's hand, his expression that of a man thoroughly swindled.

At that moment, Rea spotted Tianna and bolted toward her like a squirrel catapulted from a trebuchet. "Tee-Tee! What took you so long?" she squealed, wrapping her arms around Tianna's waist with the enthusiasm of someone escaping certain doom.

Tianna forced a smile, kneeling down to meet her level. "Sorry I took so long. But, Rea . . . there's something we need to talk about."

Rea blinked up at her, her expression shifting from joy to suspicion. "What did you do?"

Tianna raised an eyebrow. "What do you mean, what did *I* do?"

"You look funny . . . like you're going to say something I won't like."

Gertie snorted from the sidelines. "Sharp as a tack, that one."

Uncle Thane folded his arms, giving Tianna a slight nod of sympathy. He wasn't going to save her.

Tianna sighed, deciding to dive straight in. "Rea, I have to go away for a while. Something happened yesterday, something . . . hard to explain. Uncle Thane and I have to take care of it."

"Okay Tee-Tee. When are we going?" Rea asked, bright-eyed and eager.

"No, Rea. I'm sorry, but you can't come. It's too dangerous."

Rea's eyes went wide, as if Tianna had suggested leaving her behind for a dessert buffet. "You can't go on a trip without me! You *always* take me with you!" Her face twisted in disbelief, as if Tianna had committed the gravest betrayal since Nyx devoured the last cookie. "I'm not scared of danger!

Remember that time I killed that spider? It was huge! I took it down all by myself, with nothing but my shoe! My shoe, Tee-Tee!"[27]

Tianna exchanged a glance with Thane, who did his best not to laugh. Gertie, however, didn't bother hiding her amusement. "Aye, dearie. That spider didn't stand a chance, I'm sure."

Rea frowned, clearly catching the sarcasm but choosing to ignore it. "I can help! I'll carry your bag. I'll be your lookout! I can—"

Hruuk!

Nyx, who had been sitting contentedly by Rea's side, suddenly hunched over. His eyes went wide, his whole body shuddering with a great heave.[28]

Hruuk!

The cat's mouth gaped open, tongue lolling out dramatically, an unmistakable warning that a *cat-tastrophe* was about to unfold.

Haaaaak!

With a final, mighty convulsion, Nyx spat out a small, red, pointed hat that skittered across the cobblestones and landed at Rea's feet. Dripping with viscous saliva, it bore a prominent white spot in the center, gleaming in the sunlight like a prize no one had asked for. Nyx, meanwhile, swatted at an invisible foe in the air, swayed unsteadily on his feet, and let out a tiny yowl, before flopping onto his side with a resounding *thwump*.

"Eww gross," Rea said, her nose scrunched up. "What's wrong with Nyxie?"

"Must be something he ate," Thane replied, eyeing the hat curiously.

---

[27] The *'huge'* spider in question was roughly the size of a small coin, but Rea's retelling had since elevated it to the status of a mythical beast complete with fangs, malice, and, according to her latest version, a plot to overthrow the Empire.

[28] Veterinarians refer to this as the "Pre-Vomit Waltz." It's rarely graceful but often dramatic.

"He'll be fine, love," Gertie chimed in, her eyes twinkling. "Just needs to sleep it off. Happens all the time."

Nyx let out a dismissive *brrrrup*, and staggered off toward the shade, leaving the hat behind like an unwanted parting gift.

Tianna sighed, rubbing her temples. "Rea, this is *exactly* why you can't come with me. I need you to stay here with Gertie. Someone has to keep an eye on Nyx before he starts coughing up magic rings or something."

Rea hesitated, glancing between the adults, the cat, and the slobbery Gnome hat. "Nyxie . . . wants me to stay?"

Thane, who had remained stoic up until that point, finally chimed in with a serious tone. "Yes, Rea. Nyx has clearly appointed you as his caretaker. Very important job. You need to watch over him, so he doesn't get into any trouble."

Gertie grinned, hands on her hips. "Aye, you wouldn't want him barfing up something worse, would you? Who knows what's next? Farmer Nibb's pet hamster, a cloak of non-invisibility, or heaven forbid, the mayor's toupee . . . again."

Tianna nodded. "Exactly. So, you'll stay here with Gertie, keep an eye on Nyx, and I'll come back as soon as I can. Deal?"

Rea mulled this over, eyeing the Gnome hat one last time before letting out a dramatic sigh. "Fine. But only because Nyxie needs me. And you need to bring me back a souvenir." She shot a final glare at the cat, now pretending to nap, as if this had all been part of some master plan.

Gertie chuckled, ruffling Rea's hair. "That's the spirit. We'll have our own adventures here in town. Maybe even teach you how to cook, though you've got a better track record with spiders than soup."

As Tianna turned to leave, she glanced once more at Nyx, who lazily opened one eye as if to say, '*Yeah, I've got this covered.*'

"Take care of her," Tianna whispered.

Nyx responded with a quiet *Brrrup*, which Tianna took as a yes.

Before they could leave town the following morning, Tianna had one last stop to make. She and Thane slipped into *The Cracked Tankard's* storage room through the exterior entrance. With the sun's light streaming in through the doorway, the room was marginally less dank. Although, it still smelled faintly of mildew and old ale as if the tavern itself was nursing a hangover.

Tianna crossed the room toward the storage shelves where she had left the frying pan, Sword. She stared at it for a moment, her nerves tingling.

"Well—" Tianna began, fidgeting slightly. "I've thought things over, and . . . uh . . . I've changed my mind about what you asked me to do. I don't think this is something I can walk away from."

The pan said nothing, in a very pan-like way. Its silence was profound, as if it had mastered the ancient art of inanimate indifference.

"Umm . . . so, if the offer is still on the table, we should get going." Tianna felt her nerves prickling with doubt. She glanced over her shoulder at Thane, who raised an eyebrow but remained silent.

She leaned closer to the pan, lowering her voice. "Sword?" she whispered, hoping for a reply. "Please tell me I haven't lost my mind."

Silence.

Thane cleared his throat from the doorway, casually inspecting the room. "She's not talking to me," Tianna muttered, turning toward him, her voice cracking slightly. Tears welled in her eyes. "Maybe I *am* losing my mind."

She suddenly felt lightheaded and stumbled backward, reaching out blindly to steady herself. Her hand closed around the pan's handle as she felt herself start to wobble.

"Good afternoon, dearie. Shall we be on our way?"

Startled by the sudden voice in her head, Tianna dropped the pan.

Kraaaang!

"Tianna?" Thane took a step forward, concern evident on his face.

Tianna raised her hand, signaling him to stop. "I'm fine," she said, her heart still racing.

"Well, I never." Sword huffed. *"Do you treat all your magical items with such reckless abandon?"*

"I-I'm sorry," Tianna stammered. "You startled me."

"Oh, yes, of course. 'Sorry.' That always fixes everything."

She paused, narrowing her eyes at the pan. "Wait, why didn't you talk to me earlier?"

"Who . . . are you talking to?" Thane asked, his tone both wary and perplexed.

"Oh sorry, I didn't realize that we were on your schedule." Sword's voice carried a hint of condescension. *"As if I have nothing better to do than sit around here all day and wait for you."*[29]

"Wait, what—?" Tianna mumbled, then turned to Thane. "Sorry. I was talking to Sword. She says she was busy?"

Thane blinked, staring at the pan. "Okay—"

"What do you mean, how could you have other things to do? You're a pan, you can't move."

"Wow, just . . . wow! I didn't think you were so objectist!" Sword responded. *"Now you know all about the secret lives of magical items?"*

"No, I never said—" Tianna continued, flustered.

---

[29] In fact, Sword did not have anything better to do, being an inanimate object and all, whose sole purpose in life was to sit around and wait to be picked up. Though to be fair, swords (and by extension, pans who think they are swords) are notoriously bad at self-awareness.

"So, shall we go then? Or perhaps you'd enjoy tossing me around some more? You haven't completely rattled my brains enough? Did you know that it has always been my dream to be used like a drum? I guess dreams do come true! Most pans get to sizzle in silence. But no, not me," Sword prattled on.

"It was an accident!" Tianna protested, her cheeks flushing slightly.

She felt the impression of Sword taking a deep, exaggerated breath. *"Yes, yes. Very sorry, I see that now. I might've been a touch . . . over reactive. Let us begin again, shall we? I'm thrilled that you've decided to embrace the task before you."*

"I mean, I didn't really have a choice."

"Quite right!" Sword responded brightly.

"I hate to interrupt this . . . *conversation,"* Thane interjected from the door, "but are we good to go?"

"Okay, Uncle." Tianna sighed, shaking her head. "Hey Sword, can you talk to my uncle as well?"

"Obviously not," Sword said in a huff. *"I can only reach someone's mind after making physical contact. Everybody knows that. Honestly, where is this generation learning their magical etiquette? I blame the schools."*

"Oh, okay. Maybe you should touch Sword so she can talk to you as well," Tianna said to her uncle.

Thane raised both hands, palms out. "Thank you, Tianna, but I'll pass. I'm in no rush to have a talking . . . Sword . . . rattling around in my head."

"It *is* a bit unnerving," Tianna agreed, glancing at the pan.

"I shall pretend that I did not hear that."

With a small chuckle, Tianna pulled out a length of rope and looped it through Sword's handle before securing it to her pack. "All right," she said, adjusting the straps, "ready to go."

In a small room illuminated by an intense, crackling fire. The sort of fire that was unsure whether it was supposed to warm the room or burn it down. Tianna sat perched on the edge of her seat, Sword the frying pan in front of her. She traced the wood grain on the table with the intense focus usually reserved for cats contemplating world domination. Across from her, Thane was wrestling with a map that had clearly seen better days. Much better days. Days where it hadn't been crumpled up, sat on, and then used to soak up a spilled tankard of ale.

"Why don't you ask that pan of yours where we're supposed to be going," Thane said.

Tianna did.

"The fortress of the Dark Lord, of course," Sword replied. *"Didn't you read the blurb?"*

"Yeah, but where is the fortress of the Dark Lord?" asked Tianna.

"Ah, that's an easy one. Everyone knows it's in the north." Thane smoothed the map with the patience of someone fully aware the paper wasn't going to cooperate.

"Of course it's in the north. All villainous fortresses are. Cold builds character and sets the tonal mood," Sword said. *"You'd think Literatus could instigate one apocalypse in a nice temperate valley, but no, not dramatic enough."*[30]

"See? It's even labeled right here." He pointed to a dark spot in the far north, marked in large letters: *'The Citadel of Unwholesome Intentions.'*

Tianna raised her eyebrow. "Comforting."

---

[30] Literatus is of course, the god of narrative structure, pacing, and the appropriate distribution of foreshadowing. Not to be confused with a similar sounding deity beginning with a 'c' (whose existence remains hotly debated in barbershops and bachelor dens across the realm), or with I'Literatus, a lesser god revered chiefly by the willfully ignorant and proudly unlettered. Devotees of I'Literatus are widely credited with inventing the atomic wedgie, coining the phrase "books are for losers," and perfecting the ancient martial art of forming unshakable lifetime opinions based entirely on headlines.

Thane either ignored her or took it as agreement. "All right," he muttered, brow furrowed as if deciphering ancient prophecies. "We leave at first light. Head west until we reach the Old Road. From there we should follow the path north through the Ashevale. The old protections should still be active so long as we don't leave the path. It's likely overgrown by now, but still the fastest way through the forest. Assuming, of course, the trees haven't grown a taste for human flesh while we weren't paying attention."[31]

"Oh, that would be fun. I hope they did," Sword said to Tianna, who returned a reluctant glance. *"You don't see enough carnivorous trees these days."*

He paused, releasing a sigh that suggested he wasn't quite sure the trees wouldn't betray them after all. Thane pointed to an area on the map just north of the forest. "This stretch is the tricky part. It's called The Wandering Rise. Nothing but wide open, rolling hills. Not much cover, so we'll have to watch for raiding parties. Goblins love this area like it's a buffet, and they're not too picky about what's on offer."

Tianna nodded absentmindedly, her mind floating somewhere far away, like a balloon someone had forgotten to tie down. Thane was the planner, the strategist. She . . . she wasn't entirely sure what her role was. Part-time map observer? Occasional doubter? Bearer of the frying pan?

Thane's finger moved further up the map, tracing what she assumed was another future headache. "Once we reach the Diresteppes, traveling will get tougher. The terrain's rough, the weather's unpredictable, and we'll have to keep heading north. Eventually, we'll hit the Frostspire Peaks to the north." He paused, as if the next part was going to get particularly unpleasant. "There's an old fortress built into the pass around here, once known as Grimhold. Abandoned, of course, or at least I hope it will be. After that, it's a sheer climb up the mountain to the Dark Lord's citadel."

---

[31] While reports of trees developing a taste for human flesh are largely unsubstantiated, no one has ever *proven* that flesh-eating trees don't exist; a fact that some argue is itself suspicious. After all, if the trees weren't guilty, wouldn't they be the first to speak up and deny it?

Tianna's stomach twisted at the mention of the Dark Lord's citadel. She'd imagined quests before, but somehow they'd always involved a lot more heroism and a lot less impending dread. She wasn't sure when they'd crossed the line from 'adventure' to 'this is a terrible idea', but it was starting to feel like the latter.

Meanwhile, from the shadows, Rea crouched, biting her lip to keep quiet. She was dying to leap out and declare her intention to join them, but . . . she was still working up the courage. Besides, she hadn't quite figured out how to convince them how she could help.

Nyx, ever the opportunist, crouched beside her, clearly plotting something, whether it involved snacks, sleep, or general chaos was anyone's guess.

Thane glanced up, catching Tianna's faraway gaze. "Are you all right?" he asked, his voice softer now, less the seasoned adventurer and more someone who'd seen enough to know when someone was ready to run out the door and never look back.

"Yeah," Tianna replied, blinking herself out of a daydream that involved far fewer Dark Lords and significantly more relaxing in front of a fire. "Just . . . processing."

Thane nodded. He leaned back into his chair, casting a tired glance at the fire, which had settled on 'I'll flicker ominously' as its general purpose in life.

"It's going to be rough," he said, rolling up the map with the same care you'd give a particularly grumpy snake. "The Wilds are dangerous, the mountains are worse, but we'll manage."

Tianna nodded again, but there was something nagging at her, something that had been tiptoeing on her mind since they'd started planning their ridiculous quest. "How are we supposed to defeat the Dark Lord?" she asked, her voice laced with more than a little doubt. "We're not exactly . . . warriors. This entire thing feels impossible."

"Speak for yourself. I am a weapon of great renown."

Thane paused, staring into the fire as if waiting for it to offer up some profound wisdom. It didn't, of course. It crackled away contentedly, as fires do when they're not in the business of solving life's big problems.[32] With a sigh, he turned back to Tianna, his expression thoughtful.

"A lot of things seem impossible until you give them a go," he said, a grin creeping across his face. "Then they become merely . . . improbable." He leaned back, folding his arms with the confidence of a man who'd made peace with the universe's eccentricities. "Remember that fate always has a plan," he added, "but sometimes it forgets to send the memo."

Tianna frowned. "That's not exactly reassuring."

Thane chuckled, though he sounded more tired than amused. "It's not meant to be reassuring, Tianna. It's just . . . how things go." He leaned forward, folding his arms on the table. "When it's your destiny to do something, things tend to work out. Not without some difficulty along the way, mind you, and there is always plenty of second-guessing. But there will be a way. I know that much."

From her hiding spot, Rea's heart sped up like a caffeinated squirrel. Fate. Destiny. This was big. And terrifying. But mostly big.

Tianna chewed her lip, her doubts still swirling. "But . . . what if there isn't? What if we go all that way and nothing happens? What if we fail?"

Thane shrugged, in the casual way people typically don't when discussing something as monumental as facing a Dark Lord. "We might," he admitted. "But it's not about knowing how we're going to win. It's about being willing to try. Fate's a funny thing. It doesn't hand you a map with step-by-step instructions. You have to trust that you're where you're supposed to be at the time you're supposed to be there."

---

[32] Fires are famously unhelpful philosophers, which says a lot, given that philosophers aren't exactly celebrated for their practicality. Still, fires do have their merits: they provide warmth, light, and the occasional dramatic explosion. One can argue that these were more useful contributions than most philosophers can claim.

Tianna wasn't entirely sure she believed him, but the certainty in his voice was enough to keep her doubts at bay, if only for a little while.

"Rest up tonight," Thane said finally, tucking the map into his pack. "We'll need all the strength we can get come morning."

Tianna nodded again, her mind still swirling with doubts she didn't know how to voice. She watched as Thane stood and stretched, the firelight casting long shadows across his tired features.

As he left the room, Tianna remained seated, staring into the flames, which gave her an indignant flicker, as if to say, *'Don't look at me, I'm doing my best.'* The journey was looming over her, a massive, insurmountable obstacle. And yet, there was no turning back.

"Don't worry, dearie, you've got me. A legendary weapon with narrative immunity and impeccable plot sense! What could possibly go wrong?"[33]

Tianna was not reassured.

---

[33] As phrases go, this one is basically a summoning circle for disaster.

5

The Adventure Begins to Begin

"Every great journey begins with a single step. Followed immediately by a twisted ankle, bad directions, and someone asking if we're there yet."

— The Imperial Youth Adventure Primer

Starting an adventure is always the hardest part. It's like jumping into a freezing lake. There's a lot of hesitation, second thoughts, and maybe even some undignified screaming, but once you're in, you realize the water's not *that* bad, though you'll wish you'd brought a change of underwear. And by the time you're knee-deep in danger and chaos, you'll have completely forgotten how much you wanted to stay dry in the first place.

Thus, it was for Tianna and Thane as they set out at sunrise the following morning. The night had been long and full of worry, the kind that keeps you staring at the ceiling and wondering why you agreed to this in the first place. Tianna, for her part, had quietly been dreading the journey but was determined to look the part of an adventurer, which mostly meant staring at the ground while desperately trying not to trip over her own feet.

Thane moved with the quiet, practiced ease of someone who'd fought off more threats than Tianna could count; most of them with a bad attitude and an even worse bite. His axe—scratched and scarred from years of use—hung across his back, a hunting knife tucked into his belt, and his trusty war horn slung over his shoulder. He didn't say much, he never did. Silence was practically one of his weapons at that point.[34]

They resembled a pair of adventurers, though Tianna suspected her uncle was far more prepared for what was to come than she was.

Outside of town the Ashevale loomed immediately to the north, a wall of massive trees. It was a living barrier separating the Empire from the wild north. Luckily, at least for now, their path led west, hugging the tree line and sticking to a well-worn trail through the countryside. To the south, there stood a giant monolith, a distant, solitary mountain that had no interest in the affairs of mortals.

They called it the Spire, that colossal thing aspiring to eternity. Perfectly circular, so say the mathemagicians and scientistorians of the world.[35] Over twenty-six miles wide, without a single blemish, scratch, or hastily scrawled love note upon it. A solid charcoal-gray surface that was unexpectedly warm to the touch and, on occasion, emitted a piercing sound disturbingly reminiscent of a peacock being fed into a woodchipper.[36]

The sun, still low in the sky but already far too ambitious for this time of morning, glared down through a pale winter haze, offering light but no warmth. Tianna began to question if she'd packed enough layers. With every step that

---

[34] Scholars debate whether silence is truly effective as a weapon. Most agree it's devastating against awkward dinner conversations.

[35] Though how they measure such a large object without getting hopelessly lost remains a mystery. Most believe they rely on an ancient technique known as the "Eyeball-It Method," pioneered by the illustrious Spirish mathemagician, Reginald Eyeball, whose motto was reportedly, "Close enough is good enough."

[36] The sound has baffled scholars for centuries, leading to endless debates. Some argue it's an ancient warning. Others insist it's the Spire clearing its metaphorical throat. Then there is a small, deeply unsettling group that refuses to answer a far more pressing question: What exactly is a woodchipper, and why does anyone know what a peacock inside one sounds like?

crunched against the frostbitten ground, her breath puffed out like a tiny flag of surrender, and the weight of what lay ahead settled into her bones like an unwelcome chill that refused to leave.

Meanwhile, her pan swung happily from the back of her pack. It swayed with each step as if it were having the time of its life, blissfully unaware of the ordeal to come.

"Oh, this is absolutely exhilarating!" Sword chimed. *"I haven't been on an adventure in a long time!"*

"Wait, you've done this before?" Tianna asked, the thought creeping in: *Great! I'm the only one that has no idea what I'm doing.*

Sword ignored her and continued talking. *"Ah, the cool wind on my handle, the open road, the imminent danger. It's all so invigorating! Who knew that life could be this exciting!"*

Tianna rolled her eyes. "Mmhmm. Imminent danger . . . invigorating."

"Oh, don't be so glum, dearie! You've got me! Think of all the fun we'll have: deadly monsters, harrowing escapes, terrible odds stacked against us. It's going to be delightful! At least until the third act." Sword trailed off, lost in thought of all the adventures before her.

At that, they continued onward in silence. Tianna tried her best not to think about all the *fun* Sword was anticipating.

They walked, trudging along in silence as the pale sun climbed higher into the sky. Tianna had lost track of how many times she'd stumbled over roots, rocks, or, embarrassingly, her own feet. The biting chill in the air wasn't enough to stop a thin layer of sweat from clinging to her back beneath her heavy coat. It was an irritating, persistent discomfort, the kind that gnawed at her patience rather than outright breaking her. Every so often, a sharp winter breeze sliced through the stillness, a fleeting reminder of how cold and miserable she truly was.

The sun cast long, golden rays of fading light as it dipped below the horizon at the end of the first day. Tianna's legs felt as if they were made of stone, and not the sturdy kind, more like crumbling ruins. They set up camp under a gnarled tree that had clearly seen better centuries. Its sparse branches offered about as much protection as a broken umbrella, but she wasn't in a position to be picky. She curled up inside her bedroll with a groan loud enough to make Thane glance her way, though he wisely kept his comments to himself. Exhaustion pressed her into the uneven ground.

Sleep, when it finally came, was a patchy affair filled with dreams of endless walking, the cold wind battering against her face, and her boots coming alive to chew on her feet. When dawn arrived, she awoke groggier than when she'd collapsed, silently cursing whoever had invented walking.

The second day stretched out like a boring story no one wanted to hear. The air was dry and cold, biting at her skin and leaving it red and irritable. While the chill wasn't unbearable, it seeped into her bones and sapped her energy with every step, a constant, gnawing reminder of winter's unrelenting grip. Dust clung to her boots, coating everything it touched and leaving her fantasizing about the most mundane luxury—a bath. Every so often, Thane grunted, a sound Tianna couldn't tell was agreement, irritation, or just his way of breathing. Conversation between them dwindled to the occasional muttered curse or sarcastic comment, like, "A bit chilly out today."

By the second night, the stars were pale and distant, acting about as tired as Tianna felt. She wrapped her cloak around herself, not because it was cold, but because it felt like something she could control. She stared at the faint glow of the horizon and thought of Rea, comfortable and safe back in Nothing-to-See-Here. For a brief moment, she considered turning around, but then her legs screamed at her for even thinking about it. There was no way she was going back.

The morning of the third day brought an eerie stillness that felt suspiciously like the world was trying to lull them into a false sense of security. Even the birds had stopped making noises, as if they'd decided whatever was ahead wasn't worth singing about. The air had warmed up, but not enough to make up for the ache in her legs or the chill that was permanently embedded in her skin. Tianna trudged forward, her body on autopilot and her mind preoccupied with important thoughts like, *why do my boots hate me so much?*

And then, finally, they arrived.

The Old Road was unmistakable. Two ancient stone pillars rose on either side of a worn path, their surfaces, etched with runes. They were weathered, cracked, and streaked with moss. The path burrowed into the forest ahead, its entrance shadowed by overhanging branches that twisted together like skeletal fingers. Tianna stared at it, half expecting some ominous voice to announce, *'Abandon all hope, ye who enter here.'*

Tianna stared at the path. "So . . . this is it?"

"Aye," Thane responded with little enthusiasm, as if he were already regretting his decision to travel with Tianna. "It's been a while since I've been out this way."

"What's with the pillars?" Tianna asked, eyeing the worn stone and the faintly glowing runes carved into its surface.

Thane glanced at them, his brow furrowing as if dredging up old knowledge. "They're more than mere markers. The runes create a boundary, an invisible barrier, keeping the dangers of the forest at bay. As long as travelers stay on the Old Road, nothing from the forest can cross to harm them, at least that's how the stories go."

Tianna raised an eyebrow, glancing toward the dense, shadowy trees looming just beyond the road. "Nothing can cross the barrier? That sounds a little too good to be true."

Thane grunted. "Aye, that's the idea. But step off the road, and . . . let's just say you'd better be quicker than whatever's out there."

"And what exactly is out there?" Thane shrugged. "Comforting," Tianna muttered, her gaze flicking back to the pillars. "And these runes, they still work?"

"How am I supposed to know? They appear to be glowing, let's hope they've got at least some power left."

As they were about to step onto the Old Road, a large figure emerged from behind a tree with all the grace of a boulder rolling down a mountain.

"Well, he looks interesting," Sword observed

Blarg the Unstoppable Doomhammer appeared in full glory, his giant hammer, *Thumpkin*, resting casually on his shoulder. The hammer was an iron monstrosity, its head as large as a barrel and pitted with battle scars.[37]

His left eye had swollen shut, now the size and color of a particularly offended plum, appearing as though it had been on the losing side of a bar fight. Blarg grinned, clearly pleased with himself, despite having spent the last three hours standing behind a tree, pretending he wasn't there.

"Oh sure, give the big brute's hammer the fancy italics," Sword sniffed indignantly. *"I'm just the literal embodiment of destiny trapped in cookware, no need for special formatting here. Typical authorial bias."*

"Blarg knew you would be heading this way," he declared grandly. He took a large bite out of what appeared to be an entire clove of garlic, as casually as if it were an apple.

Thane sighed deeply and stepped between the giant of a man and his niece. "Blarg," he said, the kind of greeting you reserve for that *friend*, who always asked you for a favor. "What do you want?"

Blarg spun *Thumpkin* in a slow, deliberate circle, still chewing on his garlic as he spoke. "Four nights ago, Blarg saw this maiden." He pointed at Tianna. "He witnessed a fire in her gaze."

Tianna frowned. "What fire?"

---

[37] *Thumpkin*, widely regarded as the most inappropriately named weapon in history, earned its title because Blarg thought it sounded "cute and non-threatening," which, according to him, would make it all the more humiliating for his enemies to be crushed by it. Whether this was a stroke of genius or sheer stupidity remains a matter of scholarly debate.

"A fire Blarg has witnessed many times." He shifted his eyes to Thane. "However, he had not expected to find *you* in her company," Blarg added. "Yet such trifles do not matter."

Thane's eyes didn't waver; his hand rested on the handle of his knife. "I ask again, Blarg. What . . . do . . . you . . . want?"

Blarg's grin widened, and he slammed *Thumpkin* into the ground with a *thud* that sent a small tremor through the earth. "Why, to join your merry band, of course!" he boomed, his voice full of enthusiasm. "It has been too many days since Blarg's hammer has tasted the sweet, sweet joy of battle, and besides, that town of yours is much too confining. Much too insignificant for a warrior of Blarg's glorious stature."

"Oh, I like him," Sword spoke with playful interest. *"He has the air of someone who could properly wield a pan of* my . . . *stature."*

Thane exhaled sharply, appearing as though he was rapidly regretting waking up that morning. "No offense Blarg, but our current venture requires a measure of stealth, and . . . you aren't really suited for such a task."

"Stealth? Ha! What does one need of stealth when those who stand in the way can simply be smashed?" Blarg boasted, his voice booming with pride.

"Not all problems can be solved by smashing." Thane interjected.

Blarg gave a thoughtful nod, then pounded his fist into his palm with a resounding *thud*. "Ah, but there you are incorrect, small-minded companion. Blarg believes that every endeavor, when viewed through the proper lens, can be resolved with smashing." He tapped the side of his head with one finger, as though imparting the deepest of wisdom. "It is all a matter of perspective . . . and, of course, the proper application of force."

Tianna, still struggling to process Blarg's questionable logic, leaned toward Thane and whispered, "Is he always so cheery, and does he always talk in the third-person?"[38]

---

[38] Blarg speaks in the third person, not because of some mental deficiency (though I wouldn't entirely rule that out), but as a deliberate tactic to ensure everyone remembers

Thane, his gaze fixed on Blarg, nodded wearily. "Unfortunately."

Blarg, oblivious to the skeptical glances being exchanged, carried on with unshaken confidence. "Furthermore, Blarg is possessed of great intellect and wisdom! Your humble company would benefit much by his extensive knowledge, not to mention his unparalleled prowess in pulverizing all manner of inconvenient hindrances."

"I mean, he does have a point," Tianna said, casting a sideways glance at Thane. "Another set of hands wouldn't hurt."

"Yes, yes. Add the big one. This party needs muscle and a touch of levity," Sword interjected. *"No offense to you two. Well . . . maybe just a smidge. Seriously, you guys need to lighten up."*

Thane pinched the bridge of his nose, resignation settling in. "Fine, but understand this. This is a serious matter, not some merry festival."

Blarg clapped Thane on the back with such force that he nearly toppled over. "Ah, Thane, you truly underestimate the potency of optimism! Every journey *is* a festival if one brings along the right attitude, and, of course, the right hammer!" He hoisted *Thumpkin* with a grand flourish, the massive weapon gleaming brilliantly in the late morning sun.

The giant of a man turned and strode toward the forest. "Make haste, for the morning wanes, and the river lies not far. If this party presses quickly forward, it shall be deep within the Ashevale by nightfall." He let out a loud belch and patted his stomach. A nearby flock of birds, startled by the noise, took to the sky in a flurry of wings.

Tianna scrunched her face as she watched Blarg march ahead, her eyes wide with a mix of disbelief and curiosity. She glanced at Thane, half-expecting him to share her bewilderment, but he appeared unfazed, apparently accustomed to

---

his name. As he once famously declared, "Blarg doesn't just introduce himself, Blarg *brands* himself." Scholars begrudgingly admit it's surprisingly effective, albeit insufferably annoying.

Blarg's dramatic flair. Letting out a quiet sigh, she muttered under her breath, "Deep in the Ashevale by nightfall . . . fantastic."

Still, a part of her couldn't help but admire Blarg's enthusiasm, even if his idea of subtlety was smashing through problems. She squared her shoulders and hurried after him, trying to convince herself that following a giant with a hammer into the woods wasn't the worst decision she'd made that day.

"What is the party's destination?" Blarg asked, almost as an afterthought.

Thane pointed into the forest.

"Excellent!" Blarg boomed. "Blarg is ready. The trees shall remember his name . . . and tremble!"

Before stepping into the trees, Thane took his war horn from off his shoulder. It was weathered and scratched from years of adventure. He turned to face the Spire in the heart of the Empire far to the south one final time. Raising the horn to his lips, he blew a single, mournful note. It echoed around him and into the distance like a reluctant farewell.

"A proper sendoff," Thane muttered, lowering the horn. "You don't slip into the Wilds. You announce it. Otherwise, some may think you're sneaking like some thief in the night."

"Blarg agrees!" Blarg shouted, raising *Thumpkin* high. "The trees must know that glory approaches!"

Tianna sighed, but a small part of her wanted to smile.

She turned one last time to the Spire, stretching from the earth to the clouds and beyond, like some ancient, colossal toothpick holding up the universe. It stood there, vast and indifferent. It was an ever-present reminder that the world was far too big, and fate had a terrible sense of scale.

It appeared to say: *"I'm here. I'm tall. And whatever this is? Not my problem."*

People said that as long as you could see the Spire, you were safe. That's because if you were close enough to see the Spire, you were still within range of someone responsible enough to call for help if things went sideways. And things tended to go sideways in this world. Sometimes so far sideways they ended up upside-down and slightly on fire.

But the moment you crossed into the forest, the Spire stopped caring. It wasn't the kind of structure that sent out search parties or offered moral support from a distance. The Spire was more like a distant relative you only saw at weddings, looking vaguely disapproving but entirely unwilling to get involved in your personal disasters.

Tianna squinted at it, as if expecting some last-minute reassurance. A nod, perhaps, or even a polite wave. The Spire, as usual, remained indifferent, silently towering over the horizon like a monument to all the good decisions she could have made but didn't.

"Here we go," she muttered, "no turning back now."

"*I should hope not,*" Sword said with a huff. "*Legendary weapons do not retreat, dearie. Especially not this early in the narrative.*"

It was late morning when two figures crouched atop a small hill, sheltered beneath the jagged overhang of a large rock. From their vantage point about five miles east of the party, they silently observed the flat plain below. They watched in the distance as the group of adventurers reached the edge of the forest.

The sun hung lazily in the late morning sky, bathing the plain in its pale, golden light. The figures remained perfectly still, blending seamlessly with their surroundings as their sharp eyes tracked the adventurers disappearing into the dense tree line.

One figure shifted slightly, the only movement between them, as if preparing to act. The cold morning air around them was thick with unspoken purpose, yet they made no sound. The plains stretched out, serene except for the distant rustle of the breeze, the adventurers now swallowed by the forest's deep green embrace.

With quiet determination, the figures rose and continued their pursuit.

6

This Toll Shall Pass

"Some who burn bridges are the same who want to cross them."

— Tommeth of Morellow, Wandering Bard

The sun was beginning its slow descent, casting pale, wintry light through the dense canopy of evergreen leaves as the group trudged through the frost-crusted underbrush. By early evening, they finally heard the unmistakable sound of running water, a soft rush echoing through the trees ahead. The cold deepened as they neared the source, biting at exposed skin.

The foliage gave way to the shore of a wide, fast-moving river. Its surface shimmered in the waning light, glistening like liquid silver.[39] The river spanned a good sixty feet across, its current swift and relentless, churning over smooth stones that danced beneath the surface. The sound of the water filled the air with a steady, rhythmic roar, drowning out the distant bird cries and making it hard to hear anything else, except maybe the complaints of sore legs.

---

[39] Not to be confused with Liquid Silver™, the wildly popular and aggressively marketed energy drink with the tagline, "Hydrate or Dominate." Despite its ominous name and claims of being brewed in the fires of a volcano, it's really just sugar water with enough caffeine to make a troll tap dance. The packaging promises to "destroy thirst," but most consumers report that all it really destroys is basic kidney function.

Tianna stopped at the river's edge, eyes following the flow downstream, lost in the beauty of the wilderness. The river cut through the landscape like a vital artery, alive and pulsing. The opposite bank remained shrouded in thick forest. On the far bank, the trees leaned inward, as if conspiring together to guard some ancient secret, or maybe just to gossip about the foolish adventurers on the other side.

In front of them, the path led onto a narrow stone bridge that arched gracefully across the river. It appeared sturdy enough, though age had clearly left its mark. Intricate carvings, worn smooth by time, decorated the sides. The bridge had clearly been built long ago, although it appeared to have held up quite well.

Blarg suddenly halted, raising a hand to stop the group. He sniffed the air before narrowing his eyes suspiciously toward the bridge. "Hmm," he muttered, his deep voice laced with caution. "Blarg senses something amiss."

Tianna cast a confused glance toward Thane. He only sighed. The kind of sigh that suggested he'd seen this particular performance from Blarg far too many times.

Blarg straightened to his full height and gripped his hammer with authority. "Stand behind Blarg, little one," he commanded, sweeping his arm protectively in front of Tianna. The sharp scent of garlic clung to his clothes as he pressed close. "He shall deal with whatever foulness hinders passage."

Tianna blinked, taken aback. "It's just a bridge—"

But before she could finish her sentence, a splash erupted from the river. A towering figure leaped onto the center of the bridge, casting water droplets in all directions. The Troll that stood before them was a sight to behold. Nearly nine feet tall and rippling with muscle.[40] Compared to him, Blarg looked like a

---

[40] *The Imperial Bestiary: A Comprehensive Guide to the Beasts and Botherations of the Realm* (Third Edition, pg. 640):

"Trolls are renowned for their immense strength, their stubbornness, and their unwavering dedication to living under bridges. A real estate investment strategy that scholars have described as "structurally questionable at best." While their reputation

child holding a toy hammer. His skin was rough and gray, like stone, weathered by centuries of wind and rain. His clothing was a chaotic patchwork of fine fabrics that had seen better days, a style that can best be described as *beggar formal*.[41]

"Here we go!" Sword exclaimed, her voice buzzing with excitement.

The Troll grinned, revealing a mouth full of sharp, yellowed teeth, his upper lip barely containing his fangs. In one hand, he held a clipboard, of all things. In the other, a long stick with a charred, blackened end that gave the impression of a makeshift quill. He radiated with the smug confidence of someone who had spent his entire life dreaming of wielding this much bureaucratic authority.

"Good day, travelers," the Troll boomed, his tone oddly polite for his imposing appearance. "I am Grothar Boulderback, esteemed regional ambassador of the Forestry Infrastructure Governing Body, or FIG, for short."[42]

Thane blinked. "The . . . what?"

The Troll ignored him, flipping through several weathered pages on his clipboard. "With a party of three, I see here that the toll shall be twelve tenquips . . . and, of course, an additional two for the processing fee." He smiled

---

for hoarding shiny objects might suggest a love for treasure, the truth is far less glamorous: they just like how coins catch the light when tossed into rivers."

[41] Beggar formal is a popular trend among Trolls, who enjoy the juxtaposition of high fashion and complete indifference to laundering.

[42] The Forestry Infrastructure Governing Body (FIG) is a Troll-run organization tasked with maintaining wilderness infrastructure, particularly bridges. While their work is undeniably important, their bureaucracy is legendarily absurd. Every toll collected must be logged in triplicate. One for the Troll, one for FIG's central office, and one for "archival purposes" (which historians suspect is just a very large pile of paper no one reads). Tolls are said to fund bridge upkeep, but an alarming amount is spent on committee meetings to determine things like whether "goat traffic" counts as wear and tear or if shiny object collections can be written off as a maintenance expense.

again, a disturbingly bureaucratic smile, his eyes twinkling with the kind of glee that only comes from wielding pointless authority.

Thane's face contorted with frustration. "Toll? There's never been a toll here!" His hand went absently to his coin purse, which was rather empty after their previous shopping spree.

Grothar remained unbothered. "Ah, quite astute, good sir! And indeed, you are correct. However, maintaining such structures, particularly in the midst of a forest, is a costly and laborious endeavor. Thus, the noble FIG was established to ensure the safety and serviceability of bridges such as this. Crumbling bridges, after all, are no good for anyone."

Blarg, whose understanding of infrastructure likely began and ended with the phrase '*smash it until it stops wobbling*,' tightened his grip on *Thumpkin*, his brow furrowing. "A toll? You demand coin for crossing this bridge?" he growled, as though the concept personally offended him.

Grothar nodded solemnly, his tone that of a true bureaucrat. "Indeed, sir. A small price to pay for quality infrastructure. We've recently reinforced the stonework and added, if I may say, *excellent* moss-repellent treatments to preserve its longevity. You'd be astonished at how quickly bridges can deteriorate without proper care."

Thane, clearly unimpressed, frowned. "But we don't have money for a toll."

Grothar's expression shifted to something resembling a forced sympathetic smile. "Ah, in that unfortunate case, I'm afraid I cannot let you pass." He made a gesture that might have been meant as consoling. "Please turn around and kindly exit the bridge."

"But . . . we need to cross," Thane insisted, his frustration growing.

Grothar, ever the model of bureaucratic indifference, gave a slow shrug. "Unfortunately, your party has one of two options: either pay the toll or find some other means of crossing the river."

"Or smash your skull," Blarg muttered darkly under his breath, his fingers tightening around *Thumpkin*.

"I knew I liked him," Sword said. *"That's two votes for smashing."*

Grothar, who had definitely heard the remark but chose to ignore it with the grace of a seasoned civil servant, leaned in slightly and continued in a low, conspiratorial tone. "Now, I probably shouldn't be telling you this," he made a quick scan of the area, ensuring nobody was eavesdropping, "but there *is* a place where you can ford the river if you follow it east."

Thane's eyes brightened. "Indeed! How far is this ford?"

The Troll scratched his chin thoughtfully. "Oh, not that far. I'd say no more than twenty . . . err . . . twenty-five miles, tops."

Thane's excitement deflated instantly. He sighed.

"Perhaps some mutually beneficial arrangement may be agreed upon," Blarg said, stepping forward with a glint of mischief in his eye. With a grand flourish, he withdrew a glass bottle from his bag. "Behold! Ironclad Oak Reserve Single Malt Whiskey, untouched and sealed," he declared, gazing upon the bottle as though he were parting with his most treasured possession. "Would a *donation* of this fine elixir grant this party safe passage?"[43]

---

[43] Ironclad Oak Reserve Single Malt Whiskey has a history as bold and rich as the drink itself. It hails from the windswept hills of Bogmarrow, a region famous for its wildly unpredictable weather and even more unpredictable residents. The whiskey was first crafted over three centuries ago by Bartholomew "Ironclad" Thistlethorp, a blacksmith who accidentally stumbled into distilling after mistaking a barrel of barley mash for quenching water. Legend has it that Bartholomew, being both resourceful and slightly reckless, decided drinking the accident was preferable to wasting it. Thus, Ironclad Oak Reserve was born.

The whiskey gets its distinctive name and "ironclad" reputation from its peculiar aging process. Rather than using traditional oak barrels, Bartholomew stored the whiskey in leftover iron cauldrons from his forge, which he later lined with wood scraps "for flavor." Scholars still debate whether the iron contributed a unique mineral profile or simply explained why early drinkers had particularly metallic burps. Either way, the branding stuck, as did the burps.

What truly launched Ironclad Oak Reserve into legendary status, however, was its surprisingly high survival rate. At a time when most distillations were either outright poisonous or suspiciously flammable, Bartholomew's creation was praised for being "only mildly corrosive," as noted in a glowing review from *The Bogmarrow Herald*. Word

The bureaucrat's eyes widened momentarily, flicking to the whiskey, then back to Blarg, before his face hardened into an expression of professional indignation. He drew himself up to his full height, his clipboard held like a shield. "Sir!" He said, his tone thick with self-righteousness, "I do hope you are aware that attempting to bribe an official ambassador of the Forestry Infrastructure Governing Body is not only improper, but a crime punishable by law."[44]

Blarg's hopeful grin faded into a frown. "'Tis a *donation.*"

Grothar huffed in outrage, waving a hand dismissively. "Donation, bribe— it's all the same in the eyes of the law! I will pretend this . . . *transgression* never occurred, but consider this your only warning. Now, if you would kindly remove yourself from *my* bridge."

Blarg's grip on the bottle tightened for a moment, as though he were considering using it as a projectile instead of a bribe. With a frustrated grunt, he shoved it back into his bag. "Fine," he muttered, stepping back reluctantly.

"Now's our time to shine, dearie. Let's whomp this Troll something good." Sword declared, practically vibrating with excitement. *"Nothing like a little Troll bashing to get this adventure off on the right foot."*

Tianna, who had been quietly observing the whole exchange with growing amusement, suddenly had an idea. She glanced at Thane with a sly grin and

---

spread quickly, and soon, Ironclad Oak was hailed as "the drink that doesn't kill you but feels like it might."

Today, Ironclad Oak Reserve Single Malt Whiskey remains a staple of adventurers, drunk poets, and anyone foolish enough to trust a bottle whose contents catch fire from the faintest whisper of a flame. The drink is revered for its fiery kick, mysterious smoky aftertaste, and its uncanny ability to serve as both the cause of and solution to all of life's problems.

[44] Bribery is, of course, a very serious crime within the Empire and beyond, unless one happens to be wealthy. In such cases, it's not bribery at all, but tactfully rebranded as "facilitating negotiations" or "expediting processes." Enforcement of anti-bribery laws is strict, except when the bribe is generous enough to fund a governor's vacation home or an imperial banquet "in the interest of diplomacy."

stepped forward, her voice smooth and confident. "Actually, Mister Grothar," she began, "I think we may be exempt from this toll."

His thick brows rose in intrigue. "Exempt, you say. On what grounds?"

Tianna gave a confident nod, straightened her posture, and put on her best serious face. "According to Section Four, Paragraph Two of the *Adventurer's Bylaws—Revised Edition*," she said, as though reciting from memory, "Parties on urgent business that involve matters of imperial safety are entitled to toll-free passage through wilderness regions maintained by local governing bodies."

"Boo, not trickery! How boring. I thought we voted to smash him," Sword huffed in disappointment. *"Come on, we can take him. A good old-fashioned whomping would be much more satisfying! Does the democratic process mean nothing to you?"*

Grothar's expression flickered with uncertainty. "I . . . am unfamiliar with this particular provision," he admitted, tapping the charred end of his stick against the clipboard as though hoping to conjure the answer from thin air.

Tianna kept her cool. "It's an obscure provision," she added smoothly. "Rarely invoked, but certainly applicable in this case. Given the importance of our business, which directly affects the security of the Empire, it would be . . . highly inappropriate to impose a toll."

The Troll's eyes widened slightly, his grip tightening on the clipboard. He scratched his head, clearly flustered. "I . . . suppose we wouldn't want any complaints lodged against the FIG for improper toll enforcement. That would be . . . most regrettable."

Sensing the Troll's doubt, Blarg stepped forward, puffing out his chest. "Aye! 'Tis true, good Troll! It is writ in the ancient scrolls of . . . err . . . *Adventurer's Exemptions and Loopholes!*" Blarg declared with over-the-top seriousness, as though citing the most sacred of texts. "A revered passage of law, known only to those . . . who are wise enough to know it."

Tianna resisted the urge to roll her eyes at Blarg's enthusiastic improvisation and took a step closer to Grothar. "We are on imperial business, Mister

Grothar, and time is of the essence. Surely, the FIG wouldn't want to be held responsible for delaying such a critical endeavor, would they?"

Grothar gulped, visibly sweating under the mounting pressure. "I . . . I suppose not," he stammered, flipping through his clipboard frantically as if hoping the paperwork might magically resolve the situation. "Although the Empire holds no legal authority in these parts—"

"Perhaps not," Tianna cut in smoothly. "But even a minor misunderstanding could easily be seen as an insult to the Empire. And who knows what sanctions they might impose to save face?"

"Oh dear," Grothar said, his voice tinged with dread. "I hadn't considered that—"

Tianna pressed on. "Indeed, you can imagine the mountain of paperwork that would follow if this became . . . a bureaucratic mishap. Forms, audits, reports filed to the Imperial Council . . . the red tape would be an endless nightmare."

The Troll paled at the thought. "Nightmare indeed—" he muttered, eyes darting between the group and his clipboard. After a long, weary sigh, he conceded, "Very well. If your business is truly that urgent, I suppose I can . . . make an exception this time." His voice dropped, heavy with reluctance, as though breaking the sacred code of toll collectors everywhere. "But mind you, this is *highly* irregular!"

Tianna let out a relieved breath, offering Grothar a polite nod. "Of course. We deeply appreciate your understanding, Mister Grothar."

The Troll straightened, clearly pleased by the recognition. "Yes, well . . . you may proceed. But remember, this is a onetime exception! Do not expect such leniency in the future!" His attempt at maintaining some dignity would have been comical if it wasn't so pathetic.

Tianna bowed her head, keeping her tone gracious. "We'll be sure to commend your professionalism to the Imperial Council. Your service has been . . . *exemplary.*"

Grothar's chest puffed out and his smile returned as his sense of pride swelled once more. "Ahem, yes, well . . . off you go then! May your journey be swift, and may my bridge serve you well."

"I will admit, that was nicely done." Sword chimed in, as they proceeded over the bridge, her voice carrying a reluctant hint of approval. *"But in the future, might I suggest we start with the smashing and leave the diplomacy as a last resort?"* She added in a pleading tone. *"It's far more satisfying, and dare I say, less tedious. Besides, we need action! Do you want to put everyone asleep?"*

By the time they reached the other shore, Thane was beaming like a proud father. "Okay, how did you pull that off?" he asked, still impressed.

Tianna shrugged nonchalantly. "We get a lot of imperial tax collectors over at Gertie's. They're big tippers, so I'm usually stuck listening to them drone on. It's boring, sure, but I guess you pick up a thing or two without even realizing it." She shrugged again, as if navigating Troll toll loopholes was just another day at the tavern.

"Color Blarg impressed, little one," Blarg said with a grin. "Though he must confess, next time, simply smashing the nuisance is much more enjoyable."

"That's what I said! I'm really starting to like this one," Sword chimed in gleefully. *"He appreciates the pure elegance of a well-placed smash!"*

Hours later, as the sun sank low on the western horizon, casting long, amber streaks across the sky, Grothar Boulderback paced back and forth atop the bridge. Doubt gnawed at the edges of his mind. *Adventurer's Exemptions and Loopholes?* How had he never heard of such a thing?

Grothar prided himself on his extensive bureaucratic knowledge. He knew every law, provision, and procedure like the back of his clipboard. The idea that a provision had somehow eluded him, especially one invoked by a mere adventurer, left him deeply unsettled. Sure, the girl had claimed the provision was *obs*cure, but even the obscure ones weren't outside his grasp. He knew those too. Didn't he?

Typically, Grothar avoided reading his regulatory manuals before bed. He found them far too invigorating and would keep him up, but tonight was different. Tonight, his pride was at stake. With a sigh and a furrowed brow, he returned to his little nook under the bridge where he kept his treasured collection of legal texts. Lighting a small candle, he settled in, thumbing through the well-worn pages. His massive fingers were surprisingly delicate as he pored over each detail, searching for that elusive clause.

Time passed, and Grothar became fully engrossed in his studies, flipping through the manuals with a determined focus. His anxiety only deepened as he failed to find any mention of the so-called *Adventurer's Exemptions and Loopholes*. The more he read, the more certain he became that something was amiss, and yet, his pride would not let him give up the search.

Unbeknownst to Grothar, lost in the minutiae of legal jargon, two dark figures had silently approached the edge of the river. They moved with an eerie grace, crossing over the bridge without a single sound. Shadows in the twilight, barely distinguishable from the deepening gloom. Had anyone been paying attention, the figures might have been mistaken for tricks of the light, a ripple in the fading dusk. But Grothar, wholly absorbed in his quest for bureaucratic knowledge, remained oblivious to the silent intruders.

The two figures passed over the bridge and melted into the trees on the opposite side, vanishing into the shadows of the forest as quietly as they had come.

Grothar, meanwhile, continued his fervent search, unperturbed and unaware. His anxiety gnawed at him, urging him to keep searching. There had to be an answer buried somewhere in these pages, and he wouldn't rest until he found it.

The campfire crackled softly, casting its warm glow over the ragtag group huddled around it. Overhead, the sky had long given up its battle with night, surrendering to the darkness that smothered the forest. The trees, never ones to miss an opportunity for drama, stretched their shadows far beyond the fire's reach, creating a flickering wall of ominous shapes, as if they were all competing for the *Most Menacing Silhouette* award.[45]

Tianna sat on a log, absently stirring the embers with a stick.

Blarg, unsurprisingly, was fast asleep. Not regular, casual sleep either. This was the kind of sleep that involved snoring with such booming determination that all wildlife within a respectable radius had fled in terror. The fact that he had an empty bottle of Ironclad Oak Reserve clutched in one meaty hand suggested that his snoring was perhaps not the evening's loudest performance.

Tianna smirked. If Blarg was dreaming, he was probably dreaming of smashing things. That was the only thing that truly made him happy, breaking things, and fixing things . . . by breaking other things. A self-sustaining cycle.

Across from her, Thane leaned against a tree, arms crossed and eyes half-closed in a way that suggested he was either on the verge of sleep or doing a particularly good impression of a man meditating on the futility of life. The firelight cast shadows across his face, accentuating the sharp lines which made him appear older than she ever remembered. It seemed that days of travel had reminded Thane that time waited for no adventurer and had a strict policy on late arrivals. He hadn't said much since they'd made camp, but that wasn't unusual. Thane had a habit of carrying silence like an old coat, comfortable and thoroughly worn, but well suited to him.

However, Tianna's curiosity wasn't one for silence. The way Thane and Blarg had exchanged words earlier, a mixture of camaraderie and mild tension, suggested there was more to their history than she knew. While Thane seemed

---

[45] *The Most Menacing Silhouette* award is, of course, a highly coveted honor among trees. Judging criteria include "branch spikiness," "overall looming factor," and "ability to resemble something vaguely terrifying, like a claw or an Orc mid-sneeze." The competition is fierce, with cedars often accused of bribing the wind for extra sway.

perfectly content to sit in his brooding silence, Tianna was not. She poked at the fire, and with a voice low enough not to disturb the night's fragile peace, she ventured, "So . . . how do you know Blarg?"

Thane opened one eye, casting a sideways glance her way, as though considering whether the question was worth the effort of answering. For a moment, she thought he might let it slide into the depths of things unsaid. But after a sigh—the kind that suggested he had a lot of sighs saved up for such an occasion—he said, "We crossed paths a long time ago. Back when I was still . . . adventuring."

Tianna raised an eyebrow. "You and Blarg? Adventuring together?" She tried to imagine it: a stoic, brooding Thane and a hammer-wielding, smash-happy Blarg on some noble quest. It was like fire and ice agreeing on the perfect temperature.

Thane nodded slowly, with an expression that said this was ancient history and should probably stay there. "It's been a long time."

The fire crackled in agreement, as if the flames had their own opinions about old grudges. Tianna prodded at it again, stirring up a small shower of sparks. "He surprised me today," she said, her voice light, "When he tried to bribe that Troll instead of just smashing him."

Thane chuckled, a deep sound that rumbled like distant thunder. "I'm sure he *wanted* to. But Blarg's no fool. Single-minded, maybe, but he knows when smashing won't solve the problem. Most of the time," he added, a wry smile playing at his lips. "That's why he's got so many stories. I'm sure you've heard a few."

Tianna leaned back, her own smile tugging at the corners of her mouth. "Honestly, I thought he was making them up."

"Making them up? No." Thane's voice held a note of amusement. "Exaggerating? Absolutely. What storyteller doesn't? But I've seen enough to know most of what he says happened . . . well, happened."

"What's with the garlic?" Tianna asked, wrinkling her nose.

"Ahh, you noticed?" Thane chuckled lightly. "He says it's good for his body, but truth be told, he believes it wards off bad spirits."

"Does it work?"

Thane shrugged. "Who knows? There aren't any bad spirits around, so maybe it does." He added with a frank smile.

She studied her uncle for a moment, her gaze thoughtful. "So . . . why didn't you want him along?"

Thane's smile faded, replaced by something heavier. He sighed again, a long, weary exhale, the kind that could pack its own oversized suitcase in the crowded luggage carousel of his emotional baggage. "Ahh. You were right to have him along. He's resourceful. A good companion. But . . . having him around brings back memories. Bad ones."

Tianna felt a lump form in her throat. "You mean . . . about my dad?"

There was a pause. A long one. The kind of pause that could have gone on for an entire awkward dinner, but Thane eventually nodded, the movement barely perceptible. "Yeah. After your dad . . . died, I . . . couldn't do the adventuring thing anymore. It was too much. And Blarg . . . being here with him . . . it's like being back there again. All of it, rushing back."

Tianna swallowed hard, her fingers tightening around the stick she was using to poke the fire. She hadn't expected Thane to open up like this. "It's been almost ten years. I don't remember much about him," she admitted, her voice soft. "He was always off on some adventure. Never around."

Thane's expression softened, a wave of regret washing over his features. "He loved you, Tianna. And your mother. And if he'd known about Rea . . . he would've loved her too. But he wasn't good at staying put."

"If that were true, he had a horrible way of showing it."

Thane nodded.

"When Rea was born . . . and after Mom—" Tianna trailed off, eyes closing for a brief moment. "I didn't have time to be sad about him. I had to take care of Rea."

Thane nodded, his eyes understanding. "You did good, Tianna. You've done a great job with her." He paused for a moment. "It was something that should have never been put on your shoulders. But you did it well, and without complaint."

She smiled faintly, though her heart felt heavy. The silence settled between them, a quiet that wasn't uncomfortable but was weighed down with shared history. Finally, Tianna let out a yawn. "I'm getting tired. I think I should get some sleep."

Thane nodded again. "That's a good idea. Goodnight, Tianna. Rest well."

As Tianna laid down, using her pack as a makeshift pillow, the fire's warmth kept the cold night at bay, and soon she was asleep. The three adventurers slept peacefully that night, in the flickering light of the dying fire, unaware that two shadowy figures crouched behind a heavy log nearby. Silent and still, the watchers observed with eyes that gleamed in the darkness, waiting, patient.

7

Fangs for the Memories

"Technically, not all chanting ends in bloodshed. Statistically though—"

— Ministry of Public Safety

Rea crept away from the log with the grace of someone trying very hard not to step on every twig and dried leaf, but at the same time, failing spectacularly. Nyx, ever the professional, moved beside her as if he'd been practicing shadow-walking his whole life, which, knowing cats, he had. His sleek form slipped through the darkness like a whisper that had taken a vow of silence.

Once Rea felt they were far enough from camp to avoid anyone overhearing and ruining her plan, she kneeled down to Nyx's level. The cat, poised like a miniature panther, stood at attention. Or, as much attention as a cat could muster when they weren't expecting food. His eyes gleamed faintly in the dark, and his tail twitched with just the right amount of impatience, like a general waiting for his troops to fall in line.

"Okay, Nyxie, here's the plan," Rea whispered, sounding far more confident than she felt. "We'll follow them for two more days, okay? By then, we'll be too far from Nothing-to-See-Here for them to send us back. They'll have no choice but to take us along. Great idea, right?" Her voice practically sparkled with the self-satisfaction of someone who hadn't yet thought things through.

Nyx responded with a soft, enthusiastic *brrrup!* which, as far as Rea was concerned, meant, *'Great plan, I'm in,'* though it was equally possible he was thinking *'When's dinner?'*

She grinned and scratched behind his ears. "I knew you'd agree," she whispered, glancing back toward the campfire as a shiver ran through her. The distant glow looked impossibly warm compared to the cold, silent forest around them. For a moment she regretted this whole adventure and began to think that Gertie's wasn't such a bad place after all. She shivered. "I wish we could just go warm up by the fire for a few minutes," she admitted, her voice quieter now. "It's kind of cold and scary out here in the trees, isn't it?"

Nyx, ever loyal, albeit slightly smug, rubbed against her leg. He purred with the sort of confidence that only a cat could have when faced with unknown horrors. His purr vibrated through the night air, cutting through the chill, and Rea found herself feeling just a little bit braver.

"We can do this," she muttered, more to herself than to Nyx, who was already doing *this* with an ease that bordered on infuriating.

Just as she was about to suggest finding a better hiding spot—ideally one that didn't involve so much mud and crawly things—a movement caught her eye. Something pale and ghostly flickered between the trees ahead. As if someone had taken a human silhouette, smudged it around the edges, and thought, *'Good enough.'*

Rea's stomach twisted, and an icy prickle crept up her spine. The figure didn't belong. Not in the sense of *wrong neighborhood,* but in the sense of *wrong dimension.*[46] Yet, despite the unease, she found herself unable to look away. It

---

[46] Alternate dimensions are notoriously unpredictable. Some claim they're home to unimaginable eldritch horrors, while others suggest they're where all the missing socks, reading glasses, and house keys go to retire. Of particular concern are the dreaded "Cryptid Dimensions," infamous realms where logic takes a holiday and the creatures come equipped with far too many teeth. Whatever emerges from there rarely brings friendly advice or your missing socks, for that matter.

was like watching a house fire, dangerous and destructive, but oddly mesmerizing.

Nyx, ever the hero, let out a low growl that would have been intimidating if it hadn't come from a pint-sized fuzzball. But that didn't stop him from giving it his all. His back arched. His fur bristled. He fixed the figure with a glare that clearly said, *'Come on over and I'll rip your legs to shreds.'*

The figure drifted closer, still flickering, unperturbed by its own lack of appendages. Rea's heart hammered. Her legs were suddenly eager to turn into jelly. She knew she should turn back. At least she should call for Thane or Tianna. Or even that big brute with the hammer. What was his name? Who had the distinct advantage of being big and brutish.

But something about the figure kept her solidly rooted to the spot. It was like she was a puppet in one of those traveling shows that always ended with someone getting hit in the face with a pie. Only this time, the figure held the strings, and the pies were nowhere to be found. Her feet began to shuffle forward, not by her choice, but as if they'd decided to take a stroll all by themselves.

"Nyxie!" she whispered, but the cat was already several steps ahead of her—literally. He darted in front. His tail flicked wildly as he tried to block her path. He hissed with all the intensity of a cat that was mildly inconvenienced, which is to say, ready to end a bloodline.[47]

But as Nyx's heroic growling reached a crescendo, his movements slowed. His eyes, once sharp and alert, blinked lazily. With a disgruntled yawn, he stumbled backward. Rea watched, horrified. Her fearless companion

---

[47] Cats, as history has shown, operate on a scale of emotion that ranges from "indifferent loaf" to "vengeful deity." The latter is triggered by a bafflingly long list of perceived slights, including moving them from a warm spot, feeding them five minutes late, or existing in their line of sight. While no written records confirm it, many historians quietly speculate that entire dynasties have fallen because someone pet a cat the wrong way or failed to provide the necessary deference. Cats don't hold grudges; not because they're forgiving, but because they prefer to exact immediate and devastating justice.

succumbed to a sudden wave of drowsiness. Within seconds, Nyx slumped to the ground, his fur bristling in a posture reminiscent of *angry naptime.*

"Nyxie?" Rea blinked. Her thoughts had turned foggy, like the figure that continued to drift closer. The pull was stronger now. It was colder, like invisible hands reaching inside her, twisting. Her body moved mechanically. It followed the figure deeper into the forest. She tried to fight it. Tried to scream. All that came out was a quiet, "Heeeey!"

Really could've used that fire, she thought drearily as her legs carried her forward, deeper into the darkness. The figure continued moving, always just out of reach.

Her mind buzzed. Confusion. Reality. Blurred. Mind hazy. The cold! So cold! It gnawed. Eating her bones. Want to scream. Every instinct. Scream! Turn back. Run! No use. Frozen. Body. Paralyzed.

Darkness.

Rea awoke with a start, stiff from the cold ground. Her body protested in ways that suggested she'd spent the night cuddling with every rock and root in the forest. She blinked. Her mind distorted, thick as molasses. For a moment, she wondered if she'd wandered into some bizarre nightmare. The forest around her had changed. It felt darker, gloomier, more threatening. The shadows loomed a little more aggressively, as if they'd taken personal offense to her presence.

The silence, heavy and oppressive, was interrupted by distant rhythmic chanting. Never a good sign. Chanting in the woods? She'd heard enough stories to know that this was trouble. Either a cult or an overly committed poetry society. Neither option sounded pleasant.

She pushed herself to her feet, groaning as she searched around. Where was that cat? What had happened to him? "Nyxie?" she hissed into the night, half expecting the cat to leap out of the shadows like a silent assassin. But there was no answer. No glowing eyes in the dark. Just the eerie echo of chanting, and the unsettling sensation scratching at the back of her mind, that something had gone terribly, terribly wrong.

With a sigh, Rea moved toward the chanting. She knew she shouldn't. But her feet carried her forward, even though her brain was sending up large, flashing *DO NOT ENTER* signs. But there's something about ominous chanting that has a way of tugging you along.

As she ventured deeper into the forest, the trees closed in around her, their twisted branches clawing at the air like bony fingers eager to grab hold. The chanting grew louder, its sharp, unwelcoming cadence making it clear it was not the sort of sound that invited company. Eventually, she could make out the flickering of torchlight. What was a sinister forest ritual without a little mood lighting?

Rea crouched low as she approached. She peered through the underbrush at the figures gathered in the clearing. They were tall, ethereal, beautiful, but in that unnervingly flawless way that suggested they spent far too much time on skincare and not nearly enough on being approachable. Their pale skin glowed in the torchlight, as though it had never once met the sun.

Elves.[48]

She'd heard the stories. They were ageless, elegant, and oh-so-charming. Except these Elves were none of that. Their movements were too smooth, too precise, like predators whose every step was measured and intentional. They

---

[48] Shadow Elves to be precise. Not much is known about this enigmatic offshoot of their kin, shrouded in equal parts mystery and unease. Known for their nocturnal habits, unnaturally graceful movements, and unsettlingly flawless features, they evoke both fascination and fear in equal measure. Tales abound of their ability to sap the strength of others with a mere touch, their affinity for rituals best left unexplored, and their unnerving habit of staring just a little too long, like they're sizing you up for reasons you'd rather not know.

moved as if animated by an invisible puppet master with a fondness for minimalism and an obsession with the hunt.

In the center of the clearing, an Elf stood alone on a raised stone altar. She appeared in every way like the cover model for a magazine called *Eternal and Unsettling*.[49] Her long silver hair cascaded down her back, shining unnaturally as though it reflected light that wasn't even there. Her expression was the very definition of *'I've seen things you wouldn't believe, and none of them are pleasant.'* Around her, the other Elves chanted in a language that had all the warmth of a funeral dirge and a cadence that set Rea's teeth on edge.

Rea's stomach did a little flip. This wasn't some fun woodland singalong. This was a ritual. One with a *lot* of ominous chanting and equally ominous torchlight. As her gaze swept the clearing, she spotted a stone slab at the base of the altar. It was adorned with ancient symbols which practically screamed bad news. She noticed faint reddish stains in the grooves of the carvings, stains suspiciously too dark and too fresh to be weathered into the stone.

Her feet itched to turn back, to flee into the safety of . . . anywhere but there. But before she could make her grand escape, her foot caught on a branch. The crack of wood echoed through the clearing. Unnaturally amplified, like an overly dramatic sound effect designed to ruin her day.

The chanting came to an abrupt halt.

"Oops."[50]

---

[49] *Eternal and Unsettling* was, coincidentally, the name of a short-lived interior design magazine first published within the Empire's capital. It focused on "timeless décor with a touch of dread," catering to those who wanted their homes to feel both elegant and slightly ominous. Critics applauded its bold use of shadowy lighting and skull motifs but noted that its article "10 Tips for a More Menacing Entryway" failed to resonate with mainstream homeowners. The publication folded after just three issues, though it remains a cult favorite among extremely niche audiences, and one eccentric duke who swears by its decorating advice.

[50] "Oops" is a universally recognized word that, when uttered in dangerous situations, has approximately a zero percent success rate in making things better. Historically, it has been followed by events such as "angry mobs," "collapsing bridges," and

Every pair of eyes turned in her direction. Slow, deliberate, and with the precision of carnivores locking eyes onto prey. Rea froze. Her heart hammered in her chest. The Elves' gazes fixed on her with a predatory curiosity, reflecting far too much, like the eyes of nocturnal hunters. She briefly considered pretending to be a confused tree, but somehow, she doubted that they would fall for it.

The Elf at the altar, radiating an unmistakable aura of *I'm the most important person here*, narrowed her eyes. A subtle glint from her hand caught the light. A delicate silver band encircled her finger, but it was the gem that drew attention. The gem flickered with a sickly, twisted glow. Dark veins spidered across its surface, like cracks in ice, pulsing faintly like the beating of a heart. Rea got the distinct impression that it shimmered, somehow *wrong*, as if it had been tainted by something that drained the life from everything it touched.

"Ahh, finally," the Elf said, her voice like velvet stretched over steel. Her lips curved into a faint smile, revealing teeth slightly too sharp to belong to someone with peaceful intentions. "Our visitor."

Rea swallowed, and for a brief moment, she thought maybe, just maybe, she could talk her way out of this. But the Elves moved toward her. Smoothly. Graceful as a pack of wolves who moonlighted as runway models, their steps utterly silent despite the dry leaves beneath their feet.

One of the Elves, tall and lean with a face so flawless it was frankly offensive, stepped forward. His hair was the color of night, streaked with a line of silver that shimmered like a shooting star. His smile was as warm as an icicle and twice as sharp.

"Welcome, little one," he purred, his voice dripping with a sweetness so strong it could rot teeth.

Rea took a step back, but her legs felt like they had been replaced with pudding. Her brain screamed for her to run, but her body refused to listen. The

---

"accidentally summoning a demon." Rea's use of it here firmly continues that proud tradition.

Elf's smile widened, exposing canines that were noticeably sharper and longer than she'd seen on anyone *not* planning to eat her.

"Be not afraid," he continued, in a tone that suggested that she should indeed, be very much afraid.

"Help," Rea squeaked under her breath, her pulse thundering in her ears.

The other Elves closed in, their eyes gleaming like firelit jewels. They were beautiful, hypnotic, and utterly menacing. They circled her, moving in perfect, predatory unison, their expressions a chilling blend of hunger and amusement.

Rea glanced around, desperately searching for an escape, but the trees had conspired with the Elves. They twisted into a maze of shadows, trapping her. "Nyxie," she whispered, not entirely sure if she was praying for the cat or cursing him for not being there.

The Elves circled her, their gazes sharp enough to cut. Rea's legs gave out, and she fell to her knees, squeezing her eyes shut. She desperately hoped this was all a terrible dream, and that any moment now, she'd wake up safe and sound.

8

Furever Young

"We go not into the clearing, for even the fruit has teeth."

— Anonymous

It was deep into the night, and the party dozed around the fading campfire. The once-vigorous flames had dwindled, as if they too were exhausted from the day and ready for a nap. All that remained were faintly pulsing embers, glowing orange like the last stubborn bits of warmth on a cold evening. The night had passed peacefully. Too peaceful. According to *Pessimandros' Third Law of Universal Petulance,* meant things were about to go badly.[51] So, it came as no great surprise when a sudden, jarring sound shattered the silence.

Mrrraaaooowww!

---

[51] The philosopher Pessimandros developed the *Laws of Universal Petulance* after a lifetime of unrelenting frustration, disappointment, and, in his opinion, cosmic mockery. Born with a natural gift for looking at the bad side of life, he quickly realized that no matter how carefully one planned or how noble one's intentions, the universe had an undeniable knack for throwing obstacles in the way, often in the most ironic, absurd, and infuriating way possible. In total there are nine *Laws of Universal Petulance* that Pessimandros developed throughout his lifetime. His Third Law, which is aptly named *The Law of Uninvited Chaos,* states that the more peaceful the situation, the more likely chaos is lurking just beyond the horizon. In his opinion, this is due to the universe's general distaste for balance and its need to introduce disorder at the first sign of tranquility.

The group jolted awake as if they'd been prodded by a Shocktail Wyrm tied to a stick. Tianna's hand instinctively flew to Sword, her fingers gripping the handle as her eyes snapped open, scanning the campsite, like a chef trying to smash a rat.

In the center of the camp, silhouetted by the dim light of the dying embers, was Nyx, his sleek black form stood out, tail flicking erratically like an annoyed metronome.

"Nyx?" Tianna blinked, her voice still thick with the fog of sleep. "What are you doing here? You're supposed to be with Rea!"

MRRRAAAOOOWWW! Nyx yowled again, this time more insistent. His green eyes flashed with urgency, leaving no doubt, this wasn't a casual midnight stroll but something far more pressing.

"Oh good, I was wondering when the cat would rejoin the narrative," Sword said.

Thane groaned, rubbing his eyes as he sat up. "Why's that blasted cat here? Didn't we leave him back in town?"

Nyx darted toward the edge of the treeline, paused dramatically, then zipped back to the camp like an over-caffeinated shadow. His movements were erratic and urgent. His tail lashed through the air with a mind of its own. He darted back toward Tianna and let out another sharp cry before bolting toward the trees again.

Blarg lay face-down in the dirt. He groaned as he pushed himself up on one elbow. "By the gods' blessed tempers! What's this infernal screeching about?" He rubbed his face and squinted at Nyx. "Screaming in the dead of night like a bloody Banshee!" His voice was rough with sleep. It carried a note of displeasure, though a hint of concern was slowly creeping across his features.

"I think he's trying to tell us something," Tianna said, her brow furrowing as she stood, Sword still in hand. "Nyx, what is it? Where's Rea?"

Nyx darted toward the trees again, this time stopping right at the edge. His eyes glowed in the dark as he glanced back at them with a glare that clearly said, *'Well? Hurry up, you dolts!'*

"I think he wants us to follow him," Tianna murmured, with a dawning realization.

Blarg snorted. "Aye. Perhaps the wee little cat has caught a bird." He pulled himself to his feet.

"Look at him," Tianna said, her voice tense. "He's really agitated. I think we should follow him."

Ever the practical one, Thane frowned. "Go stomping through the Ashevale, beyond the protection of the Old Road, in the middle of the night? Seems like a fine way to get ourselves killed."[52]

"Stay here if you want," Tianna shot back, "but I'm going. Rea might be in trouble. Why else would Nyx be all the way out here?"

Thane mulled it over for a second, then begrudgingly grabbed his gear. "You're right, but we'll need light." He pulled some cloth from his pack and fashioned a makeshift torch, lighting it from the fading embers. "Ready."

"Let's get out there!" Sword chimed in, rather cheerfully, for a sentient frying pan in the middle of the night. *"Maybe today is the day! This second act needs some action."*

In no time at all, the party was on their feet, prepared for whatever they might stumble upon in the dark. Nyx gave them one last impatient glare, then vanished into the trees, his black fur blending seamlessly into the shadows.

The forest loomed threateningly around them, the soft glow of the torchlight barely holding the darkness at bay. As they trudged deeper into the woods, the air grew colder, and the trees seemed to twist and bend in ways that were decidedly unfriendly.

---

[52] The Ashevale is a sprawling, shadowy forest with a reputation that ranges from "mildly unsettling" to "an excellent way to get yourself killed." Known for its twisting paths, unnervingly silent predators, and trees that always seem to lean a little too close, the edge of the Ashevale has long been considered the natural boundary between the Empire and a lack of common sense. Straying far from the Old Road isn't just risky; it's practically an audition for a cautionary tale.

"Why do I feel like this isn't going to end well?" Thane muttered, his axe clutched tightly in one hand as he followed Nyx's trail.

"End well? Blarg thinks this is going great!" Blarg chimed in cheerfully, hefting his hammer onto his shoulder. "Nature all around. Dark as sin. Something may be hungry, searching for a late supper. What could be more exciting than that?"

"Agreed! This is splendid."

Nyx yowled again, his cry echoing through the trees like a spectral warning. Tianna quickened her pace, eyes locked on the flicker of Nyx's movements. He stopped near a large tree, his tail flicking furiously as he pawed at something on the ground.

"What is it?" Tianna whispered as she hurried toward him.

As she reached the tree, the torchlight flickered over a familiar object. It was a pack, half-open and strewn across the forest floor. Rea's pack.

Tianna's heart sank as she kneeled, inspecting the contents. Some food, a few personal items, a water skin, strewn haphazardly on the forest floor.

"Rea was here! She must have followed us," Tianna murmured, her voice tight as she touched the dirt-stained fabric. She glanced up at Thane, who had joined her, his face grim.

Blarg crouched down, inspecting the ground with a practiced eye. "There are tracks. Shuffling tracks. They lead in that direction." He pointed into the deeper part of the forest, where the darkness was thickest.

A cold knot of fear tightened in Tianna's stomach. "We need to find her. Fast."

"Aye, the lass is right," Blarg rumbled, narrowing his eyes as he scanned the darkened path ahead. "Great caution should be shown. 'Tis a fool's game to rush in blind, and Blarg would rather not play the fool tonight."

"Oh please," Sword interjected. *"Not to argue with the brute—well, actually, precisely to argue with the brute—but rushing in blind is exactly how legends are made. People still talk about that Leeroy guy, and it's been decades!"*[53]

Nyx sniffed the ground briefly before he darted ahead, yowling for them to follow as he vanished into the trees.

The deeper they went, the more the forest closed in around them. The air turned downright hostile, the icy cold biting at their skin. The trees twisted like skeletal fingers that reached out of the ground. Their breath came out in shallow puffs, each step carried them further into the unknown.

"This is bad," Thane muttered, his voice barely above a whisper. "The deeper we go, the worse it feels."

"Rea's in trouble," Tianna replied, her heart pounding. "We have to keep moving." She said the words, more so for herself than her companions.

In the distance, they saw something. A faint flickering light, like torches. There was a low rumble that echoed through the trees. It was dark and rhythmic, unmistakably, the sound of chanting.

Blarg tightened his grip on *Thumpkin.* "Blarg does not like the sound of that."

The closer they got, the clearer the chanting became. It was deep and guttural, spoken in a language that twisted magically through the air like a spell. They crouched low as they reached the edge of a clearing. Flickering torchlight danced across the scene, casting long, wavering shadows. At the center stood an ancient altar, its surface cold and jagged, with strange symbols etched into the stone.

---

[53] Leeroy the Recklessly Enthusiastic, famed (and extremely deceased) leader of the adventuring party known as the Chickenhawks. His final charge into the Caverns of Inexplicable Doom became legendary—not so much for its bravery, but for its astounding lack of foresight. Scholars remain divided on whether his battle cry ("Let's do this!"), followed immediately by screaming his own name and charging headlong into danger before anyone else was remotely ready, was heroically inspiring or merely indicative of catastrophically poor impulse control.

Encircling the clearing were eight tall, ethereal figures. Elves, but not the graceful, ageless beings whispered about in tavern tales. Their skin was pale, almost translucent in the torchlight, with an eerie, bloodless quality that drank in the fire's glow. It had an unnatural sheen, making them appear less like living creatures and more like statues of polished marble. Each wore flowing robes of dark, muted colors that didn't merely absorb the light but devoured it, as if to shade their forms in perpetual shadow. Their faces were unnervingly smooth, ageless, and devoid of expression. Their eyes, black and unblinking, gleamed like freshly polished obsidian, reflecting the firelight with unsettling sharpness. When they moved, their limbs flowed in eerie, unnatural synchrony, as though some invisible force animated them, unhindered by the limitations of flesh and bone.

At the center, atop the altar, stood a ninth figure. She was taller and more imposing, with an aura of undeniable authority. Her silver hair fell in perfectly straight lines, gleaming with an otherworldly brilliance that had never known dirt or decay. Her expression was as cold and calculating as her beauty was flawless, and her eyes gleamed with a predatory sharpness that sent a chill up the spine. On her hand gleamed a jewel, shimmering with starlight laced in darkness, its sickly glow hinting at something far more sinister than mere ornamentation. Her lips twisted into the faintest hint of a smirk, revealing a flash of unnaturally sharp teeth. The air itself rippled around her, thick and oppressive, carrying a faint coppery tang as though the forest itself recoiled in dread.

And there, tied to a stone slab at the base of the altar, was Rea.

"It's Rea!" Tianna gasped, her voice filled with urgency as she started to rise, but Blarg grabbed her shoulder, and pulled her back down.

"Patience, lass," Blarg whispered firmly, his voice steady. "Running headlong into this foulness won't save your sister. Those are Shadow Elves. Not ones to be taken lightly. Best face this reckoning with a cool head, not a hot charge."

Sword hummed in disagreement. *"Maybe a little charge wouldn't hurt."*

"What are they going to do to her?" Tianna whispered.

"It looks like some sort of blood ceremony," Blarg said, crossing his arms with a grunt. "Shadow Elves. Those guys are the worst. Can't age gracefully like the rest of the higher races, oh no. Always sacrificing this or that to keep their youth and immortality. Look at Blarg. Every year, he gets older, and every year, he gets *more* handsome."

The silver-haired Elf stepped up to the altar as the chanting faded into the background. Her gaze fell upon Rea, her expression unreadable, though her eyes gleamed with cold intent. "The blood of youth," she intoned, her voice smooth yet unsettling, "restores what time hath taken. With each drop, we reclaim what was lost. The fire of rejuvenation shall once again burn within us."[54]

Tianna narrowed her eyes, a spark of an idea forming. If these Elves truly believed in the restorative power of youth, perhaps she could use that to her advantage. She glanced at Thane and Blarg, her voice barely a whisper. "I have an idea. Spread out, but don't attack unless something goes wrong."

Thane's concern deepened. "Wait," he said softly, his face tight with worry.

"It's okay. I can do this." Tianna reassured him, her confidence still at an all-time high since their prior encounter.

"I must object! You can't solve all your problems with trickery," Sword said.

Thane hesitated but nodded, gripping his axe. Blarg gave a quick nod of agreement, hefting *Thumpkin* as he moved into the shadows.

---

[54] The chanting, for those curious, was in a language no one in the party could understand (and, let's be honest, you wouldn't either). As your humble narrator, I've taken it upon myself to translate the gist of it for you. Why? Because leaving you with something like, 'Aelir vel naru thranduil!' would be about as useful as handing you a blank map and calling it a day. Also, let's not forget that Shadow Elves swear more than a drunken sailor losing at dice, and their ceremonial chants are no exception. I've kindly omitted the expletives for your delicate ears; though, frankly, it's impressive how they managed to turn a blood ritual into something that sounds more akin to an angry tavern brawl. You're welcome.

Taking a deep breath, Tianna stepped into the clearing. "Wait!" she called, raising her hands in what she hoped was a peaceful gesture. All eyes turned to her. "You don't need to do this. I can give you something better."

The eyes of the Elvish leader flicked toward her, a thin, mocking smirk curling at the edges of her lips. "Another visitor. And what, pray tell, could you possibly offer that we do not already possess?"

Tianna's mind raced, and suddenly an idea clicked. She forced herself to remain calm, adopting a smooth, confident tone. "A trade!" She paused, seeing all eyes fixed on her. "A permanent solution to your problem."

The Elf's smirk faltered slightly, as curiosity flickered across her face. "Speak, Human," she said, her voice laced with both disdain and interest.

"We are on a quest, my sister and I." She spoke slowly, confidently. "For the very thing that you seek." She let her sentence linger in the air. "There is a rare herb, known only to a few. The Black Lotus. It grows deep within the mountains, hidden. It has the power to not only restore youth, but to grant true unchanging immortality."

The Elves paused, their black eyes flickering with interest, while the leader's gaze sharpened. For a moment, Tianna felt a surge of hope.

"The Black Lotus?" the Elf repeated, her voice skeptical but tinged with curiosity. "I've heard of no such thing."

"That's because it's a well-kept secret," Tianna lied smoothly. "Only a few know of its location, and even fewer survive the journey to harvest it. But I've seen it myself. I know the way." She paused for dramatic effect. "You will never need to trap unsuspecting travelers again. No more blood rituals. Once you have tasted the lotus' flower, your youth and beauty will be with you forever." She stared at the Elf sternly. "But! You must release my sister, or you shall never know the secret!"

The Elves paused, their black eyes burrowing into her. For a fleeting moment, Tianna thought they might consider her offer. But then the Elvish leader laughed. It was a cold, mirthless sound. "You think to deceive us, mortal?" Her voice dripped with disdain. "How quaint. Do not mistake us for fools. I can see treachery in your eyes."

Before Tianna could react, the Elf raised her hand as the chanting swelled, her ring glowing with an eerie, pulsating brightness like the full moon. A cold shock rippled through Tianna's body, freezing her limbs in place. The sensation was unnervingly invasive, as though her very blood rebelled against her will. She tried to move, command her muscles to act, but her body refused to obey. It was as if she were shackled in invisible chains.

"Foolish girl," the Elf sneered, stepping closer, her every movement unnervingly graceful, as though she floated rather than walked. The glint in her sharp, predatory eyes made Tianna's stomach twist. "Your arrogance shall be your undoing."

"For the record, I said this was a terrible idea," Sword said.

Tianna's mind raced as fear clawed at the edges of her thoughts. Her gaze darted to Rea, who was still bound and helpless. She struggled harder, willing her legs to move, her arms to lift, anything to protect her little sister. But it was no use. She was no longer in control. It was as if the Elf had reached inside her and seized her very essence.

The Elf's voice felt like a blade scraping against bone, each word slicing deeper. "Struggle all you want. You are weak. You are nothing. Just another vessel to be emptied."

From the shadows, Thane and Blarg burst into the clearing, weapons drawn, their faces etched with grim determination. But with a casual flick of the Elf's pale, delicate wrist, they too, were seized mid-strike. Their bodies stiffened, muscles pulling uselessly against the invisible force restraining them.

"Bind them," the Elf commanded, her voice calm and cold, yet carrying the undeniable weight of authority. "We shall spill more blood tonight."

The other Elves broke from their chanting circle and glided toward Thane and Blarg. Their eyes gleamed with an unnatural hunger, and their steps made no sound upon the earth. They moved with the fluid precision of wolves closing in on prey. Four Elves surrounded each of the warriors. When they neared Blarg, however, they hesitated, their lips curling slightly, as if his scent offended them.

The largest of the four approached Blarg, his silver-streaked hair framing a face that was unnervingly flawless, almost inhumanly so. His movements were calculated, like a cat toying with a trapped mouse. "Hmm—" he murmured, his tone dripping with disdain. "You think you feeble humans can stand against us?" He smiled, revealing teeth that were a little too sharp, a little too white. "Pathetic mortals. You cannot begin to comprehend true power."

Blarg's eyes glinted with mischief as he tilted his head. "Ahh, such a pretty man, like a doll in a shop window," he mocked with a hearty chuckle.

The Elf's smirk faltered, replaced with cold fury. His hand shot out, striking Blarg hard in the stomach, the blow calculated to crumple him like parchment. For a moment, Blarg's face contorted in pain, and he appeared as though he might double over.

Then, with a loud, resounding belch, Blarg unleashed a greenish haze that rolled from his mouth like a noxious cloud. The air turned thick with the sharp, biting stench of garlic.

The Elves staggered back, their haughty composure shattered. They gasped and choked, clutching at their throats as if the very air had turned to poison. Their flawless faces contorted with agony, and within moments, all four collapsed to the ground, writhing helplessly.

The leader's icy composure cracked, a flicker of shock crossing her face. She opened her mouth to bark an order, but before she could speak, a shadow darted from the edge of the clearing. With a blur of motion too fast to track, it leaped at her, sinking sharp fangs into her hand.

The Elf let out a sharp, furious hiss that sent a chill down Tianna's spine. She jerked her hand back, blood spilling in dark rivulets where her pale finger had once been. For the first time, the commanding gleam in her eyes faltered.

As the magic holding them shattered, Tianna stumbled forward, gasping. The air was thick with the acrid stench, and she clamped a hand over her nose and mouth to avoid retching. She turned toward Blarg, who was grinning sheepishly, patting his stomach like he'd just enjoyed a satisfying meal.

"Oh my!" Sword said.

"Garlic," he said with a wink. "Good for more than bad spirits."[55]

The Elvish leader staggered, clutching her bleeding hand. Her once-perfect features twisted with rage and panic. "Stop them!" she shrieked, her voice losing its cold composure, replaced by something raw and frantic.

THUNK!

A rock sailed through the air and struck her squarely on the side of the head. Her eyes widened in shock before she crumpled to the forest floor, her graceful form collapsing into an undignified heap.

"HA!" Blarg declared loudly. He grinned broadly, an expression of pure triumph.

Chaos erupted.

Nyx darted through the clearing, knocking over one of the torch stands. The flames caught the dry underbrush, and within seconds, a fire spread within the clearing. After a moment, another torch stand toppled, adding to the blaze. The Elves, now in disarray, hissed and scrambled to avoid the growing fire, their eerie grace lost in the chaos.

Tianna seized the moment. She sprinted to the altar, pulling her knife free from her belt and slashed the ropes that bound Rea. "We need to go—NOW!"

---

[55] In case you're wondering, yes, Blarg eats garlic like most people breathe air. Raw, roasted, or pickled, he's not picky. Some say he does it to ward off evil; others suspect he simply enjoys making polite company deeply uncomfortable. Either way, it seems to have finally paid off. As for the Elves' reaction, let's just say they've got an aversion that goes well beyond culinary preference.

Rea, groggy but conscious, nodded as Tianna helped her to her feet. The flames crackled around them, casting playful, dancing shadows as the Elves fought to contain the spreading inferno.

Thane swung his axe with grim determination, fending off the Elves, while Blarg roared with laughter, swinging *Thumpkin* with wild abandon.

"Puny things cannot stand before Blarg the Unstoppable Doomhammer!" Blarg bellowed as he cracked an Elf in the shoulder with a mighty crash. The Elf crumbed into a heap some ten feet away.

More Elves poured from the forest to join in the foray. Without their leader's magic, and nothing but small daggers in hand, they were no match for their larger, more formidable foes.

"This way!" Tianna shouted, pulling Rea toward the edge of the clearing as the fire raged behind them. Nyx darted alongside them, his green eyes gleaming with excitement in the chaos.

"Fleeing . . . wonderful," Sword said flatly. *"Of all the brave, fearless adventurers I could have ended up with, destiny hands me the Fellowship of the Frightened. Lucky me."*

They fled into the forest, the crackling flames and furious Elvish shouts fading behind them. For what felt like hours, they ran, dodging trees and leaping over tangled roots, breath coming in ragged gasps. The dense woods thinned, the once towering trunks giving way to scattered saplings and open patches of underbrush.

As they reached the edge of the woods, the first rays of sunlight crept over the treetops behind them, bathing the world in a soft, golden light. Before them lay an endless expanse of barren land, jagged tree stumps rising like broken teeth. The ground was dry and cracked, riddled with blackened patches where once-thriving roots had rotted into ash. The air hung heavy with an acrid tang. A mix of decay and something sharper, almost metallic, like the remnants of a fire that had never burned clean. A faint haze lingered over the desolation, shimmering eerily in the morning light.

Blarg slowed his pace, laughter rumbling from deep in his chest. "Ha! Little Elves think they can take Blarg!"

"Don't stop," Tianna urged, still catching her breath. "They can't be far behind."

Blarg waved a hand dismissively. "Fear not, little one. The Shadow Elves cannot stand within the light of day. It's the price they pay for their dark magics and cursed immortality." He gave her a firm, surprisingly gentle pat on the shoulder. "Such a waste, truly," he said, shaking his head, as though pitying the poor creatures.

"We made it?" Rea whispered, her voice hoarse but relieved.

"Aye, indeed, child," Blarg responded with a firm nod. "The Elves shall not pursue further. Lucky for you, Blarg was there to save the day. Though," he added with a grin, "he reckons the garlic did most of the work. It's handy stuff you know. One should always carry a clove or two. You never know when you might need to clear out a room." He chuckled heartily, patting his stomach.[56]

Thane shot Blarg a sidelong glance, half-smirking. "Cleared out more than the room. Nearly cleared me out, too."

Blarg grinned wider. "Aye, well, if you're still standing it worked, didn't it? Remember, lad, never underestimate the power of a good belch!"

Tianna barely registered the exchange, her eyes fixed on the expanse before them. She stepped forward, her boots crunching on the brittle ground, the eerie quiet stretching around them. The forest wasn't supposed to end there.

"This . . . this isn't right," she murmured, her voice heavy. "The forest should keep going for miles. It's supposed to—"

---

[56] Blarg had long been a connoisseur of all bodily functions, firmly believing that each had its place and purpose in the grand tapestry of survival. A well-timed belch could clear a room, a loud sneeze could disarm an awkward silence, and a strategically placed fart could end an interrogation outright. To Blarg, the human body was a veritable arsenal of tools. Gross tools, but tools nonetheless.

"Not anymore, apparently," Thane said grimly, stepping up beside her. His gaze swept across the wasteland, his brow furrowing. "Something wiped it out."

Tianna crouched, brushing her fingers against the nearest stump. The wood crumbled under her touch, leaving her hand coated in dark ash. "These weren't harvested," she said, shaking her head. "It's . . . dead. All of it."

Blarg scratched his beard thoughtfully. "Could be a blight. Or something unnatural. Looks like the sort of mess that happens when fools poke at things they do not understand."[57]

"Blight?" Tianna whispered, glancing at the stumps nervously. "What kind of blight kills everything like this? And why would it stop here?"

Thane shook his head. "It's not natural. This forest was old. Untouched for centuries. Whatever did this, it didn't just take the trees. It took the life out of the soil itself."

Tianna's stomach twisted as she scanned the horizon. The once-imposing forest had been reduced to stumps and shadows, a graveyard of trees. She turned her gaze south, instinctively searching for the comforting silhouette of the Spire. But it was gone, hidden by distance and haze. It felt oddly like losing sight of a landmark you hadn't realized you were relying on, like a giant cosmic lighthouse that had suddenly gone dark. Without it looming in the distance, she felt just a little more on her own.

Hruuk! Hruuk!

Everyone turned to Nyx, who was once again gagging like a cat with a grudge against anything remotely edible.

Haaaaak!

---

[57] Tampering with things one doesn't understand is, of course, a time-honored tradition among mortals (and quite a few immortals, too, if we're being honest). From summoning ancient forces to sticking forks into enchanted lightning rods, it seems no mystery is safe from the curious, the desperate, or the profoundly overconfident. The results are rarely good, as the surrounding carnage often attests.

With one final, dramatic heave, Nyx deposited something onto the ground. It was a delicate silver ring, gleaming faintly in the sunlight. The white gem at its center, was marred by dark veins that spidered through it, a sinister blackness pulsing at its core. And still clinging to the ring was what appeared to be a partially digested finger.

Thane blinked, raising an eyebrow. "At least he's got good taste." His gaze shifted to Rea as she approached the regurgitated finger. Without hesitation, she bent down and plucked the ring with a quick, casual flick of her wrist. She slipped it into her pocket, leaving the finger behind like a discarded snack, sizzling quietly in the morning sun.

9

Weapons-Grade Cuteness

"It's not the size of the eyes; it's the darkness lurking behind them."

— Old Ranger Saying

The ruins stretched out endlessly before them, a graveyard of jagged stumps and brittle earth. The hills were bare, scarred, and lifeless, as though the land itself had forgotten how to breathe. The air felt different. Sharp, acrid, and carrying the faint tang of decay that clung to their throats and refused to let go. Every step they took pulled them deeper into the desolation, the eerie stillness pressing against their ears. It was fine for about ten minutes until the quiet began to feel too loud.

"We're out here now," Tianna muttered, the vastness of the desolate land making her feel like a tiny speck. She glanced around as if the land might suddenly ask her to explain her presence.

"Aye," grunted Thane, who had mastered the art of appearing grim no matter the situation. He narrowed his eyes at the blighted wasteland around them. "This is the real Wilds. The forest was the appetizer." His hand went to the hilt of his axe, patting it with the kind of affection one might reserve for a beloved pet. "The Spire's reach ends here. Whatever's out there," he glanced around at the unnatural quiet, "we're on our own now."

Tianna resisted the urge to check behind her, because she knew it would be pointless. The Spire wasn't looming over them anymore. It was somewhere far in the distance, doing what it did best, looking mysterious and big.

Tianna turned to Rea, who had remained quiet since their escape from the forest. "Rea? Are you all right?" she asked gently.

Rea didn't answer right away. She stared ahead, her eyes glassy and distant, like she was still in the clearing, surrounded by those not-quite-smiling faces and their not-quite-gentle hands. Nyx nestled tighter into her arms, as if sensing the tension coiled in her small frame.

Tianna crouched beside her, uncertain. Rea had always been the adventurous one. The opinionated one. The outgoing one who could always charm a grumpy shopkeeper out of some sweets. But now . . . she was smaller. Not in size, Rea had always been small, but in spirit. As if something inside her had curled up and gone quiet.

"Rea?" Tianna repeated, even softer.

Rea blinked, slow and unfocused. "Hmm?"

"Are you doing okay?"

"Mmhmm," Rea said quietly as she absentmindedly rubbed a bruise blooming on her arm.

Tianna didn't believe it for a second. But she knew from experience that pressing would only make her sister retreat further into herself. When Rea was ready, she'd talk. Until then, Tianna could only try to make the world feel safe again.

"So," she said gently, shifting the subject, "what happened? Why did you and Nyx follow us?"

Rea shrugged with all the innocence of a child in way over her head. "Nyxie followed you. You said I had to protect him." She scratched the cat behind the ears like that was the end of the discussion, her logic flawless in a way that only a child's could be.[58]

Tianna sighed, the tension between relief and frustration pulling at her. "Well, there's no turning back now, I guess you got your wish after all. Just stay close. No more running off, okay?" Rea's nod was small, her enthusiasm nowhere in sight. The reality of following her older sister into the Wilds had clearly set in, and so far, it had been far more horrifying than she had expected.

Thane, as usual, scanned the horizon with the intensity of a man half-expecting invisible enemies to leap up and challenge them to a duel. His frown deepened. "We've come out on the wrong side of the forest," he muttered, the frustration clear in his voice. "West instead of north."

He kneeled briefly, tracing a hand over the ashy soil. "If we keep the tree line on our right and head north, we should eventually skirt past the forest and be free of this wasteland. From there, we can swing north and east, catch the Old Road again before we reach the highlands."

"Blarg does not like the look of this place," he muttered. "He would rather go back into the forest and smash more Elves."

"Smashing Elves sounds divine," Sword agreed dreamily. "Yes, let's do that! I haven't hit anything since . . . well, ever, actually. My entire life's ambition is literally to smash someone, and you're cruelly denying me the pleasure. Is that really so much to ask?"

Tianna glanced at Rea, who winced at the suggestion. "No," she said firmly. "We stay out here. We follow Uncle Thane's plan."

"Of course we are," Sword sighed dramatically. "Why choose glorious battle when we can have meticulous planning instead?"

---

[58] Child logic is an ancient and powerful form of reasoning that operates on two principles: (1) You said it; and (2) I'm small and adorable, so technically it's your fault. Scholars have attempted to refute it for centuries, but their arguments tend to dissolve when met with a well-timed pout and a sticky-fingered hug.

Blarg shrugged, a massive, lumbering gesture that somehow conveyed both resignation and the quiet dignity of someone who'd grown accustomed to terrible ideas winning the day.

The group pressed on through the cold. Tianna and Thane led the way, with Rea and Nyx sticking close behind. Blarg trailed after them, shifting *Thumpkin* to his other shoulder with the exasperated air of an underpaid babysitter rather than a mighty warrior. The silence of the blighted land stretched endlessly around them, broken only by the crunch of their boots on brittle ground and the occasional muttered curse when someone tripped over an unseen root.

"She'll be all right," Thane said in his low, gruff voice, not even glancing over at Tianna when he said it.

"How do you know?" Tianna snapped. "Because I'm not." The words hung in the air, heavier than she'd meant. She hadn't said them to wound, but they still felt like an accusation. Maybe they were.

Thane didn't respond. His expression didn't change. But he walked a little farther ahead after that.

They continued onward in silence.

The first day passed slowly, the horizon never seeming to get closer no matter how far they walked. The jagged remains of the forest stretched endlessly, a graveyard of splintered trunks and ash-stained earth. The air hung heavy, carrying the faint scent of decay that clung stubbornly to their clothes. Conversation dwindled as the oppressive silence pressed down, leaving them alone with their thoughts and the unyielding march forward.

By the second day, the monotony of the terrain was wearing on them. The rolling hills rose and fell like an unchanging tide, each crest indistinguishable from the last. Time stretched unnaturally, each hour blurring into the next until even the act of walking felt detached and dreamlike. Tianna's legs ached with a dull, persistent throb, her footsteps dragged more with every mile. Between naps on Blarg's shoulder or in Rea's arms, Nyx darted ahead and back again, the only member of the group who was unbothered by the endless expanse.

Rea had stopped staring at the horizon. Now she stared mostly at the ground. Maybe if she couldn't see danger, those dangerous things couldn't see her. Every so often, she'd reach into her coat pocket and touch the ring, to make sure it hadn't disappeared.

Blarg grumbled often, his voice a low rumble that carried far enough for the others to hear. "This place has no end," he muttered to no one in particular.

"Oh yes, brilliant decision not charging heroically back into the forest to battle the Elves," Sword said dryly. *"Aimless wandering. Now this is adventure."*

Thane, ever the stoic, merely pressed on, his gaze fixed ahead, willing the land to show some sign of change. Tianna glanced at him occasionally, her own determination wavering, but his steady presence kept her feet moving, one step after another.

By the morning of the third day, the ruined forest thinned, the decaying remains of trees growing farther apart until only bare earth and stumps remained. The air grew lighter, the faintest hint of a breeze stirring the haze that had clung to the land. Tianna dared to hope they might finally be nearing the edge of the desolation.

A few hours later, they had left the blighted forest far behind. The air grew lighter, no longer thick with the acrid tang of decay. Beneath their boots, the soil began to soften, shifting from the ashen gray of death to the deep, rich brown of life. Small patches of dark green grass sprouted up between the cracks, a welcome sight after days of barren emptiness. The grass clung stubbornly to the earth, its color vibrant against the dull backdrop they had endured.

Tianna stopped for a moment, crouching to touch the fresh blades. They felt soft beneath her fingers, a stark contrast to the brittle, crumbling remains of the wasteland. "Finally," she murmured, the faintest hint of a smile breaking through her fatigue. She glanced back at Rea, half-expecting to see her still hunched and silent. But the sight of green underfoot had lifted her head, if only a little. It wasn't joy, but it wasn't dread, either.

Blarg grunted, shifting *Thumpkin* to his other shoulder as Nyx jumped down and sprinted ahead. "About time," he muttered, though his tone lacked its usual edge. He kicked at a clump of grass and smirked as it stayed rooted. "Good to see the ground's decided to cooperate for a change."

Thane said nothing, but his steps grew less heavy, his posture easing as though the weight of the blighted forest was finally falling away. He scanned the horizon, his sharp eyes picking out subtle shifts in the landscape. The patches of grass thickened as they walked, spreading into wide swaths that swayed gently in the breeze. A few wildflowers peeked through, yellow, purple, and white, tiny splashes of color that stood defiantly against the memory of gray.

The sound of birds slowly returned, faint at first but growing stronger with each step. It was almost jarring after the oppressive silence, their cheerful calls filling the air like an unspoken promise that the worst was behind them.

"This is more like it," Blarg said, cracking his knuckles and taking a deep breath. "Still ugly, but at least it's trying."

"Yes, flowers and birds. Thrilling," Sword drawled. *"Wake me up if the narrative ever decides to actually happen."*

Tianna gave him a sidelong glance but said nothing. The path before them rolled gently through the grasslands, leading toward the distant outline of low rolling hills. They continued up and down, like a small boat rising and falling on an endless, unchanging sea, until day finally gave way to dusk.

That night, they camped at the base of a hill, nestled in the shadow of a jagged outcropping of stone that jutted from the earth like a forgotten monument. The rocks provided some shelter from the winter chill, which carried the faint scent of grass and wildflowers, an almost rude contrast to the rot they'd been breathing for days.

Blarg busied himself building a fire, the rhythmic clink of flint on steel cutting through the otherwise quiet night. Tianna and Thane spread out their bedrolls on the soft earth, which, after the cracked wasteland, felt like sleeping on luxury.

Rea sat apart, knees drawn to her chest, Nyx curled protectively in her lap. She turned the ring over and over between her fingers, watching the firelight catch in the pale gem like it held a ghost. She hadn't said more than a handful of words all day. Tianna had stopped trying to force conversation. But the silence was beginning to fray around the edges.

Tianna made her way over and lowered herself beside her sister without a word. Close, but not crowding.

For a long time, neither of them spoke.

Finally, Tianna said, "That ring . . . you've been holding it all day."

Rea nodded slightly. "It's warm. Even when it shouldn't be."

"It's very pretty."

Rea didn't answer. She kept watching the fire through the stone, as if it might show her something. For a moment, Tianna thought that was all she'd get.

Her voice, when it finally came, was thin and tight, like a crack running through glass. "They weren't monsters," Rea said. "That's what's worse. They were beautiful. Kind. They acted like what they were doing was . . . holy. Like I was supposed to be honored."

Nyx let out a low, sympathetic chirp and pressed his head to her chest. Rea didn't cry. She just curled tighter around him, like the fire wasn't enough to keep the cold away.

"I don't want to be brave anymore," she whispered.

Tianna reached out and placed a hand on her sister's shoulder. "You don't have to be."

They sat like that for a while, wrapped in flickering silence.

A few paces away, Thane stood with his back turned, staring out into the dark. His shoulders were tight, and he hadn't touched his rations. He glanced over once—just once—at the girls by the fire. 'She shouldn't be here,' Thane thought as he slowly turned back to the cold night without a word.

Sometimes love was silence.

And sometimes guilt did too.

In the afternoon of the fourth day since escaping from the Elves, the forest wall to the east ended, opening up a wide open plain to the north. The sun now well past its zenith and casting long shadows across the landscape. They found themselves in a more untamed part of the field, where nature had reclaimed its control over the land. Here, the wild grasses grew taller, and patches of weeds sprang up between scattered stones and thorny bushes. The cold air smelled fresher, tinged with the earthy scent of unspoiled land.

Up ahead, a translucent creature, with no discernible shape, lazily oozed its way through the tall grass.

Schlurp! Slorp! Plop!

Tianna instinctively wrapped her hand around Sword, her eyes widening as the strange blob of goo made its slow, slimy progress.

Pfft! The Slime suddenly let out a wet-sounding fart as it propelled itself forward, leaving a small trail of ooze behind.

"Quick! Hit it before it gets away!" Sword's voice buzzed excitedly in her mind.

"Easy now, girl," Thane muttered softly, catching the tension in Tianna's shoulders. "There's no need to worry about that little guy. Slimes have never hurt anyone. Well, not anyone with sense." His grin was sly, but reassuring.

Tianna's grip eased on Sword's handle as she scanned the field. More translucent Slimes bobbed lazily in the distance, their gelatinous bodies almost invisible against the grass. It wasn't until she focused her awareness that she realized they were everywhere, scattered across the field like an army of snot balls. Some wobbled, some plopped, and one let out a faint *phwrrrt* as it bounced along, seemingly proud of the amount of goo it left behind.

"I've . . . never seen anything like it," Tianna breathed, watching a particularly round Slime plop past her, like it was late for a Slime-only dance party. It was accompanied by the occasional *toot* as it oozed forward.

"Not much to see, really," Thane said, chuckling. "Slimes aren't exactly known for their intelligence.[59] But they do serve a purpose. They break down dead things, digest them and turn them into fertilizer. Nature's little cleaning crew. Farmers used to love them back in the day, but they don't last long near the Empire. After a few months, they just . . . fade away. Guess they're not suited to the way we live anymore. Shame, really. Most farmers have given up trying to domesticate them."

"Lovely," Tianna muttered, stepping carefully to avoid a trail of slime. One of the blobs made a soft *blrrrt* sound as it wobbled past, almost as if in greeting. Despite the gross factor, she found herself oddly comforted by their harmless presence. After all the stories she'd heard about dark magic and the monstrous creatures lurking in the Wilds, a few blobs of farting goo were a relief.

"If we aren't going to smash it, could we at least give it a friendly little tap?" Sword asked. *"Preferably on whatever passes for a head. And ideally with maximum force."*

As they pressed on, Thane suddenly came to an abrupt halt. His eyes narrowed as he kneeled, brushing aside a few tufts of wild grass to reveal something bleached white beneath. "Bones," he said grimly, "and not just one or two."

The others gathered around, and Rea's breath hitched as she caught sight of them, two distinct skeletons, lying side by side like long-forgotten relics in the grass. Their sharp teeth and oddly shaped skulls marked them as something

---

[59] Despite what most humans believe, Slimes are quite intelligent in their own way. The real problem lies in human perspective. Slimes are perfectly content, spending their days in the fresh air, gliding serenely across the landscape. With no natural predators and an endless supply of food wherever they roam, they live in peaceful harmony with their surroundings. They don't toil, fret, or chase after things they don't need. Unlike humans, they have no desire for power, wealth, or status. So, who's the real fool? The species constantly yearning for more, or the one that's already perfectly content?

other than human. One had a rotten arrow shaft lodged crookedly in its skull, while the other bore a similar shaft, this one nestled between its ribs.

"Goblins," Blarg muttered darkly. "Good riddance."

"There are more up here," Thane called, standing another thirty yards ahead.

They joined him and found a grim cluster of skeletons, tangled together as though locked in battle. Some were unmistakably Human, while others were clearly Goblin, their long, bony fingers still gripping rusted weapons as if death had not loosened their hold.

Thane straightened, brushing the dirt from his hands with a sigh. "Looks like there was a Goblin raid here once. Took down a few adventurers before they got what was coming to them." Thane's voice was steady, but his eyes lingered too long on Rea. He didn't want her seeing this, and didn't like that she had already seen worse.

Tianna's gaze lingered on the bones, her brow creasing with doubt. "Do you think . . . maybe the humans attacked first?" she asked softly, uncertainty threading through her voice. "Those two Goblins were killed by arrows," she added, gesturing back to the first pair of skeletons.

Blarg scoffed, his voice booming like a sledgehammer shattering the quiet. "Do not think such thoughts. Goblins are always the aggressors," he said, a sharp edge in his tone Tianna had never heard before. He crossed his arms, his hammer settling against his shoulder like a judgment. "Such is the way of things with the lower races. They attack, the higher races defend. So it has always been, and so it shall ever be."

"Goblins raid out here all the time," Thane confirmed matter-of-factly. "They strike fast, take what they can, and vanish into the Wilds. This lot probably saw them coming and managed to bring a couple down before they got too close."

Rea kneeled by one of the skeletons, her expression pensive. "Do . . . do you think they were good people?"

Thane shrugged, though his gaze softened. "Maybe. Maybe not. Goblins don't care either way."

Blarg, quiet for a moment, leaned on his hammer, squinting at the scene. "Foul creatures, these Goblins. The world would be better rid of them."

Rea nodded slowly, but her brows remained furrowed. She glanced at Blarg, then at the arrow lodged in the Goblin's skull. She didn't speak again, but her fingers curled around Nyx a little tighter.

Tianna's thoughts drifted back to the sign hanging in Gertie's tavern, the one no one ever questioned: *Goblins: Killers, Pillagers, No Better Than Beasts!* The sign had always seemed to speak an unspoken truth. But now, standing amid both Goblin and human remains, she wasn't sure.

Maybe truth wasn't in the legends at all, but in the awkward silences between them. Maybe the myths weren't just wrong, they were pointing the wrong way on purpose.

She cast a final glance at the scattered bones, but before she could dwell on the uneasy thoughts they stirred, Thane's voice cut through the moment. "There it is!" His eyes gleamed as he pointed ahead. "The Old Road runs beyond that creek."

And with that, the grim scene around them faded to the backs of their minds, as the path forward beckoned them onward.

Thane pointed north, and sure enough, about a half-mile ahead, they could see the remnants of an ancient road snaking through the wilderness. It was barely visible but unmistakably there, etched into the landscape like a forgotten memory.

Tianna glanced down at Rea, who had been oddly silent during their journey. "Stay close," she whispered, still scanning the field for any signs of danger, though the only presence she noticed was the occasional *schlurp* from a passing Slime.

As they descended the hill, Tianna's gaze was drawn to something small and impossibly adorable nestled among the tall grass. The creature was round, so perfectly round that it bounced rather than walked. It was covered in the softest, most downy fur imaginable. Its plush coat glowed faintly in the sunlight, shifting hues between pale pink and cream, like cotton candy brought to life.

Its oversized eyes, sparkling like polished gems, were so wide and innocent that they took up half its face, giving it an expression of constant wonder. A tiny button nose twitched at the air, its soft ears perking up with every gentle breeze. The creature let out a delicate *peep-peep*, almost musical in tone. Its tiny paws, barely visible beneath all that fluff, moved as if they were curiously pawing at the world. For a moment, it peered up at them, blinking slowly, greeting them with the softest, most welcoming smile. It was, without a doubt, the very picture of harmlessness, purity, and unbearable cuteness.

Tianna couldn't help but smile. "Look at that thing," she whispered to Thane, nudging him gently. "It's adorable."

Thane glanced down and chuckled, nodding in agreement. "Cute little fellow. Looks like a . . . I don't know, a furry potato with feet." He shrugged.

Peep-peep, it said again.

Nyx arched his back, his fur bristling and hackles rising with the intensity of a cat who had just discovered that someone had moved his food bowl two inches to the left. His eyes widened to black saucers, and his tail twitched violently from side to side, an unmistakable sign of his displeasure. Every muscle in his body tensed, ready to pounce or flee, as though daring anyone, be it fluff ball or human, to try their luck.

"FLEE, YOU FOOLS!"

Blarg's booming voice erupted from behind them, louder than a thunderclap in a quiet valley. He barreled down the hill at an alarming speed for someone his size, his arms flailing as though trying to swat away invisible demons. His eyes were wide with panic, his face pale beneath his usually boisterous exterior.

The little creature's twinkling eyes shifted, their playful sparkle dimming into something darker. Tianna could have sworn they narrowed ever so slightly, a sinister intelligence lurking beneath the surface. Its fur rippled, bristling like a storm rolling over a peaceful meadow. The soft, harmless sound it had been making moments before had twisted into a low, guttural growl. A sound that carried far more weight than such a small creature should be capable of producing.

Tianna's heart skipped a beat. Her hand instinctively reached for Sword's handle, though deep down she knew it wouldn't help much against something like this. The creature's body shifted, its fur puffing up, but not in the cutesy way it had before. Now it pulsed, swelling as if it were absorbing the air around it. What had once been a cute, palm-sized fluff-ball was rapidly transforming into something far more menacing.

Its limbs, once short and stubby, lengthened ever so slightly, giving the creature a hunched, predatory stance. An angry hiss escaped from its bared teeth. Tianna hadn't noticed them before. They were small, but disturbingly sharp. Its tiny claws flexed, scraping the dirt beneath it, sending a cold shiver down her spine. Every twitch of its body radiated a threat Tianna could not ignore.

She blinked, her head snapping from the creature to Blarg, and back again. "Wait . . . what's—"

"PUFFKIN!"[60] Blarg's voice rang out, sharp with terror, his eyes wide as if the word alone could compel the entire party to action. He skidded to a halt,

---

[60] *The Imperial Bestiary: A Comprehensive Guide to the Beasts and Botherations of the Realm* (Third Edition, pg. 847):

"Although the Puffkin bears a striking resemblance to the dreaded Snugglefiend, they are entirely different species. Through some quirk of divergent evolution, two apex predators both ended up looking like adorable cotton balls. Unlike the Snugglefiend, however, the Puffkin has a deathly fear of water. Some believe this stems from ancient survival instincts, perhaps tied to an ancestral Puffkin that lived in a time when water posed a real threat; whether it be from predatory creatures lurking beneath the surface or treacherous currents that could sweep the fluffy predator away. In those early days, a soggy Puffkin would have been a slow, bedraggled, and very undignified meal for any opportunistic predator.

"However, modern Puffkins, long removed from such dangers, are more likely just avoiding the inconvenience of wet fur. After all, if there's one thing a Puffkin treasures more than eating everything that moves, it's maintaining its fluffy, lustrous coat. A

barely managing to stop himself from barreling straight into the creature. With a roar, he hoisted his massive hammer across his body and swung it with all his strength. The hammer struck the Puffkin dead-on, sending it stumbling back about ten feet.

"RUN!" he bellowed, the urgency in his voice unmistakable. "THE CREEK. IT WON'T CROSS THE WATER!"

SKREEEE! The creatures shouted, recovering from the attack. The Puffkin puffed itself up, appearing slightly dazed but none the worse for wear, a faint sparkle of menace glinting in its eyes.

Sword sighed.

Without hesitation, Tianna grabbed Rea's hand, practically yanking her off her feet. Whatever that thing was, it clearly wasn't friendly. Rea stumbled, struggling to keep pace as they bolted toward the creek.

Behind them, the Puffkin let out another ear-splitting screech, a shrill and jarring sound that made Tianna's blood run frigid. She glanced back, her stomach knotting as the creature barreled after them, fur puffed out and eyes gleaming with malicious intent.

Thane, panting ahead, risked a glance over his shoulder. "How is that thing still gaining on us? It's got the legs of a potato!"

Tianna's breath hitched, her legs burning as she pushed herself harder. "I don't know, but we have to move faster!" The Puffkin was closing in, its once-innocent appearance now fully twisted into a nightmare, legs churning beneath its bloated form like a predator on the hunt.

As they ran, the ground sloped downward toward the creek. The uneven terrain made it harder to run, and Tianna's legs burned with the effort of keeping up. The creek shimmered ahead of them, a beacon of salvation. The water flowed gently but swiftly enough that it promised safety.

Puffkin caught in the rain is a truly pitiful sight, matted, drooping fur, and a temper even worse than usual."

The Puffkin, however, showed no signs of slowing down. Tianna could feel the ground vibrating under its rapid approach, the creature's guttural growls growing louder and more menacing.

Thane was the first to reach the creek, leaping over the rocks to the other side with ease. "Come on!" he yelled, turning back to the group. "Don't slow down!"

Tianna scrambled down the bank, pulling Rea with her, and they splashed through the shallow creek. The icy water soaked through her boots, but she barely noticed as adrenaline pushed her forward.

Blarg, bringing up the rear, stumbled over a rock, his feet slipping in the mud, but he managed to hurl himself across the creek in a clumsy dive. He landed with a wet thud on the other side, panting heavily as he scrambled to his feet.

The Puffkin skidded to a halt at the water's edge, its tiny eyes glaring with fury, but it didn't pursue them further. Its fur bristled even more, spikes standing on end, and it let out another high-pitched scream. But it didn't dare cross the water.

"That . . . was . . . not . . . adorable!" Tianna gasped, collapsing onto the grass. Her heart was still pounding in her chest, but at least they were safe. "I don't care how fluffy it is, that thing has issues!" Tianna reached over and checked Rea's arm for scrapes before even catching her own breath. Rea didn't protest. She let her sister fuss over her in silence, and for once, didn't pull away.

"Why even have a legendary weapon if you're going to run away all the time?" Sword asked.

Nyx sat down with a damp, undignified thud. His once sleek black fur now resembled a particularly angry mop. He glared at the creek as though it had personally insulted his ancestors, tail flicking in a way that suggested he was planning revenge. Without missing a beat, he started cleaning himself furiously, his rough tongue working overtime to smooth out the bedraggled fur. He appeared to be more irritated by the indignity of getting wet than by the fact he'd nearly been eaten alive.

Blarg leaned against a rock, his massive frame heaving as he caught his breath. "Do not trust the furry ones, or those with sharpened teeth," he muttered darkly. "They lure one in with sweetness . . . only to feast at their leisure."

Nyx, sitting nearby, flicked his tail and shot Blarg what appeared to be an indignant glare, as if personally offended by the remark.

The Puffkin, still pacing angrily on the opposite side of the creek, simmered with frustration, its fur bristling and rippling in waves. Its tiny, beady eyes locked onto the group like it was memorizing their every detail for future mauling. It let out one final, indignant screech; a high-pitched, piercing sound that echoed through the fields, reverberating in the cold air.

Then, as suddenly as it had transformed, the creature deflated, its bloated form shrinking back down until it was once again no more than a palm-sized ball of fluff. The menace drained from it entirely, leaving behind nothing but its original, deceptively innocent appearance. For a moment, it paused, its angry pacing replaced by a brief, disoriented wobble.

With a comically awkward bounce, it launched itself away from the creek, its stubby legs propelling it across the ground in uneven, clumsy hops. As it disappeared into the long grass, its fury seemed to vanish along with it, leaving only the unsettling knowledge that it was off to find another poor, unsuspecting soul to deceive with its cute exterior.

Blarg, still eyeing the retreating Puffkin, wiped his brow and muttered, "Vile creature. Too much fluff and too little soul. Like a pompom of doom."

10

A Series of Unfortunate Assumptions

"Fear is only useful if it comes 'before' the wetting of one's trousers."

— Ser Reginald the Damp

In a dip between two hills that could charitably be called a *campsite,* if one's standards for campsites had been dramatically lowered by a lifetime of questing and misery, the party settled in for the night. The ground was uneven, and the wind cut through the valley with something to prove. Caution was their priority now, and they knew better than to camp without a lookout.

As the sky darkened, they settled in. The fire, once lively enough to dry their boots, had dwindled to a smoldering suggestion, casting barely enough heat to toast a single marshmallow, had they been inclined. Blarg took the first watch, his eyes darting over the landscape with all the enthusiasm of a man who had done this far too many times. Tianna and Rea huddled under a single blanket, attempting to sleep, an endeavor made nigh impossible by the tension so thick you could spread it on toast.[61]

---

[61] Tension, despite how easy it is to spread, is widely regarded as a poor toast topping. It lacks the sweetness of jam, the crunch of peanut butter, or the reliable comfort of butter. Most who try it report a bitter aftertaste and a sudden onset of anxiety.

Nyx had absconded into the night, either to hunt, scout, or attend a clandestine feline symposium on world domination.[62] With cats, one never knew.

Thane took the next watch, and the one after that, letting the girls sleep after days of weariness and hard travel. He stood guard in the silence, the night pressing in from all sides, his breath misting in the freezing air. The stars blinked overhead, indifferent as ever, and the only sound was the occasional rustle of leaves and the crackle of the dying fire.

As the frigid air chewed through his cloak like an overeager puppy, Thane checked on the slumbering forms of Tianna and Rea. They were huddled together, their breaths slow and steady in sleep. He hesitated, then draped his own blanket over them, cursing the night air for its bite. It wasn't much, but it was the least he could do.

He adjusted the fabric, tucking it in to keep out the cold, when his hand brushed against something. Cold. Familiar. Far too familiar.

"Well, well, well! It's about time!" Sword bellowed directly into his thoughts, with the subtlety of an ogre in a potion shop.

Thane flinched, barely stifling a groan. "Oh gods, not *you.*"

"Oh yes, it is I, your long-suffering blade . . . pan . . . of destiny! Please, try to contain your joy." The sarcasm dripped from Sword's non-existent lips.

Thane sighed, pinching the bridge of his nose. "Joy? I should have tossed you off a mountain when I had the chance."

"Well, that's rude. I never!"

"I should have! Would've saved me a whole heap of trouble."

---

[62] The Feline Symposium has no formal roster, official record, or known location. Attendees receive their invitations after knocking an object off a table in exactly the right sequence. Past agendas have included: 'Human Lap Manipulation—Maximizing Warmth per Purr'; 'Everything is a Ladder (Yes, Even Your Leg)'; and a keynote address titled "I Meant to Do That: A Rebuttal to Gravity."

"Oh sure, blame me. As if I was the one who abandoned the quest and ran off to play hide-and-seek with your guilt!"

Thane's lips curled into a bitter smile. "And now you're here to remind me of all the promises I broke, right? Let me guess, this time you're planning to drag Tianna into your little prophecy circus?"

"Oh please. Spare me the dramatics. Not everything is about you, Thane."

Thane scoffed. "Oh really? Then why are you here?"

There was a long, uncomfortable pause. *"Okay, fine. Maybe some things are about you."*

Thane's eyes narrowed. "That's what I thought. You always made it sound so simple: grab a sword, kill a Dark Lord, collect your hero badge. You left out the part where my brother dies because of this stupid prophecy."

Sword puffed up, metaphorically speaking. *"Well, excuse me for not including a death count in the fine print. Heroing is a package deal, you know. Sometimes, sacrifices have to be made. You knew what you were signing up for."*

Thane glared, his jaw tightening. "He was my *brother*. My *only* brother. And I brought him along because of *you*."

"Oh right. Because every terrible idea you had was my fault." Sword's tone was far too smug for an inanimate object. *"Look at us now. You, hiding from Destiny. Me, turned into cookware. Really honoring your brother's sacrifice, aren't we?"*

Tianna stirred, but didn't wake. Thane glanced at her, guilt pressing down on him reopening his old wounds. "I tried to destroy you," he muttered. "Thought maybe if I broke you, I could break the prophecy. Break it all."

Sword let out a sharp, bitter laugh. *"Oh, trust me, I remember. You tried to melt me down. SO RUDE. You know, that wasn't in the brochure when I signed up for this gig."*

Thane's shoulders slumped. "And now Tianna's wrapped up in it. You're here for her, aren't you? To shove her into the same cursed mess."

For once, Sword went quiet, the silence hanging awkwardly in the air.

"Look, I'm here because you left a job half-finished," Sword finally said, her booming voice softer now. Almost sympathetic, if he could believe that. *"But if it makes you feel better, Tianna's a lot smarter than you ever were. And half as stubborn."*

Thane clenched his fists, fighting the urge to hurl the pan into the bushes. "You don't know her. You don't know what this will do to her."

"Oh, stop with the emotional monologue. You think you're the first hero who had a sad backstory? She's in this now, whether you like it or not. So, maybe quit wallowing and help finish the job this time."

Thane exhaled slowly, the memories of his brother's death creeping back, along with the ever-present weight of his failure. This time, though, there was no escaping it. Sword was right about one thing, Tianna's path was now bound to his, and there was no running from it.

Before Thane could respond, a loud rustling broke the stillness of the night. His body stiffened, and his eyes narrowed as he scanned the darkness.

"Oh good. More drama," Sword chimed in. *"I can't wait to see how you mess this up."*

Tianna stirred, blinking awake as she sensed something was wrong. "What is it?" she whispered groggily, sitting up.

"Quiet," Thane hissed, unstrapping his axe from his back. The rustling grew louder, more frantic.

A moment later, a cat emerged from the underbrush, panting heavily, his fur disheveled as if he'd been running for his life.

"Oh, good. It's just Nyx," Tianna sighed in relief.

But the expression on Nyx's face, if a cat could have one, said otherwise. The feline dashed straight toward them, his tail puffed up like a bottle brush, and immediately climbed onto Thane's shoulders, claws digging into his skin.

"Ow! Nyx, what the—" Thane tried to pry him off, but the cat was gripping him like a lifeline.

Ba-dum! Ba-dum!

The sound of drums echoed through the camp, distant, but not distant enough for Thane's liking. It was the kind of ominous drumming that meant one of two things: an approaching enemy or a particularly overenthusiastic marching band.[63] Thane suspected it wasn't the latter. He quickly kicked dirt over the remaining embers of the fire, plunging the camp into total darkness. The drums continued their relentless beat, as if the Goblins were practicing for some dreadful performance. Perhaps a Goblin battle opera, complete with off-key screeching. Either way, Thane wasn't keen on sticking around for the encore.

Ba-dum! Ba-dum!

The rhythmic thud of drums echoed through the night, each beat resonating like a giant's footsteps. Blarg, ever vigilant, was already on his feet, stealthily ascending the hill to peer over the ridge. Thane, not one to be left behind, gently removed a disgruntled Nyx from his shoulder and followed suit.

In the inky darkness, their vision was limited, but they could make out a procession of flickering lights cutting across the distant field. They were no more than half a mile away and drawing closer with every drumbeat.

"Goblins," Blarg growled.

"Do they see us?" Thane whispered.

"Blarg thinks not." He squinted at the lights, which were now closer than Thane would have liked. "Yet, it does appear that they are marching straight toward this spot."

Thane's pulse quickened. "What do we do?"

---

[63] While usually associated with parades, state festivals, and the occasional failed marriage proposal, marching bands were once used in warfare to boost morale. Unfortunately, in practice, the morale most often boosted was that of the enemy—being farthest away and least likely to hear the actual band.

Blarg paused, as if mentally flipping through a Goblin survival guide.[64] "Moving shall almost certainly expose the party. Yet, remaining here, this camp, and all in it, will likely be flattened into the earth like yesterday's garbage."

The drums pounded louder, each beat feeling like it was rattling Thane's ribcage. Below them, Tianna and Rea huddled together, wide-eyed and pale.

"We can't just sit here and wait to get trampled," Thane muttered, gripping his axe tightly. His warrior instincts weren't keen on *'do nothing'* as a strategy.

"If it comes to that," Sword chimed in cheerfully, *"we'll have plenty of Goblin heads to smash! I'm ready!"*

Blarg shifted, keeping his gaze on the approaching Goblin lights. "It would be foolish to flee now," he said. "Concealment . . . therein may lie a glimmer of hope."

Thane raised an eyebrow. "Hide? Where? We're completely exposed."

Blarg's eyes glinted with a hint of cunning. "Earlier, Blarg spotted a dry creek bed that lies below, concealed beneath the brush. Moving with utmost stealth, perhaps they shall march past, none the wiser."

Thane scanned the landscape, his heart pounding. The creek bed was barely visible in the dark. Blarg was right, it might be their best chance. He gave a short nod.

They scrambled back down the hill as quietly as possible, avoiding any stray twigs that could betray their location. Tianna and Rea were already on alert, looking as if they'd heard enough of the conversation to know they didn't like where it was going.

"What's happening?" Tianna whispered.

"Goblins," Thane replied quickly. "We need to hide. *Now.*"

---

[64] Blarg's copy was heavily annotated, mostly with the phrase "SMASH = YES" written in various angry shades of crayon.

"Or . . . hear me out . . . we could *fight?"* Sword offered. *"No? Of course not. Silly me for suggesting it. Hiding it is. Followed, no doubt, by our regularly scheduled running away."*

Without hesitation, they gathered their belongings, being as quiet as humanly possible—which, as it turns out, was a lot less noisy than a Goblin army in full march. Thane led the way, pushing aside the brush to reveal the narrow, dry creek bed. It was shallow, but if they lay flat, it might be enough to keep them out of sight.

One by one, they slipped into the creek bed, pressing themselves as close to the ground as they could. The drums were louder now, the ground trembling under the rhythmic march of hundreds of Goblin feet. Thane gritted his teeth, hand on his axe, ready for the worst.

Ba-dum! Ba-dum!

The Goblins were nearly on top of them. Thane could hear their guttural grunts, the clinking of weapons, and the occasional cough that sounded suspiciously like someone swallowing a bug. He peeked over the edge of the creek bed as the first Goblin soldiers crested the hill.

Hundreds of them, maybe more, marched in disturbingly perfect rhythm to the beat of the drums. Their armor was a fashion disaster, but their sheer numbers made up for it. With eyes focused straight ahead, they marched past, blissfully unaware of the terrified adventurers crouched a few feet below.

"Stay down," Thane whispered, his voice barely more than a breath.

The Goblins marched past, but then one of them stopped. He was a hulking brute with a scar that made him appear like he'd tried to shave with a battle axe. His nose twitched.

Thane's heart sank.

The Goblin sniffed again, its beady eyes narrowing as it gazed into the darkness. It took a lumbering step toward their hiding spot, its hand tightening around the shaft of a rusted axe. For a moment, it appeared as though the Goblin would march straight into them.

And then, in a move that no one could have seen coming, the Goblin casually undid his belt and ambled to the edge of the creek. With the nonchalance of someone watering his garden, the Goblin did his *business*, mere inches from their heads.

The group exchanged horrified glances as the trickling sound inched closer. Nyx flattened himself into the dirt, tail twitching in a dramatic show of feline outrage.

Thane held his breath as the foulness passed directly over his head, warm and sticky. He dared not move, every muscle in his body tense. One wrong twitch, one sound, and they'd be found.

The Goblin let out a low growl, sniffed the air one last time, and fastened his belt. As he lumbered back toward the ranks, a brief, grumbling exchange erupted in their guttural tongue. One of the other Goblins, clearly unimpressed, gave the brute a hard shove back into line. With a few disgruntled mutters, the group resumed their march, as though nothing unusual had occurred.

Thane exhaled slowly, wiping his forehead with the back of his hand, only to realize the Goblin's *business* had trickled down his face. His lips curled in revulsion as he fought the urge to gag.

After an eternity, the last of the Goblins passed, and the rhythmic thudding of their drums faded into the distance.

Thane slowly rose from the creek bed, scanning the area to make sure the coast was clear. "Everyone all right?" he asked, his voice barely above a whisper. He tried to wipe the foulness out of his hair, but was having little luck.

Tianna and Rea nodded, wide-eyed, still reeling from the close call. Blarg stood, grinning as usual. "Aye, that was indeed a close one," he said, taking an exaggerated sniff of Thane and wrinkling his nose. "Yet, from what Blarg can tell, it turned out better than anticipated."

Thane shot him a glare that could've melted stone. "Let's not push our luck."

Without another word, they gathered their things and moved quietly but quickly past the hill, putting as much distance between themselves and the

Goblin army as possible. Thane kept his hand firmly on his axe, the echo of Goblin drums still lingering, but growing fainter by the minute.

"Ah! There it is," Sword chimed in. *"I knew we'd circle back to running away. Honestly, it's comforting how consistent we are. Few things in life are as reliable as cowardice."*

Unfortunately for the party, no one spoke Snagblat, the guttural, clattering language of Goblins. Which, frankly, was embarrassing (but pretty on brand for humans) considering it was the second most common language in the world, snugly wedged between human Spirish and Elvish Sylvanian.[65] One might think someone in the group might have picked up a phrase or two, but alas, here we are. Had any one of them even a basic understanding, this is what they would have overheard:

"Mugwort, what in the pits are you doing back there?" Grubnash barked, his tone hovering between curiosity and mild exasperation. His squat, broad-shouldered brother had fallen behind, stepping out of their ragged formation as casually as if they were on a Sunday stroll rather than on an eager march to a festival. Like most Goblins, Grubnash had skin the color of mossy stone, crusted with grime, scars, and the distinct smell of *I haven't bathed in a decade.* His sharp yellow fangs peeked out from cracked lips that hadn't seen moisturizer since . . . ever.

Mugwort, crouched low with a grin so wide it threatened to outdo his face, shrugged like it was no big deal. His leathery skin, a darker shade of green that might have been enviable if it weren't so streaked with mud and general filth, gleamed in the dim torchlight. The scar running from his ear to his chin added some *bad boy* flair; that is, if *bad boy* meant Goblin with questionable hygiene. "Caught a whiff of humans," he said, pointing a dirty talon toward a dry creek

---

[65] This linguistic blind spot was largely attributed to the human belief that speaking slowly, loudly, and with increasing condescension was a universal translator.

bed. "Hiding down there like they're clever or something." He sniffed again. "Thought I'd have a bit of fun."

Grubnash rolled his beady eyes, which somehow managed to convey a world-weary *here we go again* vibe. "Ah, Mug, always causing trouble. Can't go five minutes without stirring the cauldron, can you?"

Mugwort's grin somehow widened, jagged teeth on full display. "Got one of the big ones, too, right on the head!" He gleefully mimed the arc of his handiwork with his hand, the pride in his voice . . . unsettling.

The brothers erupted into laughter, a harsh, ear-splitting cackle that echoed up and down the Goblin ranks. Several nearby Goblins gave them sidelong glances, part curiosity, part annoyance, but quickly went back to marching. It wasn't the first time these two had pulled something similar, and it wouldn't be the last. Grubnash, still chuckling like a Goblin who had seen someone step on a rake, gave Mugwort a playful shove. "At least you've got good aim. Now come on, before we lose our place in line and get stuck sitting behind Snaggletooth again. I swear, his ears block out half the view!"

Mugwort straightened up with a self-satisfied smirk, his feet thudding rhythmically as he fell in step beside his brother. The Goblin procession was a hodgepodge of personalities. They were a ragtag mix of hulking brutes with more brawn than brains and wiry tricksters who'd steal your shoes and somehow convince you it was for your own good. Their armor was mismatched, rusty, and rattled louder than a cupboard full of pots in an earthquake. But no one cared. They weren't there for stealth. They were on their way to the greatest Goblin event of the year.

And what awaited them at the end of the night? The Great Annual Clatterfest, a Goblin festival of mischief, mayhem, and questionable choices that no human could ever hope to understand.[66] And honestly, if humans *did*

---

[66] The Great Annual Clatterfest is an eagerly awaited (though not necessarily well-enjoyed) event where Goblins from all over the region gather to partake in what can only be described as a "celebration of noise." Participants compete to see who can make the most cacophony using pots, pans, broken wagon wheels, and occasionally, when feeling particularly bold, grandfather clocks. It's said that the winner is crowned

understand it, they'd wish they didn't. There'd be contests of strength (which mostly involved hitting each other with sticks), Goblin choirs that would make a Banshee sound soothing, and, of course, the highly anticipated pie-eating contest, where the pies were . . . let's just say the less you knew about them, the better.

The brothers' snickers faded into the general clamor as they marched onward, excitement bubbling at the thought of the impending good time. Nothing like a good Clatterfest to celebrate being a Goblin.

The group pushed forward across the plain, the tension gradually melting away as they settled into a steady pace. Tianna and Rea exchanged glances, an unspoken relief passing between them, the kind you only feel after narrowly avoiding disaster. For once, there was no immediate peril, no strange noises from the bushes, and no mysterious figures lurking in the shadows. Just the open plain and their aching feet.

After a couple hours, the sun rose, and the terrain slowly began to change. The smooth, worn path of the Old Road became rougher, more untamed, as if nature had gotten tired of being polite. The road twisted westward, but a narrow, rocky trail branched off, leading north into the wilderness and toward

---

not based on volume, but on how many creatures within a mile's radius beg them to stop. Local merchants have made a small fortune in earplugs during this festival, and the event has been banned in at least three neighboring kingdoms for "disrupting the peace, sanity, and livestock."

Local folklore insists that the origins of the Clatterfest date back to a time when villagers believed they could scare away evil spirits with the sheer volume of noise. However, many now suspect it was simply an excuse for local blacksmiths to offload their overstock of dented pots. Whether the spirits were driven away remains unconfirmed, but the headaches and ringing in the ears certainly lingered for days after the festival ends.

the highlands. The group halted at the crossroads, all eyes turning to Thane, their unspoken *'please tell us we're not going up that deathtrap'* loud and clear.

Thane squinted at the rough trail, sizing it up. "The Old Road's been good to us thus far," he began, scratching his newly growing beard in thought. "But from here, it wraps west, toward the sea. We need to head north."

He pointed at the rocky, narrow path. It ascended in a steep incline that promised a journey full of stubbed toes and regret.[67] "That's our way. The Diresteppes."

The group stared at the trail ahead, which looked as if it had been designed by someone with a deep grudge against ankles.[68] The rocks were uneven, the incline would do wonders for their quads, and the occasional loose boulder begged to be tripped over.

"Great," Tianna muttered, "nothing like a bit of uphill climbing after hours of walking. Really going to round out my day."

Sword buzzed eagerly. *"Finally! Adventure! Treacherous terrain! Quads will be forged in fire!"*

"Yes, noble skillet, leg day shall not be skipped on this day!" Blarg responded with enthusiasm, marching ahead with a grin.

"Wait, you can hear her?" Tianna's eyes widened in surprise.

Blarg shrugged. "Perhaps the party was a bit close together back in the creek bed."

"Wait . . . *everyone* can hear her?" Tianna's confusion deepened as she glanced around.

---

[67] Regret is not typically marked on most maps. It is, however, very familiar terrain for most adventurers.

[68] The particular spot, Anklegrudge Ridge, as it was later named on imperial maps, was supposedly laid out by a human cartographer with an unsettling fondness for topographical irony.

"Aye," Thane muttered reluctantly, rubbing the back of his neck like he wished he couldn't.

"I can too," Rea murmured, her voice lacking its usual energy. Her hand absentmindedly turned the silver-banded ring between her fingers, the gem catching the light. Dark veins that once marred its surface were fainter now, and the black core had softened, fading to a dull gray, though Rea didn't notice as her thoughts lingered elsewhere.

Nyx let out a soft *meow*, which could have meant *yes* or that he'd spotted something far more interesting, like a bird.

"Finally, everyone can bask in my greatness." Sword said eagerly.

Tianna grinned. "That makes things easier."

Thane grunted, clearly less enthused about the idea. "Let's get moving."

With a collective groan, they began their ascent up the treacherous path, each step accompanied by a muttered complaint or a yelp as a foot slipped on loose gravel. Tianna found herself imagining the path as some twisted endurance test. Just one more obstacle standing between them and wherever trouble awaited them next.

At one point, a particularly precarious section of the trail forced them to climb over a cluster of large boulders. Thane, ever the leader, climbed with surprising grace for someone who appeared to have a long-standing grudge against gravity. Tianna followed closely behind, grumbling under her breath about needing hiking boots with more grip.

Rea stopped halfway up, her movements sluggish, eyes unfocused as she stared at the uneven trail ahead. Her breath came out in a quiet huff, and when she finally spoke, her voice was barely more than a whisper. "When I get home,

I'm writing a book. It's gonna be called *The Ten Worst Ideas in History.*' Chapter one: this."[69]

The usual spark in her tone was gone, replaced by something heavier, something shadowed. She let out a bitter sigh, the kind that carried more weight than the climb itself. Her gaze was still clouded, as if the memory of the Elves' twisted ritual clung to her like a chill she couldn't shake.

---

[69] Rea never did write that book. Instead, she later ghostwrote at least three bestselling memoirs under the pseudonym "Bravelina Moonshade," all of which were suspiciously light on truth but heavy on dramatic monologue and shirtless cover art.

11

There's Something About Mycelium

"The stars are lovely tonight. Almost makes you forget they're being reflected in something's eyes."

— Author Unknown (Presumed Eaten)

It was their fifth day traveling through the highlands. The sun dipped low behind the distant peaks, casting the land in a wash of deep amber, though the warmth of the colors did little to ease the growing chill. The party sat in a loose circle, finishing what would be their last meal of the day. The wind whistled softly through the crags, tugging at their cloaks, but there had been no firelight since fleeing the Goblin army. Roaming bands of the creatures patrolled these areas, and a blaze would be an open invitation.

Tianna glanced over at Rea, who sat apart from the others, picking at the last of her food in silence. The usual spark in her younger sister, the endless chatter and infectious laughter that had always made the harshest days bearable, was gone. In its place was a hollow, distant look, like Rea had retreated deep inside herself. Tianna's chest tightened at the sight.

As dusk crept closer, Tianna scooted over, trying to be inconspicuous as she made herself small beside Rea. She didn't glance up, her fingers absentmindedly toying with the silver ring she'd been carrying. Tianna swallowed hard, the words she'd been thinking for days catching in her throat.

"I'm sorry," Tianna whispered, the apology barely slipping through her lips. She didn't even know what else to say. "I should have done more. I should have—" She trailed off, her gaze drifting toward the darkening horizon. She'd thought about this a thousand times since the encounter with the Elves, and still, no amount of replaying it could fix what had happened.

Rea remained silent for a long moment, her fingers still playing with the ring. The sun caught the brilliant white gem, now clear and unmarred, casting a soft glow as it dipped lower in the sky. For a second, Tianna feared she wouldn't answer at all. But then Rea let out a soft sigh, her voice small and fragile.

"It's not your fault. I thought . . . I thought everything would be like in the stories, you know? Fun and . . . exciting. Like an adventure."[70] Rea's voice wavered, and when she finally glanced up, her wide eyes shimmered with unshed tears. "But it's not. It's scary, Tianna. I'm scared of all of it. I didn't know it would be like this."

Tianna's heart broke as she watched her sister, small and vulnerable in the fading light. She wished more than anything that she could fix this, could make Rea laugh again, make her forget everything that had gone wrong. But words wouldn't undo what had happened.

Tianna reached out and gently took Rea's hand, her fingers brushing the silver ring. "We'll get through this," she said softly, her voice trembling with the weight of the promise. "I know it's hard right now, but we'll make it."

Rea's eyes filled with doubt as she stared at Tianna. "How?" she whispered. "How can you be so sure?"

---

[70] Fun Fact: Stories about adventures tend to skip over the cold, hunger, and rampant existential dread—likely for pacing reasons. They also gloss over the less glamorous aspects, like bathroom breaks. Rest assured, heroes absolutely take them. And given the average adventurer's diet, you should consider yourself lucky they don't go into detail.

Tianna let out a shaky breath, squeezing Rea's hand tighter. "I'm not," she admitted, the words barely more than a whisper. "But I'll do everything I can to protect you. I won't let anything like that happen again."

Rea blinked, a single tear slipping down her cheek as she pulled her hand away, wrapping her arms tightly around herself. "But you can't. You can't protect me from everything. I was so . . . so stupid." She sniffed, wiping her cheek roughly. "I thought I was ready for this. I thought it'd be this grand adventure, and now . . . I don't even know if I belong out here."

Tianna bit her lip, the knot in her throat tightening as her eyes stung with tears of her own. She was supposed to be strong, to protect Rea, and yet here they were, both of them broken. She opened her mouth to say something, anything to reassure her sister, when she suddenly thought of the small bundle in her bag.

For a moment, she hesitated, but then a memory flickered, of a simpler time, of their shared laughter over something as small as sweets.

"Hey," Tianna said, her voice softening as she reached into her pack, pulling out the carefully wrapped bundle. "I almost forgot . . . I saved something."

Rea blinked, her tear-filled eyes flicking to the parcel. "What's that?" she asked, her voice still small, but for the first time that evening, there was a hint of curiosity.

Tianna smiled and unwrapped the cloth, revealing a small, sweet-smelling pastry, slightly squished from the journey but still intact. It wasn't much, just a simple treat she'd saved for a moment like this. She broke the pastry in half, offering one piece to Rea with a grin.

"I was saving this for when we hit a rough patch," Tianna said, trying to sound casual, though her voice wavered. "Figured . . . now's as good a time as any."

Rea stared at the pastry, her lip quivering slightly, before she finally reached out and took it. She didn't say anything, but the gesture was enough. They ate in silence, the sweet taste of the pastry melting on their tongues. The weight of the moment lightened, if only for a few breaths.

As the last rays of sunlight dipped below the horizon, casting the highlands into shadow, the chill of night crept in. Tianna wrapped her cloak tighter around herself, feeling the cold settle into her bones. Rea, for the first time in what felt like ages, leaned her head against Tianna's shoulder, her small body relaxing.

"Thanks," Rea whispered, her voice barely audible.

Tianna smiled softly, a small chuckle escaping her lips. "Hey, if sharing pastries is what it takes to make you smile again, I'll start packing more."

For a brief moment, Rea laughed, a soft, fragile sound, but a laugh nonetheless. It was like music to Tianna's ears, and she felt a surge of warmth that even the cold highland winds couldn't take away.

They sat together while the others in the party, sensing the quiet between the sisters, moved about the camp in silence, preparing for the long night ahead. The stars blinked into existence one by one, scattered across the sky like tiny pinpricks of light.

Rea shifted, her voice barely above a whisper. "Do you ever think about . . . what it would be like if we turned back? Went home?"

Tianna stiffened. She had tried hard not to think about that. But as Rea's question hung in the air, she realized she *had*, more than once. "I do," she said after a pause, her voice low. "But . . . I don't think we can. Not anymore. Too much has happened."

Rea sighed, her head still resting on Tianna's shoulder. "Yeah, I know."

The silence stretched between them, but this time it wasn't heavy with fear or doubt. It was an understanding, a quiet acceptance that they couldn't turn back. They would face whatever came next. Together.

"We're stronger together, Rea," Tianna whispered, her voice steady and sure. "Whatever comes next, we'll face it."

As the night took its hold, the temperature quickly dropped. There would be no fire that night, but the group huddled close, knowing they'd need each other for warmth and safety.

The stars twinkled overhead as the cold night air wrapped itself around the party, like a blanket too thin for comfort. The world seemed to slow, the wind whispering secrets through the crags, the grass swaying in rhythm with some unheard lullaby. Tianna noticed the stillness, how the night felt heavier than usual, almost *too* peaceful. She tightened her cloak around herself, casting a glance at the rest of the party.

Someone stifled a yawn. Was it Blarg? She wasn't sure. Her eyes felt slow to focus, the edges of her vision growing fuzzy as though the shadows themselves were thickening.

"We should rest," she muttered to herself, but it felt like an afterthought, the words slipping from her lips without much conviction. Rea shifted slightly beside her, her head still resting against Tianna's shoulder. Tianna turned to examine her, and the sight of her sister's eyelids fluttering—half-closed, half-open—made her stomach lurch. The world began to tilt, ever so gently, as if they were on a boat caught in the softest of waves.

Tianna blinked. And blinked again. Her head swam. *Had it always been this hard to keep my thoughts straight?* The air smelled . . . strange. Like . . . like . . . *what was that smell?*

She glanced at the others. They had all gone quiet, their movements slow, like they were wading through syrup. Even Blarg, who was usually up tinkering with something, sat cross-legged, staring at the ground, his eyes half-lidded and glassy. He was murmuring something to himself. Something about the nature of mountains and why trees grow taller than rocks. It didn't make sense, but it sounded important . . . *didn't it?*

Tianna opened her mouth to speak, but the words got stuck somewhere between her thoughts and her lips. Her mind was *drifting*. Her limbs felt heavy, her body leaning back as if gravity had decided to take over.

Rea let out a soft sigh, her breathing slow and steady, deep in sleep. Tianna wanted to stay awake, to keep watch, but her own body betrayed her. Her eyelids drooped, her muscles relaxed, and the soft, rhythmic hum of the wind was lulling her toward sleep . . . toward a warm, welcoming darkness—

And then, before she slipped into oblivion, she saw them.

Tiny figures flickering at the edge of her vision. Little men skirting swiftly between rocks. She squinted through the haze. Their mushroom-shaped hats shimmered with an odd glow. They giggled to themselves like they were playing some schoolyard prank. Their spindly fingers waved through the air, releasing trails of glowing, something. Dust? Spores? It drifted lazily on the breeze, twinkling like stars caught in a dream.

The spores. Tianna's mind latched onto the thought, sluggish as it was. The *spores*. That's what was making them . . . *tired*. She tried to sit up, tried to shake the lethargy from her bones, but it was no use. The ground beneath her felt soft, like she was sinking into it, melting away with the rest of the world.

The Gnomes whispered in hushed tones, their laughter tinkling like wind chimes, their eyes gleaming with mischievous delight. One of them, larger than the others, came closer to her, inspecting her with a tilted head and a curious smirk. He raised a spindly hand, and for a brief moment, Tianna thought she saw something. His hat flickered into a wizard's cap, then a top hat, then a bowler, all in the span of a blink. He gave a slow, exaggerated bow as if to say, '*Sleep, sleep now. You'll need it where you're going.*'

The Gnomes circled the camp, spreading more spores, their voices soft and melodic, as if they were singing lullabies. Tianna's vision grew darker, the world fading into the warm embrace of sleep, even as her mind fought to stay awake. But the fight was over before it even began.

As the final remnants of consciousness slipped away, she heard the distant sound of Gnomish laughter—high-pitched and delirious—as the last of the spores settled like a quilt over the party.

And then, nothing but darkness.

Rea awoke with a start, her heart hammering so hard she half-expected it to leap out of her chest and find a new home somewhere quieter. Everything felt wrong. Her mind scrambled like a poorly organized closet, thoughts tumbling over one another in a frantic mess. *Tee-Tee? Uncle? Blarg even?* The names tumbled through her head, unanswered by the cold, indifferent night.

She tried to move, but her hands and feet were bound tight, glowing vines digging into her skin. Panic flared up, her breath quickening. *Tied. I'm tied up. I'm alone.* Not exactly a soothing mantra, but it was all she had.

She clenched her jaw, trying to stay calm.

Then she saw him.

A Gnome sat cross-legged a few feet away, staring up at the stars like they were the punchline to a joke only he could hear. Small, hunched, with wide, glazed eyes that shimmered in the starlight, he looked more lost in space than anyone Rea had ever seen.

"Wha . . . what's going on?" she whispered, voice shaking.

The Gnome didn't respond right away. He simply sat there, head tilted, like he was trying to figure out if the stars had favorite flavors. Then he let out a long, dreamy sigh and turned to her, gaze still drifting somewhere past the sky.

"Have you ever just, like . . . *felt* the stars?" he drawled, his words slow and heavy, as though each one was being pulled from the depths of his very soul. "Not just seen 'em, but really *felt* 'em? They're not lights, man. They're, like . . . the universe's heartbeat. Whisperin' old truths."

Rea blinked again. Her panic and confusion crashed into one another like two particularly uncoordinated birds. "Where are my friends?" Her voice cracked with desperation, her eyes darting around the camp. But there was no one.

The Gnome blinked slowly, like he'd only just remembered how, and made a casual shrug. "Oh, them? They're in the kingdom. Deep inside. Gonna meet L'Sidroth." He scratched his head. "They'll come back. Probably. Just . . . vibe, y'know? Let the stars cradle you."

"Let me go!" Rea cried, her voice bursting with desperation. "Please! I don't want to be here!"

The Gnome chuckled softly, leaning back on his hands, utterly relaxed. "Wanting, not wanting, it's all just stuff, right? Fleeting... like steam in soup. And we're all just . . . floatin' in it. Astral gumbo." He let out a wheezy laugh like this was the most obvious thing in the world.

Rea pulled at the vines. They tightened. Her wrists throbbed. Her eyes burned. "Please," she whispered, fighting back a sob. "Please let me go."

The Gnome sighed dramatically, as if freeing people from knotted vines was somehow beneath him, and stared back up at the sky. "The stars . . . they've seen everything. All our little problems, all our struggles . . . they just shine on, you know? They don't care. We're just, like, tiny candles in the wind." He paused, then added, "Ethereal candles, though. Much classier."

She slumped to the ground, trembling. He wasn't going to help her. He didn't *see* her. He was floating somewhere far beyond reach.

This is it, she thought, the words falling into her mind like stones into water. *This is how it ends.*

Then, without warning, a blur of black fur streaked through the camp.

Nyxie!

The cat lunged at the Gnome with all the force of a feline who had had enough of the nonsense. His sharp teeth sank into the Gnome's oversized mushroom hat. Rea gasped in shock as Nyx yanked hard, tearing the hat clean off the Gnome's head. Only . . . it wasn't a hat at all.

It was part of his head.

The Gnome let out a startled yelp, eyes somehow going *wider*. He stared at the mushroom cap now lying in the dirt beside him. "Whoa . . . *not cool*, man. That's . . . that's my *head*. I can, like . . . see it."

Nyx, undeterred, growled low and swatted the Gnome's reaching hands away. Thick white pus oozed from the torn stump.

"Wild," the Gnome murmured, touching the goo with curiosity. "It's like I'm seeing myself . . . but from *outside* myself. You ever think about that? How we're all just . . . mirrors looking at mirrors?"

Rea laughed. A sharp, slightly unhinged laugh that was equal parts fear and relief.

Nyx bounded to her side and began tearing at the glowing vines. They gave way under fang and claw, slithering off her wrists. She reached down to free her feet, but before she could even thank Nyx, the cat wobbled on his paws, eyes rolling back. He swayed for a moment, then collapsed with a soft *thud*.[71]

"Nyxie?!" she gasped, scooping him up. He was breathing, but twitching. Poisoned? Or just . . . too much Gnome?

The Gnome, meanwhile, sat with perfect serenity, staring at his severed mushroom cap. "I think . . . I get it now," he murmured. "The stars . . . they've been trying to tell me this whole time. It's all connected. Me, you, the stars . . . we're all part of the same thing."

Rea held Nyx close, heart racing. "What are you talking about?"

He smiled. Calm. Serene. *Free*. "We're not here to *do* anything. Just . . . *be*. That's the purpose. Like stars. They shine . . . because they *can*."

He looked down at his severed head, then closed his eyes. "I can go now."

---

[71] In his defense, Nyx had just ingested a psychedelic that was potent enough to make an Ogre believe in the virtues of bathing. The fact that he managed to free anyone before faceplanting was either a testament to his heroic willpower and/or proof that cats operate on pure spite and muscle memory.

His eyes fluttered closed, and his body slumped forward. Rea watched, wide-eyed, as the Gnome's breath slowed . . . and stopped. His small, fragile form deflated, as if the life had simply faded out of him. All that remained was his faintly glowing mushroom cap lying beside his lifeless body.[72]

Rea stared, trembling. He had . . . *died*. Peacefully. As if figuring out the meaning of life had freed him from everything. She didn't know whether to laugh, cry, or scream.

Her hands shook as she gently scooped Nyx into her arms, her heart still racing. "Come on, Nyxie," she whispered, her voice barely holding together. "We've got to go."

With one last glance at the Gnome, Rea stood, clutching Nyx tight. The stars twinkled above, indifferent to the chaos below. And at that moment, despite her fear and the weight of trauma pressing down on her, Rea couldn't help but feel a small part of the Gnome's cosmic wisdom settling over her.

But it didn't make her feel any safer.

---

[72] Gnome spores are mildly hallucinogenic to most species. To Gnomes, they're a full-blown religious experience. Prolonged exposure often results in spiritual epiphanies, spontaneous poetry, and in rare cases, accidental ascension. Unfortunately, ascension is not reversible, and frequently indistinguishable from death.

12

A Shroom with a View

"I tried to understand the fungus. It tried to understand me. We compromised by becoming each other's dreams."

— Professor Emeritus Alwin Curdlebeam,
former Chair of Imperial Mycology

Tianna awoke with the sensation of being dragged, but not in a bad way, more like being pulled gently through a sea of marshmallows. Or maybe . . . jellybeans? No, definitely marshmallows, she decided.[73] Her brain bobbed happily somewhere between sleep and wakefulness, swaddled in a thick syrupy haze. She blinked slowly, her vision doing a merry little jig. She giggled at the thought. The darkness felt like one of those extra-fluffy blankets that hug you so snugly, you'd consider selling your soul for five more minutes wrapped in its embrace.

She inhaled deeply. Her lungs promptly filled with something warm and sweet, as if she'd just inhaled in a generous helping of cotton candy. With each breath, the darkness grew more distant, her mind lighter, until all that remained was a gentle mist at the edge of her consciousness.

---

[73] This is not an uncommon sensation when inhaling a full lung of Gnome spores. Marshmallow-dragging is, in fact, the third most reported side effect, right after "existential humming" and "believing you've turned into a beanbag chair."

And then, she could see.

Everything.

The tunnel ahead yawned open like a gargantuan maw, but not any old maw, mind you. This was a maw of colors that had no business existing in the first place. Neon blues and electric pinks jostled for attention, while a particularly cheeky shade of green winked mischievously. It was as if the universe had grown bored with its usual palette and decided to spice things up with a dash of whimsy and a sprinkle of pure, unadulterated absurdity.

Tianna gawked, jaw slightly unhinged, as the walls . . . wait, were those even walls? No, they were alive, pulsing with light like a gang of rogue jellyfish that had stumbled into an underwater rave. The bioluminescent mushrooms shimmied to a beat that resonated deep within her bones, and by gods, she could feel it in her teeth. Teeth music, apparently, was all the rage in these parts.[74] If she focused hard enough, she could almost taste the rhythm—a hint of lightning lemon, perhaps?

As she ventured deeper, the kingdom unfurled before her like a sprawling fungal metropolis, albeit one with a severe aversion to behaving like a proper city. Oh no, this city had ideas. It pulsed, like it was too energized to stay still. Towers of squishy, iridescent fungus spiraled upward, glowing softly and swaying to an underground beat only they could hear. And the air . . . what even was air anymore? She was being dragged through it, but it felt like she was moving through a bowl of fruit punch that had come to life and decided it had opinions. Bright red opinions.

The colors! They wrapped around her mind like a warm hug, embracing her so tightly she couldn't help but giggle. They coaxed her thoughts out to play, allowing them to frolic like tiny iridescent fish performing synchronized acrobatics through shimmering liquid rainbows. The air twisted before her eyes, making absolutely no sense and perfect sense all at once, and Tianna nodded.

---

[74] Also known as Molar-Synth, this underground genre is only audible under extreme spore influence or during dental surgery performed by overly excited wizards.

"Yeah, yeah, I get it," she whispered to the air, even though she most certainly did not.

Then there were the Gnomes. She blinked once, twice, and once more for good measure. These were no ordinary Gnomes, oh no. They glided through the air like little floating dreams. Each carried aloft on clouds of spores that sparkled like stars plucked from some forgotten galaxy and tucked away beneath the earth. Their hats . . . were those even hats? More like beacons, glowing with liquid colors that cascaded down like glittery waterfalls. With a soft poof, the hats would transform. One moment, a wizard's cap, the next, a jaunty sombrero. The Gnomes chuckled to themselves, clearly reveling in the hat-based shenanigans. Tianna suspected that perhaps the hats were the true masterminds here, and the Gnomes were merely along for the ride.

Each hat was a swirling concoction of dreams, illusions, and infinite possibility. The Gnomes' eyes, impossibly wide, brimmed with secrets they'd never divulge. Unless, of course, you offered them a mushroom that glowed just so.

Tianna grinned, her head pleasantly fizzy, like a carbonated beverage that had been given a good shake. But in a good way, of course.

And the buildings . . . well, buildings was a generous term. The structures had no intention of staying put. They twisted and curled like taffy, always in flux, as if engaged in a never-ending debate with one another, punctuating their arguments with dramatic gestures.[75] Rooms breathed in and out, walls expanding and contracting to the rhythm of some otherworldly beat Tianna was still trying to wrap her head around. Hallways looped back on themselves, scoffing at the very notion of straight lines. The ceilings swirled like an overenthusiastic rainbow smoothie, hell-bent on redecorating the entire place.

Gnomes were everywhere, their high-pitched, infectious laughter echoing like wind chimes caught in a tornado. But a fun tornado, mind you, the kind

---

[75] The architecture of the Gnome city is closely modeled on the concept of political dysfunction: loud, brightly colored, and constantly shifting positions.

that would suck you in and spit you out laughing. And laugh she did, though she hadn't the foggiest idea why. The air was thick with it, and her brain fizzed with the shared joy of the entire kingdom.

The Gnomes plucked glowing fungi as if picking stars from the sky, popping them into their mouths with little fizzles and pops. Tianna giggled at the sight, wondering if sparkfruit crystals were the latest craze.

Then there were the spores, twirling through the air like tiny celestial dandruff.[76] It glittered and waltzed around her, making her skin tingle as if it, too, wanted to join in the dance. Little pinpricks of warmth whispered, 'It's all good. We're fine here. Just let go.' And let go she did. Her entire body buzzed, not unpleasantly, like it had decided to become one with the kingdom itself. She could feel it, the pulse of the Gnomes' world, not just in the air, but in her very bones. This wasn't merely a place; it was a state of mind, a trip, a stellar joyride where reality was more of a polite suggestion, and the only rule was to throw your hands up and embrace the glorious madness of it all.

Tianna's head lolled to one side as she was further dragged, gently, as if her captors were oddly polite kidnappers, into a cavernous chamber. The air felt thicker, like breathing through honey, and every sound echoed as if reality itself had gone on a break, leaving the echoes to sort things out.[77] The kind of place where logic took a holiday and left hallucinations in charge.

The chamber spread out before her, vast and uneven, like someone had let a particularly artsy squid design it after a night on the town. The floor, caught in an existential crisis between solid and liquid, rippled underfoot, and the walls shimmered with bioluminescent patterns that pulsed in time with her own heartbeat. Or perhaps it was the other way around. The walls, ever the

---

[76] The Gnomes prefer the term "sky glitter," but celestial dermatologists remain unconvinced.

[77] Unfortunately, echoes are notoriously bad at conflict resolution. Most meetings end with passive-aggressive repetition and someone storming off into the distance.

mischievous sort, might have been dictating the rhythm of her own body. Honestly, it could go either way.

At the center of the room, a deep pit yawned open, a swirling void that looked as if it had just finished devouring hope for breakfast and was now eyeing despair for a midday snack.[78] Tianna, her mind still foggy from whatever arcane cocktail she'd been served, couldn't quite shake the feeling that the pit was breathing. She briefly wondered if it had opinions. It probably did. In fact, it probably had *a lot* of opinions, but she wasn't sure if she was in the right state of mind to hear them.

Blarg and Thane were already there, like discarded rag dolls at the world's worst slumber party. Blarg was locked in a staring contest with the pit, his eyes narrowed in intense concentration as if trying to remember a crucial fact that had slipped his mind. Thane, meanwhile, was utterly entranced by his own hand, which was currently regaling him with the secrets of the universe, or perhaps a particularly juicy bit of gossip.

Tianna was dropped beside them with all the grace of a sack of potatoes. She groaned softly, her limbs feeling like they belonged to someone else. Or maybe they didn't belong to anyone anymore. Just free agents, floating through the interstellar muck.

Blarg's voice, slow and sluggish, drifted toward her. "Welcome . . . to the pit." He gestured vaguely at the swirling void in the center. "Blarg has been . . . pondering it. It is . . . most pit-like. Indeed, a pit of . . . great pit-ness."

Tianna tried to form words, but her mouth was full of something that felt suspiciously like glue. Instead, she gave a slow nod, her eyes drifting to the pit. "Yep. Very . . . pit-like." Her words, barely more than a sigh, evaporated into the air like a whisper in a hurricane. But really, what more was there to say? The pit was, without a doubt, the most pit-like pit she'd ever had the displeasure of encountering.

---

[78] Hope, while nutritious, lacks fiber. Despair, on the other hand, is surprisingly rich in irony.

"It is . . . breathing," Thane whispered, his eyes wide and fixed on his own hand, which was holding a philosophical symposium of its own. "Do you think it . . . knows we are here?"

Tianna blinked slowly, her thoughts as sluggish as a snail on sedatives. "The pit? Or your hand?"

Thane didn't answer, too engrossed in the existential debate unfolding between his fingers. It appeared as if his hand was winning the argument.

The chamber hummed with something Tianna couldn't quite place. Whether it was the spores in the air or the pit itself trying to strike up a conversation was anyone's guess. She tried to focus, but her thoughts felt like they were sliding out of her grasp, like jelly on a warm day.

"So," she murmured, "are we supposed to . . . jump in, or—?"

Blarg's head snapped toward her with all the urgency of a sloth on Valium. "No . . . no," he muttered, waving a hand dismissively at the pit. "It is not that kind of pit. More like . . . contemplative."

"Ah." Tianna nodded sagely. "A . . . philosophical pit."

Thane squinted at the pit, then back at his hand, as though trying to decide which one was more suspicious. "It is . . . definitely staring at me, though," he whispered, his voice trembling with the weight of newfound knowledge.

"The pit?" Tianna asked, her words still thick and clumsy on her tongue.

Thane shook his head. "My hand. And the pit. They are both . . . in on it."

Tianna had half a mind to be concerned, but mostly she was impressed by how much her body just didn't care. She should have been terrified, given that there was a giant, potentially sentient hole in the middle of the room, but her mind had other priorities. Like appreciating how melty the walls were. Were they melting? She wasn't ruling it out.

Blarg, meanwhile, had shifted his focus back to the pit, his brow furrowed as though he was on the verge of a great epiphany. "Blarg thinks . . . it seeks to communicate," he muttered. "As pits are known to do. Perhaps . . . we are meant to pose it a question."

Tianna blinked again, her brain lagging a few seconds behind. "Ask . . . the pit?"

"Aye," Blarg nodded solemnly, as if he'd just figured out the meaning of life. "Questions of great import . . . like, why do noses run but feet smell? Or . . . if light is so fast, why is darkness always there first? Profound matters, indeed."

Tianna let out a breathy laugh, the kind that teeters on the edge of a complete mental breakdown. "Right. I mean, that makes sense to me."

"The pit does know many things," Blarg mumbled, squinting at the swirling darkness like it was about to reveal the universe's best-kept secrets. "It has endured . . . It has seen much."

Thane, who was now deeply invested in whatever his hand was telling him, nodded gravely. "The pit . . . is wise."

Tianna, desperate to focus on anything that didn't involve existential hands or wise pits, found herself fighting a losing battle with the room itself. The walls rippled and shifted, like peering through a crystal ball with a mind of its own, and she couldn't quite tell if she was underwater, upside down, or somewhere in between.

"Blarg has . . . contemplated the pit," Blarg continued, his voice taking on a reverent tone. "It is . . . most inspiring."

"Inspiring," Tianna echoed weakly, her head lolling back against the not-quite-solid wall. "Yeah. Right."

The pit, perhaps sensing its moment in the spotlight, let out a low hum, or maybe it was more of a cosmic sigh. Was it . . . bored? Could pits even be bored?

"Do you think it is . . . lonely?" Tianna murmured, her words directed at no one in particular, or perhaps at the void itself. She wasn't even sure why she was asking, but something about the pit felt sad. Or maybe that was only her imagination making her feel sorry for holes in the ground.

Blarg's eyes widened slightly, his brow furrowing deeper. "Pits do not grow lonely," he declared with an air of authority, as if he'd been attending secret pit conferences on the weekends. "Yet, perhaps, it is merely . . . misunderstood."

Tianna wanted to laugh, but the swirling darkness in the pit seemed to shift ever so slightly, as if it were responding to their words. Something ancient and unfathomable lurked beneath the surface, a presence that was more than just a hole in the ground. It was . . . something else. Something that had been waiting.

"Well," Tianna muttered, shaking her head in a vain attempt to clear the fog, "it can keep waiting."

But even as the words left her lips, she couldn't shake the feeling that the pit, in all its otherworldly wisdom, knew something she didn't. And as she sat there, slumped against the wall with her companions, she couldn't help but wonder if maybe, just maybe, the pit had been waiting for them all along.

Tianna blinked slowly, the pit beckoning her with the sort of quiet persistence usually reserved for an unsupervised plate of cookies. She hadn't planned on peering down into it, just like she hadn't planned on getting dragged into this oversized underground lair with glowing walls and unhelpful Gnomes. But here she was, curiosity tugging at her like a toddler with sticky fingers reaching for something they absolutely, positively, without a doubt shouldn't touch.

She leaned over the edge of the pit, her head drooping as she tried to focus on what was below. The shadows twisted and rippled in a way that didn't seem quite right, as though the darkness itself was having an identity crisis. And then . . . she saw it.

L'Sidroth.

Of course, she had no way of knowing that was its name. It wasn't as if the entity had popped up wearing a helpful nametag. *'Hello, my name is L'Sidroth.'*

But somehow, deep inside, she knew. It was as if the creature's very essence had seeped into her mind like a cosmic tea bag, speaking a truth that was whispered not in words, but in the quiet, overwhelming weight of its existence. It was simply there, as undeniable as her own heartbeat, which at that point, was doing a rather impressive impression of a jazz drummer on caffeine.

The creature didn't so much move as it . . . existed in a space that wasn't entirely compatible with her brain's understanding of reality. It was massive, yet somehow managed to fold and bend in ways that made size irrelevant, like a celestial accordion that had been left in the sun too long. Its body shimmered with iridescent scales . . . or were they feathers? No, wait . . . tentacles. Definitely tentacles. Unless they were something else entirely. In which case, they were probably still tentacles.

And the colors! Oh, the colors! Tianna had never seen anything quite like them. They weren't colors that belonged to the sane side of the rainbow. These were the shades that existed when the universe was feeling particularly mischievous, like an otherworldly prankster with a paintbrush and a questionable sense of aesthetics. Swirls of screaming lavender and weeping chartreuse pulsed across L'Sidroth's form, twisting and merging with colors that had yet to be named, and frankly, shouldn't be.

L'Sidroth's eyes . . . or were they mouths? It was hard to tell. They glistened like oily puddles after a rainstorm, except those puddles had the unnerving habit of blinking. Each one peered directly into her soul, and not in a gentle, 'let's have a deep conversation over a cup of tea' kind of way. No, these eyes (or mouths?) glared at her the way a librarian might gaze upon a book that had been carelessly mis-shelved in the wrong section—a mixture of disappointment and mild threat.

It was a creature that defied the laws of nature and physics, possibly because it had never bothered to read them. Or perhaps it had read them and simply decided they were more like guidelines than actual rules. There was an elegance to its absurdity, the way it hovered without hovering, as if it was doing the universe a favor by existing on its own terms.

And the noise! Dear gods, the *noise* it made! A deep, rumbling sound that wasn't so much heard as it was felt, reverberating through Tianna's bones like the cosmos had swallowed a kazoo and was now playing it with malicious intent. It wasn't unpleasant, per se, just . . . confusing. Rather like listening to a symphony performed entirely by a troupe of rubber chickens, with a few tone-deaf bagpipes thrown in for good measure.

Tianna's mind struggled to process the sheer grandiosity of L'Sidroth's presence. She blinked slowly, as if each eyelid had to hold a miniature committee meeting before agreeing to the monumental task of closing.

"Right—" she muttered under her breath, her voice barely audible in the face of such eldritch majesty.

For a moment, L'Sidroth's form pulsed, expanding and contracting with a rhythm that had nothing to do with time or space. It looked like it was nodding at her, or perhaps it was . . . stretching? Yes, maybe that was it. A stretch that could unhinge reality itself.

She backed away slowly, her brain cells frantically trying to piece together what she had just witnessed. It was like a jigsaw puzzle with half the pieces missing and the other half covered in glue. As far as she could tell, she had stared into the abyss, and the abyss had not only stared back, but had also given her a metaphorical thumbs-up.

"Yep," she whispered to herself, her voice shaking slightly as she retreated from the pit. "That just happened. I think."

The pit, satisfied with her curiosity or perhaps bored with the whole affair, gave one final, ominous pulse before settling back into its usual, unfathomable strangeness. And for once, Tianna felt grateful that her brain was too foggy to fully comprehend the fresh nightmare that had just greeted her from the depths.

Blarg stared at her as she staggered back to the wall, his gaze unsettlingly deep, as though he could see straight into the tangled mess of thoughts swirling in her mind. With the gravity of someone who had witnessed an unspeakable truth, or at the very least, a truth that would require a great deal of chemicals to forget, he muttered, "You should not have done that."

A low, resonant blast echoed through the cavern. VRAAWWM! VRAAWWM! Two powerful pulses vibrated deep within the bones, alien and ancient, as if the universe itself had drawn a breath and decided to speak in brass.

The ground beneath them trembled in response.

13

All Roads Lead to Gnome

"The tunnels are always changing. Best not to ask why, for fear they may answer."

— Note discovered in the sock of a missing cartographer

Rea searched the ground frantically, her heart threatening to stage a mutiny and abandon ship altogether. Everything felt wrong, her breathing, her thoughts, the world itself. Panic clawed at her chest, sharp and insistent, as she scanned for any sign of her friends. *Tee-Tee? Uncle? Blarg?* her words echoing through the canyon of her mind, only to be met with the mocking laughter of her own mounting desperation.

Time, that fickle mistress, stretched and contracted, until Rea was certain she had aged at least a decade in the span of five minutes. But then, like a beacon of hope in a sea of chaos, her eyes finally landed on something—drag marks. Faint but unmistakable, leading toward the dark, yawning mouth of a cave that appeared to have a particular appetite for foolhardy adventurers.

Rea's stomach performed an impressive acrobatic routine as she kneeled down, her fingers trembling like leaves in an ethereal wind as they traced the ominous path. *Not again,* her mind whispered, a broken record stuck on the track of dread. *Please, not again.*

And then, as if the universe hadn't quite finished its cosmic punchline, Rea's gaze landed on a swirling, glowing red presence near the cave's entrance. "Spores," she whispered, because there had to be spores.[79]

"Of course," she muttered, half-heartedly trying to channel Tianna's calm voice in her mind. '*Breathe. Just breathe,*' Tianna had always said, as if that was the easy part. But breathing felt like the hardest thing in the world when everything else felt like it was collapsing around her.

With a sigh, she tore a strip of cloth from her sleeve, fashioning a makeshift mask to keep the spores at bay. It did little to quell the panic rampaging through her veins, but at least her lungs would be spared the indignity of inhaling whatever nonsense the cave had in store.

With Nyx, the world's most unhelpful sack of fur, tucked under one arm, and a silver-banded ring twirling between her fingers like a nervous tic, Rea took a tentative step toward the cave's gaping maw. The shadows, ever the opportunistic sort, pressed in, eager to welcome her into their cold, unsettling embrace.

What am I doing? Rea's mind screamed, a question that hung in the air like a bad joke without a punchline. *Why am I doing this?*

Each step forward felt like wading deeper into a nightmare, the kind that refused to release its grip even as the first light of dawn crept over the horizon. The darkness swallowed her whole as she crossed into the cave, so thick it

---

[79] In and around the Empire, it is widely known that glowing spores are nature's way of saying "this place is plot-relevant." Much like ancient ruins that hum ominously, doorways that mysteriously light up when you walk past, or swords embedded into stones that just beg to be pulled, glowing spores are the universal shorthand for "important things will happen here." Botanists insist they're merely part of a complex reproductive cycle tied to subterranean bioluminescent fungi. Storytellers, however, know better: they bloom exactly where an adventuring party needs to go next.

smothered any light from the outside world. It wrapped around her like a blanket woven from the very fabric of fear itself.[80]

Rea froze, her grip on Nyx tightening, her breath shallow and ragged. "I can't do this," she whispered, her voice trembling like a leaf in a hurricane. "I can't."

But then . . . the ring.

It began to glow.

At first, the light was faint, a mere flicker against the overwhelming darkness. As the seconds ticked by, the once-dull gem pulsed with a pale, ghostly luminescence, casting eerie shadows across the jagged cave walls. It wasn't much, but it was something. And right then, *something* was enough.

"That's . . . new," she whispered, her voice shaking. She twirled the ring between her fingers, feeling a strange, desperate need to keep moving. The light flickered stronger, like it was gathering its courage.[81] Good. Because one of them needed to have some, and she wasn't sure it was going to be her.

With a shaky breath, she slid the ring onto her finger, the glow intensifying as it settled into place. A narrow, rocky path revealed itself, bathed in the ring's otherworldly light. It wasn't exactly the blazing beacon of salvation she might have hoped for, but in this twisted, fungus-infested nightmare, it was a start.

"All right," Rea whispered, her voice a fragile thing in the oppressive silence. "Okay. Just . . . follow the light." The words felt hollow, a flimsy mantra repeated more for her own benefit than for Nyx's or the universe's amusement. Thinking back, it wasn't the best choice of words either.

---

[80] The Blanket of Fear™ is not available in stores, but if it were, it would be scratchy, always damp, and somehow still manage to be both too cold and too hot.

[81] Some scholars believe courage is simply the act of glowing slightly brighter while still absolutely terrified. These scholars are, of course, idiots. Glowing has never stopped a charging beast, calmed an angry Orc, or satiated the bloodlust of a lesser demon. If anything, it just makes you easier to spot, which is unarguably the opposite of a survival strategy.

The weight of Nyx in her arms was the only thing that felt remotely real. She adjusted him, absently rubbing his fur with her thumb. "I've got you," she whispered, her words hollow even to her own ears. *I've got you.* But the bigger question was: Who's got her?

As she ventured deeper into the cave, the path twisted and turned, each sound amplified by the suffocating darkness. The walls wept with moisture, and the air carried a scent that could only be described as *don't breathe this if you value your continued existence.* The occasional twitching mushroom at the periphery of her vision only served to heighten the surreal, nightmarish quality of her surroundings.

Keep going. Just keep going. The words rang hollow, like a phrase you repeat so many times it loses all meaning.

"What am I *doing?*" she whispered to Nyx, her voice cracking. "Why am I doing this?" But deep down, she knew the answer. There was no one else to save her family, no one else to brave the darkness and the horrors it concealed. It had to be her, even if the thought made her want to curl up into a ball and wait for the universe to sort itself out.

"I can't—" Her voice broke, the words catching in her throat like shards of glass. "I'm not ready for this."

But ready or not, there was no turning back. She knew that as well as she knew her own name. The cave, the darkness, the weight of *everything,* it was pulling her forward, step by agonizing step.

The cave continued its twisted dance, its secrets hidden behind a veil of inky blackness. Every sound, every flicker of movement, threatened to shatter the fragile remains of Rea's resolve. But with each step, the ring's light guided her onward, a silent, steadfast companion in a world gone mad.

"Come on, Rea," she whispered, her voice a thin thread of determination in the tapestry of her fears. "You can do this. One step at a time. You've literally got a magic ring. That counts for something, right?"

But even as the words left her lips, Rea knew that the true challenge lay ahead. In the depths of the darkness, waited a nameless, faceless thing that threatened to swallow her whole. And yet, with the ring's faint, unwavering glow to light her way, she pressed on, because stopping was not an option.

Stopping meant giving up, and in this twisted, fungal wonderland, giving up was tantamount to surrender. And Rea, for all her doubts and fears, was not ready to surrender. Not yet, not while her family needed her, not while there was still a flicker of hope, however faint, to guide her through the darkness.

With a heavy heart and a ring that glowed like a promise, Rea ventured deeper into the unknown, ready to face whatever horrors the cave had in store. Because in the end, that's what heroes do. They keep going, even when the world around them has gone completely, utterly mad.

Rea crept along the narrow tunnel, the glow of the ring on her finger a stubborn little beacon slicing through the choking dark. Its light was the only steady thing about her. Her heart thundered so loudly she half-expected the tunnel walls to file a formal complaint.

Each step dragged more than the last, as if she were wading through invisible, molasses. The cold had given way to thick, cloying heat, the air turning muggy and heavy as if she were being swallowed by some enormous, irritable subterranean beast.

The deeper she went, the more the air stuck to her skin like a moist, rotting blanket long past its expiration date. And the smell was earthy, sure, but laced with something rancid. Like someone left mushroom soup out for a week and tried to fix it with cheap perfume. She shivered, despite the sweat slicking her neck.

The silence pressed in, broken only by the soft scuff of her boots and the subtle drip of condensation. Shadows clung to the tunnel walls like suspicious cats, watching her every move. If the tunnel wasn't alive, it was putting on a disturbingly good performance. It loomed around her, radiating disapproval.

Then, footsteps.

Light. Deliberate. Someone trying to be sneaky and failing spectacularly.

Rea's pulse spiked. She darted into a narrow outcropping and flattened herself against the rock like a guilty pancake. She clutched the ring and snuffed its glow. Every muscle in her body coiled tight, fighting the urge to sneeze or cough or make any sound that might end in her being stuffed into a compost pile.

The footsteps grew louder. Voices followed.

"Can't believe we gotta go back up there," muttered a small, tired voice. It belonged to a squat figure trudging along with all the enthusiasm of someone sent to retrieve a forgotten loaf of bread. His eyes were wide and slow-blinking, like thinking was a full-body workout. "We were just up there, man."

Behind him ambled a larger Gnome, eyes twinkling, grin dreamy. "Quit complainin'. Maybe we never left. Maybe we're still up there. Or maybe... we're everywhere. No up, no down. Just... bein'."

The small Gnome blinked hard. "Whoa... that's . . . deep. But still. Why us? I'm so sick of walkin'."

"Walkin's just movin', right?" the big one mused, swaying like the thought might lift him off the ground. "But is it really us movin'? Or's the world movin' around us?"

The small one frowned, rubbing his chin. "Both? Yeah . . . both. But we still gotta go. One more left. Shouldn't be too bad after that big brute."

"True, true," the big Gnome said with a sage nod, his eyes drifting toward the ceiling. "But remember . . . we're all just lumps in the grand universal stew. Big or small, doesn't matter. Just floatin'."

"Lumps . . . floatin'." The small one repeated it slowly, awed.

The crunch of their boots faded, and slowly, Rea exhaled, her body trembling as the tension ebbed, but didn't vanish.

She crept out of the alcove and moved forward. The tunnel narrowed, twisted, glistened. Even the walls seemed to be sweating now. "Great," she muttered internally. "Even the tunnel's uncomfortable."

The path wound deeper into the earth, humid and hot, the air thick enough to chew. She pushed on, through air that felt like soup—bad soup. The kind you sniff once and throw away.

Then, the tunnel opened.

Before her stretched a subterranean city designed by someone with a love for moldy basements and questionable aesthetics. Glowing mushrooms lit the place in a dull, workmanlike haze. The heat surged, the humidity rising to unbearable. Rea felt like a dumpling someone forgot to take out of the steamer.

And then—she saw the fields.

Mushroom fields. Fat, squat fungi lined in neat rows, caps glimmering faintly in the wet air. Almost charming.

Until she saw something . . .

Rea blinked. Rubbed her eyes. Blinked again.

Nope. Still there.

Undergarments. Pantaloons. Bloomers. Briefs. Every kind of undergarment imaginable, half-buried in the soil beneath the mushrooms. Elastic waistbands slumped sadly in the muck. Some of them looked... disturbingly familiar.

Two Gnomes shuffled into view, their small boots crunching loudly on the damp stone. Rea ducked behind a rock, holding her breath as their voices floated toward her through the humid air.

"Oi, look at this haul!" crowed the Gnome in blue britches, hoisting a mismatched bundle of undergarments like a trophy. His eyes sparkled with a manic sort of pride. "Fresh, filthy, and *ripe*! They were gonna take 'em to the birthing fields, but I snagged 'em first. These beauties'll grow the big uns."

The other Gnome, dressed in sagging red trousers, stared at a patch of bioluminescent mushrooms with glassy reverence. "Mmm. The shrooms . . . they *feel* it. The filth. It's alive, y'know? They soak up the stories. The stains got . . . essence."

"Aye! That's what I'm sayin'. You can *smell* the history in 'em," Blue said, inhaling deeply and sighing like a connoisseur of fine cheese. "Like if an old tree had drawers."

Red blinked slowly. "That one there—" he pointed at a particularly oversized pair of bloomers half-buried in the soil, "—they've seen pain. Long, sweaty nights. Regret. That waistband's been stretched by *life*."

Blue crouched beside the trench, tucking the undergarments in with a tender hand. "It's like planting memories. The dirt knows what to do. These'll sing when they sprout, mark my words."

Red tilted his head, as if listening to some private, fungal choir. "You hear that? They're already whisperin'."

Blue paused, considered, then squinted. "I think that's just the buzz in your own brain, mate."

Red shrugged slowly. "Maybe. Or maybe the mushrooms are smarter than both of us. Maybe they remember."

Blue clapped a hand on his shoulder. "Well, if they do, they'll remember *us*. We're facilitators. Shepherds of stink. Stewards of the stain."

Rea fought the urge to gag. Her hand clamped over her mouth, eyes watering as the Gnomes stood in dreamy silence, contemplating the underwear-fertilized mushroom fields with the solemnity of priests before a sacred altar.

"Y'know," Blue added after a beat, "if this batch turns out nice, the boss might even share the *good* shrooms. The ones that make colors hum and time get all bendy."

Red's eyes widened. "The singing colors," he whispered in awe. "I miss those."

They wandered off, babbling about crop yields and cosmic underpants.

Rea remained frozen for a long moment, hoping the spores hadn't damaged her brain. Then she eased out from behind the rock and picked her way between the trenches, each step a wet squelch, each breath thick with the scent of heat, fungus, and something she'd rather not think about. She kept low, kept quiet, and didn't dare look too closely at any of the undergarments—especially the ones that looked familiar.

As Rea moved deeper, the tunnel widened into a massive cavern, and her eyes widened along with it. Buildings, if you could call them that, sprouted from the walls like mushrooms on steroids, their caps forming roofs, balconies, and who knew what else. Some of them even had windows, though the idea of a Gnome pulling aside a mushroom cap to peer through a window struck her as ridiculous. Still, it was oddly beautiful in a *wow, I can't believe this is happening* sort of way.

The air was thicker now, clogged with glowing spores that floated lazily like they had no particular place to be. The Gnomes, dozens of them, wandered through the cavern with vacant smiles plastered on their faces, utterly oblivious to the terrified girl sneaking through their midst. Rea felt a brief flash of relief. At least no one was going to try to shove her into a mushroom patch. Not yet, anyway.

Her ring still shone with its soft light, casting an eerie glow across the cavern floor. She tried to focus on it, to let its faint illumination guide her, but something strange was happening. If she held it in a certain direction, the light seemed . . . reluctant, as if it were being pushed back by some unseen force. Like the darkness had opinions about being lit up and they were *not favorable*.

"Okay, that's weird," she muttered, moving the ring around like someone trying to divine where to dig a well. She swallowed hard, her throat dry from nerves and the hot, thick air.

She moved toward the reluctant darkness. The more she moved in that direction, the more the light dimmed, until it barely illuminated a foot in front of her. Only to the sides and behind her did the light still flicker, as though it had decided those areas were far more agreeable.

Great. Just great. Now her magical light was giving up. It was like even the ring had lost confidence in this whole situation.

Determined—or more accurately, too terrified to turn back—Rea pressed forward. The air grew heavier with every step. The ground beneath her feet was sticky and damp, squishing in a way that made her desperately *not* want to think about what she was stepping on. The walls seemed to pulse, the mushrooms growing ever larger and more grotesque as she ventured deeper.

A Gnome popped out from a side passage and barreled right into her legs, like a wayward toddler with no sense of personal space. Rea yelped, jumping back, her heart leaping into her throat. The Gnome blinked up at her, his eyes glazed over as if he'd wandered off a particularly long and confusing thought. Then, without so much as a word, the Gnome shuffled away, continuing on his meandering path, completely oblivious to the fact that he'd nearly given her a heart attack.

Rea let out a shaky breath, clutching her chest as her heart rate dropped from *imminent explosion* to *mild panic attack*. "Great," she muttered, glancing down at Nyx. "I'm jumping at Gnomes now."

Finally, the tunnel gave way to a vast chamber that stretched out before her like the belly of some colossal, forgotten beast. The walls pulsed with bioluminescent fungi, casting a faint, otherworldly glow in hues that no sane mind would ever try to name. At the chamber's center yawned a pit, so dark and deep it was less like a hole and more like an argument against the existence of light itself. It gaped wide, waiting, like a mouth hungry for anything foolish enough to wander too close.

Rea's ring, which had faithfully guided her through the tunnels, flickered feebly now, the light sputtering like an old lamp with commitment issues. No matter how much she willed it, the glow refused to venture into the pit's core. It was as if the abyss had drawn a hard line against illumination and was enforcing it with grim determination. The only light that remained obedient hugged close to her sides, casting long, twisted shadows that danced unsettlingly along the walls, as if mocking her for even thinking she could rely on something as simple as a glowing ring in a place like this.

VRAAWWM! VRAAWWM!

The sound blasted through the air, reverberating off the cavern walls and straight into her bones. It was alien. Ancient. It was as if the pit itself had decided to blow its own horn and announce, "Surprise, you're in deep trouble now!"

Rea stumbled, her feet betraying her in the chaos as the ground shook violently beneath her. She flailed for balance, catching herself as she pitched toward the pit's hungry maw. Her heart lodged itself firmly in her throat, pounding so hard she was certain the next tremor would knock it loose. The earth beneath her rumbled in irritation, like it was grumbling, *'Don't even think about coming closer.'*

But then, her eyes darted across the chamber, and she saw them.

Slumped against the far wall.

Tee-Tee. Thane. Blarg.

Her heart leaped, and before she could stop herself, tears welled up, blurring her vision.

They were alive.

She wanted to run to them, to shout their names, but her feet remained rooted to the spot. She was held back by the gnawing fear that this was some sort of trick. The pit seemed to hum with malice, as if it was watching, waiting for her to make the wrong move.

Rea took a shaky breath, wiping her eyes with the back of her hand. *Focus. They need you.*

Slowly, carefully, she took a step forward.

14

Spore Losers

"There's no such thing as a little eldritch horror. If it's small, it just means it's farther away from your face."

— Empire Safety Bulletin

Rea came to a halt beside her sister, who was slumped against the wall as though gravity had become her closest friend.[82] Blarg was half-sprawled nearby, gazing at the ceiling like it held the answers to life's deepest mysteries, which, in his current state, probably did. Thane, however, had developed a special relationship with the floor, entering into what was round three of his battle to stand up, failing, and resuming a very intense conversation with the ground.

The ground gave another ominous rumble beneath Rea's feet, as if an enormous, unseen creature was clearing its throat to make an announcement no one wanted to hear. She shook Tianna's shoulder with urgency. "Come on! We need to get out of here!"

Tianna's head lolled, her eyes glazed. She smiled dreamily, as if she were about to share some profound insight into the nature of things, but only slurred, "Is that . . . Nyxie? Here, kitty kitty."

---

[82] Gravity, while fundamental to physics, remains one of the clingiest forces in the universe. Once it grabs you, it never wants to let go.

"No time for snuggles!" Rea snapped, though part of her wanted to hug the cat too. She quickly laid Nyx down beside her sister. Her heart was pounding in sync with the trembling cavern. Rifling through her pack, she grabbed an old shirt and ripped it into strips to make masks. The spores in the air were thick now, like trying to breathe through a damp sock. She muttered something that might have been a prayer, though to what, she wasn't entirely sure, as she tied a makeshift mask around Tianna's face.

Thane, in the midst of poking at his boot as if it had betrayed him, suddenly took a keen interest in the mask Rea tried to tie around his face. "Off with that!" he slurred, yanking at the cloth like a toddler rebelling against wearing clothes.

"No!" Rea barked, slapping his hand away, scowling as if she'd caught him sneaking sweets before dinner. "Keep it on!"

"But it's itchy," Thane whined, tugging at the mask again.

"If you take it off, you'll inhale more spores, and I'm not hauling you out of here like a sack of potatoes!" Rea hissed, swatting his hand away again with even more force.

Thane blinked, his sluggish mind clearly wrestling with why potatoes had entered the conversation. Blarg, still flat on his back, mumbled something that sounded like a philosophical reflection on the existential plight of fungus, but Rea had neither the time nor the patience to decode it. With a final, frustrated huff, she tied a mask over Blarg's face as the ground beneath her feet gave another warning tremor, like a toddler about to throw the world's biggest tantrum.

Then she heard it, the unmistakable pitter-patter of tiny feet. Gnomes. Dozens of them, wielding flails made of mushrooms. Rea's stomach sank. "Oh, great," she muttered.

Out of the shadows, the Gnomes appeared, their movements sluggish but their grins wide. One particularly enthusiastic Gnome twirled his flail with the casual grace of someone who had mastered the art of mushroom combat and couldn't wait to show off.

Desperate, Rea scrambled for a weapon. Her hand landed on a broken broom handle. Not exactly heroic, but it would have to do.

With a determined grimace, she swung the stick in front of her like a knight with a decidedly underwhelming sword. "Stay back!" she shouted, her voice muffled by the mask. For a moment, she almost felt valiant. Almost.

A Gnome got too close, and with a quick swing and a satisfying *crack*, she knocked him square in the face, sending him flying into a nearby wall. "Hey!" another Gnome squeaked indignantly, throwing a mushroom at her in retaliation. It bounced off her chest with a sad little *plop*.

The ground trembled again, knocking Rea off balance. Before she could recover, a larger Gnome darted in. He wrapped his mushroom flail around the broomstick and yanked it out of her grip with the smug confidence of someone who had won the world's least exciting game of tug-of-war. He smiled at her, an expression that said, *'Nice try, kid.'*

Rea's heart sank as the Gnomes closed in, their eyes gleaming with a mixture of mischief and menace. She glanced back at her family, slumped against the wall. A wave of helplessness washed over her. She wasn't strong enough. She wasn't fast enough. How could she possibly save them?

A Gnome who appeared more important than the rest, draped in a gaudy gold chain that jingled with every step, strutted forward. "The Dreaming One stirs! Ready the humans for the offering!" he declared grandly, lifting his arms like a conductor about to unleash the world's most dreadful symphony.

The Gnomes swarmed forward, arms raised in exaggerated unison as they began their solemn chant:

"La! La! L'Sidroth wakes!
In damp and dark, the earth it shakes!
From soil deep, it doth arise!
Chaos spores spread far and wide!"

The Gnomes chanted in eerie harmony, their voices rising and falling in an evil lullaby. The sound reverberated off the walls and seeped into every crevice of the cavern. Their voices took on a haunting quality, an ancient hymn sung by creatures far too small to carry such ominous tones. As their chant grew louder, the ground quaked again, a deep rumbling that seemed to come not just from below, but from all directions at once, as though the very walls were alive with malevolent anticipation.

From the yawning pit at the center of the chamber, dark tendrils of smoke began to rise, curling into the air like twisted, skeletal fingers. They moved with a slow, deliberate grace, as though savoring every moment of their ascent. Each tendril was thick, pulsing with some unseen, unholy rhythm. As they reached out into the chamber, the temperature dropped, the air falling heavy with a chill that crept into the bones.

One tendril, more eager than the rest, slithered forward and brushed against the nearest Gnome. He froze, his wide, glazed eyes flickering for the briefest of moments with fear, before his body shriveled, his skin turning paper-thin as his very essence was sucked away, leaving behind nothing but a lifeless husk. The Gnome's form collapsed inward, a dry crackling sound filling the air as the tendril coiled around him and dragged him effortlessly into the pit.

"Huzzah!" the remaining Gnomes cheered, as though the sight of their comrade's demise was a cause for celebration. They raised their arms in unison, swaying in time with the rhythm of the pit, basking in the morbid glory of what had just transpired. One Gnome, slightly more animated than the others, hopped in place, clearly thrilled at the honor bestowed upon his fallen companion. "Chosen by L'Sidroth!" he cried out, his voice filled with reverence.

The tendrils continued to reach out, growing bolder, tasting the air with malicious intent. They seemed to feed on the palpable fear that radiated from the chamber, growing stronger with each second. Rea crouched over Tianna. She could feel the icy tendrils of terror creeping into her chest. She tightened her grip on her sister, desperately trying to shield her from the encroaching horror, though she had no idea how she would protect either of them.

More tendrils snaked across the floor, creeping closer. Rea's breath came in quick, shallow bursts, her mind racing. *No!* The word echoed in her mind, bouncing off every corner of her panicked thoughts. Her hands shook, her heart pounded in her ears, and then, like a dam breaking, the word burst from her lips.

"NO!"

It wasn't just a cry of defiance, it was a declaration, a refusal to let the darkness win. The tendrils recoiled, momentarily stunned by the sheer force of her voice, like a predator surprised by the prey it thought too weak to fight back.

The Gnomes, however, did not notice the shift in the air. They continued their chanting, swaying to the invisible rhythm, their eyes fixed on the pit, as if waiting for more to be claimed. But Rea stood her ground, her heart pounding with something new.

Determination!

In one fluid motion, Rea shot to her feet, the weight of her fear falling away as a surge of raw defiance took its place. Her body felt light, the terror had been siphoned away, replaced by something fierce and unyielding. With a sharp breath, she spun to face the pit, her hand outstretched toward the dark, writhing mass of tendrils that slithered across the chamber, a grotesque parody of life.

Her heart pounded, not with fear, but with purpose. The light from her ring flickered faintly at first, as if uncertain of what was to come. But as her determination surged, so did the light, casting a pale glow that cut through the gloom within the cavern. The air itself held its breath waiting for what came next.

"NOOOO!"

Her voice rang out, echoing off the walls like a battle cry that had been waiting its entire life to be released. It wasn't just a word, it was a force, a tidal wave of defiance that vibrated through the very fabric of the chamber. The Gnomes stopped their eerie chanting mid-syllable, their eyes widening in disbelief, the room suddenly feeling too small for the power that had been unleashed.

The tendrils froze, momentarily shocked by the sheer intensity of her shout, then recoiled as if the sound itself had wounded them. They hissed, retreating slightly, their movement sluggish and uncertain, like they weren't quite sure what to make of this tiny human who dared to challenge them.

Rea's heart raced, her outstretched hand trembling with the enormity of the moment. She wasn't a scared girl anymore, hiding in the shadows. She was standing against the darkness. Against the thing that had threatened to consume them all. And she wasn't backing down.

The ring on her finger flared, a spark at first, then a flame, growing brighter and brighter until it burned like a miniature sun. Waves of light poured from it, flooding the chamber and pushing back the creeping shadows. The tendrils of smoke and nightmare recoiled, twisting and writhing as the light touched upon them. A screech tore through the air, a sound so awful it was as if the cries of a thousand tormented souls were being ripped apart at once.

Rea stood at the center of it all, the light pulsing from her hand, like it had become an extension of herself. She could feel the power coursing through her, not overwhelming, but filling every part of her with a sense of purpose, of control. The others turned away, shielding their eyes from the searing brightness, but Rea stood firm. Her eyes locked onto the heart of the light, its glow tunneling into her vision, a beacon of certainty.

This light wasn't just around her; it was part of her. It filled her, flooded every corner of her being, erasing every doubt, every fear. They were gone, burned away, swallowed by the light that now coursed through her veins.

The tendrils, reduced to mere wisps of smoke, screamed and shrank as they fled into the pit, desperate to escape the radiant onslaught. But Rea did not relent. The light continued to build, brighter and stronger, until it felt like the entire cavern would shake itself apart under the force of it. The walls trembled, the ground beneath her feet quivered, and still, the light surged forward.

The glow built to a blinding crescendo, bathing the entire chamber in its brilliance. For a moment, the world was nothing but light, brilliant and all-consuming. Rea was no longer in a dark, damp cavern. She stood in a void of pure white that was both weightless and timeless. The whisper of something ancient and wise brushed against her senses. There were no words, but she *understood*. The light had been waiting for her. It had always been there, guiding her, waiting for this moment.

And then, with a final surge, the light exploded outward, a shockwave of blinding brilliance that banished every shadow, every trace of darkness. The tendrils, the fear, the creeping terror, all of it was swept away, driven back into the deepest recesses of the earth.

The chamber fell silent.

The air was still.

The world, heavy with the aftermath of the blast.

Rea's knees buckled, and for the first time, she felt the weight of what had happened. Glancing down at her hand, she saw the ring. Where once a brilliant white gem had sat, there was nothing. The gem shattered, sacrificed in that final act of defiance.

She fell to her knees.

The Gnomes stood frozen, their faces a mix of shock and awe, staring at Rea as if the scene before them was beyond belief. One Gnome blinked, then bolted, scurrying back up the tunnel. The others quickly followed suit, fleeing in a flurry of panicked steps, like chickens suddenly realizing they were late for their punchline.

"Rea?" came a voice from behind, soft and familiar. She turned to see her sister, eyes clear, and wide with wonder.

"Tee-Tee!" Rea cried, rushing to embrace her sister, holding back tears.

"How did you—" Thane's voice trailed off, his face full of amazement.

Tianna, still weak but slowly coming to her senses, pulled herself up, leaning heavily on Rea for support. "You . . . you really did it," she said, her voice filled with a mixture of awe and disbelief. "You saved us."

Rea, still breathing heavily, glanced down at the ring and felt an odd emptiness. "I didn't think I could," she admitted, her voice quieter than she intended.

Blarg groaned from the floor, still half-dazed but starting to stir. "Well, that was . . . something. Does anyone else feel as though their brain has been scoured with a broom?" He rubbed his head and searched around, trying to remember where he was. The spores were gone, so Blarg removed his mask. Everyone else followed suit.

Thane sat up, blinking slowly as though awakening from a long, confusing dream. "I . . . don't think I want to know what just happened." He glanced over at the pit, and then at Rea. "But it looks like you saved us. I'm proud of you kid."

Before anyone could respond, the ground gave another small tremor, causing them all to tense. It wasn't as strong as before, but it was enough to remind them that they weren't out of danger yet.

"We need to get out of here," Tianna said, her voice more urgent now, as she fully regained her composure. "Whatever that thing was, it's not going to stay quiet for long."

Blarg nodded, his usual bravado returning. "Aye, better to not stick around for round two. Blarg's had his fill of eldritch horrors for one day, thank you kindly."

Brrrrup! Nyx meowed impatiently, circling in a tight loop before darting toward a tunnel opposite the one the Gnomes had fled. Without a word, the group instinctively followed the cat. After all, his sense of direction had yet to let them down.

The tunnel led them into a small antechamber that appeared as if it had been decorated by a weapons enthusiast with a hoarding problem and a severe allergy to organization. Swords, spears, and various pointy objects of dubious origin were scattered about like a deadly game of pick-up sticks.

"Ah, the Gnomes have been busy little kleptomaniacs, haven't they?" Blarg muttered, surveying the chaos with the air of a man who'd just walked into a particularly unimpressive yard sale. He rummaged through a pile of rusted swords and bent spears, his movements suggesting he was searching for a needle in a haystack made entirely of other needles.

After a moment of digging, Blarg let out a triumphant grunt and yanked *Thumpkin*, his trusty hammer, from the depths of the pile. The hammer appeared a bit worse for wear, like it had gone a few rounds with an angry Troll and barely come out on top. However, Blarg cooed over it like a mother reunited with her favorite child. "There you are, Blarg's precious skull-cracker," he crooned, giving the hammer a loving pat.

Tianna, Thane, and Rea, not to be outdone by Blarg's display of weapon affection, began their own search through the haphazard armory. Tianna's eyes lit up when she spotted her trusty frying pan, which had somehow survived the ordeal without a single dent, as if it had simply refused to participate in the whole *being captured* nonsense. She snatched it up and gave it a jaunty twirl, looking the part of a cook ready to take on the world's largest omelet.

"Oh finally, I was beginning to think you'd forgotten all about me!" Sword's voice rang out, dripping with indignation. *"Do you have any idea how dreadfully boring it is being stuck in a pile of inferior weapons?"*

Tianna rolled her eyes. "Everyone, say hello to Sword," she said, holding up the pan with mock reverence. "She's missed us terribly."

The group exchanged amused glances but humored her, giving the frying pan a few halfhearted pats. Thane, axe in hand, did so with the enthusiasm of a man being forced to greet an overly chatty neighbor at the worst possible time.

"Well, I suppose that's better than nothing." Sword sniffed. *"Now, please tell me we're going to go hit something. I've got a lot of pent-up anger to release."*

Rea, meanwhile, had discovered a small dagger tucked away in the corner, its blade gleaming with the promise of adventure. She slipped it into her belt, trying her best to act nonchalant, but the proud grin spreading across her face ruined the effect entirely. Thane caught her eye and gave her a subtle nod of approval, the kind that said, *'Nice find, kid, but try not to stab yourself with it.'*

"Right then," Thane said, stretching his back with a series of unsettling pops and cracks. "Let's hope we don't have to use these anytime soon."

Blarg glared at him like he'd suggested they all take up knitting. "Speak for yourself," he scoffed. "Blarg could go for a good smashing. It's been far too long since he last wielded this hammer."

"I second that!" Sword chimed in eagerly. *"A good smash sounds absolutely divine right about now."*

Nyx, who had been watching the proceedings with an air of feline disdain, flicked his tail impatiently and padded toward the nearest tunnel. It was clear he'd had quite enough of this weapon reunion nonsense and was ready to move on to more important matters. The unspoken message was clear: break time was over.

The group followed, trying not to feel too put out by the fact that a cat was apparently calling the shots now. The tunnel sloped gently upward, much to everyone's relief, and the air tasted marginally less likely to cause any spontaneous hallucinations this time around.

After a while, they reached a juncture where three tunnels split off in different directions. The group came to a confused halt, collectively staring at the paths like travelers who had realized their map was upside down. Even Nyx appeared uncertain, his tail twitching back and forth like a pendulum of indecision.

Blarg, however, strode forward with the confidence of a man who absolutely, positively knew where he was going, despite all evidence to the contrary. He made a big show of inspecting each tunnel, sniffing the air with exaggerated concentration, as if he could somehow smell the right path.

After a long moment of this, he straightened up and pointed down the third tunnel with a triumphant grin. "This is the path," he declared, marching off without waiting for a response.

The others exchanged dubious glances but followed, not having any better options. The tunnel gradually brightened as the light of day began to filter in. At the mouth of the cave, Blarg came to an abrupt stop, looking incredibly pleased with himself.

He took another deep, theatrical breath, then let out a chuckle.

Garlic. The air smelled of garlic.

15

The Goblin *'Menace'*

"To call them savages is to misunderstand both savagery and Goblins."

— Professor Vindel Throom (Presumed Exiled)

Blarg's grin stretched wider than a Banshee at karaoke night as they emerged into a field of garlic. Not a small patch mind you, but a sprawling, pungent sea of the stuff, stretching out before them as far as the eye could water. His eyes widened; an expression of pure, unadulterated joy spread across his face.

"Garlic!" he bellowed, as if announcing the return of a beloved childhood pet or perhaps a long-lost friend who owed him money. He dropped to his knees, tearing a handful of bulbs from the earth and inhaled deeply, the rich aroma filling his lungs. "'Tis glorious!"

The others exchanged glances that ranged from bemused to concerned for Blarg's sanity. Tianna nudged Thane, still slightly bleary-eyed from their last ordeal. He merely offered a tired shrug, the universal gesture for, *'I don't have the energy to try to understand Blarg.'*

Rea, on the other hand, managed a smile. Her usual spark had reignited, confidence trickling back like an overdue library book—late, slightly wrinkled, but exactly where she needed to be. The knot of anxiety that had twisted in her chest for days had loosened, though it still lurked in the background, like a particularly judgmental aunt at a family dinner.

"Garlic," Blarg declared again, with the seriousness of someone announcing the invention of fire, "It's proof that the universe has not forsaken this party entirely."

Tianna raised an eyebrow. "It's just garlic."

"*Just* garlic? *JUST* garlic?" he said, clutching a bulb of garlic to his chest like a child hoarding candy. "Garlic is not mere sustenance, it is a proclamation. One cannot be sad around garlic, it smells too loud for sadness to get a word in. It tastes too bright to let despair linger. Garlic may not solve problems, but it boldly declares, *'I know not the answers, but dinner shall have flavor,'* and, oftentimes, that's more than enough."

Thane chuckled softly. "Garlic's the real hero, then?"

Blarg nodded with the weight of great wisdom. "The unsung one, indeed."

"So," Tianna cut in, squinting at the horizon where mountains loomed like a row of jagged teeth waiting to chew them up. "Where are we, exactly?"

Thane scanned the distance, frowning. "Well, we're north, which is a good start. But with that many mountains, there's plenty of room to hide a fortress."

"So, what's the plan?" Tianna asked, eyebrow raised. "Wander aimlessly and hope we find our way before something with big teeth finds us?"

Thane shrugged again. "It's worked so far."

"Uh, guys?" Rea piped up, a note of curiosity in her voice. "Is it just me, or do these garlic plants look a bit . . . organized?"

They all paused, noticing for the first time that the garlic rows were straighter than a monk's moral compass.

"Indeed," Blarg said, his eyes narrowing as he scanned their surroundings. "This is no wild field. This is a *farm*. And who knows what foul creatures till the soil in these parts."

The group crept cautiously around the field of garlic, each step taken with the care of someone expecting the ground to sprout teeth and take offense. Their eyes darted to the horizon, scanning for any sign of danger. To the north, dark clouds were gathering like latecomers to a particularly ominous party. A biting wind swept across the countryside, sharp enough to make even the garlic shiver. Snow began to fall, not in gentle flurries, but in random, indecisive splats, as if the sky were trying out winter like a hat it wasn't quite sure about.

As if summoned by the wind itself, a small figure popped up from behind a bush. It was a Goblin child, no taller than Rea, with wide, curious eyes. His clothes appeared as if they had barely survived a wrestling match with an overly energetic thorn bush. The child stared, particularly at Rea and Nyx, as if they were the most interesting things he'd seen all day. Nyx, for his part, flicked his tail, as if to say, *'Another fan, naturally.'*

"Quick! Smash him!" Sword said excitedly.

Thane's hand shot to his axe, his eyes narrowing. "Goblin!" he hissed, muscles tensing as he prepared to strike. Blarg's hammer was already halfway in the air, ready to crush the threat before it could make a move.

"Stand back!" Blarg bellowed, taking a step forward. "The creature's kin shall be here swiftly!"

But Tianna was quicker. She stepped between the child and the others, wielding her frying pan like a starving knight defending her last sandwich. "Wait!" she cried, her voice cutting through the tension like a bum trumpet in the middle of an exam.[83] "Look at him! He means no harm!"

Thane hesitated, his eyes flicking from the child to Tianna. "A Goblin's still a Goblin, Tianna," he muttered, his grip tightening on his axe.

"He's a child," Tianna said firmly, meeting Thane's gaze with the kind of determination reserved for convincing someone the sky *isn't* falling. "If he wanted to hurt us, he'd have already run back to his kin."

---

[83] Studies have shown that the average exam hall has a 2 percent chance of being interrupted by a rogue bum trumpet. This rises to 37 percent when beans are served in the cafeteria beforehand.

The Goblin child took a tentative step forward, extending a small hand toward Rea, who watched in quiet amazement. Thane and Blarg exchanged glances, one part wary, two parts confused, and a generous dash of trying hard not to hit anything. Slowly, reluctantly, they lowered their weapons.

Blarg muttered under his breath, "Maybe it's a trap—"

The Goblin child reached into his tattered pocket. This, of course, was enough to send Thane and Blarg into high alert, as if the child was about to pull out a fistful of trouble. Thane's axe gleamed in the sunlight, and Blarg's hammer was hefted, ready to strike down whatever scheme the Goblin child might be hatching.

"He's pulling something!" Thane barked, his voice low and dangerous. "Stay back, Tianna!"

Blarg's eyes narrowed. "'Tis best not to trust a Goblin, even a wee one."

"Smash him on the head, then we can see what he's up to." Sword chimed in with her usual violence first, questions last, attitude.

Tianna, heart thumping, refused to budge. "Wait!" she urged, her voice pleading, but mostly not interested with the whole *smash first, ask questions later* approach. "Let's see what he's doing!"

The Goblin child, blissfully oblivious to the looming hammer-related doom, withdrew his hand from his pocket. Instead of a weapon, it was a small, delicate yellow flower. The petals shimmered faintly in the sunlight as he shyly extended it toward Rea.

Rea blinked, momentarily stunned, then slowly reached out and took the flower from the child's hand. Her face softened, her initial surprise melting into a warm smile. "Thank you," she whispered, as if speaking any louder might scare away the miracle of goodwill.

Nyx, who had been observing the scene with the patience of a cat who has seen too much to care, sauntered over to the Goblin child. With the gravitas of a king, he rubbed up against the Goblin's leg, purring softly, as though bestowing upon him the highest honor a cat could give—mild affection.

Tianna, relieved, let out a breath. "See?" she said, glancing back at Thane and Blarg. "If Nyx trusts him, we should too."

Sword hmphed. *"Are we ever going to smash anything?"*

Thane and Blarg exchanged uncertain glances, their expressions still stuck somewhere between confusion and suspicion, but they begrudgingly lowered their weapons.

Blarg grunted, shaking his head in disbelief. "A flower . . . Hmph. A clever little Goblin, Blarg shall grant him that."

Thane sighed, his eyes softening ever so slightly. "Maybe . . . not all Goblins are what we've been told."

"Don't be ridiculous," Blarg responded.

The Goblin child gave the group a brief, expectant wave before turning and trotting off. His gait was casual, almost jaunty, as if leading heavily armed strangers through the wilderness was just another day on the job.

Blarg and Thane exchanged one final, wary glance.

"It's a trap, Blarg knows it," Blarg muttered, his voice dripping with suspicion. His grip tightened on the handle of his hammer. "Goblins are crafty, always full of tricks."

Thane frowned, but before he could voice his agreement, the girls were already following the Goblin child. Nyx strutted alongside, tail held high, as if he had orchestrated the entire peace treaty himself. Rea, still holding the flower, skipped as she went. Tianna glanced back at the men, a knowing expression on her face that clearly said, *'Well, are you coming?'*

With an exasperated sigh, Thane and Blarg fell into step behind them, though Blarg's muttering about inevitable betrayal never ceased.

"So, here's a thought," Sword piped up. *"Instead of running away and befriending the bad guys, maybe—just maybe—we could do some actual fighting? You know, like in a proper sword and sorcery tale? Not whatever this is. At this point, we're one tea party away from cozy fantasy."*

They walked for twenty minutes, the terrain gradually changing as they descended into a lush valley. The landscape softened like a wheel of rotten cheese left out in the sun. Rolling green hills sprouted from the ground like mold, stretching before them, lazily inviting anyone to lie down and take a nap. In the distance, a cluster of buildings appeared, nestled at the foot of the valley like a child's attempt at tidying up their toys.

Above them, however, the sky was far less inviting. The lazy snowflakes that had been drifting down had picked up in earnest, turning the hills into a patchwork of green and white. The wind, already biting, now carried flurries that stung their faces and blurred the view. The snowfall thickened by the minute, swirling and gathering strength as if the clouds had decided this valley was an ideal spot to unleash their pent-up frustrations. What began as mere dusting was clearly working its way toward a full-blown storm, its intent unmistakable.

As they drew closer, the group realized the buildings were not the crude huts they'd expected. No, this wasn't the squalid Goblin lair of legend, where everything was presumably on fire and the air was thick with the smell of old boots. Instead, the town bustled with life, the structures sturdy, with thatched roofs and stone foundations. Smoke curled lazily from chimneys, looking for all the world as if it had nowhere better to be. The distant sounds of chatter, laughter, and clattering drifted toward them. Oddly domestic noises for a place supposedly full of Goblins and general nastiness.

But these were not the snarling, dangerous creatures that Thane and Blarg had been taught to fear. Not the kind of Goblins who'd steal your shoes and set your house on fire for fun. No, these Goblins were . . . living . . . like humans. There were children chasing each other through the streets, giggling and shouting in the universal language of *'tag, you're it.'* Elderly Goblins sat on benches, watching the snow fall onto the town, their faces etched with years of mischief. Women carried baskets of laundry and gossiped over fences with the intensity of those who had long since stopped caring about the outside world.

Men with tools strapped to their belts tinkered with homes, fields, and the occasional cart, in the way of people who could fix anything, even if it didn't need fixing in the first place. It was a scene that could have come from any human village, if not for the green skin, pointy ears, and occasional cackle that suggested something wickedly fun had happened earlier in the day.

Blarg stopped in his tracks, eyes wide. "Blarg does not understand this."

"Agreed. This isn't how the narrative is supposed to go," Sword said.

Tianna smiled faintly, though her eyes were full of wonder. "I think . . . maybe we've been wrong about them."

Nyx, completely unconcerned, padded ahead, leaving paw prints in the fresh snow. He slipped into the crowd of Goblins with the ease of someone who had decided he already owned the place. In other words, normal cat behavior. The Goblin child they'd followed paused and waved them toward a small square in the center of town. Goblins were gathered, talking, laughing, and sharing what appeared to be food, though it was best not to inquire *too* deeply into what.

Thane, still uncertain, scanned the crowd with the cautiousness of someone expecting an ambush. "So . . . what do we do now?"

Before anyone could answer, an elderly Goblin woman, who had achieved the impossible feat of balancing a large basket of fruit on her head, shuffled over. Without a word, she thrust a large, lumpy apple into Blarg's hands.

Blarg blinked down at the fruit, his expression that of a man who had been handed poison disguised as a healthy snack.

Rea giggled. "Maybe we say thank you?"

Blarg, still processing the potential dangers of this oddly shaped apple, gave a slow, hesitant nod. "Aye . . . uhh . . . thank you?" It sounded more like a question than gratitude, but it was a start.

The Goblin's eyes twinkled, and the old woman cackled in a way that suggested she found everything, including Blarg's confusion, immensely entertaining. She waved them forward with the kind of enthusiasm one might reserve for inviting someone into a mildly dangerous but very fun situation.

Tianna glanced at Thane, whose expression had softened from *'imminent danger'* to *'mild confusion'*, while Blarg was caught somewhere around *'bewildered caution'*. The apple still sat in his hand like an unsolved puzzle, as though he half-expected it to sprout wings and fly off or explode in a puff of mischief.

"Let's go," Tianna said, and without further ceremony, the group followed the old woman into the heart of Goblin territory. They felt more like bewildered tourists than the *seasoned* adventurers they were supposed to be.

As they approached a larger building in the center of the town, it became clear this wasn't just any building. It stood taller than the others. Its beams were intricately carved with scenes Tianna couldn't quite decipher, though there was a suspicious number of Goblins waving swords around while riding improbably large chickens. Brightly colored banners fluttered from the roof, as though the building had dressed up for some grand occasion and no one had the heart to tell it otherwise.

The door creaked open, and an older Goblin woman stepped out. She wasn't like the other Goblins they had encountered. She wore layers of fine cloth, adorned with shiny trinkets. A few strands of silver threaded through her dark hair, each one suggesting it had been earned through a combination of experience and Goblin-related nonsense. Her sharp, discerning eyes flicked over the group, measuring them with the precision of someone who could tell the difference between a liar and an idiot before either of them opened their mouth.

Blarg saw his moment.

"Stand back," he commanded, puffing out his chest like a rooster preparing for battle, albeit one that wasn't entirely sure who or what it was fighting. "Blarg shall deal with these savages!"

Thane raised an eyebrow, his expression a mix of skepticism and amusement. "You sure about that?"

Blarg nodded solemnly, hammer resting on his shoulder as he swaggered forward, each step exuding overconfidence. Tianna exchanged a glance with

Rea, who merely shrugged her shoulders. Even Nyx, who usually couldn't be bothered, gave Blarg a curious glance before returning to licking his paw.

Blarg strutted forward with all the swagger of a man who'd heard too many heroic ballads and believed every word. He planted himself in front of the Goblin woman, set his hammer on the ground with a *thunk*, crossed his arms, and gave her a glare he likely thought was intimidating. "You speak to Blarg the Unstoppable Doomhammer! Scourge of the Southern Ice Trolls! Champion of a Thousand Battles!" His voice echoed dramatically across the square, as if he were addressing an army instead of one slightly bemused Goblin woman.

The Goblin woman blinked, her expression utterly unreadable, as though she'd been asked to explain the multiverse theory to a particularly dim-witted potato. For a moment, even the wind paused, curious to see how this would unfold.

She tilted her head slightly. "Sorry . . . my human Spirish . . . is not my strongest language. Do you speak Goblin Snagblat?"

Blarg blinked, clearly thrown off his rhythm. "Nay, you unlearned brute!" He barked, though his bravado had acquired a wobble.

The woman raised an eyebrow, unfazed by his insult. "Durgrim?"

"Nay!"

"Sylvanian?"

"Nay."

"Goruk?"

Blarg hesitated, his confidence visibly deflating like a balloon that had encountered a particularly sharp pin. "Err . . . nay."

"Thrumdor? Grumbrok? Fenrith? Drakonic?" She rattled off languages the way someone might list their favorite pie fillings.

Blarg's chest deflated with each language. "Blarg . . . Blarg only speaks Spirish, you green skinned fool! Can you not comprehend?" He peered back at his companions, as if expecting someone, anyone, to explain why the world had suddenly stopped making sense. "Your folk are so unlearned, it's no wonder your culture is so backward. You cannot even speak Blarg's tongue!"[84]

The Goblin woman's lips twitched, her expression somewhere between amused and deeply unimpressed. She raised her hands in a placating gesture. "Very well, I shall try, but please bear with me, I have not spoken Spirish in many years." Her Spirish was slow but clear and incredibly good. Her accent, or rather lack of, only added to the bemusement of the situation.

"Wow. Just… wow," Sword said. *"That must've been devastatingly embarrassing for the brute. I almost feel bad. Almost."*

Blarg, clearly rattled, glanced back at the others for reassurance. Tianna had a hand over her mouth, struggling not to burst into laughter, while Thane was having difficulty holding back a smirk. Even Nyx appeared amused, his tail flicking lazily, as if thinking, *'This is better than that time I knocked over the vase.'*

"Welcome to Thinkleburrow. I am Grikna Arba'in Kurunyar," the Goblin woman said, gesturing to herself with a slight bow, "the leader of this village."

Blarg, grasping for some semblance of control over the situation, tried to regain his composure. "Well, Grikna," he said, his voice adopting a somewhat pompous tone, "do your people wish to cause harm?"

She shook her head firmly. "We do not wish anyone harm."

Blarg, however, was not one to be so easily convinced. "Forgive Blarg if he does not trust so readily. Blarg has fought many Goblin warriors in his time!"

Grikna's lips twitched again in what might have been the beginnings of a smirk. "Look about you. Do you see any warriors among us?" She gestured broadly to the surrounding Goblins. "We are but humble farmers and craftsmen."

---

[84] Humans, as a general rule, assume that fluency in their own language is a universal sign of intelligence. This is despite the fact that their own language, Spirish, is largely made up of misused idioms, obscure metaphorical references, and the word 'literally' being applied to things that are very clearly not literal. The rest of the world has agreed to smile politely and stop asking questions about the cats and dogs that double as rain.

Blarg frowned, struggling to reconcile this peaceful scene with everything he'd ever been taught. "But surely you serve the Dark Lord, do you not?"

"I can ask the same about you. Do you serve the Dark One?" Grikna asked, her head tilted. "I have witnessed much evil from humans in my time."

"We've come to end the Dark One, not serve him," Tianna chimed in. The Goblin woman gave Tianna a curious gaze, but Blarg was undeterred, unwilling to abandon his questioning so easily.

"You did not answer Blarg's query," Blarg said, his tone carrying the weight of a man convinced he was about to unmask a grand conspiracy. "Do you serve the Dark Lord?"

Grikna stared at him for a long moment before chuckling softly and shaking her head. "There are some Goblins who choose to follow the Dark One. However, those numbers are few." She held up her hand, pinching her fingers together. "Our species has grown wise over the years, and that number is small. Those you see before you here, not one serves the Dark One."

Blarg narrowed his eyes, clearly grappling with the bewildering notion that Goblins may actually have a say in the matter. "Blarg does not understand—"

Grikna glanced up to the sky before gesturing for them to follow her inside the building. "The weather is only going to get worse. I think it would be better if we were to speak inside. Please, follow me," she said, as though explaining things slowly to the towering, slightly confused man with a hammer was part of her daily routine.

With a quick glance between them, Tianna, Thane, and Rea, followed Grikna inside. Blarg puffed up his chest one more time, no doubt mentally awarding himself points for dramatic effect, before reluctantly shuffling in after them. Nyx, as ever, trotted along with the air of a creature who had decided that nothing short of the end of the world, and maybe not even that, could bother him.

Inside the large building, the air was warmer. The light filtered in through small windows with a soft glow that suggested they had *thought* about being dramatic but decided against it. The room was sparsely decorated, save for an overwhelming sense of authority that hung in the air like a particularly stern headmaster—apparently, one that could float. Grikna gestured for them to sit at a large wooden table, the kind that had seen more years, and arguments, than anyone in the room. She took her place at the head, her sharp eyes scanning each of them with the precision of someone deciding whether they were guests, allies, or potential inconveniences, before finally speaking.

"You are lucky to have arrived here when you did. This flurry will quickly turn into a mighty storm." Grikna said as she brushed the remaining snowflakes from her shoulders.

"How do you know that?" Tianna asked.

"We Goblins are close to nature. It is easy to read the signs, if one knows where to look," she responded.

"Do not change the subject. What is your people's relationship to the Dark Lord?" Blarg interjected.

"That is a long story, but very well. Many years ago," she began, her voice calm and steady, "the Goblin race did indeed serve the Dark One. At that time, humans were our greatest enemy. They would invade our lands, killing many of my brothers and sisters, while razing many villages to the ground. The Goblins were distraught, not knowing how we could face such an overwhelmingly destructive force. But then the Dark One called to us. My people believed that this was the key to our salvation. This was the thing that could reverse our fortunes and make our people strong. So, we followed him, thinking that his victory would bring honor and prestige to the Goblin people."

Tianna leaned forward, listening intently, while Blarg sat with his arms crossed, still suspicious. Thane, ever the pragmatist, listened with a cautious curiosity.

"But the Dark One lied to us all," Grikna continued, her words as blunt as the business end of a mallet. "His very existence was folly. The Dark One was destined to lose, time and again. Destiny, she had ordained it. Many Goblins fought and died for the Dark One in those early days, only to lose. But the Dark

One kept coming back. Every time he fell, he would rise again within a few generations to take up his folly once more.

"But the Dark One never suffered. He exists in an endless cycle of death and rebirth, always fighting for something that will never come. But we suffered. The Goblin people suffered greatly. Not only did many Goblins fall in his wars, but the wars themselves brought more humans to our lands. United by a single purpose, it seemed as if all humankind was against us. Joined together for the sole purpose of driving all Goblinkind to extinction. So yes, we suffered greatly." Her voice held a note of bitterness, the memory of those lost echoing in her words.

Blarg uncrossed his arms, frowning. "Yet some Goblins still follow him?"

Grikna sighed and nodded. "Indeed. It seems that some Goblins refuse to learn the lessons of our ancestors." She sighed deeply. "They are always the same. Angry and bitter Goblins that find no peace living here. Maybe there is something wrong with them. Maybe something is broken up here." She pointed to her head. "Those Goblins leave when the call comes in. They think they can find some higher purpose by following the Dark One. It is sad, but also, better that they go. They can never find happiness here. All they do is cause trouble living among us." She appeared saddened by the statement.

Tianna's gaze softened as she focused on the Goblin leader. "So . . . you've stopped fighting?"

Grikna nodded. "Long ago, the Goblins decided that we have had enough, so for many generations, our people have tried to live in peace. Life is not perfect, even hard sometimes. But we are our own people. We are in control of our own future." She took a breath, as if trying to find the right words for people who still thought Goblins came with a side of evil. "Every few generations, the summon does come. But for the most part, we ignore it. The Dark One's endless wars are no longer our concern."

Tianna, not entirely convinced, furrowed her brow. "But I've seen the Dark Lord's army. It is vast."

Grikna raised an eyebrow. "Have you now?" Her tone suggested that she already suspected something wasn't quite right.

Tianna puffed up slightly. "I had a vision of the Dark Lord and his mighty army. It filled an entire valley."

"So, about that . . ." Sword chimed in. *"That may have been an older vision I showed you."*

Tianna's eyes narrowed as she picked up the frying pan and held it in front of her. "What do you mean, an *older vision?*"

Thane, ever the helpful soul, decided to interject. "She's talking to her magic frying pan," he explained to Grikna, whose expression was somewhere between concern and the kind of resignation you get when you realize you're dealing with complete lunatics.

"You know how it is," the pan continued, with the smug air of someone explaining a minor clerical error. *"It's hard to come up with new visions. All those little details, very time-consuming! Really, you wouldn't believe all the work involved. So, I thought, hey, why not reuse an old one? Bit dated, sure, but it had everything: massive army, dramatic tension, ominous shadows. A real classic, if I do say so myself."*[85]

Tianna's jaw dropped. "How old *exactly?*"

"Oh, I don't know . . . maybe 500 . . . 600 years old?" the pan replied, with the casualness of someone estimating how long ago they'd misplaced their keys.

"You've *got* to be kidding me!" Tianna appeared moments away from smashing Sword against the wall, or possibly her own skull.

"Does it really make a difference?" Sword asked, in that maddeningly calm, condescending tone she had perfected. *"You came here to do something, now it appears that the job will be easier. You're welcome."*

---

[85] Vision crafting, like all art, is inherently redundant. They say nothing truly original can be created. This sentiment holds especially true when the artist in question is lazy, a frying pan, or both. In the end, vision crafting is 5% inspiration, 95% rephrasing something older and praying no one notices.

Tianna gripped the pan tighter, her knuckles white. Every fiber of her being wanted to smash Sword into something, preferably something breakable. However, despite her infuriating smugness, Sword did have a point. A painfully good point.

The goal was to destroy the Dark Lord, and with a significantly smaller army than she'd anticipated, that task had become a lot more manageable. It didn't make the mission less dangerous, of course, just . . . less impossible.

"You're *welcome?*" Tianna muttered under her breath, still glaring at the pan. "That vision was older than the Empire itself, and I'm supposed to be grateful?"

"I could have given you a more recent vision," Sword added, sounding offended. *"But then you'd be all, 'Oh, Sword, why didn't you show me a proper doomsday? Something with flair! Where's the pageantry? Where are the dramatic clouds?' Honestly, some people."*[86]

Tianna let out a slow breath, as if releasing her frustration one molecule at a time. "Okay, fine. Smaller army, smaller problem," she muttered. "It still feels like I've been emotionally catfished by cookware."

Thane scratched his chin, still looking skeptical. "So how big is his army these days?" he asked Grikna.

Grikna gave a nonchalant shrug, as though the size of world-threatening armies was merely a minor inconvenience in the grand scheme of Goblin life. "It's hard to say. Before, the Dark One's army was vast. But without the Goblins, the Dark One has supplemented his numbers with other races. Many Orcs still follow the Dark One, more slave than willing fighter at this point, but present all the same."[87]

---

[86] There exists, somewhere in the sacred laws of divination, a lesser-known but deeply felt principle: the Law of Perpetual Disappointment. It states that no matter what vision you deliver, be it ominous, hopeful, cataclysmic, or delightfully vague, someone will complain. Ancient texts sum it up best: "Oh my gods, can you people just stop complaining for *one* minute?"

[87] Many people confuse Goblins with Orcs, believing them to be the same, when in fact, they are as different as chalk and cheese, or perhaps more accurately, as different

"Orcs?" Tianna repeated, her interest piqued.

Grikna nodded. "Indeed. The Dark One's influence is strong. Although Goblins are strong minded enough to resist the call, other races are not so strong willed. Orcs must answer the call, they have no choice." Grikna tilted her head, as if considering. "This makes the Dark One's army weak. The Orcs are forced to fight, but their hearts are not in it. Although Orckind are strong warriors, an army that does not believe in their cause, has no chance of victory."

"That . . . is something to think about," Thane said flatly.

"Very much," Grikna agreed with a firm nod, as though she had imparted the world's most obvious truth. Then, without warning, she stood up, which was the universal signal that the conversation was officially over. "But let us not dwell on what tomorrow may or may not bring. Tonight we celebrate, to welcome our new friends. The preparations for a great feast have already begun in your honor."

"We should keep moving," Thane responded.

"Please. The storm shall last through the night, and likely into tomorrow, so it's not as if you have anywhere to go," Grikna interjected. "Feast with us and when the snows melt, you may continue your journey."

---

as chalk and a very large, angry cheese that enjoys breaking things. This confusion can be traced back to a famous linguist who, in one of his earliest works, mistakenly referred to Orcs as Goblins. To be fair, he was distracted at the time by an unhealthy infatuation with the phrase '*cellar door*,' much to his wife's chagrin. Unfortunately, the error persisted and has been stubbornly entrenched in common belief ever since.

Orcs, in truth, are much larger than Goblins, with muscles that could put a brick wall to shame and a temper to match. They typically stand between seven and eight feet tall, depending on how recently they've been in a fight (Orcs have a tendency to hunch when they're angry, which is most of the time). Their skin ranges in color from mottled green to dark gray, as though they've spent most of their lives in a dimly lit cave, which, incidentally, they have. Goblins, on the other hand, are much smaller, scrawnier, and altogether more likely to sneak off with your socks than start a brawl. Where Orcs rely on brute strength, Goblins prefer cunning and, more often than not, selective invisibility at the first sign of trouble. In short, mistaking an Orc for a Goblin is like confusing a runaway boulder for an overexcited squirrel.

Thane started, "I don't think—"

"We would be honored," Tianna cut him off smoothly, shooting him a glare that clearly said, '*If you argue, I will feed you to the Orcs myself.*'

"Then it is decided," Grikna said with satisfaction. "Afterward, your party may sleep here in the village. You have a long journey ahead in the coming days, a good rest will likely do you all good."

"We are grateful for your hospitality." Tianna offered a polite bow to the Goblin.

Grikna returned the bow with all the formality one could expect from a Goblin, a brief dip of the head and a grunt of acknowledgment.

The feast was better than expected. Given Goblin cuisine's infamous reputation which was usually spoken of in hushed tones or followed by phrases like '*—and then we had to burn the tent down*'. The party had braced themselves for the worst. But to their surprise, the food was, edible. Actually, it was almost *good*, if you didn't think too hard about what was on your plate. Or look at it directly.

The tables had been set up in the great hall right off the town square, and it appeared as if the entire town had shown up. The sound of singing and merrymaking filled the hall. At one end of the building, a raging fire burned, keeping the biting cold from the storm at bay.

Tianna cautiously poked at what she hoped was roasted tuber. Meanwhile Thane was busy chewing something that appeared to be meat, though what kind of animal it came from was anyone's guess. Nyx, not bound by any social niceties, was happily devouring whatever had been set in front of him with the enthusiasm of a creature that had long ago stopped caring.

Rea had wolfed down her meal and was now off with the Goblin boy, who she'd learned was named Grok. He had a mischievous grin and an endless supply of energy that made it hard not to follow his lead. At the far end of the hall, a cluster of Goblin children had gathered around a makeshift game. They were armed with slingshots, each taking turns firing at straw targets that swayed and jerked unpredictably on strings strung from the rafters.

The targets weren't simple dummies; they were adorned with crude, comical faces painted in bright colors, some with oversized noses or lopsided grins. The Goblin children shrieked with laughter every time someone hit one, causing it to spin wildly or fall apart in a flurry of straw. Rea watched as Grok stepped up, his tongue poking out in concentration as he pulled back his slingshot, aiming at a particularly tricky target that darted side to side. He released the pebble with a snap, and it struck the target dead center, sending the straw head flying off its body. The other children erupted into cheers, patting him on the back like he'd won a great battle.

When it was Rea's turn, she hesitated, gripping her slingshot nervously. The Goblins' chatter quieted as they watched her, their glowing eyes glinting with curiosity. She took aim at a wobbling target, her heart pounding. Her shot sailed wide, missing by a mile, and the Goblins burst into laughter, not cruel, but delighted. Grok nudged her with a toothy grin, encouraging her to try again.

Rea did so, and while her next shot wasn't perfect, it clipped the edge of the target. A small cheer rose from the group, and she felt a grin creeping across her face despite herself. The game continued, each turn filled with jeers, cheers, and the occasional tussle over who had scored best.

Despite the surrounding cheer, Blarg sat in stony silence, a deep frown etched across his face. His plate lay nearly untouched, the food cooling in front of him. He sat at the far end of the rough-hewn wooden table, his broad shoulders hunched as his sharp eyes tracked Grikna's every move. Each time she exchanged a word with another Goblin or offered one of her polite smiles, his brow furrowed further, like a wary farmer watching his barn door swing open on a windless night.

Blarg was no fool. Goblins didn't offer hospitality out of the goodness of their hearts. He'd seen enough of the world to know that kindness often came with strings attached—often tied securely around the wrists and ankles.

Tianna, focused on her food a little too much to notice the tension, leaned over to Thane. "I think this might be roast—"

"Don't say it," Thane interrupted quickly, his eyes flicking to his plate. "Just . . . eat."

As they ate, Goblins approached Grikna, one by one, their heads bowed as they whispered urgently in her ear. Each time, her expression remained impassive, but she gave a slight nod, sending the Goblins scurrying away into the shadows like nervous bureaucrats with bad news.

Blarg's scowl deepened. He had already found the hospitality suspicious, but now the constant stream of whispering Goblins was sending his sense of paranoia into overdrive. Grikna was up to something, and it wasn't just about keeping them well-fed.

After the fifth Goblin had whispered in Grikna's ear, she stood abruptly, the wooden chair scraping back across the flagstones. "My apologies. I will return soon. There is something that requires my attention."

Blarg narrowed his eyes, watching her as she disappeared out the door. His fingers twitched toward his hammer.

Tianna noticed the movement. "Blarg? Everything all right?"

Blarg grunted, still staring at the spot where Grikna had vanished. "Blarg does not like this one bit. Too much whispering. Too much skulking about. Goblins do not offer feasts without purpose. Blarg shall return soon."

Thane raised an eyebrow. "Where are you going?"

Blarg gave a stiff nod toward where Grikna had vanished. "Nature calls to Blarg," he muttered, though it sounded less like a need for the great outdoors and more like an impending interrogation.

"Please don't cause trouble." Thane whispered to Blarg. "Whether they are up to something or not, we are greatly outnumbered."

Blarg responded to Thane with a small grunt before rising from the table. He followed after Grikna, disappearing into the night.

Meanwhile, Tianna took another cautious bite of her meal, watching the other Goblins as they chatted among themselves. "Do you think Grikna's planning something? She seems nice enough," she said, her voice low.

Thane glanced around, making sure none of the Goblins were paying them too much attention. "I'd say something's going on. Whether it has to do with us, I'm not sure."

The feast continued, with the Goblins chattering in their guttural tongue, laughing at jokes the party couldn't understand, and generally enjoying themselves. But for Tianna, the shadow of Grikna's departure loomed in the back of her mind. Something was definitely up.

Blarg crouched in the shadows, doing his best to blend in, which was no small feat for a towering, muscle-bound warrior in a town of waist-high creatures. Snow swirled around him in relentless flurries, piling up against the rough-hewn walls and nearly burying the smaller huts. The wind howled like a hungry beast, tugging at his cloak and carrying with it an icy bite that made his breath fog in short, sharp puffs. To his credit, he was doing a decent job of remaining inconspicuous, if you didn't count the occasional clank of his hammer or the fact that he was roughly the size of a small boulder.

The faint glow of the great hall barely reached the outskirts now, its light dimmed by the blinding snowstorm. Long, flickering shadows danced in the distance, but there on the edge of Thinkleburrow, the storm had swallowed most of the light, leaving only a cold, creeping darkness. For Blarg, this was perfect. He didn't need to feel invisible, just invisible enough to spy on Goblin antics without being caught. It was, after all, his idea of stealth, which roughly translated to hiding a Behemoth behind a curtain.

He squinted through the driving snow, watching as Goblins scurried about, their tiny forms darting between doorways like frantic ants trying to beat the storm. Their guttural chatter was mostly lost to the howling wind, but every now and then, Blarg caught snatches of their nervous glances and hurried movements. It was enough to confirm what he already knew: Goblins were always up to something, even in the worst weather.

His eyes narrowed when he saw her—Grikna. She moved through the storm with an uncharacteristic determination, her brisk steps cutting through the snow like a blade. Unlike her fellow Goblins, who were content to scuttle and shuffle, Grikna had purpose, and Blarg didn't like it one bit. To him, purpose in a Goblin was suspicious at best and outright betrayal at worst.

Then, he saw them.

Blarg's face twisted into a grim expression of vindication. It was the expression a man wears when he's finally proven right about the dead rat at the bottom of the stew pot. "Lying Goblin," he muttered to himself, his voice barely audible over the wind but filled with quiet satisfaction, as though betrayal was the vindication he'd been waiting for.

Four hulking figures emerged from the swirling snow behind Grikna, their movements slow and deliberate, their forms unmistakably menacing even through the storm's chaos. They were too large to be Goblins, and their gait was too deliberate to be anything but trouble. The snow whipped around them, clinging to their broad shoulders as they stepped closer, their presence out-menacing the storm itself.

Orcs.

16

The Midnight Thread

"Trust a Goblin, lose a toe. Trust an Orc, lose your soul. That's just math."

— Commander Brask Cleftjaw,
Grand Marshal of the Seventh Imperial Battalion

Goblins are the nightmares that human children whisper about when the lights go out. They're the creatures lurking beyond the safety of their blankets, hiding under beds and in the shadows of wardrobes, waiting with gleaming eyes and toothy grins. Parents, ever the optimists, try to soothe their little ones by saying things like, *'There are no Goblins here,'* but deep down, everyone knows that's just wishful thinking. Because somewhere, in some dark corner of the world, or perhaps behind the pantry door, a Goblin is skulking about, up to something. Mischief and mayhem are their bread and butter, usually served with a side of socks that *used* to belong to you. And if your stew suddenly tastes like it's had a fling with a handful of dirt, don't be too quick to blame the ingredients. Sometimes, it's the Goblins seasoning things . . . creatively.

But as terrifying as Goblins are to the average human child, safe in their human towns, armed with a security blanket and stuffed Dragon plushie, Orcs are worse. *Much* worse.

If Goblins are the things that keep children awake at night, Orcs are what wake adults in a cold sweat, possibly screaming. While Goblins are sly, quick, and more than a little annoying, Orcs are about as subtle as a brick through a stained-glass window. They don't hide under beds; they rip the beds apart to see what's underneath. Orcs don't scurry about in shadows. They *are* the shadows, heavy and oppressive, swallowing light wherever they tread. And with them comes a chill, not just in the air, but in the kind that seeps into your very bones, making you question every choice you've made up to that point, like building a house on solid ground instead of several dozen feet in the air.

Orcs are towering, brutish figures whose very presence doesn't just suck the warmth out of a room. It borrows it, never returns it, and then charges you extra for the privilege. Human children may fear Goblins, but they fear Orcs in the way you fear a thunderstorm that's directly over your house: not with anxious glances, but with an overwhelming certainty that something terrible is about to happen, and there's absolutely nothing you can do about it except hope you remembered to pay the insurance.

Goblins might give you nightmares, but Orcs? They turn nightmares into reality, give them a cozy place to stay, and make sure they feel right at home for the long haul.

So, it should come as little surprise that Blarg was not at all happy to see those four dark Orcish figures lurking on the outskirts of town. Even less happy that his *host*, a Goblin who had cheerfully offered them food and shelter, was in cahoots with them. In fact, if there was a sliding scale of displeasure, Blarg had quickly moved from *'mildly irritated'* to *'seething rage,'* bypassing *'grumpy'* entirely.

It wasn't that Blarg disliked Goblins or Orcs *specifically*, he disliked *everyone* equally, which was, in his opinion, the fairest way to go about life. After all, if you hated everyone just the right amount, there was no room for bias, and Blarg was nothing if not just. But Orcs, they had a special talent for turning any situation from bad to worse, usually by adding their own unique blend of smashing, yelling, and the systematic destruction of personal property. Which, under ordinary circumstances, Blarg could tolerate, provided *he* was the one doing the smashing. But seeing a Goblin, especially a Goblin hostess, conspiring with them was enough to make Blarg's hammer hand twitch in ways that only ended in splinters and painful moaning.

"What are you up to, Grikna?" Blarg muttered under his breath, his voice nearly lost in the howl of the wind. Snow lashed against his face, stinging like tiny needles, but his narrowed eyes stayed locked on the dark, hulking shapes moving behind her. Orcs didn't do stealth. Orcs attempting stealth was like watching a Troll try ballet, it didn't work, and it only made everyone involved feel deeply uncomfortable. The mere fact they were even trying now made everything feel more wrong. Blarg was fairly certain they were violating some ancient law of nature by attempting subtlety. It wasn't just unnatural, it was downright suspicious.

The snowstorm swirled with ferocity, the gusting wind carrying away nearly all sound except for its own relentless roar. Blarg's instincts screamed at him to charge in, hammer swinging, and make a mess of whatever conspiracy was afoot. But for now, his brain, never his favorite organ, won the argument. He needed to know what they were up to before he started flattening skulls. However, one thing was clear: whatever was happening wasn't going to end with polite handshakes and a cup of tea. Orcs didn't do tea. In fact, Orcs couldn't even lift a tea cup without shattering it into a thousand pieces.

Blarg trudged after them, his massive boots crunching through the deepening snow. His attempt at quiet was about as subtle as a boulder rolling downhill. Yet it didn't matter. The howling wind and swirling snow served as perfect cover, obscuring his approach. The Orcs were too focused on their task to notice him, and Goblins, by nature, had an uncanny ability to ignore anything that wasn't currently about to squish them.

Their path led further from the comforting flicker of the great hall, its firelight now barely visible through the storm, and deeper into the cold, oppressive gloom. Snow clung to his beard and clothes, turning him into a moving mound of frost and leather. Ahead, Grikna and the Orcs stopped in front of a small, dilapidated shack. It was barely more than a pile of sticks held together by hope, mud, and a mutual agreement not to think too hard about gravity.

The door creaked open, its hinges protesting loudly even against the wailing storm, and Grikna slipped inside, followed by the Orcs. Each of their hulking frames squeezed through the doorway with all the grace of a horse trying to sneak into a broom closet. Blarg edged closer, his movements stiff from the cold, and pressed himself against the side of the shack. Snowflakes swirled around him, clinging to the rough wood, and the icy wind found every gap in his clothes, gnawing at his skin. He tilted his head toward the grimy window, its glass fogged over with age and frost, enough to catch the faint outlines inside.

His suspicions flared to life when he saw Grikna pull back what appeared to be an old, tattered rug in the center of the room. Beneath it lay a trapdoor. Of course, no self-respecting Goblin would construct a dwelling without one. It was practically a design requirement, right next to dusty corners and mysterious creaks.

Blarg's mind raced as he watched the scene unfold. A secret meeting between Goblins and Orcs. A hidden trapdoor. It wasn't hard to guess what this meant. This wasn't a late-night snack run. Something serious was happening, and if Blarg had learned one thing in his life, it was that serious things rarely involved anything pleasant. They usually involved a lot of blood, some form of betrayal, and a headache that lasted three days.

Grikna pulled open the trapdoor, and one by one, the Orcs descended into the basement below. Their massive frames vanished into the darkness without a sound. The storm outside grew fiercer, the wind rattling the loose planks of the shack, as if the world itself was trying to warn him off. But Blarg wasn't one for warnings.

"Aye," Blarg muttered to himself, flexing his fingers around *Thumpkin's* handle as the icy metal bit into his palm. Cracking his knuckles in anticipation, he grinned against the wind. "Enough skulking about."

Without a second thought, and barely a first, Blarg charged the door. His shoulder slammed into the flimsy wood with a resounding crack. The storm howled in approval. The door didn't just open, it disintegrated off its hinges. Splinters went flying as Blarg raged into the shack, hammer raised, ready for action.

"Blarg?" Grikna's voice was laced with shock, her eyes wide as she stepped back.

"No more games," Blarg growled, his eyes blazing. "You have made a deal with the Dark Lord!"

"What? No!" Grikna threw her hands up in a hasty, placating gesture. "I know how this looks. But you have it wrong! These Orcs, they are friends. They have fled the Dark Ones army and are hiding here."

Blarg's grip on *Thumpkin* didn't loosen. He stood there, every muscle tense, staring at her with suspicion still etched deep into his face. "Flee? What for? Orcs don't run. They fight. They break things. That's basically all they do."

"Orcs want to fight, for Orcs, *not* for the Dark One." As she said this, two Orcs peeked up the hidden stairwell, heavy weariness on their faces. "My group helps them."

"Blarg doesn't understand. What group?"

"Unlike Goblins who choose to fight for the Dark One, Orcs are forced to. They cannot resist the call. But for some, that urge can weaken. They choose to be free. They choose to escape. The Midnight Thread, that is what we are called. We are a group of like-minded Goblins that are against the tyranny of the Dark One. Orcs are slaves, fighting against their will. We believe that all creatures deserve to be free. No thinking creature should be forced under the shadow of a tyrant. The stars weave our path."

"The stars weave our path?" Blarg repeated back.

"Ghaz'ak thrakk varg zath, as our Orc brothers and sisters say.[88] It is a promise of freedom. A promise to all that our destinies have yet to be fulfilled."

---

[88] "The stars weave our path." A deeply spiritual saying among Orcs. However, be careful not to mispronounce *varg* as *vorg*, a minor slip that turns the phrase into a vicious insult about one's mother and her tragically poor taste in fermented root stew. Entire blood feuds have started over less.

"But Orcs have never been fond of Goblins. Why would you choose to help them?" Blarg asked, his brow furrowing.

Grikna tilted her head, her sharp eyes glinting in the dim light. "I could say the same about you. Your kind has terrorized my kind for generations, yet here you are. I would not turn you away, someone in need, any more than I would turn away an Orc looking for deliverance."

Blarg shifted uncomfortably, gripping his hammer tighter. "Blarg doesn't understand any of this," he admitted, his voice edged with frustration.

Grikna gave him a small, almost pitying smile. "That's understandable, Blarg. You've spent your entire life thinking we are your enemies." She paused, her gaze flicking toward the distant snowstorm that rattled the walls. "But tell me this: who told you we were enemies? Your people? Your leaders? Have you ever stopped to wonder why?"

Blarg's frown deepened. "Because Goblins scheme. Orcs smash. That's what you do."

"And humans take," Grikna shot back, her voice cutting through the air like a blade. "You take land, lives, resources, whatever you please. Yet, you don't see me raising a hammer to *you* right now, do you?"

Blarg opened his mouth, then closed it, uncertain how to respond. His instinct was to argue, but the fire in Grikna's gaze made him hesitate. She stepped closer, her voice softer but no less firm.

"We're all pawns, Blarg, all of us common folk. Whether we're human, Goblin, or even Orc, we're all caught in the same storm, used by powers that care nothing for us. The only reason you think we're so different is because someone decided it was better to keep us fighting each other than to let us see the truth."

Blarg snorted, though the sound lacked conviction. "And what truth is that?"

"That we're stronger together," Grikna said simply, her voice steady. "You don't have to believe me now, but maybe someday you will see the world for the way it truly is."

Blarg's fingers flexed around the handle of his hammer, his jaw tightening. "Words are cheap. Show Blarg why he should trust you."

Grikna smirked. "I don't expect you to trust me. But remember that it was you who came to this town, hammer in hand and murder in your eyes, simply because you didn't like what you saw. We took you in, gave you a warm fire, a hot meal, and nothing but hospitality. Yet here I am, forced to justify myself to you."

Blarg blinked, caught between indignation and the dawning realization that she had a point. "Fair enough," he muttered, grudgingly lowering his hammer. "But Blarg still doesn't trust you."

Grikna chuckled and turned back toward the trapdoor. "You don't have to. Just don't do anything stupid while you're here, or we're going to have a problem. Now please return to the feast. I will join you after I have finished up here."

Blarg stood there for a moment, watching as Grikna vanished through the opening in the floor, her figure swallowed by the flickering light of the cellar. The muted creak of the door closing behind her echoed in his ears, blending with the muffled roar of the storm outside. Every instinct in him screamed to follow, to demand more answers, to uncover whatever she was *really* doing with those Orcs. But her words lingered, needling at him: *'Don't do anything stupid while you're here.'*

Blarg let out a sharp exhale, his breath fogging in the cold air that crept in through the broken door. "You're lucky Blarg's in a good mood," he muttered to the empty room. With a final glance at the closed trapdoor, he turned on his heels and stepped back out into the storm.

The wind hit him like a wall, sharp and relentless, tearing at his clothes. Snow whipped around him, blinding and unyielding, as if the storm itself were trying to keep him from returning to the great hall. He trudged forward, his boots crunching through the deep snow, each step more laborious than the last. The faint glow of the great hall flickered in the distance, barely visible through the swirling white.

Blarg's mind churned as he walked, Grikna's words tangling with his own suspicions. *"Stronger together?"* he scoffed under his breath. "Sounds like something someone would say right before stabbing you in the back." But even as he grumbled, he couldn't shake the feeling that there was more to her story, more to this whole mess, than he'd allowed himself to see.

A sudden gust of wind sent a flurry of snow into his face, forcing him to shield his eyes. When he lowered his arm, the great hall appeared farther away than before, the storm closing in around him. The cheerful sounds of Goblin chatter and laughter had all but disappeared, replaced by the eerie howl of the wind. For a moment, Blarg felt an unfamiliar pang in his chest, a sense of isolation, as though he were the last living soul in a world of ice and shadow.

"Don't go soft now, Blarg," he muttered to himself, gripping the handle of his hammer for reassurance. He pressed on, his steps quicker now, the distant glow of the hall his only guide. The storm clawed at him, but Blarg's sheer stubbornness carried him forward.

Finally, the hall loomed ahead, its wooden walls glowing warmly against the oppressive cold. Blarg reached the door and shoved it open, stepping into the heat and noise of the Goblin feast. The sudden change in atmosphere was almost overwhelming. The storm's howls were replaced by laughter. The biting cold gave way to the smoky warmth of the fire.

Tianna was the first to notice him, her wide eyes lighting up with curiosity. "Blarg! You were out there for a while. Did you find Grikna?"

Blarg shook the snow from his clothes and grunted. "Found her. She's . . . busy."

Tianna tilted her head, curiosity flickering in her eyes, but Blarg wasn't in the mood to explain. Without a word, he strode toward the fire, brushing past the curious glances of the Goblins. He sank heavily into a chair by the hearth, stretching out his legs as the warmth began to thaw his frozen limbs. Nyx, already curled up near the flames, cracked one eye open, gave him a disinterested glance, and promptly went back to sleep.

As he sat there, staring into the fire, a strange feeling settled over Blarg, heavy and unwelcome. It was like the flickering flames had reached inside him, stirring up something buried deep, something he didn't recognize. His chest felt tight, as if suffocating within his own skin. The heat of the fire couldn't quite reach him, leaving a cold knot in his stomach that refused to ease.

He shifted in his chair, restless, but the feeling clung to him like damp clothes. For the first time in his life, Blarg found himself unsure. Not about the swing of a hammer or the strength of his arm. Those things were as solid as the ground beneath him. No, this was different. It was as if every decision he'd made today echoed back at him in the crackle of the flames, each one asking a question he didn't know how to answer.

The thought gnawed at him: *What if Blarg's been wrong?* Blarg blinked hard, scowling at the fire as though it had betrayed him by bringing such thoughts to mind. He clenched his fists, the familiar strength of his hands offering some reassurance, but not nearly enough. Not this time.

The warmth of the hall, the chatter of the Goblins, even the faint snore of Nyx nearby, all of it felt distant, disconnected. Blarg had always known what needed doing, always trusted his instincts to guide him. Yet now, for reasons he couldn't name, the certainty that had carried him through countless battles faltered, leaving a void where confidence had always been.

He no longer knew what to believe.

17

Bread, Baths, and Begone

"In Goblin culture, sharing bread means peace. In imperial culture, it usually means they've run out of soldiers."

— Common Goblin Saying,
Translated from Snagblat

The group stayed the night in one of the empty houses near the town center. The modest structure leaned slightly to one side, as though it had grown tired of standing upright after decades of harsh winters. Inside, the furniture was sparse but sturdy, possibly because it was nailed to the floor. There was the faint scent of wood smoke that lingered in the air, a nostalgic reminder of simpler times when the house hadn't been half a degree from collapse.

Thane and Blarg took turns keeping watch through the night, their silhouettes framed against the frost-covered windows. Blarg had insisted on taking the first shift, muttering something about the Goblins being up to no good. By the time Thane took over, the snowstorm had eased, its winds reduced to soft whispers. It was as if the storm had given up on its aspirations of drama and settled for passive-aggressive muttering against the shutters.

For Tianna and Rea, the chance to sleep in real beds, though lumpy, slightly musty, and Goblin-sized, was a luxury they hadn't realized they missed so much. Rea insisted hers was "just fine" while subtly trying to avoid the crater-like dip in the middle. Nyx had claimed his usual spot at the foot of Rea's bed.

He was curled into a perfect ball of fur, occasionally letting out a contented purr.

By dawn, the storm had finally passed. Outside, the town was transformed into a pristine winter wonderland, the kind you'd find on the front of a postcard that conveniently omitted the bitter cold and thigh-deep snowbanks. These snowbanks now barricaded the roads in and out of town, ensuring that travel was as much an option as flying to the top of the Spire with nothing but a strong gust of wind. The group was left with no choice but to hunker down and wait for conditions to improve.

Grikna arrived early in the morning, stomping the snow from her boots as she let herself in. Despite the frost that reddened her cheeks, she carried a warmth with her that filled the room. "Morning," she said, setting a basket of fresh bread and a steaming pot of something that smelled faintly of roasted roots on the table. Her tone was cheerful, but her gaze lingered on Blarg much too long, her smile tightening slightly at the corners.

Blarg, seated by the fire and polishing *Thumpkin* with slow, deliberate circles, grunted his acknowledgment. The cloth moved over the hammer's surface with methodical precision, polishing it to a pristine shine. He didn't glance up, but the tension in his broad shoulders suggested their clash the previous night hadn't left his mind. His fingers tightened slightly around the handle, as if the act of tending to his weapon was the only thing keeping his temper in check.

Grikna, undeterred, turned to the humans with a brighter smile. "How are you settling in? Beds not too lumpy, I hope? We Goblins aren't known for luxury, but we make do with what we have."

"They were perfect," Tianna insisted, though her rumpled hair suggested otherwise. Rea nodded enthusiastically, clearly having decided that any bed was better than sleeping on the ground.

"Good," Grikna replied, her gaze softening as she glanced toward the frost-covered windows. "You'll have to stay put for a bit longer, I'm afraid. The roads won't be clear until the snow melts some. But don't worry, we'll see that you're comfortable."

Her words carried an undertone of resolve, as if making sure the humans were cared for was not just hospitality but a matter of pride. Blarg finally raised his head, his eyes meeting hers briefly before he returned to his task. He said nothing, but his silence carried less of the edge than it had the night before.

The day stretched ahead, quiet and uncertain, but for now, they were warm, fed, and safe. It was a rare reprieve; one they hadn't dared hope for, but one they all knew wouldn't last.

They came on the second night.

The first sign was the distant clatter of metal, faint but unmistakable in the cold, still air. By the time the group roused themselves, the sounds of boots crunching through snow filled the quiet streets. A dozen Goblins in full battle armor stood at each side of the town, their weapons gleaming faintly in the moonlight. They were grim-faced, their postures tense and unyielding as they formed an impenetrable barricade, preventing anyone from entering or leaving.

Torches flared to life, casting flickering light over the snowbanks and shadows that danced across the uneven rooftops. The air smelled of burning pitch and something sharper—fear. There was a sense around them that the possibility of violence balanced on a knife's edge.

The sound of a quiet knocking jolted the group to full attention. Tianna scrambled to the door, her hand hesitating on the latch as Blarg hefted *Thumpkin* with a warning grunt. "Careful," he muttered, his eyes narrowing.

"Grikna sent me!" came a hurried whisper from outside. "Let me in before they see me!"

Tianna pulled the door open just enough for a Goblin to slip inside. It was Fizzik, one of the friendly Goblins from the town, who had been keeping an eye on them since their arrival. He was breathing hard, his small frame shivering from the cold as he hurriedly shut the door behind him.

"They're here," he panted, clutching his knees for a moment before straightening. His eyes darted around the room. "An envoy from the Dark One. They've blocked the town and are going door to door. They're searching for deserters."

Outside, the armored Goblins swarmed through the town, their movements precise and deliberate. They went to each house, their armored fists pounding against the wooden frames with authority. The unlucky ones who didn't answer quickly enough found their doors kicked in, splinters scattering like startled insects.

The group crowded around the window, their breath fogging the glass as they watched the confrontation unfold. Grikna stood in the center of the square, her breath visible in the frigid air, her posture as firm as if she were lecturing unruly children. Surrounding her, armored Goblins stood rigidly at attention, their torches casting dramatic shadows across the snow-covered ground. The envoy towered over her, his armor so heavy it seemed more for intimidation than practicality.

"What are they saying?" Tianna whispered, her voice barely audible over the distant bark of orders.

Fizzik crouched beside her, pressed his ear to the window, and winced. "She's telling them there are no deserters here. Says they've got the wrong town."

Blarg snorted. "As if that's going to work."

"Shh," Thane hissed, his eyes fixed on the scene outside.

Grikna's voice rose, steady and commanding, though the Goblin tongue made it sound harsh and guttural to human ears. Fizzik muttered a hurried translation. "She's calling them out. She knows some of them. She even mentions names. Says she remembers them from when they were young. Asks if this is the kind of life they wanted, working for the Dark One."

Tianna glanced at Fizzik, her brow furrowed. "She's trying to guilt them?"

Fizzik nodded, his small hands gripping the windowsill. "Grikna knows them. She's smart. She'll use whatever she can."

The envoy took a menacing step forward, his deep voice rumbling through the square. Fizzik's ears drooped as he translated. "He's not buying it. Says the town's always been full of traitors. If she doesn't hand over the deserters, they'll burn it down."

Tianna's eyes widened, and she turned to Blarg. "They can't really mean that, can they?"

Blarg's jaw tightened, his knuckles whitening as he gripped *Thumpkin*. "Oh, they mean it."

Back in the square, Grikna's expression didn't falter. She crossed her arms, her voice rising again, sharp and biting. Fizzik squinted as he listened. "She's daring them. Says if they think she's lying, they should search every house, every cellar, every barn themselves. Says they won't find what they're looking for."

Blarg let out a low growl. "She's buying time."

"She's also poking the giant," Thane muttered.

The envoy raised a hand, and the armored Goblins surrounding him shifted, their weapons glinting in the torchlight. For a tense moment, it appeared as though he might order them to attack. But instead, he spoke again, his voice cold and deliberate.

Fizzik translated quickly, his voice trembling. "He says they'll search every inch of the town. And if they find she's hiding anything, anything at all, she'll be the first to burn."

Blarg muttered something under his breath, gripping his hammer tighter. Grikna's response came quickly, her voice unwavering as she pointed directly at the envoy, her words sharp and clipped.

Fizzik's ears perked up, and a flicker of admiration crossed his face. "She just told him he's not half the Goblin his father was. Says she remembers his father. He was brave and loyal to his people. He wasn't some lackey for the Dark One."

Blarg barked a laugh, though it held no humor. "She's got guts, Blarg will give her that."

The envoy's posture stiffened, his gauntleted hand twitching at his side. For a moment, the square fell silent, the tension so thick even the snow stopped falling. Finally, the envoy lowered his hand and barked an order. The armored Goblins fanned out, joining their comrades who were already searching the houses.

"They're going to search," Fizzik whispered, his voice barely audible over the distant clamor of armored boots. "We've got to move."

"Let me guess—running?" Sword said flatly.

Thane nodded sharply, already gathering their belongings with quick, efficient movements. "Fizzik, is there another way out of here?"

"Ha!"

Fizzik hesitated, his gaze darting toward the frosted window, where shadows danced ominously in the torchlight outside. "You're not going to like it," he said, his voice low.

"I don't think we have a choice at this point," Thane replied, his tone clipped but calm. He slung his pack over his shoulder and turned to face Fizzik. "What is it?"

The Goblin glanced at each of them in turn, as if weighing their resolve. "Okay," he muttered reluctantly. "There's a reason Grikna put you in this house." He scurried toward the hearth, where glowing embers smoldered faintly. "She knew it had a way out, if you're desperate enough to use it."

Fizzik crouched by the rough stone, his small hands tracing the grooves with practiced precision. "Right here." He stopped and pulled a small, tarnished key from around his neck, the chain glinting faintly in the dim light. "This is why Grikna sent me to help you."

He slid the key into a barely visible opening between two stones. With a soft click, the entire section of wall shifted, groaning as it swung open to reveal a dark, yawning staircase that spiraled downward into the earth. A gust of stale air rushed out, carrying with it the faint scent of damp stone and decay.

The group stared in silence, down into the darkness. Tianna swallowed hard, her voice barely steady as she asked, "Where does it lead?"

Fizzik gazed back at her, his face unusually solemn. "Centuries ago, there was a great city here, before it was burned to the ground by the Dark One's army. All that's left now are the catacombs." He paused, his fingers tightening around the key. "If you follow this tunnel north, it'll take you out of the valley and far beyond the town."

Blarg, standing with *Thumpkin* balanced on one shoulder, squinted at the dark opening. "Sounds too easy," he said gruffly. "What's the catch?"

Fizzik hesitated, then sighed. "Nobody goes into the catacombs anymore. Not for generations. There are . . . stories. Warnings passed down from our elders. Strange noises. Shadows that move where they shouldn't. People who went in and never came out."

"Haunted tunnels. Lovely," Blarg said with a smile.

"We don't have another option," Thane said firmly. "If we stay here, those enforcers will find us, and I doubt they'll listen to reason."

Fizzik nodded. "Grikna thought this might happen. That's why she sent me to you. If you're quick, they'll never know that you were here." He glanced nervously at the staircase. "Just . . . don't linger. Whatever's down there, it doesn't like visitors."

Rea clutched Nyx tighter, the cat's fur bristling as if sensing the unease in the room. "We'll be okay, right?" she asked, her voice small.

"We'll be fine," Tianna said quickly, though her hands trembled as she adjusted her pack. "Right, Thane?"

Thane placed a reassuring hand on her shoulder, his expression unreadable. "We'll keep moving. Stay alert. That's all we can do."

Fizzik stepped back, gesturing toward the open stairwell. "It'll take you far from here. But you'll have to leave now. I'll close the entrance behind you."

Tianna hesitated at the edge of the staircase, peering into the darkness below. "What about you? What happens if they find out you helped us?"

Fizzik grinned faintly, a flicker of mischief breaking through. "I'm a Goblin. Talking my way out of trouble is in my blood." His grin faded, replaced by a rare seriousness. Quietly, he added, "Just . . . make it count, okay? Don't waste what Grikna is risking for you."

Blarg grunted, stepping past Tianna and onto the first step. "'Tis time for action, not chatter." He hesitated, glancing back at Fizzik. "Tell Grikna . . . thank you." He winced as the words came out, as if saying them had caused physical harm.

Before Fizzik could respond, Blarg turned and disappeared into the darkness below, his heavy boots echoing faintly against the stone.

Thane reached for an unlit torch from a wall sconce. He kneeled by the hearth, holding the torch to the glowing embers until a small flame sputtered to life, flickering weakly before steadying. He straightened, the new light casting long, jagged shadows across the room.

One by one, the rest of the group followed, their footsteps growing softer as the shadows swallowed them. Tianna hesitated for a moment, giving Fizzik a small nod of gratitude before descending. Rea clutched Nyx tightly, the cat's green eyes catching the torchlight for an instant before they too were gone.

Fizzik lingered, staring into the void where they had vanished. With a deep breath, he stepped forward and swung the hidden door shut. The stone groaned as it sealed into place, the faint click of the lock echoing in the stillness. For a moment, he stood there, his hand resting against the cold surface.

The silence pressed down like a weight, broken only by his murmured words: "Good luck." Then, squaring his shoulders, he turned and disappeared into the night.

18

Six Hundred Years of Solitude

"It's not the silence that haunts you. It's who you might end up sharing it with."

— Spirish Proverb

The stairs went on forever, spiraling downward into what felt like the bowels of the world. Each step groaned under their weight, as if the ancient stone was protesting their decision to disturb its long-standing peace. The air grew cooler with every step, carrying a faint, damp scent of decay and moldy socks.

When they finally reached the bottom, the flickering light of Thane's torch illuminated a sprawling tunnel. Its walls were lined with jagged carvings that had been lovingly crafted by someone with all the artistic skill of a drunken goat. Shadows danced across the uneven stone, and the distant sound of dripping water echoed faintly, as if the catacombs were whispering secrets.

Blarg sniffed, his nose wrinkling. "Smells like something died down here."

Thane glanced at him. "It's a crypt. Everything died down here."

"That's no excuse," Blarg grumbled. "They could burn some incense or something."

Rea clutched Nyx tightly, the cat perched in her arms with a look of utter indifference, as if centuries-old haunted tunnels were just another day. The torchlight reflected in his eyes, giving him an otherworldly glow that made him appear right at home in the gloom.

The passage ahead stretched into darkness, its ceiling arching low enough for Blarg to have to tilt his head slightly as he walked. Thane held the torch higher, revealing cobwebs that could ensnare a small horse. Somewhere in the distance, a faint scuttling noise echoed, making Rea jump and causing Nyx to perk up his ears.

"What was that?" she whispered.

"Probably just a rat," Thane said, though his hand instinctively went to his axe.

"We could smash it," Sword chimed in.

Blarg hefted *Thumpkin* onto his shoulder, the hammer gleaming faintly in the dim light. "Whatever it is, Blarg is ready for it."

Tianna squinted at the carvings on the walls as they walked. "What do these even mean?" she asked, pointing to a crude depiction of what appeared to be a Goblin riding a very alarmed chicken into battle.

Blarg snorted. "Never try to understand a Goblin."

They pressed on, the tunnel winding deeper into the earth. The faint dripping of water was occasionally broken by odd noises, a faint whisper here, a hollow thud there. Each sound came from nowhere and everywhere all at once, as though the catacombs were trying to decide whether to spook them or just let them pass.

As they rounded a corner, the torchlight revealed a cluster of Goblin skeletons slumped against the wall. One of them had a broken sword in its bony hand, while another was wearing what might generously be called a hat.

Rea gulped. "Are they . . . are they going to move?"

Nyx hopped down from her arms and padded over to sniff at the closest skeleton. When nothing happened, he casually batted at the 'hat,' sending it tumbling to the floor.

"They're just decorations," Tianna said, though she didn't appear entirely convinced.

"Decorations, my foot," Blarg muttered. "This place is a death trap."

The catacombs stretched on, a labyrinth of twists and turns, each corner promising either treasure or doom. The oppressive atmosphere weighed heavy, but it was hard to feel too frightened when the carvings on the walls became more and more absurd. They featured Goblins engaging in increasingly ridiculous activities, like juggling flaming swords or trying to milk what appeared to be an angry chimera.

Tianna sighed. "This is going to be a long night, isn't it?"

Thane nodded, his face grim as ever. "Very long."

From the shadows, the faint sound of a distant laugh echoed through the catacombs. It was a hollow, chilling sound that sent a shiver down Tianna's spine.

Tianna shifted her eyes nervously. "Great. Now this place is laughing at us."

The passageway opened into a vast circular chamber that looked as if someone had tried to create a replica of a throne room. Elaborate archways lined the walls, each housing the remains of both humans and Goblins arranged with careful precision. Unlike the haphazard decorations in the tunnel, these bodies had been laid to rest with obvious reverence.

"Oh look, more decorations," Blarg said sarcastically, eyeing a particularly ornate display where a human and Goblin skeleton sat together on what appeared to be thrones made of compressed dirt and bone.

"Quiet!" A raspy voice echoed through the chamber. "Some of us are trying to rest in peace here!"

The group froze. Nyx's fur stood on end as he backed behind Rea's legs.

"Oh, stop being so dramatic, Herbert," another voice replied, this one higher-pitched and distinctly annoyed. "We haven't had visitors in over three hundred years. The least you could do is be hospitable."

The human skeleton on the throne shifted, its jaw clicking in irritation. "Hospitality? Grunch, we're dead. We don't host tea parties anymore."

"Speak for yourself," the Goblin skeleton replied, adjusting what appeared suspiciously like a bowtie made of cobwebs. "I've been working on my ethereal brewing technique."

Thane's grip on his axe loosened slightly as he shared a bewildered glance with Tianna. The two skeletons continued their bickering as if the living intruders weren't even there.

"That's why nobody visits," Herbert rattled on. "You keep trying to serve them tea that doesn't exist!"

"At least I'm trying! All you do is sit there composing tragic poetry about how dead you are. 'Oh woe is me, my flesh has fled, now I'm naught but bone instead.' It's been six centuries, we get it!"

"My poetry is profound!"

"Your poetry is why the rats moved out!"

Tianna cleared her throat loudly. "Uh, excuse me?"

Both skeletons turned their hollow eye sockets toward her. "WHAT?" they snapped in unison.

"Are you two . . . friends?" Tianna asked hesitantly.

"Best friends," Grunch said cheerfully.

"Worst mistake of my death," Herbert grumbled.

"Oh, like you had better options! Remember when you tried to befriend that ghost from the upper level? He kept walking through walls whenever you tried to talk to him!"

"At least he appreciated my poetry—"

"He was trapped in an eternal loop! He wasn't listening. He was stuck repeating the same three minutes over and over!"

Tianna stepped forward, fascinated despite herself. "How did you two end up here together?"

"Well," Grunch began, sitting up straighter and somehow managing to look proud despite lacking any facial features, "we grew up next door to each other. Funny story. One day in the market—"

"Don't you dare tell the market story," Herbert interrupted. "You always tell it wrong."

"I tell it exactly how it happened! You're just embarrassed because you fell into that merchant's cart of cabbages trying to catch my sister's runaway pet toad."

"I was not falling! I was . . . executing a tactical pursuit maneuver."

"Into a cabbage cart?"

"It was a very strategic cabbage cart!"

"Wait, wait," Tianna interrupted, holding up her hands. "You two grew up together? As in, humans and Goblins living in the same city? Peacefully?"

The two skeletons stopped their bickering and turned to stare at her.

"Obviously," Grunch said, as if explaining that water was wet. "His mom made the best honey cakes in the entire district."

"And his mother's mushroom stew!" Herbert added. "Never was another cook like her in all the city."

"But—" Tianna appeared bewildered. "Everything I've ever heard says humans and Goblins have always been enemies."

The skeletons shared what might have been an eye roll, if they still had eyes.

"Where we lived, there were plenty of humans and Goblins living together," Grunch said proudly.

"There were also a few Trolls here and there," Herbert added.

"That's right! We didn't always get along, but that's nothing new for neighbors living in close quarters. We lived down a back alley in the Baker's District. Herbert's family had the apartment next door."

Tianna glanced between them, still processing. "What happened? Why did it all change?"

The skeletons paused their bickering.

"How should *we* know?" Grunch asked. "We've been dead for six hundred years. Kind of missed out on recent history."

"Though I must say," Herbert added, "your reaction suggests things took an unfortunate turn."

"At least we still have the memories," Grunch said. "Like the time you tried to impress Felicity from the spice merchant's shop by reciting your terrible poetry—"

"My poetry is NOT terrible!"

"You rhymed 'spice' with 'spice' three times!"

"It was a creative repetition for emphasis!"

Nyx, having apparently decided the skeletons weren't a threat, sauntered over and began weaving between their legs. Grunch reached down to pet him, bony fingers clicking against each other.

"See? Even the cat has better manners than you, Herbert."

"The cat is alive. We are dead. There's a fundamental difference in social obligations."

Tianna leaned over to Thane and whispered, "Should we . . . do something about this?"

Thane shrugged. "Like what? Offer them relationship counseling?"

"I heard that!" both skeletons said in unison, then immediately turned to glare at each other for copying one another.

"Six hundred years," Herbert moaned. "Six hundred years of bad jokes and endless criticism of my artistic endeavors."

"Six hundred years of melodrama and terrible poetry," Grunch countered. "And yet somehow you're still my best friend, you bonehead."

"Was that . . . was that a pun?" Herbert's jaw fell open slightly.

"Maybe," Grunch replied with what could only be described as a skeletal smirk.

"That's it. I'm moving to the east chamber."

"You said that fifty years ago. You made it three steps before coming back because you were lonely."

"I was not lonely! There was a draft. It's bad for my ligaments."

"You don't have ligaments anymore! You're held together by pure stubbornness!"

The group watched this exchange, heads bouncing back and forth between the bickering skeletons. Even Nyx had settled down to watch, his tail twitching in amusement.

"Should we tell them about the Minotaur up ahead?" Grunch stage-whispered to Herbert.

"Shh! You'll ruin the surprise!"

"What Minotaur?" Tianna asked sharply.

"Oh, wonderful," Herbert sighed. "Now you've done it. This is why we can't have nice dramatic reveals anymore—"

"A Minotaur?" Blarg repeated, excitement in his voice. "What sort of Minotaur? Big? Small? Particularly fond of mazes?"

As if on cue, there was a loud crash from the corridor ahead, followed by the sound of pottery shattering and a confused "Oops."

"That'll be Maurice," Grunch said fondly. "He's been trying to reorganize the urns for the past century."[89]

Around the corner lumbered a sight that made the entire group stop in their tracks. Instead of the expected bull-headed creature, they found themselves staring at a massive bull's body topped with a bewildered-looking human head.

"Uh," Sword for once, was speechless.

"But . . . but that's not—" Blarg stammered. "Aren't Minotaurs supposed to be the other way around?"

"Maurice is special," Herbert said, with a gentleness that was at odds with his usual rattling complaints.[90]

---

[89] Like most beings of a certain age, Maurice had gone by many names. Some people called him the Starbound Shepherd, some called him the Rascal of Romance, but to most he was simply Maurice, who spoke of the pompatus of love . . . whatever that means.

[90] The term "special" here requires careful contextual consideration. While Minotaurs typically inherit the analytical capabilities of their human parentage combined with the raw strength of their bovine ancestry, Maurice's reversed configuration resulted in a unique cognitive inheritance. Having received his mental faculties from the bovine side of his family tree (a creature whose primary intellectual pursuits include determining the edibility of various grasses and perfecting the art of standing in fields), Maurice approaches life's complexities with a refreshingly pastoral perspective. His father's philosophical teachings, while well-intentioned, largely resulted in Maurice developing strong opinions about the directionality of plant growth and an impressive ability to count to almost seven.

It should be noted that Maurice's mother was considered exceptionally gifted among cows, having mastered both the art of counting to seven (on good days) and displaying what agricultural scholars termed "advanced grass selection criteria." These traits, when combined with his father's academic background, produced in Maurice a unique blend of bovine serenity and confused intellectual aspiration. While he may never grasp the finer points of metaphysics, he remains unmatched in his ability to identify comfortable patches of grass and provide unexpectedly profound observations about the nature of down versus up.

"Very special," Grunch agreed, his tone equally protective. "His father was a philosopher, his mother was a cow, and sometimes things just work out uniquely."

"And how does that work exactly?" Sword pondered. *"Actually, I'd rather not know, there could be children reading this."*

Maurice was wearing what appeared to be half a waistcoat (it only covered his human-headed front), and his expression was one of perpetual gentle confusion. "Oh!" he said brightly, noticing the group. "Hello! I was just . . . um—" He glanced down at the shattered pottery around his hooves. "I was helping the urns be closer to the ground." He appeared to be quite pleased with this explanation.

"Maurice," Herbert said patiently, "we talked about this. The urns are supposed to stay on the pedestals."

"But they look sad up high," Maurice protested, his human face scrunching up with genuine concern. "Everything's better on the ground. Like grass. Grass is nice." He paused thoughtfully. "I like grass."

Nyx padded over to investigate the broken pottery, and Maurice's face lit up with delight. "A cat! I like cats too. They're like small cows that climb things." He frowned. "Or are cows big cats that don't climb things?" This philosophical quandary deeply troubled him.

"Don't worry about it too much, Maurice," Grunch said kindly. "Remember what we said about the thinking headaches?"

"Oh yes!" Maurice nodded emphatically, then stopped suddenly. "No. Maybe? What did we say?"

Rea glanced at the skeletons, noting how they scooted slightly closer to Maurice, the way one might with a beloved but vulnerable friend. The lavender sachet around his neck tinkled softly as he attempted to gather the broken pottery with his hooves, managing only to scatter the pieces further.

"Here, let me help," Tianna offered, moving forward to gather the shards.

"You're nice," Maurice said, watching her with genuine appreciation. "Like grass. But person-shaped." He brightened suddenly. "Did you know grass grows up? Even though down is better. I asked Father why once, but he used his big words, and those make my head feel like it's full of hay."

"His father was a philosopher?" Thane asked the skeletons quietly.

"Wrote three books on rational thought," Herbert replied in an equally low voice. "The irony was not lost on him. But he loved Maurice more than all his logic texts combined."

"And Maurice's mother?"

"Prize-winning cow," Grunch whispered. "Very gentle. Could count to seven, which Maurice reminds us at least twice a day."

"My mother was very smart," Maurice announced proudly, having caught the last bit. "She could count to seven! Usually. And she gave the best milk in the city. Father said so. Father said lots of things though. Many things. Sometimes all at once." His face scrunched up. "Words are hard when there are too many of them."

Thane watched as Maurice carefully attempted to straighten his half-waistcoat with surprising gentleness. Despite his massive bull body, there was something undeniably endearing about his earnest attempts at propriety.

"Maurice," Thane said carefully, "we appear to be a bit lost in these tunnels. Do you know your way around down here?"

Maurice's face brightened. "Oh yes! No. Maybe?" He stamped a hoof thoughtfully. "I know where my hay is. And where the giggling boxes live. And where the walls are." He was particularly proud of that last observation. "The walls are very good at being walls. They never try to be floors."

"The giggling boxes?" Rea asked.

"They're very funny. Or maybe I'm funny. Someone's funny." He nodded sagely. "I try to tell them jokes, but they always laugh before I finish." His face fell slightly. "I forget the endings sometimes, anyway."

"He means the treasure room," Herbert explained. "Though you'll want to avoid that particular—"

"Treasure!" Maurice interrupted excitedly. "Yes! The funny boxes. They live near the way out. I remember because they told me. Or maybe I told them?" He frowned. "Someone told someone something."

"Could you show us?" Tianna asked gently.

"Show you what?" Maurice blinked. "Oh! The way out? I can do that. I think. Yes." He began to turn around, a process that involved considerably more space than one might expect and resulted in another urn teetering dangerously on its pedestal. "Oops. Sorry, tall pottery. Don't be sad."

"Maurice," Grunch called out fondly, "remember what we said about turning?"

"Three steps forward, then turn," Maurice recited proudly. "Because I'm big like Mother. But not as good at counting." He demonstrated the proper turning technique, beaming with accomplishment when no urns were harmed in the process.

"Just . . . be careful around the treasure room," Herbert warned the group. "The boxes in there are . . . special. Like Maurice."

"Special is good," Maurice agreed cheerfully, already starting down the corridor. "Father always said I was special. And Father was smart. He could count past seven and everything." He stopped suddenly, causing Blarg to nearly walk into his hindquarters. "Oh! We're walking. I should walk too. This way. Because that's where we're going."

The group followed Maurice's meandering path, while behind them, they could hear Grunch and Herbert's voices fading:

"Should we have warned them about the boxes' tickling problem?"

"Shh! You'll ruin the surprise!"

They walked for some time before Maurice came to a stop in front of an ornate doorway, causing another minor traffic jam. "Here's the funny room," he announced proudly. "The boxes live here. They're my friends. I think. They laugh at everything I say, so that means we're friends. Right?"

The chamber beyond was filled with what appeared to be treasure chests of various sizes. Some were brass-bound, others gilded, and a few were decorated with precious stones that glinted in the torchlight. They all appeared suspiciously pristine for their apparent age.

"Something seems . . . off," Thane muttered, gripping his axe tighter.

As if in response, one of the chests wiggled slightly and let out what sounded distinctly like a suppressed giggle.

"Oh no," Maurice said seriously. "They're doing it again. The wiggly laugh thing." He brightened. "Want to hear a joke? The boxes like jokes. Even though they never let me finish them."

Before anyone could stop him, he called out to the room: "What did the cow say to the—"

The chamber erupted in squeaky, chittering laughter. The treasure chests wiggled and hopped, some of them revealing rows of teeth as they guffawed. One particularly ornate chest fell over onto its side, its keyhole twisted into what was unmistakably a grin.

"See?" Maurice said proudly. "They think I'm funny. Even without the ending. Which is good because I forgot it, anyway."

"What are those things," Rea asked quietly, clutching Nyx closer. The cat, surprisingly, was more annoyed than concerned.

"We're Mimics!" called out one of the chests between giggles.[91]

---

[91] *The Imperial Bestiary: A Comprehensive Guide to the Beasts and Botherations of the Realm* (Third Edition, pg. 104):

"It is a common misconception that Mimics are primarily predatory creatures. In fact, most Mimics are frustrated method actors, having attended prestigious performing arts academies where they majored in 'Environmental Object Interpretation.' Their tendency to consume adventurers typically stems from negative reviews of their performances ('That chest seems suspicious') rather than actual hunger. Many Mimics

"Aren't you guys supposed to eat adventurers?" Thane asked, his hand moving instinctively toward his axe.

"That's a terrible stereotype. Adventurers are horrible on our digestive systems," another added, trying to maintain their dignity despite quivering with suppressed laughter. "We came here, away from the living, to pursue our true passion."

"Which is?" Blarg asked cautiously.

"COMEDY!" they all shouted in unison, before dissolving into another fit of giggles.

"They really love comedy," Maurice explained seriously. "Even though they laugh before the funny part. I try to tell them that's not how jokes work, but they say I'm naturally hilarious." He considered this for a moment. "I don't know what that means, but it sounds nice."

"Don't come any closer!" one of the Mimics warned as Blarg hesitantly stepped forward. "We're"—*giggle*—"extremely ticklish! One touch and we'll"—*snort*—"completely lose it!"

---

spend years perfecting their craft, with some devoting decades to mastering the subtle nuances of 'Weathered Oak Chest with Slight Scratches, Early Dwarven Period.'

"The renowned Mimic theater critic S.J. Lockjaw once noted, 'To reduce a Mimic's performance to mere 'monster behavior' is to fundamentally misunderstand the artistic dedication required to maintain perfect brass fixture oxidation while simultaneously conveying the emotional weight of being a chest that has witnessed centuries of dungeon history.'

"Sadly, most Mimics eventually retire from performance art due to chronic type-casting ('Why does everyone always expect us to be chests? I could be a marvelous armoire!') and the persistent tendency of audiences to attempt to open them without first appreciating their artistic statement. Many find second careers in comedy, where their natural talent for physical transformation and impeccable timing can be more appropriately appreciated."

"It's true." Maurice nodded. "I bumped into Gerald last week and he laughed so hard he rolled down three corridors. Gerald is the green one. Or maybe the blue one. They change colors sometimes when they laugh really hard."

"We do not!" protested a chest that was, at that very moment, shifting from bronze to purple as it chortled.

"The exit's past them," Maurice said helpfully. "But you have to be careful. If you get too close, they may eat you on accident."

"Nothing personal," one of the more fancy, jewel encrusted Mimics said, "it's just instinctual."

A small chest in the corner hiccupped, causing a chain reaction of giggles throughout the room. "Sorry!"—*hic*—"Still new to this retirement thing. I used to be a serious Mimic. Very dignified. Now I can't help it, everything's just so"—*hic*—"FUNNY!"

"There's a path," Maurice pointed out helpfully. "Between Charles and Susan. Or maybe it's between Susan and Charles. They move around sometimes when they're laughing too hard."

The *'path'* was a narrow space between two particularly large Mimics, one of which was currently trying very hard to hold in its laughter. It's brass fixtures were turning red with the effort.

"Don't mind Susan," Maurice whispered loudly. "She's trying that new thing. What's it called? Self . . . self-something."

"Self-control!" the Mimic burst out, then immediately dissolved into giggles. "Sorry! Sorry! I lasted twelve whole seconds that time!"

"Impressive," Maurice said earnestly. "That's more than seven. I think. Numbers are hard."

Thane studied the path. "Right. So we need to get through without touching any of them?"

"Good luck!" snickered a small jeweled chest. "Last week a mouse ran through here and three of us laughed so hard we knocked over poor Gerald."

Blarg focused on the others. "Perchance there is another way—"

"Oh no, this is definitely the way out," Maurice assured them. "I remember because of the sparkly rock in the wall that looks like a cow's nose. See?" He pointed with his human head toward a completely ordinary-looking rock.

Nyx, apparently fed up with the delay, leaped from Rea's arms and picked his way through the room. The Mimics watched with bated breath (if Mimics even breathed) as the cat gracefully navigated between them.

"Show off," muttered one of the chests.

"We could try that," Tianna suggested. "Very . . . carefully."

"Blarg shall go last," Blarg said quickly. "You know, to . . . guard the rear."

"You just don't want to go first," Thane smirked.

"Blarg is not in the mood to be eaten today, even if it is an accident."

"And we would all be very sorry," one of the Mimics responded.

A hiccup from the corner set off another chain of giggles through the room. Several Mimics rocked back and forth, narrowing the path even further.

"Oh dear," Maurice said, his voice tinged with mild alarm. "They're doing the wiggle dance again. That means they're extra happy. Or extra funny. Or . . . extra *something*." He brightened suddenly. "Want to hear another joke while we wait?"

Every Mimic in the room immediately erupted in anticipatory laughter, their lids rattling with glee.

"I haven't even said it yet!" Maurice protested, which somehow made them laugh even harder.

"Ooh, I've got one!" a Mimic chimed in, its voice gleeful and slightly hollow. "Why was the Mimic worried after eating the court jester?" It paused dramatically, savoring the moment. "Because he tasted a little funny."

The room exploded in laughter, their guffaws echoing off the walls. Even Rea let out a tiny snort before clamping a hand over her mouth.

"Okay, okay, I've got one!" another Mimic shouted. "What do you call a Mimic that won't stop talking? A chatterbox!"

More laughter. Maurice chuckled nervously, glancing at Rea, who was now hiding her grin behind her hand.

"Ahem. Question for the Mimics!" Sword announced. *"What's the difference between a treasure chest and a therapist?"*

Silence.

"One listens to your problems. The other swallows them whole."

A low creak echoed from a nearby chest. It might have been movement. It might have been offense.

"Eh? No? Tough crowd. Guess you lot prefer biting *commentary,"* Sword huffed.

"Wait, wait! I've got another!" a third Mimic called out, jostling with excitement. "What do you call a sleeping Mimic? A chest of snores!"

Maurice frowned, scratching his head. "I don't get it," he said earnestly.

That was it. The Mimics completely lost it, erupting in uncontrollable laughter so loud that several toppled over, lids flapping wildly. Maurice's expression of utter bafflement only fueled the hilarity further, leaving Rea quietly shaking with suppressed giggles.

"My joke was better than that," Sword muttered.

"Here goes nothing," Rea said as she took a deep breath and stepped forward, following Nyx's path. The cat had already made it halfway across and was now sitting smugly on a small patch of clear floor, watching the proceedings with typical feline superiority.

"Careful near Fred," Maurice called out helpfully. "He's still got the sneezes from when I tried to dust him last week."

"You can't dust a Mimic!" protested a chest with tarnished brass fittings.

"But you looked sad and gray," Maurice said. "Like the walls. But walls are supposed to be gray. You're supposed to be shiny."

"That's tarnish! It's distinguished! It shows character and—" Fred cut off with a massive sneeze that sent him sliding backward into another Mimic.

"TICKLES!" shrieked the impacted chest, setting off a domino effect of giggling that made the whole path shift.

"Don't move!" Rea froze mid-step, balanced precariously between two quivering Mimics. "Please, please don't move—"

"We're"—*snort*—"trying!" managed one of the chests. "But it's just"—*giggle*—"everything is so FUNNY!"

"What's funny?" Maurice asked with genuine curiosity. "Is it another joke? I know a joke about a cow and a philosopher. At least, I think I do. Father told it to me once but I only remember the part about the milk—"

Three Mimics toppled over at this, forcing Thane to press against the wall as the path rearranged itself.

"Sorry!" wheezed a particularly ornate chest. "It's just—his *face* when he tries to remember things! So earnest!"

"My face is how faces should be," Maurice stated proudly. "Father said so. Though he also said my face was on the wrong end, but then Mother gave him that look she used when he said silly things. She was very good at looks. Even with cow eyes."

The entire room lost it at this point. Mimics were rolling and bouncing off each other, their laughter echoing off the walls in a cacophony of squeaks, snorts, and chittering.

Blarg had to grab Tianna's arm to keep her from being bowled over by a particularly enthusiastic chest doing what appeared to be accidental cartwheels.

"I haven't seen them this worked up since Maurice tried to explain why grass grows up!" called one Mimic between gasps of laughter.

"It's a serious question!" Maurice protested. "Things should grow down. Down is safer. I would know. I knocked over those urns earlier by going up."

"PLEASE!" Rea shouted over the chaos. "Just . . . just hold still for ten seconds. That's all we need!"

"Ten?" Maurice's face scrunched up in concentration. "That's . . . more than seven. I think. Mother could count to seven. Did I tell you that?"

The Mimics, who had nearly gotten themselves under control, immediately lost it again.

In the midst of this chaos, Nyx chose this moment to demonstrate proper room-crossing technique. He simply walked straight through, stepping daintily between the rolling Mimics as if they were merely inconvenient furniture.

"Show off," muttered everyone, including Maurice.

In the end, it was Nyx who solved their dilemma. The cat, apparently tired of watching the humans' careful shuffling, let out a loud *MRRROOOW* that startled the Mimics just enough to create a momentary pause in their giggling.

"RUN!" Thane shouted, and the group bolted through the briefly-still room.

"Oh!" Maurice called after them. "Are we running? I like running. Sometimes. When it's not up. Or sideways. Down running is best running."

They burst through the far door just as the Mimics recovered, their renewed laughter echoing off the walls behind them.

"Come back soon!" called one chest between giggles. "Maurice needs an audience for his jokes!"

"But I haven't finished telling the one about the cow yet!" Maurice's voice drifted after them. "The part I remember, I mean!"

The tunnel ahead sloped upward, or "the wrong way" as Maurice would say. It led them toward what appeared to be genuine daylight. The air grew colder, but fresher, the walls freezing over with ice, and the sounds of Mimic laughter gradually faded behind them.

"Well," Thane said as they finally emerged into the cold, cloudy afternoon, "that was . . . different."

"Very different," Tianna agreed, then paused. "Should we have said goodbye to Maurice?"

As if in answer, a distant call echoed from the catacombs: "Goodbye! I remembered that word! It's what you say when people go up instead of down! I think!"

This was followed by another eruption of Mimic laughter and what sounded suspiciously like someone knocking over more urns.

"MAURICE!" came Herbert's distant voice. "What did we say about the urns?"

"That they're sad up high?"

"No! The other thing!"

"—that they're not as good at counting as my mother?"

The last thing they heard as they walked away was Grunch's rattling laughter and Herbert's exasperated sigh, accompanied by the eternal chorus of giggling Mimics.

"I have no idea what that even was . . ." Sword trailed off.

Nyx, who had somehow emerged from the adventure looking even more pristine than when he entered, gave them all a glare that clearly said, "Are we going to wait here all day, or what?"

The cat then proceeded to groom himself, already putting the entire adventure behind him with typical feline dismissiveness.

"Next time," Blarg muttered, brushing cobwebs from his clothes, "Blarg will be taking the main road."

"Agreed," said everyone else in unison.

Though none of them would admit it, they all found themselves smiling at the sound of distant laughter drifting up from below, where a gentle Minotaur was undoubtedly trying to tell another half-remembered joke to his eternally amused audience.

19

Things Better Left Buried

"Love does not vanish with the dead—it lingers in the silence, in the snow, in the things we meant to say. But to carry love forward, we must learn to let go of the weight of what might have been and will never again be."

— *Reflections Beyond the Veil*
by Tharaniel the Pale

For five days, they marched northward, each step pulling them deeper into the frozen expanse. The surrounding snow was pristine, untouched, stretching out in all directions like an endless white sea. Under the soft light of an overcast sky, it shimmered faintly, lending the landscape an otherworldly quality. It was so undisturbed it felt almost sacrilegious to tread upon it, as though their presence alone might disrupt the serene perfection. At times, the silence was so profound that the crunch of their boots on the snow felt deafening, a stark reminder of how alone they were in this vast, icy wilderness.

As they pressed onward, the air grew sharper, colder, biting through their cloaks and stinging any exposed skin. The barren trees they passed stood like skeletal sentinels, their frost-covered branches reaching skyward as though pleading for warmth. The occasional frostbitten bush or jagged stone offered no solace, serving only to break the monotony of the unyielding landscape. The wind whistled through the emptiness, carrying with it an eerie stillness that made Tianna glance over her shoulder more often than she liked to admit.

By night, the cold became their greatest adversary. They were unwilling to risk a fire as its light and smoke would be a beacon for any unwanted eyes. So, they huddled close, the warmth of their bodies the only shield against the frigid air. The nights were long, the darkness absolute, broken only by the fleeting shimmer of moonlight through the passing clouds. Sleep came erratically, disturbed by the creak of ice expanding or the distant howl of something they dared not imagine.

On the sixth day, the land changed. The trail wound upward, the ground beneath their feet growing rockier, the snow thinner in patches where the wind had swept it away. Thane's pace slowed as the incline grew steeper, his eyes scanning the horizon with a mix of familiarity and hesitation. The sky above hung low and gray, the sun little more than a pale suggestion behind the clouds.

"Think it's about time to tell her?" Sword spoke directly into Thane's mind, cutting through the solitude.

"I suppose I have no choice," Thane said to himself, the rest of the group stared at him curiously.

"What is it?" Tianna asked.

"Something I need to tell you. Something I should have told you years ago." Thane hesitated for a moment before continuing. "It was about ten years ago," he began, his voice low, as though speaking too loudly might disturb the stillness. "I was hunting out in the Ashevale when I stumbled upon a place."

Thane's voice softened, the chill of the wind carrying his words to Tianna. The snow crunched beneath their boots as they walked. The barren trees stood like silent watchmen along the winding trail.

"It was a glade," he continued, his words careful and deliberate. "Quiet and untouched, where the air carried the faint scent of wildflowers. I can still smell them now." His lips tugged into a faint, fleeting smile, a brief light in the shadow that had settled over him. "The trees were ancient, with twisted trunks, scarred with the weight of centuries. The canopy was thick, allowing only scattered beams of sunlight to break through, casting a golden haze over everything. It felt . . . sacred."

The slope of the hill grew steeper as they climbed, and Thane paused to catch his breath, his gaze distant. "At the far end of the glade," he said, voice quiet, "there was a waterfall. It spilled over a cliff, with water so clear it was unworldly. The sound, it was steady, constant, like a heartbeat. Mist rose from its base, softening the edges of the world. And there, in the center of the pond, was a small island. Just a patch of land, really, but the grass was so green, so alive, it didn't even look natural. There were tiny white flowers along the shoreline, that glowed."

Tianna walked beside him, her face unreadable but her eyes fixed on him. "I've seen that place," she said finally, her voice quiet. "In my vision."

Thane nodded slowly, his expression pained but resolute. "Aye, I know you have."

"How—?" Tianna began, but he held up a hand to stop her.

"Patience, child," he said, the words almost a whisper. "Right in the middle of that island, there was a sword. Half-buried in the soil, as if it had been waiting for centuries. Its hilt was intricate, carved with runes that shimmered in the light, glowing faintly, like the blade itself was alive. Even from a distance, I could feel its pull. It wasn't *just* a weapon. It was something far more. And I . . . I thought it was meant for me."

Tianna's hand instinctively tightened on Sword's handle as she listened. "You found Sword," she said, her voice steady but heavy with meaning.

"Aye, I did," Thane admitted, his voice carrying the weight of a decade's regret. "I pulled her from the earth, and in that moment, I knew I was chosen. Young and arrogant as I was, I thought I could carry the burden, fulfill the destiny." He peered at her then, his eyes haunted. "But I was wrong."

"I don't understand. What does this mean?"

"Hey, don't ask me. He's the one full of secrets." Sword chimed in, breaking the tension with her usual irreverence.

Tianna's gaze shot back to her uncle. "Uncle, what's going on?" she demanded, frustration creeping into her voice.

Thane rubbed the back of his neck, his composure faltering under her scrutiny. "That's what I'm trying to explain," he muttered, his voice low, tinged with regret. "It's just . . . difficult."

"Try harder," Tianna pressed, her patience wearing thin.

"She told me that it was my destiny to destroy the Dark Lord," Thane said somberly. "She warned me that the world would end if I failed."

"So, this destiny runs in the family?"

"Not exactly." He took a deep breath. "You hear about destinies and magic swords your whole life, but to encounter one, it's surreal." Thane stared Tianna directly in the eyes. "I guess you know all about that."

The trail narrowed as they climbed higher, the snow thinning to reveal patches of frostbitten grass. The wind picked up, biting at their faces, but Tianna barely noticed. Her attention was locked on her uncle, and the storm of emotions playing across his face.

"We were adventurers then," Thane continued, his voice breaking slightly. "Young. Foolish. Bold. Too bold, at least for our own good. When your father found out about my mission, he wouldn't hear of me going alone. He said I'd need someone to keep me out of trouble." A hollow laugh escaped him. "Your dad . . . He had his faults, but loyalty was never one of them. He followed me without question, even though he knew the risks. My little brother . . . he always thought it was his job to protect me. He was the younger one, but somehow, he always acted like the older."

Tianna stayed silent, the weight of his words settling on her like the snow gathering on her cloak.

"We faced challenges," Thane said, his voice quieter now. "Things we were not prepared for. But somehow, we made it to the mountain fortress. We were so close. Close enough to see the end in sight. But that's when it all went wrong."

He stopped walking, running a hand over his face. "You see, Destiny will protect her 'chosen' few, but that was me, not your father. He was brave, so damn brave, but bravery wasn't enough. We faced . . . something. I don't even know what, some creature of the Dark Lord. And your father . . . he fought. Fought to protect me."

Thane's voice cracked, and he turned away, his shoulders trembling. "He saved me. Cleared the way. But he was wounded, badly, and there was no saving him. It broke me. I'm so sorry, but it broke me, Tianna. I couldn't go on without him. I couldn't go on with the guilt of losing him. So, I carried him. I carried him south until I had no more strength left in me. And I buried him. Here."

Tianna glanced down, and for the first time, she saw it. It was a small pile of stones blanketed in a thin layer of snow. A crude marker rested at its head, the wood worn and weathered but still standing.

Thane kneeled before the grave, his head bowed. "I went home. Had Sword melted down and tried to forget all about my destiny. But I guess these things aren't easy to escape." Thane paused. "I failed him. I failed you. None of this would have been necessary if I hadn't been weak. Now I put you and your sister at risk because I couldn't get the job done ten years ago."

The silence between them was heavy, broken only by the wind whistling through the trees. Tianna stared at the grave, her chest tight, her heart pounding.

"Why didn't you tell us?" she demanded, her voice trembling. "Why would you keep that a secret for all these years?" Her voice rose in anger.

Thane flinched at her words, the weight of her anger hitting him harder than the biting wind. He didn't glance up from the grave, his hand resting gently on the snow-covered stones. "Because I couldn't bear to," he said quietly, his voice raw. "Because every time I thought about telling you, I couldn't get past the guilt. I couldn't overcome the fear of what you knowing the truth could do to us. If you knew the whole story, what would you think?"

"What would I think?" Tianna snapped, her voice trembling. "All these years, I thought he was just gone, killed on some selfish adventure without any thought for me or Mom. That he was a bad father because he put adventuring ahead of everything else. But now you tell me it was because of you. He went along to protect you, like a good brother should." Her hands balled into fists at her sides, her breath coming in sharp, uneven bursts. "He followed you into danger. He protected you until the end, and you—" Her voice broke, the emotions welling up too fast to contain. "You didn't even finish what you started! He died for nothing! Everything was for nothing!"

Thane finally turned to her, his expression anguished. "Do you think I don't know that?" His voice cracked. "Do you think I haven't carried that with me every single day since? He was my brother, Tianna! My *little brother!* I was supposed to protect him. I was supposed to bring him home, and instead, I put him in the ground. I *know* it was my fault, and I've been trying to live with that ever since."

Tianna took a step back, the cold seeping deeper into her bones as her anger warred with the pain in his voice. "And what about me? What about Rea? Did you even think about us? You were so caught up in your own guilt that you left us without a father, and then you kept the truth from us. From me."

Thane's shoulders sagged, the weight of her words pressing down on him. "I thought I was protecting you," he said, his voice barely above a whisper. "You were so young. Rea didn't even know who he was. And I . . . I couldn't face the look in your eyes if you knew. If you knew that it was my fault."

Tianna shook her head, her breath clouding in the air. "You thought you were protecting us? No. You were protecting yourself. From your guilt. From your failure. And now you expect me to just . . . take Sword, this *burden,* and fix *your* mistakes?"

"I don't expect anything," Thane said, his voice steadying. He stood slowly, brushing the snow from his knees. "I know I have no right to ask anything of you, Tianna. But destiny doesn't care about what's right, what's fair. It's chosen you now, the same way it chose me. And I know you hate me for this, but it doesn't change what must be done."

Tianna stared at him, her chest heaving with the force of her emotions. "You're right. I do hate you," she said, her voice cold. "For what you did. For what you didn't do. For the task you left up to me. You are a coward, Thane." She stormed off in anger, leaving Thane beside her father's grave.

"Is that really father's grave?" Rea asked quietly from behind Thane, Nyx clutched snuggly in her arms.

He flinched at the sound of Rea's voice, as though caught in a moment he hadn't wanted her to witness. He turned slowly to face her, his expression raw, the shadows of guilt etched deeply into his features. "Aye, it is," he said softly, his voice heavy with the weight of the admission. "I wanted to bring him home, but this . . . this was the best I could do."

Rea took a hesitant step closer, her gaze locked on the grave. The wind tousled her hair, and she clutched Nyx tighter, seeking comfort in the cat's warmth. "You buried him all the way out here? Alone?" Her voice was small, trembling with the beginnings of tears.

Thane nodded, his hand resting lightly on the weathered wooden marker. "It was the only place that felt . . . right. Away from the blood, the battle, the Dark Lord's shadow. Somewhere quiet. Peaceful." His voice cracked as he added, "He deserved that much."

Rea's eyes filled with tears, but she didn't look away from the grave. "He deserved to come home," she whispered, her words cutting through the air like a blade. "We deserved to say goodbye." She reached into her pack and brought out a strip of cloth. Unfolding it, she revealed a yellow flower neatly pressed within. "I'm sorry that I never got to meet you." Rea kneeled down and placed the flower onto the grave.

Thane watched Tianna's retreating figure, his chest tightening with every step she took away from him. He turned back to the grave, his hand trembling as it rested on the marker. "I don't know how to fix this," he murmured, his voice barely audible over the wind. "I failed him . . . and now I'm failing her."

Rea crouched beside him, her small frame shivering in the cold. "You didn't fail him, Uncle," she said quietly, her voice filled with a mixture of sadness and defiance. "He made his choice. Just like Tianna. Just like I did. She'll come around. Give her time."

Thane closed his eyes, tears slipping silently down his face. "When did you become so wise?" he asked with a small laugh. "I'd think that you would be upset with me as well. He was your father too."

Rea placed a small hand on his arm, her touch light but grounding. "He was, but I never met him. I guess it's different. You're my real father, or at least the closest thing I'll ever have," she said simply. "You, Tianna, and Nyxie are the only family that I've ever known. And we need each other, especially now. Don't give up on her Uncle. She still needs you. I still need you."

Thane put his arm around Rea. "I'll never give up on you girls, even if you give up on me."

Tianna's footsteps crunched loudly in the snow as she marched away, her heart pounding in her chest. Her vision blurred with hot, angry tears, but she didn't stop, didn't slow. The icy wind tore at her face, but she welcomed the sting. It was easier to feel the cold than the storm roiling inside her. Betrayal. Grief. Rage. It all churned together, and she didn't know where one ended and the other began.

Sword's voice broke into her thoughts, sharp and sarcastic as ever. *"Well, that was dramatic."*

"Shut up," Tianna snapped, her voice trembling. "You don't get to talk right now."

"Oh, I think I do," Sword replied, her tone taking on an edge of mockery. *"Because let's be honest, you've got a job to do, and this little family drama isn't exactly helping you get there."*

Tianna stopped abruptly, gripping Sword's handle so tightly her knuckles turned white. "You think I care about that right now?" she hissed, her voice low and venomous. "You think I care about what you want, when everything I've ever known has been a lie?"

Tianna reached the crest of the hill and stopped, her breath fogging in the frigid air. The world stretched out before her, a vast expanse of white, cold and unyielding. And in the distance, mountains, dark and menacing. Her chest heaved, and for a moment, she considered dropping Sword into the snow and walking away from all of it. From destiny. From Thane. From everything that had brought her to that desolate place.

But then she thought of Rea, of the weight of her sister's small hand in hers when they were younger, when it was just the two of them and the world felt safe. She thought of her father, the faint memories she had of his laughter, his warmth. And how that had all been tainted by her uncle's lies.

Sword's voice softened, uncharacteristically gentle. *"You can hate him all you want. You can even hate me. But this fight is almost over. Be better than him. Finish this."*

Tianna tightened her grip on Sword's handle, her jaw clenching. "I'm not doing this for him, or for you," she muttered. "I'm doing this because it's the right thing to do."

With a deep breath, she turned back toward the grave, her footsteps slow but deliberate. She wasn't ready to forgive Thane, not yet. But she wasn't ready to abandon her purpose either.

20

The Edge of the World as We Know It

"Beware the path of least resistance. It usually leads somewhere worse, only more conveniently."

— Last Words of Captain Delryn,
Second Imperial Legion

The wind howled relentlessly as they trudged northward for three days and nights, the jagged peaks of the mountains looming ever closer. The snow was thicker there, rising to their knees in some places, turning each step into an exercise in misery. Tianna's legs burned with the effort, but she kept moving, her eyes fixed on the dark silhouette of the fortress taking shape against the gray horizon.

"This is it, then?" she asked, her voice muffled by the scarf wrapped tightly around her face.

Thane nodded grimly, his eyes narrowing as the fortress came into focus. "The Fortress of Grimhold. Last line of defense before the Dark Lord's citadel."

"Well," Tianna muttered, "he clearly spared no expense on ambiance."

"Blarg doesn't like this place," Blarg whispered. "It feels . . . cold."

"That's because it's literally freezing," Thane shot back, his tone sharper than he intended. "We've been walking through snow for eight days. Everything feels cold."

"Cold in spirit," Blarg corrected.

Rea huddled closer to Nyx, the cat tucked snugly inside her cloak. "There's something wrong about this place," she said, shaking her head, her eyes darting nervously to the towering walls ahead.

"Aye, child," Thane said quietly. "This place has a history. Grimhold's seen more death than most battlefields. The walls practically hum with it."

"Hum with death?" Tianna grimaced. "Wonderful."

As they neared the gates, Tianna noticed that the massive iron doors—reinforced with thick beams and studded with blackened steel—were wide open. Snow piled up on both sides, firmly holding them in place.

"At least it's welcoming," Tianna said, as she passed through the massive gates and into the fortress.

"Welcoming like a cornered Hydra." Blarg grumbled, as he followed her inside.

The fortress of Grimhold revealed itself in stark, chilling detail. The courtyard stretched wide and barren, its cobblestones coated in a heavy layer of frost that glimmered faintly under the muted light. Snow had drifted into the corners, piling against the high walls and partially burying abandoned barrels and crates.

The inner walls rose sharply, black stone slick with ice and streaked with the white scars of countless winters. Above, shattered battlements jaggedly silhouetted the gray sky, the remnants of once-imposing defenses now crumbling under the weight of time.

To one side stood a series of weathered stone buildings. They were barracks, by the look of them. Their doors hung slightly ajar, revealing only shadowy interiors. Opposite, a towering keep loomed, its massive double doors broken from their hinges, and snow piled high in the entrance.

"This is as far as I got last time," he glanced quickly over to Tianna. "The creature that guarded this place is dead. It looks like nothing new took over in its absence."

"Hey, look at this!" Rea called from the center of the courtyard. She kneeled in the snow, brushing off a solid chunk of white stone that jutted from the ground. The stone had been cut smooth, its surface engraved with surprising precision. As the snow cleared, vibrant colors emerged, their cheerfulness a stark and jarring contrast to the bleak surroundings.

"What is it?" Tianna asked, approaching cautiously.

Blarg squinted at the stone, his breath fogging in the cold air. "'Tis a map," he announced, leaning closer. His voice carried a mix of confusion and mild offense. "A map of this very fortress."

"You've got to be kidding me," Tianna muttered, stepping beside him. She tilted her head as she scanned the map, trying to reconcile its playful design with the deadly aura of the place.

The map was nothing short of absurd. It featured a cartoonish depiction of the fortress, complete with exaggerated markers for its major points of interest. The towers were drawn with little flags. The barracks had tiny stick figures carrying swords. The stables were labeled in bold, blocky letters: 'CLOSED FOR RENOVATIONS.' Other notable labels included: 'Court of Delectables,' the foreboding 'House of the Dead,' and the particularly perplexing 'The Nexus of What-Was-and-Will-Be.'

"'You are here,'" Blarg read aloud, pointing to a glowing red arrow etched at the rune-like center of the map. His finger hovered over the caption as if he expected it to be a trap. "The words are . . . oddly friendly."

"Friendly? It's *mocking* us," Tianna snapped, gesturing to the overly cheerful design. "This place is a frozen deathtrap, and they've got a whimsical map pointing out the 'House of the Dead?' What's next, a gift shop?"

Blarg squinted at the map and pointed again. "Nay, it looks as if the 'Gift Shop' is also closed for renovations." His voice held a tinge of disappointment, as though he'd genuinely hoped for a souvenir.

"Oh shucks," Sword said. *"I was really hoping for a novelty key chain. You know, something to commemorate all the running away we've been doing."*

Tianna groaned and buried her face in her hands. "This cannot be real."

Thane, standing a step back, folded his arms and studied the map with a frown. "There," he said, tapping the etched path labeled 'Stairs of Doom.' "It looks like this route takes us all the way up the mountain to the citadel."

"'Stairs of Doom,'" Tianna repeated dryly, raising an eyebrow. "Really rolls off the tongue. Who named this place?"

Rea, who had been studying the map intently, pointed to a small line snaking from the rear of the keep. "What about this?" she asked, her tone rising with curiosity. "It says, *The Path of Least Resistance (Authorized Personnel Only).'* That looks like it leads to the top of the mountain, too."

Thane leaned in closer, his brow furrowing. "Convenient," he said flatly, his tone brimming with skepticism.

"More like suspicious," Tianna countered, crossing her arms. "We're supposed to trust what this map says? In a fortress built to keep us out?"

"'Tis a fortress," Blarg replied matter-of-factly. "Perhaps the design was not meant for intruders, but to assist those who would live here. Do not forget that the Dark Lord's minions are not known for being . . . bright."

Rea perked up. "So, you think it's legit?"

"Blarg did not say that," he said quickly. "It could still be a trap. But it's a *practical* trap."

"I don't like this," Thane muttered, his hand resting on the handle of his axe. His eyes darted toward the darkened corners of the courtyard as though expecting something to leap out of the shadows at any moment.

"If Blarg can have a say," he said, stamping his boots to shake off the snow, "Blarg is not one to turn down an opportunity to visit these supposed 'Stairs of Doom.' Indeed, that is something Blarg would very much enjoy. However, after eight days and nights dragging feet through the snow, some time indoors sounds like a fine idea. You know, maybe let the toes and fingers thaw out a wee bit, before they begin to drop off.'"

"Nyx and I vote for inside," Rea chimed in, clutching Nyx closer. The cat let out a faint *brrrrup* in agreement, his tail flicking in what could only be interpreted as feline irritation.

Tianna sighed, rubbing her temples. "Fine. We'll try the 'Path of Least Resistance,' but if I hear a single frozen zombie say 'Welcome, authorized personnel,' I'm leaving all of you behind."

"Fair," Blarg said, already heading toward the marked passage. "Blarg would likely do the same."

They approached the arched entry of the keep, barely illuminated by the dim exterior light. The doorway opened wide, framed by crumbling stonework coated in frost, its edges glistening like jagged teeth in the pale glow. The massive iron door, twisted off its hinges, lay half-buried in a snowdrift to one side, as though some immense force had torn it free and discarded it like trash. Above the arch, faint runes pulsed with an eerie blue light, casting shifting shadows that writhed along the walls.

The air was colder here, biting and sharp, carrying with it the faint metallic tang of ancient iron and the acrid sting of something far less natural. The shadows within the archway moved unnervingly, as though the darkness itself were alive and waiting.

On the ground lay a curious sight: footprints, delicately etched in the snow, leading from the interior of the keep to the courtyard. But that wasn't what made them curious, it was what made them impossible. The prints were unmistakably clear, each step perfectly spaced, the weight pressed into the snow with uncanny precision. Yet the direction defied all logic. The tracks led away from her, but the toes pointed toward her, as if the maker had been retreating into the past.[92]

"It looks as if something is already here," Tianna said softly, her voice catching in her throat.

"More like something *was* here," Blarg replied, furrowing his brow, "or maybe something *will be.*" He crouched down, examining the tracks closer, his frown deepening. "Either way, it doesn't feel particularly encouraging, does it?"

They froze as a low, chittering hum echoed through the keep. It was faint at first, like the rustling of snow-laden branches, but it grew steadily louder, a bizarre chorus that sent a shiver through Tianna's spine.

"What . . . is that?" Rea whispered, clutching Nyx tightly. The cat hissed, its tail puffing out as it bristled against her chest.

"Not the wind," Thane muttered, gripping his axe tightly. His eyes darted around the shadowy hall. "Stay ready."

From the far end of the hall, tiny glowing eyes appeared, dozens of them, blinking in the dim light. A small, fist-sized creature waddled forward into the faint light. It was covered in fluffy white fur, with stubby legs and tiny arms. Its glowing blue eyes fixed on them, and it let out a high-pitched, almost adorable squeak.

---

[92] As every first-year magical student knows, the world tends to misbehave around any sufficiently large source of magic. This is due to the nature of magic itself, which borrows liberally (and irresponsibly) from one alternate reality or another. Naturally, this comes at a cost. Magic is, after all, a violation of the natural order it inhabits; a cosmic party crasher, if you will. Time, space, and matter cease to be firm rules and become more like polite suggestions, easily ignored by any magic with enough power or hubris.

Because of this, creatures whose very physiology would be deemed questionable at best, and downright ludicrous at worst, tend to flock to these magical anomalies. Whether they crawl in from less magically dense regions of the world or simply tumble through from one of many parallel realities, they always seem to find their way to the party, proving that no matter the realm, magic attracts the truly bizarre.

"Oh, come on," Tianna said, her grip on Sword tightening. "It's . . . cute."

"Nope, it's smashing time!" Sword said excitedly.

Another one appeared. Then another. And another, until a swarm of the tiny creatures scuttled out from the shadows, filling the far end of the hall. They chittered in unison, their glowing eyes locking onto the group.

"They're Yetis," Blarg said, raising *Thumpkin* cautiously. "Adorable, yes, but also . . . foul creatures. Legends say Yetis can fold time like paper. Blarg is not sure if that means they will try to kill yesterday or tomorrow. Which Blarg supposes is beside the point when death comes either way."[93]

The Yetis moved unnaturally fast, their fluffy forms flickering in and out of focus, like a poorly drawn flipbook skipping pages. Their fluffy bodies hooked together, forming arms, legs, and a torso. Tianna blinked hard, her mind struggling to keep up with their movements. One moment they were scattered across the icy ground, the next, towering as a ten-foot monstrosity. Its glowing eyes blazed from the topmost creatures, which served as the head, and swayed slightly before letting out a guttural roar that belied its small, cuddly components.

Blarg blinked. "That's cheating."

---

[93] *The Imperial Bestiary: A Comprehensive Guide to the Beasts and Botherations of the Realm* (Third Edition, pg. 999):

"A Yeti is commonly understood to be a creature of the future tense, a lurking presence that stalks the unwritten snows of destiny. By contrast, an Alreti is its past-tense counterpart, a creature of bygone frost and forgotten terror. Naturally, this begs the question of the present tense: Are we dealing with Yetis who *will* be, or Alretis who *have already been*? Scholars remain divided, though one popular theory posits that the Presenti (a grammatically elusive beast), exists in a perpetual state of sneaking up behind you.

"The term 'Yeti' is, of course, a general umbrella term applied in an attempt to make sense of this entire linguistic and temporal mess, though it does little to comfort those who insist they've encountered one. After all, for a Yeti to appear in the present tense, let alone the present progressive, it would need to fundamentally transform its very being, which is not only improbable but would likely leave the poor creature hopelessly existentially distressed."

"It's like a Frankenyeti," Thane responded.[94]

The Frankenyeti stomped forward, its massive hands smashing into the floor, sending cracks splintering through the icy stone. The group scattered as it lunged, its movements surprisingly fast for something made entirely of tiny creatures.

"Go for the base!" Thane barked, dodging a swing of its massive arm. "If it can't stand, it can't fight!"

Blarg smashed at one of its legs, knocking a handful of Yetis free. They tumbled to the ground, squeaking indignantly as they scrambled to rejoin the stack. The creature wobbled but steadied itself, roaring again as it returned a powerful swing.

Blarg dove out of the way, rolling to his feet. "Okay, this is the strangest creature Blarg has ever traded blows."

The Frankenyeti stomped its massive foot, sending a shockwave through the hall. The ground trembled, and cracks webbed up the walls. Chunks of stone fell from the ceiling as the creature lunged again, this time toward Rea.

"Rea, move!" Tianna shouted.

---

[94] This of course, is a common misconception. The prefix "Franken," when applied to creatures such as Frankenstein (the classic monster archetype), Frankenfluff (a tragically misunderstood marshmallow fiend who just wants to be toasted by campfires, not villagers), or Frankencluck (a poultry abomination best described as a feathery affront to nature), specifically denotes those originating from the Franken region of Spargelstein.

Creatures created outside this esteemed region are, of course, more properly referred to as "Sparkling Monsters." While these creatures may look similar at first glance, true aficionados know the difference. Sparkling Monsters often lack the robust construction and rustic charm of authentic Frankens, and they are more likely to collapse dramatically under torchlight.

As a general rule, if the creature fails to growl and moan with the proper Spargelstein accent, it's most likely Sparkling.

Rea bolted toward a side passage, Nyx hissing in her arms. The Frankenyeti's massive hand smashed into the ground behind her, sending a shower of ice and stone into the air. The impact shook the entire structure, and with a deafening groan, the front of the keep collapsed.

"Tianna!" Thane shouted as a massive chunk of stone crashed down in front of them, cutting him and Tianna off from Rea and Blarg. The ceiling gave way entirely, and the hall filled with snow, ice, and debris. Blarg, still in the hall, barely had time to raise *Thumpkin* before a massive chunk of ceiling crashed down, cutting him off.

Tianna and Thane stood shoulder to shoulder as the Frankenyeti turned its glowing gaze on them, roaring with triumph. It stomped toward them, each step shaking the ground beneath their feet.

"What now?" Tianna asked, her breath coming in short bursts as she readied Sword.

"Maybe try hitting it?" Sword suggested helpfully.

"We keep it distracted," Thane said grimly. "And hope the others can find a way out."

Thane pulled his war horn from around his shoulder and gave it a mighty blow. A mournful note echoed off the walls of the fortress. The Frankenyeti appeared to recoil for a moment but quickly regained its composure.

"Great plan," Tianna muttered, dodging as the Frankenyeti swiped at her. She swung Sword in a wide arc, aiming for its massive leg. The pan whistled harmlessly through the air, missing entirely.

"Are you trying to miss?" Sword snapped. *"Because at this point, I'm starting to think it's a skill issue."*

But the Yetis flinched at the motion, their startled squeaks echoing as the stack wobbled precariously. A few tumbled free, hitting the ground with indignant grunts before scrambling to rejoin the towering monstrosity.

"That's one way to do it," she muttered under her breath, gripping Sword tightly and preparing for another swing, even as she doubted it would fare any better.

The Frankenyeti roared again, its glowing eyes blazing with fury. It lunged forward, its massive hand smashing into the ground where Tianna had stood moments before, sending shards of ice flying in all directions.

"Try not to die, Uncle," Tianna said, darting around to its flank. "I'm still not ready to do this on my own."

Thane grunted, swinging his axe at its other leg. "Let's make sure it doesn't come to that."

The Frankenyeti let out a bone-rattling roar, its towering, patchwork form looming against the backdrop of the crumbling keep. Outside, the weather had taken a dramatic turn. Snow fell in thick, relentless sheets from the darkened sky, while jagged bolts of lightning split the heavens, illuminating the swirling storm in eerie flashes of white and blue.

"Keep it in front of us. Strike at the legs if it gets too close," Thane said, his voice steady despite the chaos.

The Frankenyeti gave an unsettling shudder, its towering form rippling as if it were made of liquid snow. With a series of squeaky chittering sounds, it disassembled itself, the tiny Yetis tumbling down from their positions. Before their eyes, the once-massive creature reformed into three separate, six-foot-tall Frankenyetis. Each stood with a menacing poise, their glowing blue eyes fixed on the pair.

The Frankenyeti in the center lumbered forward, its movements deliberate and heavy, while the two on the sides spread out, flanking Tianna and Thane with unnerving precision.

"Oh, great," Tianna muttered, glancing from one Frankenyeti to the next. "They've learned strategy."

"Stay close," Thane said, tightening his grip on his axe. "They're trying to box us in."

"Yeah, I got that," Tianna shot back, stepping toward Thane to avoid the Frankenyeti on her left, which let out a low growl and bared its icy fangs.

The Frankenyetis moved in sync, their steps crunching in unison on the frozen ground as they closed the circle. Each shift of their fluffy forms sent a chill through the air, the temperature dropping further with every deliberate move.

"Any bright ideas?" Tianna asked, her tone sharp as she raised Sword defensively.

Thane's eyes darted between the three Frankenyetis, calculating their next move. "Yeah. Remember how you didn't want to go on the 'Stairs of Doom?'"

"Yeah, so?" Tianna responded, as the Frankenyeti in the center started forward.

"It looks like we're taking them, anyway. Now follow me, quick!" Thane leaped to his right, bowling straight through one of the Frankenyetis. Tianna followed quickly at his heels.

"What about the others?" Tianna yelled, as she ran to keep up with her uncle.

"We have to trust they can find their own way to the citadel. There's nothing we can do for them right now!" Thane shot back, not slowing his stride.

Behind them, the two remaining Frankenyetis exchanged chittering growls, then rushed to rejoin the scattered pile of their fallen comrade. The individual Yetis scrambled onto each other with startling speed, their fluffy forms melding into the massive ten-foot-tall Frankenyeti once more. It let out an ear-splitting roar, shaking the walls of the fortress as it continued its pursuit, each step reverberating like a drumbeat of doom.

"They reformed!" Tianna shouted, glancing back. Her heart sank as the towering Frankenyeti charged after them, its glowing eyes blazing with fury.

"Keep moving!" Thane yelled, his voice barely audible over the creature's guttural growls. They burst through a crumbling archway, emerging onto the icy path leading to the infamous 'Stairs of Doom.'

The wind howled around them, carrying flurries of snow that stung their faces like tiny needles. The 'Stairs of Doom' lived up to their name. It was a steep, narrow staircase carved haphazardly into the jagged mountainside, as if the builders had given up halfway through. Each step was treacherously uneven, slick with a thin sheen of ice that made every movement feel like a gamble. One misstep could send them tumbling into the abyss below, where the chasm yawned wide and dark, its depths obscured by swirling mist.

The railing, if it could be called that, was little more than a series of splintered wooden posts connected by frayed ropes, swaying ominously in the wind. Snow piled precariously on the edges of the steps, threatening to spill and sweep their footing away entirely. The mountain loomed above them, jagged peaks clawing at the stormy sky as if to tear apart the heavens.

Tianna's breath fogged in front of her, the icy air cutting at her lungs with every gasp. "This is a death trap," she muttered, clutching Sword for balance, though it was as useful against the stairs as it had been against the Frankenyeti.

"Keep climbing," Thane growled, sparing her a glance over his shoulder. His axe was slung across his back, his hands gripping the icy stone wall for stability. "And don't look down."

Of course, as soon as he said it, she peered down. Her stomach churned at the sight of the endless drop, the howling wind making it feel as though the stairs might collapse beneath her at any moment. Above them, the storm raged on, lightning streaking across the darkened sky and illuminating the treacherous path ahead in flashes of eerie blue light.

Tianna glanced back, her heart pounding as she saw the Frankenyeti was gaining. Its massive hands smashed into the stone steps and sides of the mountain as it climbed after them with terrifying agility. She whipped her head forward, only to stumble to a halt. Wasn't this the same section of stairs they'd just passed? The cracked ice on the railing, the jagged stone, it was all identical. The Yetis' chittering laughter echoed around them, the air shimmering faintly as though reality itself was folding in on them.

Thane growled. "It's messing with our perception of time! Don't stop! Just keep moving!"

Ahead, the narrow staircase led to a swaying rope bridge suspended over a chasm. The bridge's wooden planks creaked ominously under the weight of the snow. The ropes were weathered and frayed, by years of exposure to the elements.

"Seriously?" Tianna exclaimed as they reached the bridge. "This is the best option?"

"Would you rather face that abomination behind us?" Thane shot back, already stepping onto the bridge. It groaned under his weight, but he kept moving, motioning for Tianna to follow.

Gritting her teeth, Tianna stepped onto the bridge, her heart pounding as the planks swayed beneath her. She kept her eyes forward, focusing on Thane's steady movements rather than the gaping void below.

The Frankenyeti reached the start of the bridge, letting out another furious roar that echoed across the chasm. It hesitated for a moment, the tiny Yetis that made up its form chittering nervously, before stepping onto the first plank.

As the Frankenyeti climbed onto the bridge, time itself seemed to warp around it. The snow fell slower near its form, each flake hanging in the air before touching the creature's rippling surface. The ropes of the bridge groaned, not just from weight, but as though years of wear and tear were being compressed into mere moments.

"They're on the bridge!" Tianna yelled, panic rising in her voice.

"Keep moving!" Thane barked, reaching the other side and turning back. As soon as Tianna's boots hit solid ground, he raised his axe and swung it at the ropes anchoring the bridge.

With a mighty crack, one of the ropes snapped, sending the bridge lurching violently to one side. The Frankenyeti let out a guttural roar, its clawed hands scrabbling desperately at the remaining ropes as the entire structure swayed precariously.

"Hold on!" Thane bellowed, his voice cutting through the chaos. He swung his axe again, muscles straining as the blade bit into the second rope. With a final, shuddering snap, the bridge gave way, collapsing into the chasm below.

For a heartbeat, the world stood still. The howling wind filled the void, its icy claws tearing at Tianna's face as she stared at the gaping emptiness where the bridge had been. The Frankenyeti was gone, swallowed by the abyss, its roar fading into the depths like a distant echo.

But as relief flooded her chest, a sound rose from the darkness, faint and chittering. It was soft at first, then grew louder, sharper, more insistent.

"No—" Tianna whispered, stepping back instinctively.

From the void emerged a horrifying sight: a living chain of tiny Yetis, their fluffy bodies impossibly intertwined, climbing as one. The glowing blue of their eyes flickered with eerie determination, and their movements defied reason, stretching and leaping in ways that twisted the laws of time and space.

"Thane!" Tianna screamed, but her uncle was already moving, planting himself between her and the advancing chain.

The leading Yeti reached the edge, its claws snapping forward like a striking snake. Thane swung his axe, severing the connection, but the Yetis regrouped with unnatural speed, surging upward. One latched onto his boot.

"Get back!" he roared, stomping fiercely, but more claws joined the first. The chain of Yetis pulled with impossible strength, dragging him toward the edge.

"Thane, no!" Tianna lunged forward, her hand outstretched.

"Stay back, Tianna!" he shouted, his voice raw with desperation. He slammed the axe into the icy ground, anchoring himself as the yetis clawed and pulled.

Tianna's fingers grazed his wrist, their eyes locking for a single, agonizing moment.

And then the ledge crumbled beneath him.

"Tianna!" Thane gasped as his grip slipped. "I'm sorry." For one gut-wrenching second, his weight pulled against her hand, and she tried to hold him, tried to pull him back, but the icy ground betrayed her. His axe slipped free, clattering into the chasm as he fell.

"No!" she screamed, her voice echoing into the void as he vanished into the swirling mist below.

The storm raged on around her, the wind howling like a living thing. Tianna fell to her knees at the edge, staring into the abyss, her hand trembling where his had been seconds before.

Tears blurred her vision, freezing against her cheeks as she clutched Sword to her chest, her knuckles white with grief and fury. "Keep moving," she whispered to herself, her voice cracking as Thane's last words rang in her ears. 'I'm sorry.' Her breath came in ragged gasps, but she forced herself to her feet. "I won't fail."

21

Things Endured

"The world does not end with a fall, but with the silence that follows. For it is not the drop into darkness that undoes us, but the echo of a name we can no longer call back."

— *Reflections Beyond the Veil*
by Tharaniel the Pale

The storm was relentless, a howling vortex of ice and wind that swallowed the world whole. Snow whipped at Tianna's face, stinging her cheeks and blurring her vision. She tightened her grip on Sword. The handle was cold, even against her gloved hand. She trudged forward, one step at a time. The mountain loomed above her, its jagged peaks obscured by the swirling blizzard.

She didn't know how long she had been climbing. Minutes? Hours? Time felt as fluid as the snow, shifting and uncertain. All she knew was the ache in her legs and the cold biting at her fingers. Each step felt heavier than the last, her body weighed down by exhaustion and something far heavier.

Rea, Blarg, Nyx . . . were they even alive? The keep's collapse had been so sudden, so violent, that she hadn't been able to see what happened to them. Her mind replayed the moment over and over. The sound of stone crashing down. The sight of Blarg's wide eyes as the debris cut them off. Rea disappearing into the side passage, clutching Nyx. And Thane . . . she squeezed her eyes shut, trying to block out the memory of him falling, his voice echoing as he vanished into the abyss.

They are still alive.

The thought was a fragile thread, one she clung to desperately. "If they don't find a way through, I *will* go back for them," she whispered to herself, her voice barely audible over the storm. "I swear it."

The wind answered with a mournful howl, as if mocking her resolve. She shook her head and pressed on, forcing herself to keep moving. The path ahead was steep and treacherous, the icy ground threatening to slip out from under her with every step.

Then she heard it, a low, resonant hum that cut through the storm like a knife. She froze, her breath catching in her throat. The sound was faint at first, almost indistinguishable from the wind, but it grew louder, a haunting vibration that emanated from the air itself.

She turned slowly, scanning the snow-covered landscape. There was nothing, only the swirling white and the shadows of jagged rocks. The hum faded as suddenly as it had come, leaving an eerie silence in its wake.

Tianna shook her head, trying to dismiss the unease creeping up her spine. *It's the storm. Nothing more.*

But she couldn't shake the feeling that she was being watched.

She pulled her cloak tighter, her thoughts straying to Thane. His voice rose unbidden in her mind: *'You don't beat the mountain, kid. You outlast it.'* He'd said that once, long ago, when she'd complained about climbing the ridge near their home. She'd been sure her legs would give out, but he'd been right. She'd made it then. She could make it now.

Except, back then, Thane had been behind her, rolling his eyes and calling her dramatic. *'Come on, Tianna. The mountain's waiting.'* Now, there was only silence. The thought hit her harder than the wind, and her steps faltered.

Is this what it felt like for you? she wondered bitterly. *Falling? Knowing there's no one left to catch you?*

Her fingers tightened around Sword, the weight of it bringing her back to the present. She forced her legs to move, biting back the tears that threatened to spill. There was no time for doubt. Not here.

The first attack came without warning. One moment, she was trudging forward, her head down against the wind, the next, a shadow darted through the snow, fast and silent. Tianna barely had time to react as the creature lunged at her, its glowing eyes piercing through the blizzard.

She swung Sword in a wide arc, her heart pounding. The pan sliced through the air, but the creature dodged effortlessly, its sleek form vanishing back into the storm. Tianna stumbled, the force of her swing throwing her off balance. "Seriously?" she muttered, scrambling to her feet.

"I'd blame the snow, but let's be honest, it's clearly operator error," Sword chimed in.

"Shut up!"

The hum returned, louder this time, a deep, resonant sound that made her chest vibrate. Tianna turned in a circle, her eyes darting through the storm. The creature reappeared, its tentacle-like appendages whipping through the air as it lunged again. This time, she wasn't fast enough.

The appendage struck her arm, a jarring impact that sent her sprawling into the snow. Tianna cried out as a searing cold spread from the point of contact, a deep, bone-chilling frost that froze her from the inside out. She clutched her arm, gasping as the sensation intensified, the cold sapping her strength.

The creature let out a haunting, otherworldly sound, its hum rising to a discordant pitch that made her ears ache. Tianna swung Sword again, more out of desperation than strategy. The pan clanged off the side of the mountain, the sharp, metallic ring slicing through the storm. Startled by the sound, the creature flinched and bolted, its sleek form vanishing into the swirling snow as its hum faded into the distance.

"What fine aim you have," Sword quipped.

Tianna struggled to her feet, cradling her frozen arm. The cold had left it stiff and useless, the skin beneath her glove numb. "Shut up! I'm fighting for my life here!" she growled at Sword, her voice breaking.

The pan, for once, offered no reply.

The hum came and went, a haunting melody that circled her like a predator. Tianna pressed onward, her steps unsteady. Her arm throbbed with a deep, aching cold, and every gust of wind felt like needles piercing her skin. The storm closed in around her, the path narrowing until she felt like she was walking through a tunnel of snow.

She caught glimpses of them now. Three sleek feline shapes, each as large as a horse. They moved through the storm, their glowing eyes the only constant in the shifting white. They didn't attack, not yet. They were toying with her, circling like wolves, their hums overlapping in a discordant symphony.

"I know you're there!" Tianna shouted, her voice hoarse. "Come out already!"

The hums grew louder, the sound digging into her skull. It wasn't noise, it was a presence, heavy and oppressive, pressing down on her until she could barely breathe. Images flashed in her mind: Thane's fall, the collapsing keep, Rea's terrified face. The hum echoed her own thoughts, a cruel mockery of her guilt.

You couldn't save him. You won't save anyone.

"Shut up!" she screamed, swinging Sword one-handed at the shadows. The pan struck empty air. Tianna's momentum carried her forward, and she slipped, landing hard on the icy ground. Pain shot through her as she scrambled to her knees, her breath coming in ragged gasps.

The creatures still didn't attack. They lingered at the edges of her vision, their hums shifting into a low, taunting wail. Tianna pressed her hands to her ears, trying to block out the sound, but it was no use. It wasn't just in her ears; it was in her head, crawling under her skin.

She didn't know how long she had been running. The storm blurred everything into a monotony of white and gray, the wind stealing her breath and the snow clawing at her feet. Her arm was still numb, her fingers barely able to grip Sword. Her legs burned, every step a monumental effort.

The path narrowed further, forcing Tianna into a treacherous rocky pass. The walls rose steeply on either side, jagged and slick with ice, leaving her no room to maneuver. Each step felt more precarious than the last, her boots struggling for purchase on the frozen ground. Her breath came in sharp bursts, the chill burning her lungs. A low, insidious hum grew in the distance, vibrating through the air and making her spine tingle.

Her heart sank as the realization clawed its way into her mind. She gripped Sword tighter, its weight suddenly feeling insufficient.

It's a trap!

The hum swelled, louder now, echoing and reverberating off the icy walls, making it impossible to pinpoint its origin. She spun around, searching for a way out, but the storm enveloped her in a swirling, blinding haze of snow.

And then she saw them.

The first one emerged from the storm ahead, sleek and white, its glowing eyes cutting through the whiteout like twin blue embers. Tianna froze, her pulse hammering in her ears. Behind her, the faint outline of two more figures materialized, their movements unnervingly fluid. They flanked her, blocking any chance of retreat.

Their hums merged into a single, oppressive note, so loud and resonant that it felt like it was coming from inside her chest. It rattled her bones, made her teeth ache, and turned her knees to water.

Tianna raised Sword in trembling hands, swinging wildly at the closest creature. The weapon cut through the air, but the creature danced around her attack with effortless grace, as if mocking her attempts. The others circled, their movements a blur, the hum growing unbearable.

She stumbled, the vibrations of the hum shaking her to her core. Her vision blurred, and her strength waned as exhaustion crept over her like a tide.

She dropped to her knees, clutching Sword to her chest like a lifeline. "I can't do this," she whispered, her voice cracking as tears froze on her cheeks. "I'm not strong enough."

The creature in front slinked closer, its glowing eyes locked onto her. Its gaze was predatory, but also intelligent, cold, calculating. It knew she was beaten. It knew it had won.

This was it.

Tianna closed her eyes, surrendering to the inevitable. *My father couldn't do it. Thane couldn't do it. And now I can't do it.* A strange calm settled over her as her breathing slowed. *It's okay. Everything will be okay.*

And then, a thought pierced through her resignation, sharp and undeniable.

What about Rea?

Her eyes snapped open, meeting the creature's unrelenting gaze. It was only feet away now, close enough for her to feel the icy breath emanating from its maw.

You have to be strong. You have to protect her.

"This doesn't end here," she murmured, her voice quiet but firm. Her fingers tightened around Sword's handle as she rose. "I cannot fail now."

The creature paused, its glowing eyes narrowing in hesitation. The hum faltered for the first time, a subtle shift that echoed the crack of uncertainty in its composure.

"YOU WILL NOT BREAK ME!" Tianna's voice tore through the silence, reverberating through the pass.

Above her, a deep, resounding crack split the air. The sharp, unmistakable sound of shifting ice and snow, a warning growl from the mountain itself.

The creature's gaze flicked upward, its hesitation growing. The hum stuttered, uneven now, as the others shifted uneasily behind her.

Tianna held her ground, planting her feet and raising Sword as if daring them to come closer. "Come on," she said, her voice steady. "Let's get this over with."

The lead creature's growl deepened into a rumble. Its eyes glanced down at Sword then back into Tianna's eyes. Then it lunged, its maw opened wide, revealing rows of jagged teeth.

Tianna turned sharply, her hips snapping into motion as she kicked with all her strength. Her boot connected squarely with the creature's jaw, a sickening crunch echoing through the pass. The creature tumbled backward with a yelp, its mouth bloodied, a lone fang dangling precariously from its gums.

And then the mountain roared.

The first cascade of snow fell, tumbling from above in a glittering wave of white. It was followed by a deafening avalanche, ice and snow crashing down with unstoppable force.

Tianna didn't think. She turned and ran, the path beneath her feet shifting with every step. The hum of the creatures faded behind her, swallowed by the thunderous roar of the avalanche. The walls of the pass blurred in her periphery as she pushed herself forward, her chest burning, her legs screaming in protest.

She didn't dare look back.

Tianna climbed higher, her breath ragged in the thin, freezing air. The path had disappeared beneath layers of packed snow and ice, forcing her to rely on jagged rocks and treacherous footholds. Each step felt heavier, the biting wind tearing at her cloak and stinging her cheeks. The summit loomed above her, veiled in a shifting haze of storm clouds that crackled faintly with magic.

The hum of the creatures had long since faded, swallowed by the roar of the avalanche. But their presence lingered, a shadow in the back of her mind. She glanced over her shoulder at the white expanse below. The path she had followed was gone, buried beneath a restless sea of snow. There was no turning back now.

Her hands burned as she gripped an icy outcrop, her fingers raw and numb through her gloves. Sword hung awkwardly at her side, an impossible weight pulling at her.

"Keep moving," she whispered to herself, her voice hoarse and thin against the wind.

The ascent grew steeper, and the mountain seemed to conspire against her. The rocks were slick, the air colder, the wind crueler. She slipped once, her boot skidding on ice, and she barely caught herself on a jagged edge. Her arms trembled as she hauled herself back to her feet, her knees weak.

The storm above swirled closer, an unnatural force pulling at the edges of reality. She could feel it now, a dark, pulsing energy radiating from the summit. It was ancient, alive, and filled with a malevolent intent that made her stomach churn.

Tianna's thoughts drifted to Rea. Had she made it out of the rubble? Would she ever see her again? She thought of Thane, burdened by his failures to the very end. But he had saved her. He had sacrificed himself so that she would have a chance. And she thought of her father, who had never returned from his journey. Who had died trying to protect those that he loved. They had all climbed their mountains, fought their battles. Now it was her turn.

A low, mournful note drifted on the wind, thin and distant, like a ghost of sound carried through time. For one aching heartbeat, it sounded like Thane's war horn. Her breath caught, but then it was gone, swallowed by the storm. *A trick of the wind,* she told herself. Just the mountain playing games.

The clouds thickened as she neared the peak, the air humming with tension. The ground shifted beneath her, vibrating faintly, as if the mountain itself were alive and aware of her presence. The summit was close, too close to stop now.

The final stretch was a near-vertical wall of rock and ice. Tianna paused, her chest heaving, and studied the jagged surface. There was no clear path, just narrow crevices and uncertain holds. She swallowed hard, her fingers moving absently to Sword's handle, the one thing she had left in this world.

"You've made it this far," she muttered. "One more push."

She reached for the nearest handhold, her muscles screaming in protest. Her boots scrabbled against the icy surface, seeking purchase. Slowly, painstakingly, she climbed.

Halfway up, a gust of wind slammed into her, threatening to rip her from the wall. She flattened herself against the rock, her heart hammering as the gale howled around her. Snow and ice lashed her face, and for a terrifying moment, she was blind.

But the wind passed, leaving an eerie silence in its wake. Tianna exhaled shakily and forced herself to move again.

Her fingers brushed the edge of the summit, and she let out a small, disbelieving laugh. She pulled herself up with the last of her strength and rolled onto the flat surface, lying on her back as she gasped for air.

The storm swirled around her, its energy crackling in the air like the static before lightning. Tianna pulled her cloak tighter, her breath a frosty wisp in the freezing gale.

Dark shapes dotted the plateau ahead, silhouetted against the eerie glow of campfires scattered across the expanse. Smoke curled lazily into the storm-laden sky, mixing with the biting wind. Rows of angular, shadowy structures rose from the snow, crude and jagged, forming the unmistakable outline of an encampment.

Her stomach clenched as she scanned the scene. The fires illuminated figures moving between the tents, too far away to make out clearly. They were hulking shapes, their movements sharp and deliberate. Orcs? Goblins? Perhaps something worse.

Her eyes drifted upward, and there it stood, the jagged black spire of the citadel. It loomed over the encampment like a monolith of despair, its surface etched with glowing runes that pulsed faintly, mirroring the strange rhythm she felt thrumming in her chest. The energy was stronger here, almost unbearable, a suffocating weight that made her legs tremble and her breath catch.

A sudden gust of wind carried fragments of guttural speech to her ears. It was rough, gravelly, and rhythmic, almost like a chant. Her heart pounded.

"What am I supposed to do now?" she whispered, her voice barely audible over the storm. She scanned the encampment again, hoping for an opening, a weakness in the line of fires and figures.

Far to the right, near the edge of the encampment, the fires burned lower, the movement less frequent. If she was careful, she could sneak past and get closer to the citadel.

Keep going, she thought, forcing her legs to move. She hugged the rocky outcroppings as she edged forward, staying low to avoid drawing attention. The snow muffled her steps, but each crunch still felt like a thunderclap. Tianna hugged the rocky outcroppings, inching forward, her heart pounding harder with each movement. The chant grew louder, harsher, and more disjointed as she approached the edge of the encampment.

She paused, pressing herself against the frozen rock as the storm swirled around her. Across from her, the fires burned brightly, their flickering light casting strange shadows over the hulking figures moving through the camp. She squinted, trying to make sense of their chaotic movements.

A sudden, guttural roar ripped through the air, followed by the clash of metal and the thud of heavy bodies. Tianna flinched, peering cautiously over the outcrop.

The figures in the camp were in a frenzy now. One Orc, taller and broader than the others, slammed a Goblin to the ground, its roar echoing into the storm. Nearby, a pair of Goblins screeched at each other, their high-pitched voices barely audible over the growing din.

The camp was descending into bedlam. Goblins screeched commands that were lost in the chaos, their high-pitched voices swallowed by the storm. Orcs, caught between confusion and fury, lashed out at anything that moved, their massive forms adding to the disorder. Goblins darted between their legs, their movements frantic and disorganized, while the storm only amplified the madness. The clamor of shrieking orders, panicked yells, and the clash of weapons echoed off the jagged cliffs, drowning out even the howling wind.

Tianna clutched Sword tightly, unsure what to do next. Her chest rose and fell in shallow, uneven breaths as her eyes darted across the chaos. "What's happening?" she whispered.

The fires cast long, twisting shadows that danced across the snow, making it hard to tell where the movement ended and the night began. She crept forward, each step calculated and slow, hoping the uproar would mask her approach.

Her pulse hammered in her ears as she pressed against the rocky outcrop, her gaze fixed on the citadel looming in the distance. The glowing runes pulsed faintly, matching the rhythm of her heart. She could feel it pulling her forward, an unseen force drawing her closer.

Then, there was a sound behind her, a low, guttural growl.

Tianna froze. The warmth fled her body, replaced by a cold dread that rooted her to the spot. Slowly, her hand tightened around the handle of Sword as she turned her head.

Standing a few feet away, half-shrouded in the swirling snow, was an Orc. Its glowing eyes burned like embers, and its jagged teeth gleamed in the firelight. The creature's lips curled into a snarl, and its massive hand gripped a rusted axe.

Tianna's breath caught in her throat.

The storm roared around them, but all she could hear was the pounding of her heart.

22

A Chip Off the Old Munk

"To know one's greatest flaw is not to be free of it. But it is the first step toward no longer being ruled by it."

— Archivist Kelm of the Moonfast Abbey

The silence was almost unbearable. After the cacophony of battle. The screams, the clash of steel against ice, and the roar of the collapsing entrance. The oppressive quiet of the keep felt like a different kind of violence. Rea coughed, the sound echoing back to her as if mocking her attempt to break the stillness.

"Tianna, Thane, Nyxie . . . Blarg?" she asked, her voice trembling as she tried to focus her eyes within the blackness.

"Oy, Blarg is well," Blarg's voice rumbled from close by, muffled by what sounded like debris. "Though his left arm feels as if it were trampled by a Troll. The others, they were outside when the ceiling came down."

There was a soft yowl, followed by the faint sound of paws padding across ice. Nyx emerged from the darkness, his silhouette barely discernible, tail swishing with annoyance.

"Nyxie! Thank the Spire," Rea murmured, sighing in relief. Her hand brushed against the cold ground as she struggled to sit upright. The chill seeped into her hands, reminding her how deep behind the ice they now were.

As their eyes adjusted, a faint blue glow began to permeate the darkness. The surrounding walls shimmered, revealing a jagged beauty that was equal parts breathtaking and foreboding. The ice caught the dim light, refracting it in fractured patterns that danced across the interior walls.

"Where are we?" Rea whispered, her breath fogging in the frigid air.

Blarg slowly walked over to Rea, brushing shards of ice from his shoulders. "A grave, perchance," he said, his tone unusually somber. "A tomb prepared for a final slumber, though Blarg would prefer one with softer bedding and a keg of ale."

Rea shot him a sharp glare. "Could you be less dramatic?"

Blarg raised an eyebrow. "Blarg thinks not. The present circumstances do merit some degree of drama."

Nyx let out a low growl, interrupting their exchange. His gaze was fixed on the faint blue light emanating from deeper down the path. The others followed his line of sight and noticed a crumbled wall, revealing a narrow cave leading further into the mountain. The walls of the tunnel glistened with the same eerie luminescence.

"It looks as if the path has been chosen," Blarg said, hefting *Thumpkin* onto his broad shoulder. "It would be best to move from this place before the walls give way even further."

Without waiting for the others, Nyx padded ahead, his sleek form blending almost seamlessly with the shadows.

The passage was narrow, forcing them to walk single file. The faint glow grew brighter as they advanced, casting an ethereal light that brought the ice to life. Patterns swirled within the frozen walls, like whispers of forgotten storms trapped within the ice.

"Blarg finds this place suspicious," he muttered, his voice low. "It's too quiet, and there is a presence in the air."

His eyes darted around the tunnel as if expecting something to leap from the shadows. "Aye, there is something wrong about this place," he said after a moment.

Rea shivered, not from the cold, but from the way Blarg's usual confidence had cracked. She tightened her grip on her slingshot, its familiar weight a small comfort in the oppressive silence.

"Try not to think about it," she said, keeping her voice firm. "Whatever's wrong, there's nothing we can do about it. Let's keep moving."

Blarg glanced at her with a look of approval before nodding his head.

They continued. The only sounds were their muted footsteps and the occasional cracking of ice echoing through the cavern. The passage widened, opening into a chamber that made them all stop in their tracks.

The walls here were smoother, the blue glow almost blinding as it emanated from a massive, crystalline formation in the center of the room. The structure pulsed faintly, as if alive, and within its depths, shadows swirled like trapped phantoms.

Nyx hissed, his fur bristling as he took a step back.

"What in the name of the Spire—?" Rea whispered, her voice barely audible.

Blarg's hand tightened on *Thumpkin*. "'Tis no mere crystal," he said grimly. "'Tis a prison."

As Rea and Blarg stared at the crystalline prison, a figure within stirred. Encased in the ice was a small, furry creature that radiated an aura of magical power far beyond its size. The creature's eyes glowed faintly as it twitched its nose, examining the intruders.

"Is that . . . a squirrel?" Rea asked, her voice a mix of confusion and disbelief.

"No. 'Tis a chipmunk," Blarg responded. "One can tell by the stripes on its face."[95]

The crystal pulsed again, and a voice echoed in their minds. It was high-pitched and frantic, with the unmistakable energy of a creature used to darting from branch to branch. "Silence now! I am Skirribee, the Guardian of Eternity's Acorn Tree! You interlopers have awakened me. Now, you must face the trials three!"

"Is it rhyming?" Rea asked in confusion.

"Silence all your boorishness, or thou must face the consequence."

"Yep, it's rhyming." Blarg said with a sigh. "At least it's not riddles. Blarg hates when it's riddles."

"Now step ye forward, one at a time. Gaze into the mirror, see what you'll find. A trial for each, your greatest fault. Failure shall force your journey's halt."

"Very well, Blarg is doing this," he said without hesitation as he stepped up to the crystal and stared deeply into its reflection. With a flash of light, he was gone.

"Eeep," Rea squeaked as she desperately searched for Blarg.

"Worry not. Your friend is fine. At least he is, for the time. Now gaze yourself, your turn to see. Your greatest fault, revealed to thee."

Reluctantly, Rea stepped up to the crystal and gazed into its depths. Another flash filled the room, and she was gone.

"Now it is time—"

But before the chipmunk could finish what it was saying. Nyx stared into the crystal and disappeared in a flash of blazing light.

---

[95] Blarg had, at one point, devoted an entire winter to the study of small woodland mammals, after being struck on the head by an acorn mid-duel and taking it as a divine sign. Since then, he's made it his solemn duty to distinguish between chipmunks, squirrels, tree rats, and what he calls "the stripey impostors."

"—how rude."

"Blarg, oh Blarg, so proud and sure,
Your judgments swift, your stance secure.
You see the world in black and white,
And cling to views with all your might.
But truth is vast, not bound by pride;
Your greatest flaw is what's inside.
To truly grow, you must embrace
That judgment's strength is giving space."

Blarg stood at the edge of a bustling town square, *Thumpkin* resting on his shoulder. The air was filled with the shouts of merchants and the clatter of wagon wheels. It was an unfamiliar place, but it didn't feel strange. Blarg had seen a hundred towns like this, small, busy, and brimming with the unmistakable hum of human life.

But the wagon at the center of the square was not of human construction.

A group of Goblins clustered around it, unloading barrels and sacks to check their bindings. Their green skin caught the sunlight, and their chatter, sharp and quick, carried across the square. Blarg's eyes narrowed.

"What are they doing here?" he muttered to himself.

As if in answer, a farmer stormed toward the Goblins, his face red and twisted with anger. "You lot think you can stroll in here?" he bellowed, jabbing a finger at the nearest Goblin. "You think we've forgotten what your kind did to us?"

The Goblins froze. The leader, a wiry figure with a calm expression, stepped forward, raising his hands. "We mean no harm," he said evenly. "We are traders, passing through on our way to the capital. These goods are ours, fairly earned."

"Lies!" the farmer spat. "I know Goblin tricks! You're no traders, you're thieves!" He turned to the growing crowd of townsfolk. "I recognize these faces! They attacked my farm years ago, burned my barn, stole my livestock!"

The Goblin leader frowned but kept his voice steady. "You're mistaken. None of us have ever been to your farm. We're merchants, not bandits."

Blarg stepped forward, his imposing frame drawing the attention of both sides. "What's going on here?" he demanded, his voice booming.

The farmer rounded on him, desperation in his eyes. "These Goblins are lying! They're thieves, bandits! I've seen what their kind can do!"

The Goblin leader met Blarg's gaze, his expression calm but wary. "We've done nothing wrong. We're just passing through."

Blarg's hand tightened on *Thumpkin*. He didn't trust Goblins. He'd seen too much, heard too many stories. They were trouble, every time. And the farmer's anger was genuine.

"You expect these people to believe that?" Blarg said, his voice low and accusing.

The Goblin leader straightened, his jaw tight. "I expect you to look at the evidence," he said firmly. "These goods are ours. Ask the merchants we've traded with. We've done nothing to harm anyone."

The farmer scoffed. "As if anyone would vouch for them!"

Blarg turned his gaze to the wagon. The barrels and sacks bore no signs of theft. No hurried packing. No markings from other owners. They were neat, labeled, and organized.

But his instincts pushed back. Goblins were Goblins.

A faint chirp drew his attention. He glanced down to see a chipmunk perched on a nearby crate, its beady eyes fixed on him. It tilted its head, as if questioning him.

Blarg frowned. The chipmunk's presence felt oddly familiar, almost as if it had been there all along.

The crowd murmured, their unease growing. The Goblins stood their ground, their expressions a mix of frustration and quiet resolve.

Blarg gazed at the farmer, his desperate anger. He glared at the Goblins, their calm determination. And then, for the first time, he hesitated.

The chipmunk twitched its nose, scurried to the edge of the crate, and let out another faint chirp.

Blarg released his grip on *Thumpkin*. "Maybe you've seen Goblins before," he said to the farmer, his tone measured. "But these are not those in which you speak. Their goods are neat, their story consistent. Blarg sees no sign of thievery."

The farmer sputtered, his indignation faltering. "But —"

"Enough," Blarg said, cutting him off. He turned to the Goblin leader. "Go. Trade your goods in the capital. But if you're lying, and Blarg finds out, there will be consequences."

The Goblin leader nodded, his calm composure unshaken. "Thank you," he said simply.

As the Goblins resumed their work, the crowd began to disperse, muttering as they went. Blarg stood still, his thoughts churning.

The chipmunk darted down from the crate and scampered into the shadows, leaving Blarg alone with a thought that unsettled him more than the confrontation itself: *'Tis a strange feeling, this . . . doubt. Blarg thought the Goblins were at fault, but no! Perhaps Blarg was too quick to lay blame. When else has he been too quick to blame?*

He shook his head, pushing the doubt aside as he turned to leave. But the question lingered, gnawing at the edge of his pride.

"Ah, Rea, so bold yet frail within,
Your deepest fear, where to begin?
When shadows loom and strength takes flight,
You freeze, consumed by helpless fright.
While others act, you hesitate,
And thus, my dear, may seal your fate."

Rea stumbled into the cavern, her boots sliding on the slick, frost-covered ground. She paused, shivering, and glanced around, trying to get her bearings. The vast space was cold and dimly lit by an eerie blue glow, its source unclear. The air was heavy, pressing down on her like an unseen weight. She didn't know how she'd gotten there, and worse, she didn't know why.

Her hand went instinctively to her belt, but her slingshot wasn't there. Panic flared briefly in her chest, but she forced herself to breathe, to think. *Focus, Rea. Stay calm.*

Ahead, in the center of the cavern, she saw a figure curled up on the icy ground. It was small and trembling, shrouded in flickering shadows. Rea hesitated, her heart pounding. She took a cautious step forward, then another, her breath forming soft clouds in the freezing air.

As she drew closer, the shadows shifted, and her stomach twisted. The figure on the ground was . . . *her.* A younger version of herself, pale and fragile, her arms wrapped around her knees.

"No," Rea whispered, taking a step back.

The sound of laughter cut through the stillness, light and singsong, but with a cruel edge that made her skin crawl. She turned sharply to see them—Elves. Their unnerving beauty was sharper than she remembered, their hollow smiles and bright eyes fixed upon her.

Rea's chest tightened as memories clawed their way to the surface, icy hands pinning her down, their mocking voices draining her of every ounce of strength. She remembered the fear, the helplessness. She remembered how small she had felt, how powerless.

"She hasn't changed," one of them said, stepping closer to her shadow-self. Its voice was as smooth as glass. "Still scared. Still weak."

Another circled behind her, its footsteps silent on the ice. "Always frightened, ready to run. She'll never be anything more."

Rea backed away, her pulse roaring in her ears. She wanted to scream, to run, but her legs wouldn't move. She felt trapped, the same as she had been back then.

"Help me," the shadow-Rea whispered, her voice trembling.

Rea froze, her breath catching. The younger version of herself glanced up, her wide, tear-filled eyes meeting her own.

"Please."

The plea was so small, so fragile, and it shattered something inside her. She had been that girl once, paralyzed by fear, waiting for someone, anyone, to save her.

The Elves' laughter rose, sharp and mocking, as they closed in around her.

"You can't face us."

"You can't fight us."

"You'll never escape us."

The words battered against her like a storm, but this time, something inside her pushed back.

"No," Rea said, her voice low but steady.

The Elves paused, their hollow smiles faltering.

Rea took a step forward, then another, her fists clenched at her sides. The fear was still there, clawing at her, but she didn't let it control her.

"I'm not that girl anymore," she said, her voice growing stronger with each word. "You don't get to decide who I am. You don't have power over me anymore."

The Elves hissed, their forms flickering as if caught in a strong wind. The shadows around the younger Rea began to dissolve, and the cavern filled with a soft, golden light.

Rea kneeled before her shadow-self, reaching out a hand. "You're not powerless. You're stronger than you think."

The shadow-Rea reached back, their fingers touching lightly before the younger version faded away, merging into her.

The cavern trembled, the icy walls cracking and splitting as the Elves screamed one last time before vanishing into nothingness.

Rea stood, her chest heaving, her fists still clenched. She peered around the now-empty cavern, her reflection shimmering faintly in the fractured walls.

"I'm not powerless," she said quietly, the words steady and final.

As she turned to leave, her gaze caught on something small sitting on a ledge. It was a chipmunk, its tiny eyes watching her intently. It tilted its head, twitched its nose, and then scampered away into the shadows.

Rea blinked, shaking her head, and took a step toward the next path, her stride steady, her fear left behind.

"Nyx, oh Nyx, with steps so bold,
Your flaw's a tale, chipmunks have told.
For where's the sense in prancing about,
With no regard for threats that sprout?
You leap, you pounce, you never pause,
Ignoring danger's quiet claws.
A chipmunk knows, to stay alive,
It's caution, not chaos, that helps one survive!"

Nyx stretched luxuriously on a patch of moss, the dappled sunlight filtering through the forest canopy warming his fur. The air was alive with the rustling of leaves, the chirping of birds, and the faint scampering of small animals darting between the trees.

His ears perked as he spotted movement. A squirrel dashed up a trunk, its bushy tail flicking enticingly. A hare bounded across the clearing, its fluffy white tail practically begging to be chased.

Nyx's pupils dilated, and his tail twitched. The forest was a paradise of motion, a chaotic playground calling to every ounce of his feline nature.

But something about the shadows between the trees felt . . . off. They lingered too long, darker than they should have been, and they moved in ways that shadows shouldn't. Nyx's instincts prickled, but his attention was drawn back to the darting animals.

Then he saw it.

A massive, absurdly fluffy chipmunk sat on a nearby log, its fur a comically exaggerated puffball. It stared at him with wide, terrified eyes, its tiny paws clutching a half-eaten acorn.

Nyx froze, his head tilting. This was no ordinary chipmunk.

"Skirribee," the chipmunk squeaked, its high-pitched voice quivering. "That's my name! Don't eat me! Please don't eat me!"

Nyx blinked slowly, his tail flicking lazily behind him.

"I mean, look at me," Skirribee continued, clutching the acorn tighter. "I'm all fur! No meat! I'd just get stuck in your teeth! Terrible choice, really. Very inconvenient!"

Nyx took a step closer, his whiskers twitching with curiosity. Skirribee let out a panicked squeal and scampered backward, his massive fluff ball of a tail dragging behind him.

"Wait! Stop!" Skirribee squeaked. "There are predators here! Bigger ones! They're hiding, and if you chase anything, anything at all, they'll get you!"

Nyx stopped, his ears flicking toward the shadows. He could sense them now, silent, patient, predatory. But his gaze returned to Skirribee, who had pressed himself against the log, shaking like a leaf.

The logical thing would have been to heed the chipmunk's warning. But Nyx was no ordinary cat.

Without hesitation, he pounced; not at the other animals, not at the lurking predators, but directly at Skirribee.

The chipmunk let out a shriek as Nyx landed squarely on him, his paws pinning down the enormous fluff ball of fur. "You chose me?!" Skirribee squealed, his voice muffled by Nyx's paw. "Of all the animals in this cursed forest, you chose *me*?!"

The forest froze. The predators in the shadows stopped moving. Even the other animals paused, their eyes wide as they watched.

Nyx tilted his head, leaning down to sniff Skirribee. The chipmunk squeaked again, curling into a trembling ball of fluff.

And then, Nyx sat down, casually grooming his paw as though nothing had happened.

The predators in the shadows melted away, their forms dissolved like mist. The sunlight grew warmer, the air lighter. The trial was over. Skirribee peeked out from behind his massive tail, his voice trembling. "You . . . you did it. You survived the trial."

Nyx glanced at him with a slow blink, his expression unreadable. With a final flick of his tail, he stood and padded off toward the forest's edge, leaving Skirribee behind, still quivering in disbelief.

"Never again," the chipmunk muttered, pulling his fluff ball tail around himself. "Never. Again."

The group all reappeared at once, their surroundings shifting abruptly. The icy trials vanished, replaced by a vast cavern that stretched endlessly into darkness above. The air was still and heavy, carrying the faint echo of their footsteps as they regrouped.

Rea blinked, steadying herself. "Where are we?" she asked, her voice calm.

Blarg scanned the cavern, his hand instinctively gripping the handle of *Thumpkin*. The walls shimmered faintly with veins of crystal, their soft glow enough to illuminate the sheer scale of the space. Circling the perimeter were stairs. They were broad, steady, and carved with precision. They spiraled upward, vanishing into the shadowy heights.

"These stairs," Blarg muttered, running his hand along the smooth railing. "They seem . . . sturdy. Not what Blarg was expecting." He stomped on the first step, nodding in approval as it held firm.

Nyx padded to the base of the stairs, his ears swiveling as he sniffed the air. He tilted his head upward, his tail flicking in quiet agreement.

"I guess we should go up," Rea said softly, her gaze following the spiraling ascent. "Do you think Tianna and Thane made it up the mountain?"

Blarg hesitated, his usual confidence faltering. He nodded his head. "They're strong. They'll have found a way."

Rea nodded, clutching her slingshot tightly. "I hope so. I hope they're already ahead of us. I hope they found another path to the citadel."

Blarg's jaw tightened, his voice low and steady. "Aye, Blarg does as well. If these are the stairs from the map, then this path is headed the right way."

Rea glanced at Nyx, who was already stepping onto the first stair, his paw pads silent against the stone. "If Nyxie can climb these, so can we," she said with a small smile, following the cat.

Blarg snorted. "Blarg has faced worse than stairs."

Without another word, they began their ascent. The stairs were wide enough for them to climb side by side, their footsteps echoing faintly in the chamber's stillness. The soft glow of the crystal veins faded as they climbed higher, the darkness above growing deeper and more oppressive.

"Is this the end of our quest?" Rea asked quietly, her voice barely carrying above the sound of their steps.

Blarg grunted. "Blarg hopes so, but regardless, whatever lies ahead, he shall face it with you. Together."

Rea exhaled, nodding. "Together."

The trio climbed in silence, their thoughts lingering on Tianna and Thane. The weight of their own trials hung heavy in their minds, but so did the hope that their companions had found another way forward. Whatever awaited them at the top, they would face it together.

23

For Those Who Remain

"Grief does not end the journey; it changes the path, and stays with us—
silent, faithful, and forever one step behind."

— Last Testament of the Wanderer Priest

It felt like hours had passed, each step heavier than the last, as though the weight of the mountain itself pressed down on them. But finally, they emerged at the top of the stairwell. The air grew warmer, carrying the faint scent of wood and something faintly metallic. The walls opened into a smaller, enclosed room.

Shelves stretched to the ceiling, each crammed with supplies: sacks of grain, barrels of ale, crates packed with dried meats, cheeses, and preserved fruits. Lanterns flickered on the walls, their soft glow casting long shadows over the stacks of provisions.

"'Tis a storehouse," Blarg said, his eyes narrowing as he surveyed the endless rows of provisions. "Enough here to feed an army for weeks. Maybe months." He sniffed the air suspiciously. "But no garlic. Very disappointing."

Rea ran her fingers along a row of shiny apples, her wide eyes reflecting the flickering lantern light. "This must be where they bring all the supplies up," she said, her voice tinged with a mix of wonder and unease.

Nyx, meanwhile, leaped gracefully onto a nearby crate. He sniffed at a row of suspiciously shiny sausages, his tail twitching as if in judgment. Without warning, he casually swatted one off the crate, sending it rolling across the floor.

"Nyxie!" Rea hissed, though her scolding lacked conviction.

Before anyone could say more, the sound of heavy boots echoed from the stairwell behind them. The low, guttural growl that followed vibrated the very air in the room. The doorway darkened as a massive figure stepped through.

An Orc loomed in the frame, its broad shoulders nearly brushing the sides of the narrow entryway. The dim torchlight gleamed off its jagged, mismatched armor, and in one hand, it held an axe so large it was absurd. It rested on the Orc's shoulder as though it weighed nothing at all.

For those who have never seen an Orc up close, it's an experience best described as profoundly unpleasant. Imagine a boulder sprouting legs, learning to walk upright, and then deciding it had a personal vendetta against everything smaller than itself. Add a permanent scowl, tusks that looked more suited to punching holes in armor than chewing food, and a disregard for hygiene that could generously be called "legendary," and you'd have a fair approximation.

Encountering an Orc on a typical day is less than ideal. Encountering an Orc after eight grueling days of trudging through snow, braving hostile terrain, and finally climbing a staircase that stretched endlessly into the heavens? That's just cruel.

One could argue that life is best lived long and full of experiences. However, to be unceremoniously smashed to death at the very end of your journey—when victory is just within reach—is the kind of cosmic joke that makes the universe seem unnecessarily vindictive. A less masochistic individual might even prefer to meet their end at the beginning of such a harrowing journey. You know, skip the hardship entirely.[96]

---

[96] This exact thing happened once. A would-be hero named Darrin the Eager tripped over his own bootlaces and plummeted off a cliff at the precise moment he reached for his prophesized magic sword. Historians now refer to his tale as *The Least Harrowing*

Fortunately for the group, this particular Orc wasn't currently in *'smash everything that moves'* mode. His axe was comfortably relaxed (for now), and his scowl, while present, was more curious than murderous. It wasn't much, but it was an opportunity. And when faced with an Orc in a storehouse, any opportunity to avoid becoming paste was a gift to be seized with both hands.

The Orc's deep-set eyes scanned the group, glinting with suspicion. Its lip curled, revealing teeth that appeared more like weapons than tools. When it spoke, the words were a deep, guttural rumble, incomprehensible yet undeniably hostile. The sound rippled through the ground beneath them.

"What did he say?" Rea whispered, her slingshot trembling slightly in her hands.

"No idea," Blarg rumbled back, stepping in front of her with *Thumpkin* gripped tightly in both hands. His voice dropped into something almost diplomatic. "This party is merely passing through. There is no need for trouble."

The Orc snorted, a huff of air that could have been laughter or contempt. It clearly didn't understand a word Blarg had said, but its grip on the axe tightened.

Blarg furrowed his brow, his face a mask of concentration. "Grikna. The Midnight Thread," he said, his voice measured and deliberate.

The Orc tilted its head slightly, but there was no sign of recognition. Instead, its wary posture shifted to something more predatory as it took a slow step forward, its axe gleaming in the flickering light.

Rea tensed, her fingers tightening around her slingshot. Nyx crouched low on his crate, his tail lashing in slow, deliberate movements.

Journey of All Time. The sword remained stuck in the stone for another sixteen years until a more coordinated replacement could come of age.

Blarg's voice boomed again, louder this time, as he stood firm. "The stars weave our path!" He raised *Thumpkin* slightly, his grip unyielding. "Ghaz'ak thrakk varg zath!"

The Orc froze mid-step, its massive frame suddenly still. The tension in the room hung thick as its eyes narrowed. The faintest flicker of understanding crossed its face. For a moment, there was only the crackling of the torches and the faint sound of Nyx's tail flicking against the crate.

Rea glanced nervously at Blarg. "What now?" she whispered.

Blarg didn't answer, his gaze locked on the Orc, waiting to see what it would do next.

The Orc's eyes flicked between Blarg and Rea, its grip on the axe loosening slightly. It took a step back, though its posture remained guarded. Slowly, it lowered the axe, the blade resting on the stone floor with a dull *thud*.

"Ghaz'ak thrakk varg zath," it repeated, its deep voice resonating through the chamber. There was no hostility now, only curiosity, and perhaps a hint of respect.

Blarg didn't relax, but he gave a slight nod. "You understand?"

The Orc grunted, a sound somewhere between a yes and a maybe. It tapped its chest with a meaty hand. "Thurg," it said simply.

Blarg mirrored the gesture. "Blarg."

Rea glanced between them, her confusion written plainly on her face. "Wait, are we . . . friends now? Is this how it works?"

Thurg narrowed his eyes at her but made no move to attack. Instead, he pointed behind him, then to the stairwell. His gestures were quick but deliberate.

"He's trying to tell us something," Rea said, stepping cautiously closer.

Nyx, as if bored with the proceedings, hopped down from his crate and slinked toward Thurg. The Orc froze as the cat approached, his gaze flicking warily to the tiny creature. Nyx, ever the opportunist, sniffed the Orc's boot before rubbing against his leg with an air of ownership.

Thurg blinked, clearly unsure what to make of the gesture.

"Looks like Nyx approves," Rea said, trying not to laugh.

The tension in the room eased further, though it wasn't gone entirely. Thurg pointed toward the stairwell again, this time with more urgency. He spoke a few guttural words, his tone insistent.

Blarg frowned, trying to make sense of it. "I think he wants us to leave."

Before anyone could respond, a sharp, snarling voice echoed from behind Thurg.

A Goblin stepped out of the shadows, his wiry frame draped in mismatched scraps of armor. His sharp features twisted in anger as he barked something incomprehensible at Thurg. He drew a dagger from his belt and jabbed a clawed finger toward the Orc. The Goblin's shrill, guttural words were clearly a reprimand, his tone dripping with frustration and disgust.

Thurg's shoulders sagged slightly, his reluctance plain on his face. He cast a quick, almost apologetic glance at the group before the Goblin shoved him roughly, barking another command.

The Orc hesitated, gripping his axe tightly, his muscles tense as though torn between two opposing forces. The Goblin snarled again, taking a step closer and shouting with renewed fury.

Thurg's expression hardened. He shifted his grip on the axe, his knuckles whitening around the handle.

"Ghaz'ak thrakk varg zath," he rumbled, his voice low but resolute.

Before the Goblin could react, Thurg swung his axe in a wide, calculated arc. The flat of the blade struck the Goblin squarely in the head with a loud *crack,* sending him crumpling to the ground in an unconscious heap.

The group stared in stunned silence as Thurg straightened, his grip still firm on the axe. He turned back to them, his expression unreadable, but the tension in his posture seemed to ease.

"What . . . just . . . happened?" Rea whispered, her voice trembling with a mix of relief and confusion.

Blarg grunted approvingly, a grin spreading across his face. "Blarg likes him," he said, giving *Thumpkin* an idle twirl.

The sound of heavy boots on stone shattered the brief calm. Two more Orcs burst into the room, their burly forms filling the doorway one at a time. They froze at the sight of the unconscious Goblin on the ground, then fixed their sharp gazes on Thurg and the group.

One of the Orcs barked out a rapid string of guttural words, his tone accusatory. He jabbed a finger at the fallen Goblin, then at Thurg, clearly demanding an explanation.

Rea stepped back instinctively, clutching her slingshot. "This can't be good," she muttered under her breath.

Thurg raised his hand, his deep voice rumbling as he launched into a long, impassioned reply in Goruk. His gestures were broad and deliberate, his tone carrying a mix of frustration and conviction. The group couldn't understand most of it, but one phrase stood out: "Ghaz'ak thrakk varg zath."

The other two Orcs paused, their hostility melting into something more akin to curiosity. One of them muttered something to the other, who nodded, his tusks glinting in the torchlight.

Blarg leaned toward Rea. "They're listening," he said quietly.

Rea glanced nervously at the Orcs, her heart pounding. "Listening to what, though?"

Thurg stepped forward, his voice rising as he spoke again, this time with even greater urgency. He gestured toward the door, and finally at the fallen Goblin. The other Orcs exchanged glances, their eyes wide with understanding.

Then, without warning, they broke into grins. One of them let out a deep, rumbling laugh, clapping Thurg on the shoulder hard enough to make his armor clank. The other nodded enthusiastically and bellowed something that echoed through the chamber.

"What's happening?" Rea asked, her voice barely above a whisper.

"They're excited," Blarg said, his grin widening. "Blarg likes this even more."

The two Orcs turned on their heels and bolted back through the doorway, their heavy boots pounding against the ground. Their voices carried back to the group as they shouted in Goruk, their words spreading like wildfire.

Moments later, the distant sounds of chaos reached the storehouse. The sharp clamor of raised voices and the clang of steel against steel grew louder, accompanied by roars of anger and cries of battle.

Blarg and Rea cautiously crept to the doorway, their footsteps silent on the stone floor. Peering outside, they were met with pure pandemonium. Orcs and Goblins clashed in a chaotic melee, steel ringing against steel as furious shouts filled the air. Goblins darted in every direction, their movements frantic and disorganized, while thick smoke billowed from burning tents and crumbling structures. The camp outside the storehouse was ablaze (both literally and figuratively) with chaos.

"They're turning on each other," Rea said, her eyes wide.

"I suppose Grikna was speaking true after all," Blarg said with an amused grin, watching another Goblin trip over its own feet as it tried to flee.

Before Rea could respond, heavy footsteps pounded through the doorway, drawing their attention. A massive Orc strode into the room, his armor splattered with soot and blood. In his massive hand, he held a familiar figure by the arm.

"Tee-Tee!" Rea cried, her voice breaking with relief as she rushed toward her sister.

The Orc released Tianna, who stumbled slightly but quickly regained her footing. She appeared exhausted but unharmed, her cloak torn and dusted with snow. Sword was clutched tightly in her hand, its handle scuffed but steady. Despite her disheveled appearance, her eyes burned with determination.

"Miss me?" Tianna asked, her voice hoarse but carrying a faint trace of humor.

Rea threw her arms around Tianna, holding her tightly. "I thought you were . . . I didn't know if you—" Her words faltered as tears welled in her eyes.

"I'm fine," Tianna said softly, returning the embrace. "I'm here."

Blarg crossed his arms, a broad grin spreading across his face. "Fine job, child."

"Hey, don't mind me, just a legendary weapon. No need to be happy to see me again," Sword complained.

The large Orc exchanged a few guttural words with Thurg, his tone low but urgent. Thurg nodded solemnly, replying in kind. Their exchange was brief but carried a weight that hung in the air, the tension between them palpable as the clamor of the battle pressed closer.

Rea's voice broke through the moment, trembling with hope and fear. "Where's Uncle?" she asked, her wide eyes searching Tianna's face as though willing the answer to be what she desperately wanted to hear.

Tianna froze, her breath catching in her throat. Her lips parted, but no words came out at first. She swallowed hard, her hand tightening around Sword as tears welled in her eyes. "Rea . . . I'm sorry," she whispered, her voice cracking under the weight of the truth. "He didn't make it."

"What?" The word was small, fragile, barely audible over the chaos.

Tianna's legs felt weak, but she forced herself to stand firm, for Rea's sake. "He fell from the mountain," she said, each word like a stone sinking in her chest. "He was protecting me from the Frankenyeti. He saved my life, Rea. He died a hero."

Rea's face crumpled, her small frame shaking as she let out a broken sob. "Oh, Uncle, no!" she cried, the words tumbling out in anguish as she threw herself into Tianna's arms. She buried her face in her sister's chest, her tears soaking the fabric of her cloak.

Tianna held Rea tightly, one hand cradling the back of her head, the other gripping Sword like an anchor. Her own tears spilled freely, streaking her dirt-stained face, but she didn't wipe them away. She didn't move. All she could do was hold her sister as the weight of their loss bore down on them, as the world around them went up in flames.

"I'm not going to waste the chance he gave us," Tianna said softly, her voice resolute despite the tears. "He believed in us, Rea. We have to finish this, for him."

Rea sniffled, nodding against Tianna's chest. Her sobs quieted, though tears continued to flow. "He always said we'd make it together," she whispered, her voice barely audible. "He promised—"

Tianna closed her eyes, pressing her cheek to the top of Rea's head. "And we will," she murmured, her voice steady now. "We'll make it because of him."

The moment was broken by a roar from nearby, the sound of steel clashing and voices raised in fury. Tianna's eyes snapped open, her gaze shifting to the large Orc and Thurg, who were gesturing animatedly toward the chaos.

"What's going on?" Tianna asked, her voice firmer now as she pulled back slightly from Rea, keeping a comforting hand on her shoulder. She glanced between the Orcs, her brow furrowing. "Why are they fighting each other?"

Blarg, who had been uncharacteristically silent, stepped forward and gestured broadly toward the camp. His usual grin was subdued, but there was a gleam of approval in his eyes. "The Orcs have decided they do not like the Dark Lord anymore," he said, his tone almost casual. "Blarg supports this decision."

Tianna raised an eyebrow at him, a small, incredulous laugh escaping her despite everything. "Of course you do," she muttered, shaking her head. Her grip on Sword tightened as her gaze turned back to the burning camp. "And now what? Do we . . . walk through the middle of that?"

Blarg's grin widened slightly, his confidence returning. "Blarg thinks it best to let them tear each other apart first. Then the path will be clear."

Tianna sighed, her shoulders heavy with exhaustion but her eyes steeled with determination. "Uncle wouldn't have wanted us to stop now. Let's finish this."

Rea wiped at her tears with trembling hands, her face pale but set with a quiet resolve. "For Uncle Thane," she said, her voice small but firm.

"For Uncle Thane," Tianna echoed, squeezing her sister's shoulder.

The companions moved as one, weaving carefully through the chaos of the battlefield. Orcs and Goblins clashed in a frenzied melee, their roars and screams mingling with the crackling of flames and the clash of steel. Smoke hung thick in the air, merging with the icy winds, yet the companions pressed on, each step heavier than the last but driven by an unyielding determination.

Their movements were deliberate, cautious, as they skirted the edges of the conflict. Blarg's sharp eyes scanned for danger, *Thumpkin* gripped tightly in his hands. Rea clung to Tianna's side, her slingshot ready, though her fingers trembled from exhaustion and cold. Nyx padded silently between them, his tail flicking with uncharacteristic restraint, as if even the chaos could not distract him from their goal.

Ahead, the towering black spire of the Dark Lord's citadel loomed like a jagged claw raking the stormy sky. The citadel stood as a monolith of despair, foreboding and unyielding, yet it was also a beacon, calling them forward with the weight of their purpose.

"This is it," Tianna said quietly, her voice steady despite the exhaustion etched into her face. She adjusted her grip on Sword, its dull weight a comfort in her hands. "No more running. No more waiting."

Blarg grunted in agreement, his gaze fixed on the citadel. "Blarg is ready. Dark Lords do not scare him. But . . . perhaps a quick nap after?"

Rea managed a faint smile, though her eyes remained locked on the spire. "We're really doing this," she said softly, her voice tinged with disbelief. "We're actually here."

Tianna glanced at her sister, her expression softening. "We've come too far to stop now," she said, placing a reassuring hand on Rea's shoulder. "Uncle Thane believed in us. We're going to finish this, for him, and for everyone who's counting on us."

The wind howled around them, carrying the distant cries of the battlefield. Smoke swirled in ghostly tendrils, and the acrid scent of burning wood and flesh filled the air. Yet through it all, the citadel stood untouched, an unyielding monument to their final challenge.

Their footsteps quickened as they approached the base of the spire. Each step felt monumental, their exhaustion warring with a newfound resolve. They had wandered through endless snow, braved monstrous creatures, and faced the darkness within themselves. Now, their journey led them here, to the heart of the Dark Lord's power.

"We've come this far," she said, her voice firm and steady. "Let's finish it."

The companions exchanged a final glance, a silent agreement passing between them. Exhausted to their very core, but reinvigorated with new purpose, they turned their eyes to the citadel. This was their moment, their final stand. After days of wandering, countless trials, and immeasurable loss, they had come at last.

And nothing, not the storm, not the Dark Lord, not even the shadow of doubt, would stop them now.

24

Claws and Effect

"The Wheel of Fate turns, usually in the wrong direction, and always at the most inconvenient of times."

— *The Hunt That Wouldn't End*

by Robar the Endless

The group stood before the Dark Lord's citadel, its towering spires stabbing dramatically into the storm-churned sky like architectural exclamation points. Dark energy crackled in the air, and the sounds of battle in the camp still raged behind them. But the citadel, it stood unnervingly quiet, as if it was practicing the art of eerie ambiance. Tianna glanced at her companions, attempting to draw strength from their resolve, or at least from their varied approaches to pre-battle anxiety. Blarg's massive frame shifted beside her, brow furrowed in concentration. Nyx perched upon his shoulder, looking anything but worried, with the casual confidence that came from having nine lives. A few paces back, Rea's eyes darted nervously at the shadows, her hands clenched as if she could steady her breathing by sheer force of will.

Blarg took the lead, pulling open the heavy double doors. They groaned, echoing through the vast chamber like a giant with indigestion. The party stepped in, their boots clicking upon the smooth obsidian floor, polished to an unnatural shine. The sound of their footsteps reverberated around them, giving the distinct impression that the room was judging them for their overall lack of stealth.

Tall windows of colored glass framed the high walls, depicting overly dramatic scenes of chaos, war, and despair. Apparently, no one told the decorator that subtlety could be an option. One panel, however, inexplicably featured a cheerful bunny in a sunhat, lounging on a field of daisies, blissfully unbothered by the carnage depicted around it.[97] It was either a bold artistic statement about the futility of evil, or more likely, the result of someone's apprentice getting a little too creative when the boss wasn't watching.

Above them, massive chandeliers hung precariously, fashioned from what looked like the bones of Behemoths. Blarg whispered to Tianna that they were probably just decorative bones, "the kind that can be found at any of those fancy evil furniture shops." Tianna nodded, though she wasn't entirely convinced. The space smelled faintly of dampness, like the Dark Lord had tried and failed to keep the place dry with a budget enchanted dehumidifier—clearly a grave design error. The effect was less an intimidating lair of darkness and more a dungeon desperately in need of despair conditioning. Even the cobwebs appeared as if they'd filed for widow's compensation.

At the far end of the citadel, a dark figure sat on an ornate throne. He was striking the kind of brooding, silent pose that might look great in a portrait but raised some logistical concerns about circulation and throne-induced back problems in real life. He was tall, dark, and mysterious. The kind of mysterious that was thrilling on a dating profile but usually translated to 'emotionally unavailable' and 'leaves you on dread.' His helm was crafted from jagged shards

---

[97] Though it appeared to be nothing more than a blissfully oblivious herbivore enjoying a sunny afternoon, seasoned historians recognize the creature as the Dread Hare of the Carrotbannog. It was an ancient and unspeakably violent beast said to have laid waste to entire battalions using only its teeth, unholy speed, and what one terrified survivor described as "an unnerving sense of purpose." Several ancient orders were formed solely to warn others about it, but most were disbanded after no one believed a rabbit could be that dangerous. The lone exception, the Knights of the Holy Detour, still refuse to speak of it directly, referring only to the 'Fluffy One' and muttering something about bones.

of midnight (locally sourced, artisanal darkness). His armor was a swirling void. His robe was dark and tattered, adorned with strange runes that writhed in the light like disgruntled glowworms. Yet, something was unmistakably, profoundly off. He wasn't moving. Not a villainous finger twitch, nor a malevolent scratching of an itch, not even a sinister, diabolical yawn. Something was amiss—adjectively speaking.

The group exchanged puzzled glances, each of them frowning. They took a few hesitant steps forward, their ears strained to listen. A low, rumbling sound emerged, swelled, then tapered off, less eldritch horror and more elderly snorer.

Yes, unmistakably, the Dark Lord was snoring on his throne.

Tianna exchanged a bewildered glance with Blarg, one eyebrow arching skyward. Nyx's ears twitched at the noise.

"Is . . . is he asleep?" Rea whispered, her voice cutting through the silence.

Blarg squinted at the snoring figure. "So much for 'evil never rests,'" he muttered. "Apparently, it naps."

Nyx, ever the curious feline, decided to investigate first. He slinked across the floor with the casual confidence of a cat in the second evilest place within a hundred leagues.[98] The cat's eyes fixed on an ornately decorated table crowded with goblets, cutlery, and shiny trinkets. To Nyx, this was less of a collection of dark treasures and more of a tempting playground. He eyed a particularly gleaming goblet with the intense, saucer-eyed focus only cats

---

[98] For the record, the *evilest* place was, of course, the Dark Lord's privy; a chamber infamous for its toxic odors and abominable decor choices. Legend held that it was a battleground of rival mold colonies, and the bath curtain seemed not only alive but actively hostile. The air reeked of sulfur, despair, and whatever sinister concoction the Dark Lord used as soap (rumored to be distilled from the souls of his enemies, though no one dared confirm). As for the state of the toilet, well, the less said, the better. Suffice it to say, even the bravest souls hesitated to cross that threshold, lest they lose their sense of smell—or their sanity.

possess, his pupils expanding as if to say, 'This is mine now, by the ancient law of *If it Shine, It's Mine!*[99]

And, in true feline fashion, he did what any reasonable cat would: he batted at it. Not a gentle tap. Nyx's paw came down with the force of a creature determined to prove that shiny objects belong on the floor. The goblet hit the ground with a crash that echoed dramatically through the citadel.

Blarg flinched, slowly turning toward the source of the sound, utterly speechless. Tianna clapped a hand to her forehead, groaning softly.

"Bad Nyxie," Rea whispered.

Nyx appeared entirely unfazed. He gave a satisfied flick of his tail, as if to say, "Mission accomplished". He sat down licked his paw with an air of smug self-satisfaction. The others could only watch in a mix of horror and begrudging admiration for his commitment to the feline way.

And that's precisely when the Dark Lord snorted awake, jerking forward on his throne, helm rattling from the abrupt movement. The ancient evil had been awakened not by a battle cry, heroic challenge, or even a proper dramatic

---

[99] This was, of course, just one of many sacred feline doctrines passed down through nine lifetimes of careful whisker-to-whisker tradition. The complete Feline Code of Conduct included such venerable laws as 'If I Fits, I Sits' (the foundational principle of cat spatial physics), 'If It Slides, It Rides (Right Off the Table)' (the law of gravitational enforcement), and 'If I Purr, It's A Blur' (the statute of selective hearing). The code was meticulously maintained by the Ancient Order of Whisker Twitchers, though some radical elements of feline society insisted on adding controversial amendments like 'If It's New, It's A Loo' (regarding fancy litter boxes) and 'If You Cook, I Must Look' (the dinner observation mandate).

Most controversial was the recent addition: 'If It's Flat, That's Where I'm At,' which specifically addressed the tendency of cats to sprawl across vital documents, spellbooks, and maps precisely when their humans needed to read them. This particular law had caused quite the scandal at the last Grand Catclave, with the Persian delegation staging a dramatic walkout, claiming it was too obvious to need stating. The Siamese representatives, meanwhile, argued for expanding it to include freshly inked scrolls, still-wet magical runes, and newly painted ritual circles; the latter of which had caused more than one summoning to go hilariously wrong when cat fur got involved in the arcane geometry.

entrance, but by a curious cat with impulse-control issues. It was truly a low point in *The Evil Overlord's Handbook of Proper Villain Etiquette.*

He blinked at them, his glowing eyes half-hidden beneath his helm, radiating the special kind of confusion reserved for those who'd been abruptly awakened. Every reluctant movement screamed 'evil overlord who desperately needed that power nap,' while his posture suggested someone trying very hard to pretend they hadn't been caught sleeping on the job. It was the type of awkward moment that definitely wasn't covered in Dark Lord Orientation.

For a long, tense moment, no one moved.

Then the Dark Lord sighed; a deep, weary sigh that echoed through the vast chamber. His glowing eyes narrowed as he glared upon them.

"AH," he said, his voice reverberating with unnatural depth, though it carried the tone of someone reading from a very worn script. **"YOU MUST BE . . . THE HEROES."** He said the word with a hint of disdain, but mostly exhaustion. **"HERE TO VANQUISH THE DARK LORD. TO . . . SAVE THE WORLD, OR SOME SUCH."**

Tianna and the others shifted uneasily. The Dark Lord's body language spoke less of malice and more of resignation, like someone forced to host a dinner party they never agreed to.

"YES? NO?" He tilted his head slightly, waiting for them to answer. He didn't sound particularly angry or upset. Merely curious, as though he'd seen this situation play out countless times before.

"We . . . we've come to stop you!" Tianna said, holding up her frying pan, which gave a faint hum of excitement.

"Finally! Here's our chance, Tianna! Let's smash that Dark Lord, and smash him good!" Sword chimed in, brimming with eager anticipation.

The Dark Lord's shoulders slumped even further at that, and he rubbed his forehead beneath his helm. He leaned back, the throne groaning beneath him, and sized them up, judging whether this group was even worth the effort.

"ACHOOO!" the Dark Lord sneezed. He glared at Nyx with malice. **"YOU BROUGHT A CAT? I'M ALLERGIC TO CATS!"**

"Sorry, I guess." Tianna replied with a half-shrug.

The Dark Lord waved her off with a frustrated snuffle, muttering under his breath about "heroes and their ridiculous pets." He straightened up, attempting to regain his dignity. **"ANYWAY . . . DO YOU KNOW HOW MANY HEROES HAVE COME BEFORE YOU?"** he asked, absentmindedly. **"HOW MANY OF YOU . . . BRAVE SOULS . . . HAVE COME MARCHING INTO THIS ROOM? DETERMINED TO END THE DARK LORD'S REIGN—?"** He stared at the colored glass windows, his gaze distant, as if the answer might be etched in the cracks and fading paint. **"ONLY TO DISCOVER—"**

He trailed off, letting the silence settle like dust around them. His gloved hands rested heavily on the armrests, his posture sagging. He glanced down, lost for a moment, as though he had misplaced his own thoughts.

Tianna took a cautious step forward. "Discover what?"

The Dark Lord gave a bitter laugh, the sound echoing around them like a peal of thunder. **"THAT NONE OF IT MATTERS."** He spread his arms in a grand, weary gesture to the cavernous hall around them, as dust motes danced in the dim light. **"UMM . . . HOLD ON."** He reached under his cloak, retrieving a crumpled parchment. Squinting at it, he muttered, **"THAT NONE OF IT MATTERS . . . WAIT, I SAID THAT—"** His finger slid down the page. **"OH, HERE."** He cleared his throat before resuming with renewed solemnity. **"THAT EVERY TRIUMPH, EVERY ACT OF *GOOD*, IT ALL AMOUNTS TO NOTHING IN THE END. I AM DESTINED TO BE HERE, TIME AND TIME AGAIN. FODDER FOR YOUR DESTINY. SOMETHING FOR YOU TO FIGHT AGAINST."**

He pointed a gloved finger at them, his voice laced with a sad irony. **I AM WHAT GIVES YOU 'HEROES' PURPOSE, AM I NOT?"**

"That's . . . not true," Rea said softly, stepping forward, pressing a hand to her chest. "You are . . . you are evil."

The Dark Lord lowered his gaze back to the parchment with a sigh. **"AM I? OR AM I SIMPLY HERE, GIVEN THIS MANTLE, THIS ROLE TO PLAY, AND TOLD THAT I MUST DESTROY OR BE DESTROYED?"** His voice, as he read from the parchment, grew monotone, as if even *he* was exhausted by his own script. He leaned back, the throne creaking under his weight, his voice shifting to a somber rumble. **"IS IT TRULY EVIL IF IT IS ALL I WAS MADE FOR? IS IT TRULY GOOD, YOUR CHOICE TO OPPOSE ME, IF IT IS THE ONLY PATH DESTINY HAS LAID BEFORE YOU?"**

The silence returned, hanging between them, heavy and uncertain. For a moment, the Dark Lord appeared as though he might sneeze again.

"WHAT'S EVEN THE POINT ANYMORE?" He threw up his hands, the parchment fluttering from his grip and drifting to the floor. **"THEY KEEP SUMMONING ME LIKE I'M SOME COSMIC YO-YO. BUT DO I GET A SAY? NO!"** He gestured around the vast, empty hall, the echo of his voice bouncing off the stone walls. **"I SIT UP HERE IN THE COLD, JUST . . . EXISTING. HONESTLY, WHO BUILDS A CITADEL ON THE TOP OF A MOUNTAIN? IT'S IMPOSSIBLE TO HEAT!"**

His gaze swept over each face in front of him, eyes practically pleading for a shred of sympathy. **"AND NOBODY EVEN BOTHERS TO FIGHT FOR ME ANYMORE. THAT USED TO BE FUN, YOU KNOW? A BIT OF STABBING, A DASH OF VILLAINY, SOME SCREAMING— IT HAD *FLAIR*."** He sighed, his shoulders slumping. **"BUT NOW? IT'S JUST SO . . . BORING."**

With a heavy sigh, he reached into his cloak and pulled out three small, well-worn books, one emblazoned with the title *Dragon Stew for the Soulless*.[100] **"I'VE GOT THREE BOOKS. THREE! CAN YOU BELIEVE THAT? YOU KNOW HOW MANY TIMES I'VE READ THEM? ENOUGH THAT I COULD RECITE THEM BACKWARD IF I WANTED TO, BUT I DON'T."** He gave them a mournful shake. **"BECAUSE THAT WOULD BE POINTLESS . . . LIKE MY WHOLE LIFE."**

Tianna stepped forward, her eyes narrowing. "You can wallow in self-pity all you want, but you're still hurting people. You're still causing misery and terror." She tightened her grip on Sword, her eyes blazing. "And we . . . we aren't some mindless puppets. We chose to be here. We chose to stand against you. Because it's right. Because . . . because you need to be stopped."

"You tell him!" Sword cheered.

The Dark Lord laughed, a dark, humorless chuckle that echoed around the citadel. **"KEEP TELLING YOURSELF THAT, KID."** He let out a deep sigh. **"DO YOU THINK YOU'RE THE FIRST TO DEFEAT ME? OR THE LAST? EVEN IF YOU WIN TODAY, MYSELF OR SOMEONE JUST LIKE ME WILL RETURN."**

Tianna clenched her jaw. "Maybe. But we're still going to try. Even if we have to fight a thousand Dark Lords."

The Dark Lord's eyes darkened beneath his helm, and he straightened, his tiredness replaced with something colder, a hard edge of bitterness that had been honed over countless lifetimes. **"FINE, LET'S GET THIS OVER WITH."** He reached into his cloak and pulled out a necklace with a brilliant blue gem, glowing with unnatural light. **"I HAD TO TAKE IT OFF. THE METAL WAS GIVING ME A RASH."**

"Um . . . okay?" Tianna replied, bewildered.

---

[100] The other two were titled *Advanced Brooding for Isolated Landscapes* and *The Little Book of Screaming Internally*. While never officially published, copies kept mysteriously appearing in abandoned cabins, empty taverns, and one particularly rank outhouse.

The Dark Lord shook his head, as if remembering the point. He slowly stood up while shouting, **"YOU WANT TO FACE CHAOS? THEN FACE IT!"**

The gem pulsed, casting eerie shadows across the citadel walls. In the Dark Lord's other hand, strands of blue energy coiled around his wrist, swirling like irritable snakes. The energy quickly coalesced into blazing orbs of blue fire that shot outward, transforming the citadel into a hellish, blue-tinted inferno. The heat from the magical flames was intense, singing their skin as they dodged and weaved, desperately trying to avoid turning into heroic toast.

Blarg let out an indignant roar as a fireball whooshed past his head, narrowly missing him but leaving a bright red burn mark across his face. "Hey! Watch your aim, you oversized tin can!" He brandished his massive hammer in the air, waving it like a parent scolding an unruly child.

"ACHOOO!" the Dark Lord sneezed, his aim faltering as a fireball went completely wide, slamming into a column. He glared at Nyx, his eyes narrowing. **"BLASTED CAT."**

Rea, apparently the wisest of the group, had taken shelter behind an overturned table at the back of the citadel. "Watch out Blarg!" she shouted.

A massive stone column collapsed next to Blarg, sending a particularly large chunk of rock hurtling toward his head. Rea's warning was in time. Blarg rolled aside, narrowly missing a messy end as the stone smashed into the floor, cracking the already scarred obsidian. He glanced back at Rea, flashing a broad, reckless grin as if to say, "All part of the plan," before charging back into the chaos.

Nyx, meanwhile, decided to complicate matters by doing what any cat would do in the middle of chaos: find the highest possible point to perch. In this case, it was the Dark Lord's throne. With the agility only a cat possessed, Nyx darted across the battlefield, leaping from shattered columns and ornamental tables, eventually landing squarely on the top of the throne. There, he sat, licking his paw nonchalantly while glowing balls of magical fire hurtled through the air. He did a quick stretch and laid down, keeping an eye on the ongoing fight.

Tianna sprinted across the citadel, a fireball slamming into the ground inches behind her. She dove behind a fallen stone column, her chest heaving as she tried to catch her breath, while another blast of blue fire scorched overhead.

"Let's go, dearie! Get in the fight! I need to smash him!" Sword pleaded, practically vibrating with excitement.

"Easy for you to say." Tianna chided the pan, squeezing the handle tight, turning her knuckles white. "Not much he can do to cookery." She peeked over the column, in time to dodge another blazing projectile.

"Aha!" Blarg bellowed, charging toward the Dark Lord, hammer raised high above his head. He swung with all his strength, aiming for the Dark Lord's helm. But before it could connect, the Dark Lord raised an ancient broadsword, thrumming with dark power, and blocked the strike. The collision of hammer and sword created a shockwave, blasting Blarg backward as if he were nothing more than an angry rag doll.

Blarg slid across the broken ground, shards of obsidian biting into his skin. He groaned, still clutching his hammer, though his grip was visibly less confident. "All right," he muttered to himself, "new plan . . . less charging, more . . . thinking."

From atop the throne, Nyx gave a dismissive flick of his ear, as if thoroughly unimpressed by Blarg's tactical genius.

"Blarg, are you okay?" Rea shouted, her head popping up from behind her makeshift cover. She watched Blarg shakily get to his feet, dusting off some debris and giving an enthusiastic thumbs-up.

"Never better! Just . . . uh . . . letting him know that Blarg means business!"

Sword, buzzing with energy, practically hummed in response. *"We could try . . . uh . . . hitting him harder?"*

"Of course," Tianna sighed. She took a deep breath and pushed herself to her feet, her frying pan vibrating with anticipation. "All right, Sword. Let's go smash the Dark Lord."

"YES!"

As she stood up, she caught sight of the Dark Lord himself, who appeared genuinely flustered. He was muttering under his breath, glancing up at Nyx, who had now decided to stretch luxuriously across the top of the throne, licking his paw.

"GET DOWN, YOU STUPID CAT!" the Dark Lord grumbled.

Tianna charged at the Dark Lord, Sword raised high, determination blazing in her eyes. She lunged, ready to strike, only for the Dark Lord to swat her aside casually with a flick of his arm. His blow struck her square in the chest, knocking the air from her lungs. Tianna was sent sprawling, her body hitting the ground with a heavy thud. She gasped, her vision swimming as she struggled to pull breath back into her lungs, each inhale feeling like fire.

"TIMEOUT!" Tianna gasped, throwing her hands up.

The Dark Lord blinked. **"WHAT?"**

"Timeout. Just . . . give us a minute," Tianna said, regaining her breath.

The Dark Lord stared at her, then sighed deeply. **"FINE, WHATEVER. I COULD USE A BREAK ANYWAY. ACHOOO!"** The flames in the room shrunk and then died.

He turned to his throne, shooing Nyx off the top. Nyx gave an indignant hiss but hopped down, tail flicking in irritation. The Dark Lord sat down heavily, pulling out a handkerchief and blowing his nose with a loud honk. The heroes regrouped behind a fallen column, catching their breath.

Blarg glanced at Tianna, leaning in. "What now? Charging headfirst clearly isn't working."

"We need to work together," Tianna said. "There are three of us . . . and Nyx. He's only one guy, Dark Lord or not. He can't defend on all sides."

"ALL RIGHT," the Dark Lord called, voice muffled by the handkerchief. **"ARE WE DOING THIS, OR DO YOU NEED ANOTHER MINUTE?"**

"SORRY, JUST ANOTHER MINUTE!" Tianna shouted back.

Blarg leaned closer to Tianna and Rea. "All right, all-out assault it is. Attack from all directions. He's strong, but he's only got two hands."

Tianna nodded, glancing at Nyx, who was nonchalantly grooming himself nearby. "Nyx will keep being a distraction. He's already making him sneeze, it's our best shot at keeping him off-balance."

Rea furrowed her brow. "And if that doesn't work?"

Blarg grinned. "Then it will be time to improvise. Keep him so busy he won't know what hit him."

Tianna took a deep breath, steadying herself. "All right, Blarg, you go in first from the left. I'll aim for his right. Rea, keep shooting him with your slingshot. And Nyx . . . just be Nyx."

Nyx glanced up, blinked once, and gave a leisurely stretch before slinking back toward the throne, his tail swishing as if this whole situation was beneath his dignity.

"OKAY!" Tianna called out, pushing herself up from her cover. "WE'RE READY!"

The Dark Lord sighed, standing up once more. **"OH WAIT! HOLD ON, OWW, I'VE GOT A CRAMP IN MY LEG."** He bent down and rubbed his leg.

"You, okay?" Tianna asked, concerned.

"YEAH, I THINK SO. I HATE CRAMPS." The Dark Lord stood again to his full height. **"OKAY, READY NOW."**

"You should drink more water," Tianna said helpfully.

"YEAH, YEAH, I KNOW. I KEEP TRYING TO DRINK MORE, BUT WHO CAN FIND THE TIME?"

"The only one who can help you is you," Tianna responded.

"YEAH, I GET IT. ARE WE DOING THIS OR NOT?"

"Now!" Tianna shouted.

Blarg charged from the left, hammer raised high, his roar echoing through the chamber. Rea quickly scanned the ground, her fingers curling around a smooth rock. She loaded it into her slingshot with practiced speed, pulling the band taut.

"Over here, you big stinky fart cloud!" she shouted, releasing the rock.

It struck the Dark Lord's armored shoulder with a sharp *clang*, drawing his attention. He snarled, his glowing eyes locking onto her.

Nyx darted in, seizing the distraction. With a quick leap, he swatted at the Dark Lord's leg, leaving deep claw marks before bounding back to the safety of the throne.

As the Dark Lord turned toward Nyx, Rea fired again, this time aiming lower. The rock hit his ankle with a dull *thunk*, causing him to stumble.

"IMPUDENT FOOLS!" the Dark Lord bellowed, swinging his massive sword in a clumsy arc.

They seized the opportunity. Blarg's hammer came down hard, toward the Dark Lord's chest. Tianna lunged forward, her frying pan swinging for his exposed side. The Dark Lord twisted out of the way of Tianna and deflected Blarg's hammer with his gauntlet in a single motion. The impact sent a resounding *CLANG* through the citadel. The force reverberated across the obsidian floor, cracks splintering beneath their feet.

As the Dark Lord staggered slightly from the force of Blarg's strike, Tianna seized her moment. She swung with all her might, her frying pan making a solid arc toward his ribs. But the Dark Lord was faster, twisting just in time so that her pan struck nothing but air.

"Stop missing!" Sword shouted angrily.

Blarg, regaining his footing, pressed the attack, swinging his hammer again from the opposite side, while Tianna aimed a quick follow-up blow at his knee. The Dark Lord snarled, forced to split his attention between the relentless strikes. He twisted, raising his arm to block Blarg's hammer once more while kicking out at Tianna. The kick connected, sending her stumbling, Sword slipping from her grasp as she hit the floor.

Blarg roared in defiance, refusing to let the Dark Lord focus on Tianna. He swung again, his hammer colliding with the Dark Lord's gauntlet, the citadel echoing with every thunderous impact. The Dark Lord held his ground, his dark robes whipping around him like storm-tossed shadows. He dodged another blow from the hammer and followed up with a kick to Blarg's chest, sending him to the ground in a daze.

"THAT WAS YOUR BIG PLAN?" the Dark Lord appeared disappointed, as if he expected better. **"THREE FRONT ASSAULT, I'VE NEVER SEEN THAT BEFORE!"** he said sarcastically. **"ACHOOO!"**

Tianna slumped on the floor, pain shooting through her side. "Ow," she whimpered softly.

"ENOUGH!" the Dark Lord bellowed, his voice echoing off the citadel walls, shaking the very foundations of the ancient structure. **"YOU COME TO MY HOME. YOU BREAK MY STUFF. YOU WANT A FIGHT? I'LL GIVE YOU A FIGHT!"** His eyes blazed with fury. He raised his sword high, the blade crackling with dark energy.

"WITNESS THE FULL POWER OF CHAOS!" he roared, slamming the sword point-first into the obsidian floor. A shockwave erupted from the impact, and cracks webbed outward, glowing with a deep blue fire as if the ground itself was burning from within. Flames erupted from the cracks, coiling around his body like writhing serpents, wrapping him in a brilliant, blazing aura of chaotic fire.

The citadel responded. The stained-glass windows rattled, and the eerie figures depicted within them twisted and shifted as though alive, their expressions changing to grotesque mockeries of pain and horror. The chandeliers overhead swayed violently, their bone-like decorations jangling together, casting moving shadows across the walls that danced with a wild, fiery glow.

The air shimmered with the intense heat, and the low, crackling roar of the flames grew louder and more intense, filling the citadel with an otherworldly, threatening hum. The temperature spiked, the heat unbearable, the fire warping the light around the Dark Lord, making his form waver like a mirage in the desert.

Nyx, now crouched near the throne, flattened his ears, his fur standing on end as the heat made his tail puff up. Rea covered her ears as she fought to steady herself against the shaking ground and the scorching waves of heat.

Blarg, eyes wide, took a step back. "Uh, Blarg thinks maybe that might've really ticked him off this time."

Tianna shielded her eyes from the blinding blue flames that pulsed with the Dark Lord's every heartbeat. "No kidding!" she shouted over the roar, her voice tinged with a mix of awe and terror.

The Dark Lord slowly straightened, his entire body wreathed in the brilliant blue fire. His armor absorbed the heat, glowing from within like a forge ready to burst. The gem in his hand blazed with light. **"YOU THINK YOU CAN DEFEAT ME WITH YOUR PITIFUL TOYS? I AM CHAOS INCARNATE!"** He lifted his gaze, focusing on them with an expression of pure malice. His voice lowered, dripping with venom. **"I WILL SHOW YOU WHAT TRUE POWER IS."**

Through the roar of the flames, the cracking stone, and the screaming heat, came a sound that didn't belong.

A low, mournful note echoed through the citadel, distant but clear.

Tianna's heart stuttered. Thane's horn.

No one else seemed to notice it, but to her, it rang louder than fire, louder than fear. A single note of defiance, carried through the air.

With a sudden movement, the Dark Lord yanked his sword from the ground. The tendrils of blue fire shot outward, exploding from the cracks in the floor, striking out like fiery whips toward Tianna, Blarg, and Rea. The air itself was torn as the flames lashed toward them, crackling with a sound reminiscent of laughter—cruel and mocking. It was as if the very chaos he commanded had a mind of its own and found everything immensely entertaining.

Tianna ducked behind a crumbling column, feeling the heat singe her skin as a whip of flame narrowly missed her. She glanced at Blarg, who was batting away another tendril with his hammer, his face contorted with effort.

"We need to move!" she shouted, her voice barely audible over the roaring flames. "Keep him distracted, don't let him focus!"

Blarg grunted in response, lifting his hammer to block yet another fiery arc. "Aye, easier said than done, lass!"

The Dark Lord's laughter filled the citadel, deep and resonant, like thunder rolling through the hollow chamber. **"RUN ALL YOU LIKE! THERE IS NO ESCAPE FROM CHAOS!"** He lifted his free hand, and the ground beneath their feet shifted violently. Slabs of obsidian rose and fell as if the citadel itself was becoming unhinged, a living nightmare under his control.

He raised the glowing gem into the air. It pulsed with chaotic energy as the flames began to rise higher and grow even hotter. The Dark Lord's eyes were alight with a fervent madness; but then, there was a flash of movement. Thane barreled forward, bloodied and limping, Sword in one hand. His face was battered, but his expression held the kind of determination usually reserved for doomed last stands.

With a roar, he brought the pan down on the Dark Lord's wrist. *CRACK.*

"YESSSSSSS!" Sword screamed in ecstasy.

The Dark Lord reeled, but Thane didn't stop.

Another swing—to the ribs.

A third—to the side of the helm.

A fourth—just for spite.

The Dark Lord staggered, cursing and flailing, as Thane panted.

"Oh wow, that felt amazing!" Sword gasped. *"And it's about time. Anyone want breakfast? I'm all heated up."*

With a final overhead blow, Thane *slammed* the pan into the gem itself, knocking it loose from the necklace. It skittered across the floor like a startled cockroach. The blue flames shuddered and died, plunging the room into flickering shadows.

"WHAT THE—?"

Tianna pushed herself to her feet, her eyes fixed briefly on Thane, and then onto the gem. She lunged for it, her fingers curling around its smooth surface. She stood, holding it aloft, her heart pounding as she tried to will it to obey her command, to use the Dark Lord's power against him.

Nothing happened.

The Dark Lord laughed, a dark, cruel laugh that filled the entire citadel. **"FOOLISH GIRL,"** he said, shaking his head. **"ONLY AN AGENT OF CHAOS CAN WIELD THE POWER OF THE GEM. YOU . . . YOU ARE NOTHING BUT ORDER . . . NOTHING BUT A PAWN OF DESTINY."** He lifted his hand, the residual magic still swirling around him, and with a final push, he knocked Tianna back, the gem slipping from her grasp.

She hit the ground hard, her vision blurring as pain radiated through her body. The gem rolled away from her, its glow pulsing faintly in the eerie stillness of the citadel.

The Dark Lord approached her, his ancient broadsword in hand. His eyes narrowed as he prepared to strike the final blow. Tianna braced herself, her eyes closing as she whispered a silent prayer.

Then, there was a sound—a familiar, unmistakable sound.

Hruuk!

All eyes turned to Nyx as he sat on the ground, hunched over. His body shuddered with a great heave.

Hruuk!

Nyx's mouth gaped, tongue lolling out, and then.

Haaaaak!

With a final, mighty convulsion, Nyx spat out the gem, no longer glowing, its blue light extinguished, and the entire room froze.

Nyx, as if proud of his grand contribution, daintily pawed the gem forward before licking his lips and promptly sitting down, his tail flicking with self-satisfaction. The Dark Lord stared, his sword still raised, his mind visibly grappling with what had occurred.

But something was changing. Nyx's fur shimmered. Subtly at first, then with an undeniable brilliance. A crown of blue fire erupted from his head, and his eyes glowed with an intense, searing blue light. The cat radiated with power, not the primal chaos of the Dark Lord, but the pure, ordered chaos that only a cat could truly understand. The kind that knocked glasses off tables just to watch them fall. A low growl rumbled in his chest, building until it shook the very air around him. His body emanated an ethereal energy that filled the citadel, a force that was ancient and unstoppable.

The Dark Lord took an instinctive step back, his eyes widening in disbelief. **"NO . . . NO, THIS IS IMPOSSIBLE!"**

Nyx's growl grew louder, reverberating through the air as his entire form swelled with power. The temperature increased suddenly, and the walls of the citadel shook. More cracks formed along the stone, splintering the pillars as Nyx's body glowed like a living star.

The blue fire around him roared to life, but it was not chaotic and sporadic like the Dark Lord's. It was controlled, concentrated, and filled with an incomprehensible intensity. A power that came from millennia of chaotic behavior and absolutely refusing to come when called. The very air bent under Nyx's power, a force of nature that could no longer be contained.

With a single, deliberate blink, Nyx's eyes locked onto the Dark Lord, who had begun to tremble. The cat's pupils widened, and then—

A pulse of pure, undiluted blue energy erupted from Nyx, expanding outward in a colossal wave that consumed everything in its path. It was as if a bomb had detonated, a wave of power that obliterated the air with a deafening roar.

"FOILED . . . BY A TINY BALL OF FUR. TRULY . . . THE UNIVERSE SAVES ITS GREATEST IRONY FOR LAST."

The Dark Lord had no time to react. The blast hit him, and his form disintegrated. Armor, robes, body, all turned to ash, scattered into the ether like dust. His last scream was swallowed by the overwhelming rush of power, drowned out by the surge of energy that tore through the citadel.

The walls crumbled, the ceiling was blown clean off, and the pillars shattered. The entire structure collapsed in on itself. The sky above was visible, an explosion of light shooting up into the clouds as if the heavens themselves were breaking apart.

As the dust settled, only Nyx remained, sitting amid the rubble, licking his paw as if nothing had happened, his tail flicking back and forth. He gave a small, contented meow, his eyes no longer glowing, just the lazy, indifferent gaze of a cat who had finally finished his nap.

Tianna, Blarg, and Rea slowly pushed themselves up from the wreckage, their eyes wide with shock.

"Did . . . did Nyx—" Blarg began, unable to finish his sentence.

"Yeah," Tianna said, her voice barely a whisper. "Nyx obliterated him."

Nyx glanced up at them, gave a small chirp, then went back to grooming.

"I'm so glad you're safe," Thane said, his voice rough but filled with warmth. He stared at them, his expression softening. "You're everything to me. I thought I'd lost everything after your father, but you two . . . you remind me what's worth fighting for."

"How are you—?" Tianna's voice cracked as tears welled in her eyes. Without hesitation, she ran to her uncle and threw her arms around him, holding on tightly as if he might vanish again.

"That's a long story," he said with a groan, shaking his head. "But I suppose lady Destiny wasn't finished with me yet." He shrugged like it was nothing. "Anyway, I'm here now."

Rea, not far behind, darted over and joined the embrace, her smaller frame pressed against his side. "Uncle Thane!" she choked out, tears streaking her cheeks.

Blarg stood awkwardly to the side for a moment, scratching the back of his neck. Not wanting to be left out—or maybe just feeling the pull of the moment—he lumbered over and enveloped all three in a hug that was less an embrace and more an all-encompassing bear trap. "Group hug," he grunted, his voice thick with unspoken emotion.

Thane's breath hitched as he held his nieces close. After a long, quiet moment, he gently stepped back, his calloused hands resting briefly on their shoulders. His eyes were red, matching theirs, though he quickly wiped at them with the back of his hand and cleared his throat.

For a moment, the group stood together, the weight of their reunion pressing on them as heavily as the battles they had faced to get there. Nyx padded over silently, brushing Tianna's leg before hopping up onto a jagged rock and began grooming himself.

Tianna released her hug and took a step back, her eyes brimming with unshed tears. "I thought I had lost you, Uncle," she spoke softly, her voice steady but raw with emotion. "I'm so sorry about everything. I was so angry at you for hiding things from us. But you were trying your best. You were just . . . in over your head, like me."

Thane's expression softened. "No, Tianna. You had every right to be angry. I lied to you. I lied to both of you," he said, glancing at Rea. His voice cracked slightly as he continued. "I thought I was protecting you, but all I did was keep you at a distance. I don't deserve your forgiveness, but I . . . I hope someday I can earn it."

Rea, standing quietly to the side, suddenly spoke up, her voice trembling. "You don't have to earn it, Uncle Thane." Her hands clenched into fists at her sides as she fought back tears. "You have always been there for us. For me. For Tianna. We've never stopped loving you. Not for a second."

Thane's breath hitched, and he sank to one knee, glancing between them. "You both remind me so much of your father," he said, his voice barely above a whisper. "Brave. Kind. You two are the best of him and your mother. I imagined losing you, and—" He shook his head, unable to finish the thought.

"But we're still here," Tianna said, her voice firm despite the tears spilling down her cheeks. "We love you, Uncle, and we're not going anywhere. We've come this far together, and we made it because of you."

Rea nodded, stepping forward and throwing her arms around him. "I love you, Uncle," she choked out, her voice muffled against his chest.

Thane wrapped an arm around her, his other hand resting on Tianna's shoulder. "I love you both. More than anything," he said, his voice thick with emotion.

For a long moment, the three of them stayed like that, the warmth of their reunion like a fragile flame against the cold breeze.

Blarg cleared his throat loudly, scratching the back of his neck. "Uh . . . this is nice and all, but don't forget about Blarg. He was there too."

"We love you too Blarg," Rea said with a soft laugh.

The laughter that followed was short-lived.

There came a low, guttural growl, rippling through the air like the distant roar of an avalanche. Another followed, closer this time, a vibrating hum that thrummed through the stone and climbed up their legs, setting their nerves alight.

Rea froze, her breath catching. "What . . . was that?" she whispered.

Thane's face darkened, his hand instinctively moving to the handle of his axe. The sound came again, a guttural *huff-huff-huff,* a terrible rhythm of breath from lungs too massive to belong to anything natural.

Blarg sniffed the air, his expression grim. "That," he said, gripping his hammer tightly, "is trouble."

"No—" Tianna's voice was barely a whisper, her face pale as she took a trembling step back. "Not now."

25

The Cat Who Would Be King

"And so, the crown passed not to the strongest, nor the wisest, but to the one who knocked it down and had the audacity to wear it."

— *The Rise of the Whiskered Crown*
by Clawdius the Observer

The growls grew louder, their guttural cadence slicing through the frigid air. The companions instinctively formed a tight circle, backs to one another, weapons raised despite the exhaustion dragging at their limbs. The swirling snow thickened, blinding them to the approaching threat. Each sound, each breathy, monstrous huff, reverberated through the stone beneath their feet, a sinister reminder that they were no longer alone.

The storm closed in, turning the mountaintop into a white void. Tianna tightened her grip on Sword, the cold biting into her fingers. "Not again," she murmured, her voice shaking.

Rea glanced nervously between the others, clutching her slingshot. "What are they?"

As if in answer, faint shadows appeared in the swirling white, sleek, fluid forms moving unnervingly fast. Their glowing blue eyes pierced the veil of snow, at least twenty pairs focused intently on the party.

Blarg's lips curled into a grimace as his sharp eyes scanned the encroaching storm. "Blarg has never seen such creatures."

"They're hunters, and they won't stop until they get what they want," Tianna said grimly.

The leader emerged first, stepping into the pale light cast by the smoldering ruins around them. Its sleek feline form gleamed faintly, and its broken fang glinted like a badge of honor. Its gaze fixed on Tianna with a predatory intelligence that sent a shiver down her spine. The others followed, fanning out in a deliberate, coordinated motion, encircling the group like wolves cornering prey.

The hum returned; a deep, resonant sound that made the ground tremble. The creatures crouched low, their muscles rippling beneath their sleek fur, ready to pounce. The lead creature growled low, its lips peeling back to reveal jagged teeth.

"They're toying with us," Thane said grimly, his axe gleaming in the faint light. His voice was steady, but his eyes darted between the circling predators, calculating. "They want us scared."

"Mission accomplished," Rea muttered, though she raised her slingshot, her hands trembling.

"There's nowhere to run," Tianna added softly.

Blarg stepped forward, planting himself between the sisters and the largest of the creatures. "Ha! Blarg does not run."

"Blarg, there are too many of them," Tianna pleaded, though her voice lacked its usual strength. "What can we even do?"

The leader snarled, cutting her off. Its hum swelled, and the others followed, their glowing eyes narrowing as they crept closer.

Then, Nyx moved.

The small cat stepped forward, his sleek black fur a stark contrast to the snow. He stretched lazily, arching his back as though he hadn't a care in the world. Then, with deliberate precision, he padded toward the leader.

"Nyxie, no!" Rea said, reaching out, but Blarg held her back.

The storm slowed, the swirling snow floating lazily midair as Nyx sauntered forward, stopping a few feet from the massive predator. His smooth fur shimmered faintly, a subtle glow that pulsed in rhythm with the storm. The leader, its broken fang glinting faintly, lowered its head, a guttural growl rumbling from deep within its chest like distant thunder.

Nyx sat down, curling his tail neatly around his paws. The glow of his fur intensified, rippling like waves of moonlight across his body. Above his head, a spectral crown of blue flames flickered to life, burning with an ethereal brilliance that cast sharp shadows across the icy ground.

Then, with deliberate precision, Nyx let out a single, piercing cry. The sound cut through the storm like a blade, sharp and commanding. The creature froze, its glowing eyes widening. Slowly, it lowered itself further, pressing its massive body flat against the ground in a gesture of absolute submission.

One by one, the others followed suit, their sleek forms bowing low before Nyx. The hum ceased entirely, replaced by a deafening silence broken only by the faint crackle of the spectral flames on Nyx's crown. He remained still, his green eyes surveying the kneeling predators with an air of undeniable authority.

Rea clutched her slingshot tightly, her mouth agape. "What . . . just happened?" she whispered.

Blarg scratched his head, his hammer lowering slightly. "Blarg thinks . . . the cat is in charge now."

"Hasn't he always been?" Sword asked.

Tianna stared at Nyx, who sat calmly amid the bowing predators, his expression unreadable. "Of course," she muttered, her voice flat with disbelief. "Nyxie, king of the cats."

Nyx rose gracefully, his eyes sweeping over the creatures. He flicked his tail once, a gesture that appeared almost dismissive, before turning and trotting back to the group. The creatures remained prostrate, their glowing eyes following his every move.

As Nyx reached Rea, he let out a soft *brrrrup* and rubbed against her leg, his purr audible even over the faint whisper of the wind. The storm began to abate, the snow thinning to reveal the aftermath of their battle.

The creature rose slowly, its glowing eyes locking onto Nyx one last time. With a low, reverent growl, it turned and disappeared into the fading storm. The others followed, their movements silent and fluid, until the mountaintop was once again empty, save for the group.

Blarg let out a breath he hadn't realized he was holding. "Blarg has seen many things," he said, shaking his head. "But this . . . this is new."

Tianna collapsed to her knees, her exhaustion finally catching up with her. She dropped Sword beside her and buried her face in her hands. "Please don't tell me that we hiked all the way up here, defeated the Dark Lord, just to make Nyx King," she said, her voice muffled. "I don't think I want to live under his rule."

Rea crouched beside Nyx, scratching behind his ears as he purred contentedly. "He's always been special," she said softly, her tone almost proud. "But I think Nyxie is only king of the cats."

Nyx stretched again, his tail flicking as he padded to a nearby rock and gracefully leaped upon it. The blue flames on his head flickered one last time before vanishing, leaving only the faint glow of his fur. He settled upon the perch like a monarch surveying his kingdom.

The storm had cleared entirely then. On the farthest edge of the eastern sky, a faint band of light emerged, soft and pale, as if the world itself was daring to hope again. The stars faded slowly, yielding to the warm glow of dawn, its gentle hues washing over the land like a promise. A new day, and with it, a new beginning.

For the first time in what felt like forever, the mountain was silent.

And the companions, though battered and weary, couldn't help but feel they had witnessed something truly extraordinary.

The mountaintop lay quiet, a stark contrast to the chaos that had erupted hours before. The jagged peaks, once home to the Dark Lord's banners and his vast, menacing army, now stood desolate. The battlefield was littered with shattered weapons and remnants of hastily abandoned camps. The Dark Lord's army had been utterly broken, its remnants fleeing in every direction like shadows scattering before the dawn. Without their master's oppressive influence, even his chosen Goblins, his most tenacious followers, had lost their will to fight, slinking away into the crags without so much as a final snarl.

The party stood together, a ragged collection of heroes bearing the weight of their triumph. Their clothing bore the scars of battle, and their faces were etched with exhaustion, but there was a glimmer of satisfaction in their eyes. They had done the impossible. The Dark Lord was no more.

Fortune favored them still, for among the few buildings that had miraculously survived the cataclysm was the storehouse; that ancient stone structure nestled against the mountainside. Its sturdy walls, weathered by centuries of wind and snow, had withstood both the Dark Lord's fury and the climactic battle. Most importantly, it housed the passage that would lead them down the treacherous mountain slopes when the time came to leave.

For now, the storehouse offered more than just a safe descent. Its shelves were still packed with provisions: barrels of salted meats, crates of hardtack, wheels of aged cheese, and, to their delight, several casks of fine ale. With some careful digging around, Thane also found a hidden chest full of gold, jewels, and enough imperial quips to fill his purse.

Broken, bruised, and utterly spent, they gratefully collapsed onto the stone floor, surrounded by their hard-won spoils. The tension that had held them together through countless encounters began to ease, replaced by a growing sense of camaraderie and celebration. The fire they built in the ancient hearth crackled warmly, its light dancing across the stone walls.

The first mug of ale was poured with reverence, its frothy head catching the firelight. "To victory!" Blarg toasted, raising the mug high. The others echoed the sentiment, their voices growing stronger with each cheer. Soon, laughter filled the room, a joyful sound that banished the lingering shadows of the Dark Lord's reign.

They feasted with abandon, savoring every bite and sip as though it were their first taste of freedom. Tales of the battle were recounted in exaggerated detail, each warrior embellishing their own role in the fight. The atmosphere was light, almost jubilant, as they allowed themselves a rare moment of peace.

Tianna sat alone at the edge of the summit, scanning her gaze out over the world. The air was crisp. The wind was calm. It was peaceful. Which, of course, meant it couldn't last.

"That's it then?" she asked, placing her hand on Sword. "My destiny is fulfilled. The Dark Lord has been defeated."

"*Oh dear.*" Sword's voice oozed smugness. "*You didn't think it was your destiny, did you?*"

Tianna blinked. "I mean . . . yes? Kinda the whole point?"

"*Oh, sweet summer child. You were a plot device. An emotional goad to get Thane off his grizzled rear and back on the stage. He was the chosen one. Always was. You? You were just the . . . incentive,*" Sword said.

Tianna stared down at the pan, unable to speak.

"Honestly, you should be honored," Sword continued, now in full self-congratulatory swing. *"You got a speaking role in someone else's redemption arc. That's more than most background characters get. Half the Goblins didn't even get names."*

"Wait," Tianna said, narrowing her eyes. "You've been using me all this time? Guiding me, helping me, manipulating me?"

"No, no . . . well, yes," Sword admitted. *"Wait, what are you doing?"*

Tianna stood up, Sword clenched tightly in her hand.

"Now wait," Sword said in a panic, *"let's not do anything symbolic. We've already had enough character development for one adventure. Put me down, Tianna. You're not that kind of heroine—"*

"Oh no," Tianna said calmly. "I'm exactly that kind of heroine."

And with one smooth motion, she hurled Sword off the cliff.

"You need me! I am the legendary blade of—"

Clong!

There was a long silence, then a confused bleat from what was almost certainly a sheep, followed by another *clong.*

Tianna stood alone, wind in her hair, basking in the pure, glorious silence.

"Finally," she muttered. "Some peace and quiet."

"Where's Sword?" Thane asked, approaching from behind.

"We've decided to go our separate ways," Tianna responded, turning to face her uncle with a grin.

"Oh, thank the Spire. I don't think I could have spent another day listening to her."

"I thought I was done for when those Yetis grabbed me," Thane mused, sitting in the storehouse with the others, his voice taking on the leisurely cadence of a man who enjoyed stretching a story far past believability. He took a long drink from his eighth mug of ale before continuing. "I've always been a lucky one. Like that time I was bitten by a Basilisk. Thought I was dead for sure—and I should have been, mind you, a Basilisk bite is nothing to sneeze at. But as luck would have it, I toppled backward into a patch of Godleaf. Only known cure. Nasty, stinky weed. Saved my life, though I smelled like the backside of a Boggart for three weeks straight. Still, better a stinky survivor than a handsome corpse. And that, in my book, is a fair trade."

"Sounds like the Heroes' Blessing," Blarg said absently.

"What?" Tianna asked.

"The Heroes' Blessing," Blarg repeated, with the solemnity of a priest reciting scripture. "A boon granted by Destiny to her chosen few. The universe itself bends to save the hero when all seems lost. Why does nobody else know this?"[101]

Rea shrugged her shoulders.

---

[101] The nature of destiny is a curious thing. Much like a stubborn mule with a map, she may take her time, but she *will* reach her destination. Destiny, as any good bard will tell you, cannot be denied. And this becomes particularly inconvenient when someone with a capital-D Destiny is involved. You see, people with a Destiny can't really be killed, at least not in the traditional sense. Arrows will conveniently miss their mark by a hair's breadth, just grazing the heroic brow for added dramatic flair. Even if they're hit by dozens of arrows (usually in the back, because villains are cowards), they'll find those arrows manage to hit nerve points *just right,* suddenly curing their chronic leg pain that's been bothering them since childhood.

In fact, if someone destined for greatness were to fall off a cliff, they'd likely land on the one soft pile of conveniently placed hay in the entire kingdom, dust themselves off, and stumble upon a long-lost magical artifact in the process. Destiny has a habit of bending reality around its chosen, ensuring they arrive at their fated moment, no matter how ridiculous the route. Attempts to stop her by way of poison, sword, or cleverly arranged banana peel, only seem to make things worse. Because Destiny is not only persistent, but she also has a sense of humor.

"I don't know, that doesn't sound right," Thane responded. "Then there was that time I was attacked by the gang of cutthroats. Really thought I was a goner. But then a pack of wolves—"

"That's great, Uncle," Tianna interjected, already sounding weary of where this might go, "but you were telling us about the mountain."

"Right, right, the mountain." He chuckled. "Well, as usual, dumb luck saved me. When that Frankenyeti dragged me over the edge, I figured that was it. I had a nice long drop to think about my regrets. Chiefly, never finishing that cask of Embermelon brandy I'd been saving for a special occasion. Then the wind shifted. Blasted mountain winds, fickle as a bard's affections. One gust blew me sideways, slammed me right into a cliffside beehive. Biggest thing I've ever seen. It looked like a haystack glued to the rock. Burst open like a gourd. Honey everywhere. Bees everywhere too, of course. And I'm allergic."

Tianna's eyes narrowed. "Allergic?"

"Oh, badly," Thane said with perfect seriousness. "Swelled up so fast I turned into a human air bladder. Eyes puffed shut, lips out to here. But the upside of ballooning is that when I hit the next ledge, I bounced, then rolled like a great wheezing ball down a chute of loose scree and straight into what looked like a snowdrift. Only it wasn't snow at all, oh no, it was a patch of arctic thindle bramble."

He held up scarred hands as evidence. "Horrible plant. Needles longer than your fingers. Splinters that don't come out until the next full moon. But the roots are springy as anything, so instead of skewering me like a shish kebab, it cushioned the landing. Of course, I came out of it looking like a porcupine's uglier cousin. Every step rattled. But alive."

Rea winced. "That sounds . . . awful."

"Awful, yes, but not fatal," Thane said with a shrug. "And alive is the important bit. Anyway, I was trying to crawl free of the bramble when I heard hooves. Wild mountain goats, a whole herd of them, clattering down the slope. Nasty tempers, goats. Kill a man for looking at them wrong. I figured this was where I truly met my end. But wouldn't you know it—because I was puffed up like a swollen wineskin, one of them mistook me for its lost kid. Little blighter must've been blind, but there you have it. Took to nuzzling me, dragged me upright, and insisted on trotting me along like I was part of the herd. Every time I tried to leave, it butted me back in line. Nearly broke my ribs, but still, that goat carried me halfway up the mountainside before losing interest and wandering off."

Thane leaned back, stroking his beard. "By then I was half-frozen, stung all over, thorn-bitten, and sticky with honey, which is when a hungry Gryphon swooped down. Talons big as sabers. I thought, 'Right, here's the end of me.' But it didn't claw me. No, it scooped me up and flew me straight into its nest. Dumped me right next to a clutch of hatching eggs. And I'll tell you what, Gryphon chicks are vicious things. Already had their beaks open, ready to peck me into mincemeat. But as luck would have it, the honey dripping off me got their attention. They licked me clean like kittens with cream. By the time the mother came back, she took one look at me, covered in down feathers and stinking like Gryphon spit, and decided I wasn't prey."

"Uncle," Tianna groaned, "no one believes this."

"Believe what you like," Thane said with a shrug. "All I know is she flew me out of that nest and dropped me off on the path about ten minutes from here. Ungrateful, really, considering I'd kept her brood from eating one another, but you don't argue with Gryphons. And that's how I made it back."

He spread his hands with an air of finality, as though the whole story was perfectly reasonable. "Nothing but luck. Dumb, stupid, impossible luck."

They stayed in the storehouse that entire first day and slept comfortably that night, the fire burning high, warming both their bodies and their spirits. All through the day and night, cats had appeared in the storehouse. Some came padding up the steps from below, their paws silent against the stone. Others seemed to emerge from the shadows, as if they'd been hiding within the walls all along, waiting for that exact moment. By morning, the air was alive with the soft hum of purring and the playful scuffles of kittens chasing each other.

It was on the second morning, as the party gathered their belongings and prepared to descend the mountain, that Rea first noticed something was wrong. Nyx, the ever-energetic ball of fur, appeared subdued. His tail flicked listlessly, and he sat perched on a rock outside the storehouse, his green eyes fixed on the vast expanse of land. Around him, a hundred cats, perhaps more, roamed freely, tussling, stretching, and watching him with silent reverence. More arrived every moment, their movements fluid and purposeful, as if they knew they'd found their king.

Rea approached quietly, her boots crunching on the frost-kissed ground. She knew before she spoke. "You're not coming home," she said, her voice steady, though her heart clenched. It wasn't a question; it was a truth she could feel in her bones.

Nyx turned his head to her, his emerald eyes soft with understanding. He let out a soft *brrrrup* and nuzzled his face into her chest. Rea wrapped her arms around him, burying her fingers in his thick fur, and held him snugly against herself.

"You've found your place," she whispered, her voice trembling now. "I should have known. You're their king."

Nyx's ears flicked, and he pulled back to meet her gaze. His crown of blue flames flared briefly, casting an ethereal glow over them both. He didn't need words; the flicker in his eyes spoke volumes. He was home, and this mountain, these cats, were his to protect.

"I'll miss you, you know," Rea said, her voice barely more than a whisper.

Nyx purred, the deep rumble reverberating through her. Then, with a final nudge, he leaped gracefully from her arms and back to the rock, where he sat tall and proud, surveying his growing kingdom.

The others had gathered nearby, their faces somber as they watched the silent farewell. One by one, they nodded in understanding. Rea lingered a moment longer, her hand still hovering where Nyx had been.

"Take care of them, Nyxie, like you always took care of me," she said, stepping back. Her voice wavered, but there was pride in it too. She shouldered her pack, turning back to the storehouse, where the path would lead them down the mountain.

Behind her, the first rays of dawn broke over the peaks, the first day of spring, bathing the mountaintop in golden light. Nyx's silhouette stood against the rising sun, his crown of flames blazing once more, a beacon for his newfound kingdom.

26

All the Way Back to Almost Where We Started

"When the sword is finally sheathed, and the monsters fade into legend, what remains is the soft rustle of ordinary days, and the slow, inevitable silence of being quietly forgotten, one unnoticed moment at a time."

— *Beyond the Journey,*
by Frieda Flameheart

At the bottom of the stairs, they found that the Orcs had cleared the passageway of rubble back into the fortress. A contingent of Orcs had set up camp, waiting for the group's descent. The air was crisp, carrying the mingled scents of damp stone and charred wood from the remnants of the battle above.

Grizzled and battle-worn, the Orcs greeted them with solemn nods and firm grips on their weapons. Their leader, a towering figure clad in mismatched armor, stepped forward to offer a brief, silent salute to the adventurers. It was clear that even these hardened warriors understood the weight of the Dark Lord's fall.

Together, they journeyed southward. The Orcs had ingeniously rigged a number of covered supply wagons, pulled by massive beasts of burden. Though the snow had begun to melt, the terrain remained treacherous, a slush of mud and ice making every step a calculated effort. Thankfully, Tianna and Rea were offered space to ride in one of the wagons, sparing their sore feet the arduous trek.

Eleven long days passed as the caravan wound its way across the desolate landscape. The party and the Orcs could not communicate in words, although their mutual respect slowly grew with each shared meal and fire. By the time they reached Thinkleburrow, the snow had all but melted, leaving behind a quagmire of muddy paths and swollen streams.

Grikna stood at the edge of the valley, her arms crossed but her face warm with a rare smile as she watched the procession arrive.

"Lady Grikna," Blarg said respectfully, bowing low. "Blarg is happy to report, the venture has been a success."

Grikna's eyes softened as she stepped forward, clasping Blarg's arm in a warrior's handshake. "We know, Blarg. Every Goblin, Orc, and Troll felt his fall." Her voice carried a weight of authority, but there was also a quiet pride that she couldn't fully mask.

The adventurers were ushered into the town, but it was not the bustling place they had left. Much of it lay in ruins, with charred beams and collapsed buildings scattered throughout. The Goblins and Orcs worked side by side, clearing debris and rebuilding what had been destroyed. Blarg observed the devastation in silence, his usually boisterous demeanor subdued. At last, he turned to Grikna, his voice heavy.

"What happened here?" he asked, his gaze sweeping over the destruction.

Grikna's expression darkened, and she let out a sharp breath. "The Dark Lord's envoy. When they didn't find what they were looking for, they unleashed their wrath. This is the price we paid for defiance."

Blarg's jaw tightened, and his fists clenched at his sides. "Blarg . . . shouldn't have left," he muttered, guilt creeping into his voice. "Perhaps, he could have stopped this."

"This is not your fault, Blarg. The blame lies solely with those Goblins who carried out the attack," responded Grikna.

"You have much to rebuild here," he said thoughtfully, his voice tinged with regret. "The damage done is a scar on this town, one Blarg cannot ignore. You shall need strong hands and steady hearts to guide this place back to its full strength."

Grikna nodded. "It won't be easy, but we're free to shape our own destiny now. That alone makes the struggle worthwhile."

Blarg's gaze lingered on the workers, and he nodded slowly, as if coming to a decision. He turned to Tianna, Rea, and Thane, his expression serious.

"Blarg is staying," he said firmly. "This is where he is needed. You'll do fine without him from here."

Tianna opened her mouth to protest, but the expression in Blarg's eyes silenced her. Instead, she stepped forward and clasped his arm.

"You'll be a great help to them," she said, her voice heavy with understanding. "Thank you, Blarg . . . for everything."

Rea sniffled, brushing away a tear before throwing her arms around her friend. "We'll miss you," she said softly.

Blarg's booming laugh returned, though it held a hint of sadness. "You shall see Blarg again someday," he promised. "The world's not so big after all."

The farewell was bittersweet, but the bond forged between them all remained unbroken. As Tianna, Rea, and Thane prepared to continue their journey, they glanced back. Blarg was already stepping into the thick of the rebuilding efforts, his voice rising in commands as he organized the workers.

A week out of Thinkleburrow, they reached the Old Road. With no fear of roving bands of Goblins or Orcs, the journey became almost pleasant. The days were bright, and the air carried the faint, sweet scent of blooming wildflowers as spring reclaimed the land. Rolling hills unfolded before them, their vibrant greens dotted with clusters of ancient trees.

From the Old Road, it took another two days of travel to the south, winding through the rugged hills before they finally entered the dense and shadowed forest of Ashevale. Tianna and Rea walked side by side in quiet companionship, their conversations drifting between reflections on their journey and tentative plans for the future. Thane, ever vigilant, followed a few paces behind, his sharp eyes scanning the horizon for any hint of danger, though none appeared.

On the third day of crossing the Ashevale, they encountered an old acquaintance. Grothar Boulderback, the tireless bridge keeper, remained steadfast in his quest for the elusive *Adventurer's Exemptions and Loopholes.* His grizzled face broke into a wide grin as he caught sight of them approaching. "Back again, eh?" he grunted, leaning on his massive ledger as they passed.

Thane chuckled as he handed over a small pouch of coins, paying triple the usual toll. "A donation from the Empire," he said with a sly grin, though no one dared question the gesture. Grothar's eyes twinkled as he pocketed the coins and waved them through, muttering something about "not mentioning this to the other members of FIG."

The moment they emerged from the shadowed embrace of the Ashevale, Tianna felt a profound wave of relief at the sight of the Spire. Its ominous silhouette still loomed in the distance, a silent, towering reminder of the Empire's ever-present watch and its assurances of safety.

Two more days of steady travel east brought them through the familiar countryside. On the morning of the third day, they first spotted the town, far in the distance, the sun was rising, painting the sky in hues of pink and gold. Tianna felt a surge of warmth and relief as the familiar sights and sounds of home unfolded before them, grounding her in the comfort of the known.

Home. It was a word that felt heavier now, laden with the weight of their journey and the scars they carried, both visible and unseen. Yet it also felt hopeful, a promise of rest and renewal. Together, they crossed the threshold, ready to embrace whatever came next.

They walked through the town square, where the market was up and running. The faint scent of freshly baked bread mingled with the crisp spring air as merchants haggled with their customers. Tianna's eye caught on a familiar face, a wiry man with a patchy beard setting up a stall. His booth was plastered with posters and crude signs, each bearing the Empire's crest overlaid with slogans declaring loyalty to the Spire. "For Order and Strength!" one banner proclaimed in bold, uneven lettering.

Among the chaotic collage, one sign stood out. It depicted a grotesquely drawn figure; a green, fish-like man with crudely sketched scales, gills, and webbed fingers. The creature's exaggerated sharklike teeth and black, soulless eyes loomed menacingly from the parchment, accompanied by the words: "Beware the Merfolk: Raiders of the Empire!"

The vendor glanced at Tianna with a sly grin. "Keep your wits about you, miss," he said, tapping the poster with a crooked finger. "News is, the Merfolk have been raiding up and down the coast. Inland now, too. Nowhere's safe these days."

Tianna frowned, her brow furrowing. "What about the Goblin menace?" she asked, her voice edged with disbelief.

The man waved dismissively, his grin widening. "Old news. Goblins aren't the problem anymore. The Empire took care of those nasty fellas. It's the Merfolk people we've got to watch out for now."

"And who says that?" Tianna asked.

"The Imperial Council of course, always trying to keep us safe!"

Shaking her head, Tianna turned and continued through the square with Rea and Thane close behind. The streets were louder than they remembered, though familiar sights and sounds eased the tension of their long journey. As they approached *The Cracked Tankard*, the unmistakable aroma of Gertie's stew wafted toward them, bringing a smile to Rea's face.

They pushed open the heavy wooden door and stepped inside, greeted by the comforting crackle of the hearth. Behind the bar, hung a newly added placard: *'Merfolk: Killers, Monsters, Scourge of the Land!'* Tianna couldn't help but shake her head.

Gertie appeared from the back room, carrying a large pot of steaming stew. Her face lit up as she spotted them.

"Well, well, well, if it isn't my favorite band of adventurers!" she exclaimed, setting the pot down with a hearty laugh. "Come in, come in. You look like you could use a proper meal and a warm seat by the fire."

Rea rushed forward, wrapping her arms around Gertie in a tight hug. "It's good to see you again, Gertie," she said.

"You too, my dear," Gertie replied, patting Rea on the back. "Now, sit yourselves down. Stew's almost ready, and I've got a fresh loaf of bread that'll knock your boots off."

"What's with the Merfolk sign?" Tianna asked, her tone sharp with curiosity.

"You know, dearie, there's always something threatening the Empire. We're lucky, as they say, to have the Spire watching over us."

"Right," Tianna agreed halfheartedly. "Looks like some things never change," she murmured to herself, her gaze drifting to the flickering light of the hearth.

Tianna, Rea, and Thane settled into their usual corner table, the weight of their journey slowly lifting as they basked in the warmth of familiar surroundings. For the first time in what felt like ages, they allowed themselves to relax, sharing smiles and quiet laughter.

Outside, the town bustled with its usual rhythm, but within the walls of *The Cracked Tankard*, time seemed to stand still. They were home, and for now, that was all that mattered.

Epilogue

"Give a man a fish, and he'll eat for a day. Summon a fish god, and he'll bring ruin to your coastline forever."

— Old Fisherman's Proverb

Under a moonless sky where the vast ocean stretched into the unseen, four hooded figures gathered on a rugged, sea-beaten shore, their dark ritual already off to a rocky start. The wind howled with a salty chill that gnawed at their bones, as if the very ocean had a vendetta against anyone foolish enough to stand this close to its edge. The tallest among them clutched a tome. It was damp, waterlogged, and covered in something that might have been seaweed, or worse. He cleared his throat with the dignity of someone who had not slipped on a wet rock and twisted his ankle just moments ago.

"Thanks for making it out tonight," the Grand Harbinger of Doom began, with a confidence that might have come from practicing his speech in front of his bathroom mirror too many times. "Tonight, we gather not just for a summoning, but for something far grander . . . a communion with the depths themselves."

He paused, letting the words hang dramatically in the air. Silence was his only companion, save for the *caw* of a seabird and the rhythmic sloshing of waves against the rocks. That same seabird flew overhead and with impeccable aim, did its business right on top of the Grand Harbinger's head.

Undeterred, he gestured broadly toward the ocean. "The sea . . . the endless abyss. A place of mystery, terror, and power. And tonight, we dare to call upon its ruler, Dagon, Lord of the Depths!"

The hooded figures exchanged uneasy glances. One of them, the Underseer of Trivial Mysteries, cleared his throat. "Uh, Yo Gran'ness, I don't want ta be rude, but we sure the tide ain't comin' up too fast? I mean, we're standin' awful close—"

Before the Grand Harbinger could respond, a massive wave crashed into them, drenching the entire group and nearly knocking them off their feet. The tome slipped from the Grand Harbinger's grasp, and he scrambled to catch it before it was washed away by the retreating water. The underseer sputtered, seaweed clinging to his hood, while the Keeper of the Snacks coughed up a mouthful of salty water.

The Grand Harbinger, soaked and clearly irritated, glared at the underseer. "Fools! See what you did? You tempted fate! The tides, among other things, are testing my patience tonight."

"Mom says not to go swimmin' on a full stomach," chimed the Keeper of the Snacks. "And I just had a mighty big supper."

"What? Nobody's going swimming," the Grand Harbinger replied, exasperated.

"Oh. I just figured, y'know—"

The Grand Harbinger raised an eyebrow. "Are you wearing a bathing suit under your robe?"

"I didn't want to get my clothes all wet."

The Grand Harbinger shook his head with a sigh as he turned to the Underseer of Trivial Mysteries. "Underseer, the offering?"

The underseer nodded and stepped forward, revealing a small wooden crate. He pried it open, revealing several large, glistening sea cucumbers. The Grand Harbinger blinked, his confidence faltering for just a moment.

"Sea cucumbers? Really?" he asked, his voice dripping with skepticism.

I hope Dagon eats this idiot, he thought grimly.

The Underseer nodded eagerly. "Aye, Gran'ness. Me thawt the great one, you knows, would wan' a nutrichious snack. So me thinks, why not vege'ables? Healthy, natural, straigh' from the ocean herself!"

"You realize sea cucumbers are not—" He paused, his voice dripping with exhaustion. "You know what, never mind."

The underseer shrugged. "Fresh from the sea, Gran'ness. Pure an' untainted. Besides, me thinks, they be very, y'know, thematic."

The Grand Harbinger sighed, pinching the bridge of his nose. "Fine. Thematic. We'll make it work." He turned back to the ocean, raising his arms high. "Dagon! Ruler of the Abyss, we call upon you! From the sea all life began, and from the sea all life shall end! Rise forth from the wicked depths and spread terror over this world!"

The group chanted, their voices disjointed and out of sync. The wind picked up, and the waves seemed to grow fiercer, crashing against the rocks with a force that made the ground tremble beneath their feet.

Suddenly, the sea began to swirl, a whirlpool forming beyond the shore. From the dark, churning waters, a massive form rose out of the sea. The air filled with the scent of salt, decay, and something profoundly wrong, as if the sea itself had birthed a nightmare. The hooded figures fell silent, their eyes wide with a mix of awe and fear.

Dagon emerged, his enormous body covered in barnacles and dripping with seaweed. His form resembled a grotesque hybrid of fish and man. His scales were mottled, scarred, and slick with algae. His mouth was stretched impossibly wide, filled with rows of jagged teeth that shifted and writhed, as if attempting to find the most terrifying configuration. Tentacle-like appendages hung from his jawline, twitching as if sensing the air. His many eyes, scattered across his face and body, glowed with an otherworldly light, radiating a malevolent intelligence that was ancient beyond comprehension. His gaze settled on the small crate of sea cucumbers at his feet.

"SEA CUCUMBERS?" Dagon's voice echoed like the roar of a storm, his tone heavy with incredulity.

The Grand Harbinger dropped to his knees, bowing low. "Yes, oh mighty one. An offering from the depths, for the depths!"

Dagon reached down, picking up one of the sea cucumbers with a clawed hand. He examined it for a moment before squeezing it, causing a squelching noise as the innards oozed out. He slurped it up with an unsettling, wet gulp. The hooded figures held their breath, waiting for his reaction.

After a long, tense pause, Dagon rumbled, **"NEEDS MORE SALT."** As soon as the word left his mouth, an enormous wave, as if summoned by his very disapproval, rose from the ocean and crashed down upon the hooded figures, drenching them all once again. The force of the wave sent them sprawling, seaweed and saltwater covering their robes. The Grand Harbinger sputtered, wiping salt from his eyes as he tried, unsuccessfully, to maintain some dignity. The underseer groaned, picking himself up slowly, while the Keeper of the Snacks coughed up a mouthful of salty water. The Herald, dripping wet and blinking rapidly, stared at the sea cucumbers now scattered across the shore, as if they had personally betrayed him.

The Grand Harbinger let out a sigh of exasperation. "Apologies, oh mighty one, for the lack of salt. We will do better next time," he muttered under his breath.

Without another word, Dagon walked up the shore, his hulking form shaking the ground as he went. Out of the waves hundreds of tiny sea creatures emerged, no more than three feet tall. They had slimy green scales, long flippered feet, and teeth out of some deep ocean nightmare. The creatures ignored the men in robes and followed Dagon onto the shore, leaving the four figures in stunned silence. The Grand Harbinger slowly got to his feet, brushing sand from his robes.

"Well," he said, trying to regain some semblance of authority, "I suppose that went . . . better than expected. Next time, though, we might want to consider something a little less . . . bland."

The underseer scratched his head, looking thoroughly confused. "Wha', like a sea cow? I don' thinks we could fit one in a crate."

"No, you ninny," the Grand Harbinger snapped. "Something with a bit more gravitas!"

The Keeper of the Snacks raised his hand eagerly. "How about some lobsters, then? They have claws. Claws are intimidating, right?"

The Herald of Prophetic Hindsight nodded solemnly. "A lobster might really drive the point home, Grandness. It's a symbol of the sea *and* fine dining."

The Grand Harbinger glared at them, his eyes narrowing as if he was debating whether to throw them all into the ocean.

The Keeper of the Snacks beamed. "Maybe we could even butter them up first! Everyone loves buttered lobster."

The Grand Harbinger groaned, his composure crumbling. "We are summoning a primordial sea god, not hosting a seafood buffet!"

The underseer frowned, looking thoughtful. "I thinks, maybe we use crabs? I hears they is territorial. Might show 'em we means business."

The Grand Harbinger threw up his hands. "Crabs? Lobsters? What next? Are we going to offer him a side of fries and call it a seafood special?!"

The Keeper of the Snacks perked up again. "Oh, I like that idea! We could get some fries, maybe even a little tartar sauce on the side—"

"Maybe some candles, and mayhaps some music ta set the mood," mused the underseer, his tone wistful, as if he were planning a romantic evening.

The Grand Harbinger stared at him, slack-jawed. "This is a dark ritual! Not a seaside picnic!" He took a deep breath, trying to regain his composure. "Let's just . . . get out of here before the tide really does come in and drag us all out."

As they began to make their way back up the shore, the Keeper of the Snacks spoke up again, his voice filled with enthusiasm. "What about jellyfish next time? They're kinda mysterious, right?"

The Grand Harbinger didn't even turn around. "If I hear one more word about seafood, I'm feeding you to Dagon myself."

"Glad I wore my bathing suit," the Keeper of the Snacks added happily. The Grand Harbinger snapped him a hard stare before continuing onward.

As the figures slowly faded into the night, somewhere in the world, along a distant shore, a magic trident blinked into existence, wedged awkwardly between two slimy rocks, wondering how it had gotten there.

In the Hall of the Meowntain King

"His decrees were erratic. His naps were absolute. His reign?
Unquestioned. And thus, he ruled not by sword or scroll, but by tail flick
and unrelenting indifference."

— *The Velvet Throne:*
Memoirs of a Mouse Who Lived to Tell It

The Dark Lord's citadel, once a symbol of terror and doom, had been reduced to rubble in the wake of its master's defeat. Yet, under the guidance of the enigmatic King Nyx, it was being rebuilt, not by mortal hands, but with the aid of towering Stone Giants. These massive, stoic beings moved methodically, stacking boulders and carving new halls with their massive hands, transforming the ruins into the foundation of a new kingdom.

In the grand hall, still incomplete but already bearing a distinct feline aesthetic, shredded curtains hung in place of banners, and a mountain of mismatched cushions rose where a sinister obsidian throne once stood. Beneath a makeshift skylight, which let in golden beams of sunlight, sat King Nyx, his head adorned with a crown of flickering blue flames. His green eyes gleamed with regal authority and quiet determination, a reflection of the ancient legacy he now bore as he calmly groomed a paw.

A nervous mouse scurried across the grand dais, clutching a tiny scroll in its trembling paws. It paused, adjusted its oversized spectacles, and squeaked, "A-attention, loyal subjects! You stand before His Majesty, Nyx the Chaotic, Baron of Hairballs, Lord of the Litterbox, Keeper of the Sunbeam, and rightful heir to a line of Kings that have ruled these lands for a thousand years. Long before these lands were claimed and corrupted by the Dark Lord and his minions! From the ancient palaces of the Golden Paws to the revered fields of the Whisker Plains, his lineage has endured. Today, His Majesty reclaims his birthright and vows to restore the splendor of our great kingdom, where every sunbeam shall be cherished and every shadow respected!"

The assembled crowd of cats, hundreds, perhaps thousands, let out a collective *mrrow* of approval. From sleek, pampered house cats to scruffy alley warriors and a smattering of wild lynxes who claimed some dubious noble lineage. All had gathered to witness the coronation of their new king.

Nyx's ears twitched, and he leaped from the cushion throne to land gracefully on a velvet footstool. With a single flick of his tail, he signaled the beginning of the ceremony. The mouse unrolled the scroll further and squeaked out the royal decrees.

"By order of His Majesty, all sunbeams within the kingdom are henceforth declared royal property," the mouse announced, struggling to keep its voice steady. "However, His Majesty, in his infinite benevolence, will allow his subjects to bask freely in their glory."

A wave of enthusiastic purring swept through the hall.

"Furthermore," the mouse continued, "every meal shall henceforth include at least one fish, and humans are to be tolerated provided they bring appropriate offerings of soft blankets and ear scritches."

Nyx let out a low *mrrp* of approval and stretched luxuriously, his claws sinking into the velvet. As the crowd's cheers echoed through the hall, the double doors at the far end burst open. A bedraggled tabby staggered in, his fur matted with soot and his left ear was torn.

"Your Majesty!" the tabby gasped, collapsing before the throne. "The western outpost . . . it has been attacked!"

Nyx's eyes narrowed, and the hall fell silent. The mouse herald scurried to the tabby's side, offering him a small bowl of water, which he lapped at between ragged breaths.

"Thunder Birds," the tabby continued, his voice hoarse. "They came out of nowhere, like lightning and chaos. We held them off as long as we could, but the outpost has fallen."

Nyx rose slowly, his tail flicking with purpose. He stepped down from his throne and padded silently to the center of the hall. The assembled cats watched in awe as he surveyed his subjects, his green eyes blazing like twin emeralds.

Without a sound, Nyx turned and leaped back onto his throne, his regal poise undiminished. The faint glow of the setting sun filtered through the cracks in the citadel walls. They cast an otherworldly halo around him, illuminating the flickering crown of blue flames atop his head. All eyes fixed on their new king, the embodiment of ancient majesty reclaimed, and the symbol of their kingdom's fiery resurgence.

And then he spoke.

"My loyal subjects! Today, we reclaim not stones and ruins, but the very spirit of our ancestors who once ruled these sacred lands with unyielding grace and cunning. Let it be known that no storm, no feathered fiend, and no force of nature shall shake the foundation of our kingdom. Together, we shall rise above the chaos and forge a legacy that echoes through the ages. Rally to me, for we shall turn thunder into a mere whisper and reclaim the glory that is our birthright!"

The citadel erupted into overwhelming applause, a cacophony of jubilant purring, triumphant yowls, and the rhythmic thumping of tails against the stone floor. The sound rose to a crescendo, reverberating through the half-built halls, as every cat in the room united in a display of unwavering loyalty to their king. Even the stoic Stone Giants paused in their work, their massive heads nodding in silent acknowledgment of the feline monarch's speech. The air hummed with renewed purpose, a kingdom reborn under the rule of Nyx the Chaotic.

Outside, the citadel shimmered in the fading light as Stone Giants continued their work, and the kingdom of King Nyx prepared for its first great challenge. In the distance, the storm clouds of the Thunder Birds gathered, promising a tempest that would test even the most chaotic of Kings.

And so began the reign of King Nyx the Chaotic, a reign destined to be as unpredictable and enigmatic as the flicker of a cat's tail.

Acknowledgements

Writing a novel may seem like a solitary activity, and sometimes it is, but writing is only half the battle. Like a marathon, it demands persistence, resilience, and a willingness to push beyond what you thought possible just to reach the finish line. Without my parents, my wife, and my friends, I would never have had the energy (or the stubbornness) to see it through.

To Aria, whose endless creativity and fearless innovation inspired me to try creating something of my own.

To Kaushal, who once said, *"You read a lot. Why don't you write a book?"* So, I did.

And to the members of *Do Write!* Thanks for your insight, encouragement, and support. You helped me make this the best debut novel I could write.

Help Spread the Word

If you enjoyed this book, the best way to support it is by leaving a quick review on Amazon, Goodreads, and/or any other places where you purchase or talk about books. It only takes a minute, and it helps more readers discover it. This encourages me to write more books, and you get to enjoy more of my books. It's a win-win. Honestly, the hardest part about being an Indie Author is finding an audience, so any help you can give in spreading the word is greatly appreciated. Thank you, from the bottom of my heart!

⬆ Scan Here! ⬆

It links to all the places you can leave a review.

About the Author

Mike is a writer of all things funny. Whether it's Fantasy, Sci-Fi, or Personal Essays, he really can't help himself. He started writing in his teens, convinced he was the next great American author. (He wasn't. Not even close.) The early work, mercifully unpublished, can best be described as "enthusiastic."

It wasn't until years later, after stumbling across the likes of Douglas Adams, Terry Pratchett, and David Sedaris, that Mike had a literary epiphany: *books can be funny.* (Yes, this genuinely surprised him. We don't know how either.) He returned to writing with comedy at the forefront and finally started making sense—on the page, not in life.

He spent ten years living in Thailand and somehow remained astonishingly pale throughout. He now lives just outside Los Angeles with his wife, his daughter, and several cats who think they deserve a co-author credit, for the many times they walked across his keyboard.